What readers are saying...

"Intense, riveting, and spiritually challenging, Dark of Night will keep you on the edge of your seat. You don't want to miss the latest from Carrie Cotten!"

Jamie H. Ogle - Author of historical Christian fiction.

"Carrie Cotten once again takes us into a world where dreams can prove just as dangerous as real life, and leads us on an intense journey from untamed anger to redemption, revealing just how imperative family and the Word of God truly are. With edge-of-the-seat suspense and time running out, this book is one you won't want to put down."

Abigail M. Thomas - Christian writer and blogger

"Dark of Night is coming home to all of the beloved characters (and villains) from Dreamwalker–and then stepping onto a roller coaster with them. Still learning how to be a team, Andy and Will give each other the courage to run straight toward the danger and risk everything for the sake of the mission, even as their own deepest fears and inadequacies threaten to swallow them whole. Carrie Cotten never takes the easy way out, crafting a story that is as emotionally raw as it is suspenseful through characters that leap off the page. Truth shines in this unique tale, and light overcomes the darkness. Jump onto this ride, and hang on tight!"

Heather Wood - Author of Until We All Find Home
and Until We All Run Free

"A heart-pounding story of faith, even in the darkest of times."
Megan T. Dorman - Critique partner and ARC reader

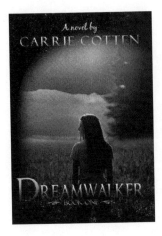

Book One of the DREAMWALKER series available on Amazon and
www.carriecotten.com

Even among special agents, Andromeda Stone is special. Her unique ability to walk in the dreams of others has placed her in the services of a secret government research and defense facility known only as The Agency. She always assumed it was because of her gift that she felt out of place, even among her family. But as she faces an entirely new and dangerous mission, she begins to wonder if perhaps it's something deeper that sets her apart.

What readers are saying...

"The book grabs your attention from the very beginning. The characters feel like you could easily meet them in real life. The plot is tightly woven and suspenseful throughout the entire book. Good versus evil is the battlefield, and the players are for keeps. I dare you to try and put it down."

"I love a good mystery, and this is a suspenseful page turner! You will definitely find that with Dreamwalker! I could picture all the images so clearly and could not put the book down! It is full of action, and with each chapter more and more of the story is revealed."

"Right from the start I was drawn into this book! Carrie made the characters come to life, and the suspense throughout felt real. She also did a phenomenal job of weaving in the Gospel message and Biblical truth from start to finish!"

"This story grabbed a hold of me from the first page and by the end, I didn't want it to let go! Walking in dreams is just the beginning of Andromeda Stone's gift. Andy stole my heart as I bonded with her in so many ways, I felt it on a spiritual level. She yearns to find her true purpose as she learns about faith, love, and mercy amidst fear and chaos. I was definitely on the edge of my seat and couldn't wait to turn each page throughout the entire story!"

Dark of Night

A Dreamwalker Novel

BY:

CARRIE COTTEN

CARRIE COTTEN

Gripping Christian Fiction

www.carriecotten.com

DEDICATION

As always, this story is dedicated to my King, without whom I would be nothing, do nothing, and have nothing.

To my husband, my protector and friend: you will always be my favorite.

To my children: I hope that you see your parents being obedient over being sacrificial, and that your faith truly consumes you.

It is all that matters.

ACKNOWLEDGEMENTS

Once again, this is a rookie novel by a rookie writer, whose pages are bound together with prayer and friendship. But don't for a minute think it delicate; the glue is strong, and the binding firm.

First and foremost, I owe all gratitude to God–always and forever! He put these words in my head and the strength in my fingers to get them down.

Thank you to my friends and family who put up with endless random quotes in text messages and strange questions at all hours of the night and day. Thank you for still believing in me and this story.

Thank you to my mom, who is my biggest fan and best salesperson! I don't know even one of her friends who didn't receive a copy of Book 1! Thanks, Momma!

Thank you to my tireless editing and beta team: seriously, you are saints. I wish I could promise you I'd get less spastic...buuuuut I can't. Thank you, Jamie and Abigail for your thrice readings and valuable feedback.

And lastly, thank you to all the amazing friends, family, and fans who took a chance on a no-name author and some weird fiction book. I never in my wildest dreams could have imagined the length or breadth of this journey, but it has been incredible.

I pray we have many more adventures together. So, buckle up, keep your hands and feet inside at all times, and hang on tight. The ride is about to begin.

PROLOGUE

August 21, 2002

*B*ang!

I jumped. Somewhere, a girl screamed and a man made a big laugh. Next to me, Lily's skirt swished and the circle sequins on the bottom flashed up under bright lights. Her sandals and my bare feet crunched across the dry grass.

Those were sounds I knew, things my eyes had seen before, but everything else was strange. New. New people, with faces I didn't recognize. All over–flashing lights, clanging, ringing, talking, and laughing. My eyes got big with each new sight. I sniffed in a long breath, trying to make a memory of all the new smells. There was a salty, buttery one, a sweet one, and one that kind of smelled the same as when Lily cooked pancakes in her black skillet.

My fingers were still sticky from the fluffy blue stuff I'd touched earlier, and I kept smooshing them together, liking the way it was kind of hard to pull them apart. It was supposed to be candy, but it looked like the furry mold that grew on a yucky orange I found once after it rolled under the seat in our van and was lost for a long time.

I had looked up at Sebastian and made a frown.

"Bash! You tricked me! It's not candy!"

He only laughed a big belly laugh and said, "Cotton candy!"

When it touched my tongue it disappeared, and I made a face but ate the rest of it anyway. Bash said it was blueberry, but it didn't taste like any blueberries I'd ever had.

Just ahead, a man stood next to a small cart—at least, I thought he was a man. He had arms and legs and a head like a man, but he also had bright white skin and a big red ball for his nose. A curly poof of rainbow-colored hair sat on top of his head, and his clothes were funny: puffy, like Lily's dress that one time when she walked in the river and it got all filled with air. Bash said she looked like a bee-loon but I had never seen a bee like that before.

The funny man held a bunch of strings in his hand and tied to the ends were big, round floating things of all colors. I wanted to touch them. They looked like glass, and I wanted to know how they could be floating in the air like that.

That's why I'd stopped. I walked towards him, and he smiled at me.

"Lily, what are those?" I pointed to the funny circles bobbing up and down on top of his strings.

Lily didn't answer. I turned real fast. Lily wasn't there. I was used to being on my own, but still—some little something told me I should find her.

"Lily?" I called, looking up at all the faces passing by. None of them belonged to her.

There were always new people where we lived; coming and going, staying and leaving. But I didn't know any of these faces. My tummy got a little rumbly.

"Bash?" I turned fast again in a circle, looking for his long silver-grey hair. My Bash was tall. I would be able to see him over the tops of all the grownups. He was wearing a...what color was his tunic again? Green...or maybe...blue.

I walked around some more. There were too many things to look at, and I quick forgot to find Bash and Lily. I stopped at a big machine that moved in a circle and people sat in buckets to ride it around. It looked high up when they got to the top. It didn't look like a happy thing to me.

I passed by a long row of tables where people stood throwing balls into buckets, and shooting pointy sticks with feathers at more of those colored circles. They made a loud pop when the stick hit them. There were big toy animals hanging up behind the games, and I heard a girl scream real loud when her friend tossed some rings around green glass bottles. She did a bunch of jumps and hugs, and the game man gave her a pink elephant that was bigger than she was.

Lots of people walked around, but none of them were Bash or Lily. The sky was dark now, and more lights came on all over. They were too bright, and made my eyes go squinty when I looked up high. I couldn't see the stars. Lily said when you could see the stars it was a good time to rest, but I could stay up if that's what felt right to me. Sometimes I would stay up and then feel grumpy the next day. Grownups knew things; I wished they would just tell us so we could know too. That would make me happy. Finding Bash and Lily would make me happy, too. Being by myself didn't feel right to me. I looked around for them again, but they weren't there. My tummy got real rumbly then, and I felt a new feeling.

I didn't like this new feeling—it made my heart hurt when it bumped, and there was a stinging thing in my throat when I tried to swallow. My eyes got tears, and I didn't like that either. I remembered that we didn't walk far to get to this new place; camp was close. It was a new camp, but camp was always home. It was near that stripey tent where the lady in the purple dress had a shiny glass ball and told Lily about her grandma. She said Grandma Sue was happy, and that made Lily cry. Lily said they were happy tears and hugged that lady two times then gave her some dollars.

If I could find the ball lady, maybe I could find our camp. I stood up high on tiptoes, trying to see over the grownups and looking for the red and white tent. The grownups were too tall, though. Over a little ways, I saw a circle fence with ponies inside. I ran over and started to climb up.

"Hey! No climbing on the fence!" A frowning man with a black beard and a red hat shook his finger at me. I didn't like him; he made my skin cold.

But I needed to be on the fence. I needed to see, so I pushed up higher.

"I said get off the fence, kid!"

That pony man pushed my shoulder and my foot slipped off the bottom rail. I went down to the ground fast and a hard thing hit my chin. It hurt real bad and so did the rocks I landed on. When I touched my face, it was wet and there was red on my fingers. My eyes got more tears. My tummy was awful rumbly now. Lily said the carnyville was a happy thing, but this was not happy to me.

"Are you lost?"

I looked up and saw a boy. Those stingy tears made him blurry, but his voice was kind. He was older than me, and had a box of popcorn in his hand.

"I need to find the ball lady," I said. My words were shaky.

"Here." The boy stuck out his hand.

I stared at it for a second and then put my hand out too. He pulled me up, and a little zippy thing went up my arm when his fingers touched mine.

"Are you 'lectric?"

"What?" He laughed, but he was looking at his hand too. "Who are you looking for?"

"The ball lady. She has a purple dress, and I can't find Bash and...and..." It was hard to make the right words. I sniffed and rubbed my arm across my face to wipe it dry.

"You're bleeding," he said.

"The pony man pushed me."

"I saw that. Here, put this on it."

He handed me a white paper napkin. I tapped it on my chin real soft; there was a big red dot on the paper when I looked at it again.

"So...are you looking for your parents?"

"Uh huh, but we came from the ball lady."

"You mean the fortune teller? She's over there."

I looked to where his finger pointed and saw the red and white stripes of the ball lady's tent. My heart did a jump and I smiled big, but it hurt my chin, so my smile went away.

"Do you want me to walk with you?"

"Okay."

The nice boy walked next to me; he was tall so he could see over the grownups, and he said the way to go.

"You want some popcorn?"

I nodded and he tipped his box so I could get a handful. It was salty and kind of sweet too.

"Good, right?"

I made a big nod and he laughed.

"What's your name?" he asked.

"My name is An– there she is!"

Some grownups moved just then, and I saw her standing there, looking all around with her skirt bunched up tight in her hands. Lily dropped her skirt and put her hands up together on her chest when she saw me. She ran over and scooped me up quick.

"Oh, you scared me! I turned around and you were gone!"

"There was a man with rainbow hair. What were those floating things he had, Lily?"

"This isn't camp, Andromeda. You can't wander!" She set me down and put her hands on my shoulders. Her mouth made a frown.

"The floating things were happy."

Most of the mommas at camp didn't make that face—they didn't tell the kids what to do. We did the happy things, but sometimes the grownups didn't like the same things we did. I didn't like those times because the grownups would talk loud and I would have to cover my ears

I was afraid Lily would talk loud now, but she didn't.

"Oh...what happened to your face?"

"The pony man pushed me, but the nice boy helped me and shared his pop-a-corn."

"What boy?"

I turned to point to the boy with the big brown eyes, but he was gone.

"Well never mind, you're safe now. Come on, Bash is waiting at the roller coaster!"

"What's a cola roaster?" I looked up at her. She did a giggle and held my hand; she squeezed a little tight, but I held on tight too.

"It's a ride. It's scary, but also exciting."

"Is it a happy thing?"

"I think so!"

We rode three times. I never could decide if it was a happy thing. When our cart went up, it was fun and bumpy, but the cart would click, click, click as it got to the top, and I knew the down part was coming. That made my tummy go tight. The down parts were scary, but after the first time I knew they would be over fast quick. Sometimes the cart was jerky around the corners, but Bash and Lily were there, and I squished into them so it didn't hurt. When our car rolled into the gate at the end, I was happy to get off but a little sad too, because there was one part on the ride where we weren't going up or down; we were just going straight, real fast, and it felt like I could fly.

Chapter 1

"**D**id you hear that?"
I looked over my shoulder. No one was there.
Annndddyyyyyy.
There it was again. I scanned the trees for movement. Still...nothing.

"Hear what?" Will said, slowing his pace, turning to jog backwards.

"I thought I heard...never mind." I sped past him, laughing as he yelled after me.

"Hey! That's cheating!"

I meant to keep up my sprint and gain a strong lead ahead of him, but my laughter only slowed me down, and he was on my heels in seconds.

"Nice try, Mrs. Carter," he joked as he passed and disappeared over the hill.

I slowed to a walk, placing my hands on my hips and tipping my head back to take deeper breaths, wincing as I swallowed down cold, dry air. We'd been running for at least thirty minutes now, and I was ready to head back but wasn't ready to admit it. I was still trying to prove to Will that I was returning to normal…whatever that meant.

I noticed a thin deer path that cut through the trees and looked to be a promising shortcut. With a sly smile, I took off down the steep trail, determined to beat my husband back to the trailhead.

I could hear the pounding of his feet on the dirt, breaking twigs and crushing leaves as he ran ahead, but the trail made a wide arc, looping back around to the bottom of the hill. I could cut straight across and beat him by several minutes.

This way was much steeper and rugged than the trail, but the vision of his face as he rounded the bend and saw me waiting at the sign far outweighed any thoughts of danger. I half-ran, half-slid down the thin path, which was still muddy from recent rains. An excited giggle escaped my lips as my footing slipped and I rode the trail down a particularly steep section on my backside. That excitement ended abruptly when I reached the end of the ride and was met with a sharp drop off. I would have sailed straight over the edge, had I not seen it seconds before and turned on my side, frantically grabbing at branches and dirt in an effort to slow my descent. Finally, my fingers settled around the rough, wet roots of an uprooted tree. They stretched and groaned against my weight, but the gnarled tendrils remained intact and I jerked to a stop with my palms on fire and my legs dangling over the edge of a muddy precipice.

"Okay…maybe this was a bad idea." I chastised myself out loud.

Will was nowhere in sight, and while I was quite certain he would find me eventually, I was not certain my grip would last that long. Plus, I didn't want to endure the lecture that would come with such a rescue, not that I could blame him. After almost losing me to a poisonous snakebite, a near drowning, and to the clutches of a villainous monster, he had reason to worry. It had been over a year, but neither of us had forgotten even one minute of that nightmare. Looking over my shoulder, I could see it wasn't actually that far to the ground below. If I lowered myself as far as I could using the roots as a rope, I could drop down. I still might even have a chance of beating him to the end.

With arm muscles that screamed every inch of the way, I moved down, hand under hand, until I was fully over the edge. After one deep breath and a desperate prayer that my foolishness wouldn't end in a broken ankle, I let go, landing on the soft brush-covered ground with a grunt.

I looked myself over and found, surprisingly, no injuries. I was filthy, but other than raw, red flesh on my palms, there wasn't even one scrape to show for my impulsiveness. My celebration didn't last, however. A sharp snap echoed through the trees, causing me to turn quickly.

I scanned the woods for movement but saw nothing. I also saw that the trail I'd been following had ended at the cliff above, and I was facing a blind downward climb through thick underbrush.

I jogged on in the direction I thought would lead me back to the trail. A cool wind snaked through the trees, sending a chill up my spine that raised the hair on my arms. Suddenly, I had the horrible, sickening feeling that something was right behind me. *Keep going...just keep moving forward, Andy.*

The air, once crisp and fresh, now smelled like smoke. It burned in my nose and I coughed, trying to expel the discomfort. It was persistent; invisible and sourceless, just like the mysterious voice that was calling out again.

I heard my name, except it wasn't actually my name–it sounded as if someone was saying Andromeda and Joanna at the same time. The two words grated against each other, like gears that didn't quite fit. An irreconcilable conflict between the past and the present, drawing my shoulders together and making me cringe. I wanted to be one or the other– not both. I'd been Andromeda Skye Stone my whole life. Until I wasn't. I shivered at the memory of brown and ice-cold river waters that had enveloped Andromeda and given birth to Joanna, which was my name at my actual birth. Yet another chill shot down my spine and brought with it a shiver that clung to my skin even under the layers of fleece and cotton.

My jog was now a run, and my knees resisted the speed at which I was coursing downhill. I finally hit the trail, but it was more overgrown than I expected. Had I lost my way? With every step, my heart pounded harder, its rhythm pushing hard against my eardrums. Something was wrong... terribly wrong. Even though there was nothing but trees every time I looked over my shoulder, I couldn't shake the feeling that I was being followed. And my pursuer wasn't friendly.

The path split, and I skidded to a stop. This wasn't on the trail map.

"Which way?" I whispered to myself, breathless and panicked.

Another snap echoed through the empty woods and I spun, frustrated and afraid. My clumsy dance came to a sudden halt. Something moved in the woods. I squinted, trying to see what it was.

"Will?" I called. *Please be Will.*

No answer.

"William Graham Carter, this isn't funny!"

No…it wasn't him. I'd gotten off the trail; I was deep in the woods and it could be any number of things, the scariest of which a bear or wolf. I remembered the smoky, burning smell; something must be nearby. Could it be another cabin, or one of the many mountain sawmills? Maybe I was just on another trail, an old one not on the map, and our cabin was close.

Without looking back, I started down the path that appeared less overgrown. searching through the trees for any sign of the reddish-brown logs of our cabin.

Our spontaneous vacation had brought us to the mountains of North Carolina. The house Will had rented was remote and peaceful, a perfect escape from downtown Alexandria. While Christ Church was not the biggest tourist hot spot, especially in the winter, there was a constant buzz of city life all around us. It was nice to take a break from honking horns, revving engines, and the never-ending sounds of urban life. While I'd referred to it as our honeymoon since we'd never really taken one, Will refused to accept that, promising he had something else in mind to earn that title.

We'd set out on a trail run just half an hour before–before I heard the strange voice in the wind, before I had the silly idea of winning some imaginary race, before I tried to prove that I was fine. The barely-there trail turned completely nonexistent, and I was simply lost in the woods. Always in the woods. I heard that grating sound again, the metallic scrape of my two names fighting against each other. I clasped my hands over my ears, staring into the trees, still trying to determine the source. My brain turned trees into men, and shadows into monsters. I swallowed hard, my throat burning from the cold winter air. Something shifted in the distance. That definitely wasn't my mind playing tricks–there was a figure in the woods. My hands moved from my ears to my mouth, and I stumbled backwards.

I'd seen enough of horror movies to know not to call out the cliché "Who's there?" that surely meant certain death. Instead my feet were moving, and I was making my own path. I wanted to shout for Will.

If it was a bear, I needed to make noise in order to scare it away, but if it was a wolf, that might bring it closer. I decided to remain quiet, although I could hear the muffled chinking sounds of the bear bells in my pocket. When we left the cabin, we'd headed east. I glanced down at my watch, the little "W" letting me know I was headed in the right direction.

Here I was, running scared through the woods…again. The last time was with Will as we ran together from The Agency, and before that, from a monster in a dream. Could he be chasing me again? Could Taklos have escaped and found me? *No…it's not him. He's just a man…just a man.* Of that, I was sure. Was my fear causing me to imagine things? Was I losing my mind? This felt like a nightmare. Was that what this was? Could I be dreaming? If I was…

Without stopping, I reached my hand out, willing the branches in front of me to bend backwards. While the leaves quivered a little, the branches did not obey. No. This was not a dream–I was awake, and this was real. I kept moving, trying to calm the panic that was rising, threatening to overtake any reason that remained. I could hear the thud of my steps on the earth, the shush of the leaves as I pushed through, and the high-pitched wheeze of my terrified breaths. Why did I agree to a vacation in the woods? Nothing good had ever happened in the woods.

Just ahead, a splotch of bright white appeared through a gap in the trees; I hurried towards it. The Something was closing in behind me. It was making no attempt at stealth, but I refused to risk a glance behind. Whatever it was, it was angry and strong, matching my pace step for step. *Get to the building…get inside…get safe. Focus on the mission.*

I stumbled from the thickness of the forest into a brightly sunlit clearing, pleased to find that the building was actually a small and very old church. I sprinted across the lawn toward its arched double doors. Locked! I hammered against the wood with my fists, despite the fleeting logical conclusion that it was abandoned. I moved around the corner and pressed flat against the wall. White flakes of chipped paint scratched my skin. My lungs burned, my breaths came shallow and ragged. I knew I should turn and face whatever was chasing me, but I couldn't. I was frozen, my eyes squeezed tightly closed.

It was close now–I could feel it.

"Mrs. Carter?"

I jumped and my eyes flew open, surprised to see a woman. A real one.

"Are…aren't you Mrs. Carter?" she asked from where she stood at the other corner of the building. My eyes rushed to take her in, desperate to gain some sort of impression. Brown hair fell straight and soft at her square shoulders; she was thin but her sweatshirt hugged tight around her upper arms. This was a woman of hidden strength. She tilted her heart-shaped face, encouraging a response with a concerned expression.

"Yes."

"Are you okay?"

"Something was…there's something out there."

She stepped back and looked towards the woods.

"I don't see anything."

"I heard…I thought I heard something." I realized I was clutching my lion pendant with both hands.

The woman stepped closer. I didn't know her, but I wasn't afraid.

"I'm Samantha Prescott. I rented the cabin to your husband," she said, placing her hand on her chest. I didn't respond; she seemed genuine but after that impulsive attempt to outwit Will, I didn't trust my instincts. "I hear things in the woods all the time too. It can be really scary. Do you want to come inside?"

"It's locked," I said.

"The front is, but the back is open. Come on, it's actually really lovely inside."

My heart was still pounding, but I peeled myself off the wall and walked toward the woman with the kind face who was urging me closer with an outstretched arm. She was older, I guessed about ten years my senior, and was dressed comfortably in faded jeans, a hooded sweatshirt and brown hiking shoes. She looked absolutely normal. As I got closer, I noticed she had the most beautiful hazel eyes. Her golden irises were rimmed with green, and I was suddenly warmed by the compassion that flowed from them like a waterfall. She was safe.

"What is this place?" I asked as she ushered me around the corner to the back of the chapel.

"It used to be Parker's Mill Chapel, but they moved to a new building closer to town and now it's just another old place that time forgot. I come out here sometimes…just to pray and be alone." She smiled as she spoke, looking around the dusty church with affection.

"Oh…I'm sorry, Mrs. Prescott, I didn't mean to disturb you." I suddenly felt silly for being such a coward.

"No! Oh, don't feel bad, really. I was actually just leaving, so I'm glad I got to meet you," she said, smiling and sticking out her hand, which I shook. "Please…call me Sam."

I laughed softly. For some reason, I felt a connection to her.

"Hi, Sam. I'm Andy."

"Andy." She repeated my name, her laugh matching mine.

"Um, so do you live near here?" I explored the center aisle, running my hands across the backs of broken pews.

Sam sank down onto one of the few sturdy benches near the entrance.

"Yes, our farm is just over the hill from the cabin. I'm surprised you haven't heard the roosters," she said.

"You have a farm?" I asked enthusiastically.

"Yes." She laughed again. "My husband and I bought it several years ago."

"I've always wanted to have a farm. Do you and he farm full time, then?"

Her smile faded a little, and I felt like I'd just said something wrong, immediately recognizing the powerful combination of fondness, sadness, and bittersweet loneliness that pulsed from her. They were the same emotions my great uncle, Jubal Jones, felt when he'd talked about his late wife, Marie. I would never forget that heart wrenching moment, when I first realized I could feel someone else's strong emotions as if they were my own. It was a "gift" from Dovanny Taklos, an unwelcome exchange as he attempted to siphon off my ability to walk in dreams.

I cut my eyes away from hers, already knowing what she was going to say.

"My kids and I do. My husband, Michael, passed away. Tuesday will be four years and five months."

"I'm so sorry. I didn't mean to…" My hand fluttered to my mouth.

She looked down at her left hand and rubbed her thumb across her fingers, a pale line still visible where a ring had been. I had a feeling she'd only recently removed it.

I suddenly felt an urge to hurry back to the cabin. Saying Will would be worried would be a huge understatement.

"Thank you." She sucked in a deep breath and shoved her hands into the front pocket of her sweatshirt. "And really…it's okay. I miss him every day, but learning to live without him has taught me so much about myself and about the sweet, unexplainable comfort of my Savior."

Her words were genuine, and I wished I could sit with her for hours, learning to have the kind of faith I could feel radiating from her heart. It wrapped around her, shielding and protecting her like a blanket against the bitter cold.

"I can't imagine," I said.

Her hazel eyes met mine, a gentle understanding reflecting back.

"I know. It's not something you can ever prepare for, losing someone you love so much. It makes you question everything; I can't even explain the depths of doubt I nearly drowned in. It feels like you can't breathe... until one day, you can. It never really gets easier, but you learn to live through it, to abide in the truth of God's love, to have joy in the midst of the pain. You really learn the meaning of hope, and what it means to long for home."

I didn't have words to respond.

"I'm sorry...you really didn't come here for a sermon," she said, then laughed as her eyes traced the lines of ancient walls that once housed a vibrant congregation. "Or did you?"

Her honesty and vibrant joy diffused any remaining discomfort. She felt like an old friend.

"I'm just in awe of your faith," I said sincerely. "I don't know if I could..."

"You can't." Her quick response startled me. "But God can. Trust me, I tried. I'm a little ashamed of how long I tried. And I'll be honest, I have my good days and bad days, but God is always faithful–even when I'm not." She glanced down at her watch and stood.

"I really wish I could stay longer, Andy, but I've got to meet the ladies' group at church. We are expecting the new youth pastor next week, and we are going to get the parsonage ready."

I followed her to the door and out into the clearing.

"Will you be able to find your way back?" she asked, hesitating.

"Um...could you point me in the right direction?"

"Sure." She pointed in the opposite direction from which I had come. "It's just over that ridge."

"Thanks," I said. "And thank you for letting us stay. It's really beautiful here."

"Oh, of course. I'm glad I got to meet you." She pulled me in for an unexpected hug.

I hugged her back and when she stepped away, her cheeks were flushed. "Sorry...I'm a hugger."

"Never apologize for that," I said, unable to hide the smile on my face.

I waved as she disappeared into the trees that lined another path leading away from the church.

"Andy?" called a familiar, deep voice from behind me.

I turned to face the confused and slightly aggravated face of Will Carter.

"I turned around and you were gone."

He stood just a few feet away, red faced, his hands on his hips and chest heaving as if he'd just run a marathon. "I've been looking for you for an hour."

An hour? Surely I wasn't off the trail that long. I blinked at him for a brief second before realizing we were out in the open. I scanned the woods. They remained still–there was nothing there.

"Seriously, Andy...you can't just disappear like that. I thought..." He shook his head and ran a hand through his dark hair, which dripped with sweat. I knew what he thought; he didn't have to say.

"I'm sorry," I said automatically. "Wait...how did you know where I was?"

He shrugged.

"I just..."

"You just knew," I finished for him. Of course he did. That was Will–finder of lost things, rescuer of the needy. The first time he rescued someone, it was his brother, and it was also the exact day and time I was born. There were so many things about our lives we didn't understand, so many mysteries, but he understood he was meant to protect me, and he took that calling very seriously.

The disapproving look faded and he turned his attention to the building behind me.

"What is this place?"

"Uh...an old chapel," I said, looking once again towards the woods. "I think she said it was called Parker's Mill."

"Who?"

"Sam...er, Ms. Prescott. She owns the cabin."

"Oh, yeah, she's nice." He walked towards the church.

"I wonder what congregation met all the way out here," he mused while looking through one of the broken windows. "Looks ancient."

His brown eyes fell on mine, and whatever he saw there caused his brows to draw together.

"Are you alright?"

"Yeah...I guess I got lost."

I slipped my arms up and locked my hands behind his neck. He drew me close, pulling me up to my tiptoes. It was bright, he was here, we were safe…everything was okay. I closed my eyes and let deep breaths of cool winter air fill my lungs.

"I'm always finding you in the woods." He laughed softly.

I opened my eyes again, and from my view over his shoulder, I could see into those woods. While I was in the chapel with Sam, I'd forgotten about it, but now that dreadful feeling of being watched returned, and I squeezed my arms tighter. Will returned the gesture.

Whatever had been chasing me was still there–spying from some place hidden, I could feel it. In the distance, deep in the shadows of the trees, I thought I saw…something impossible.

I gasped.

"What's wrong?" Will pulled back from our embrace, holding me by the shoulders.

"I…uh…thought I saw something." I blinked hard, challenging my eyes to prove what my brain imagined. When I looked again, there was nothing. Will turned, following my gaze into the trees.

"What was it?"

I searched the trees again, shaking my head. "Nothing, I guess. I must be imagining things."

I took his hand and pulled him away from the building. "Come on, take me home."

"As you wish, Mrs. Carter."

As we walked across the clearing, I chanced one last glance over my shoulder. Whatever I'd seen was gone, but the image still burned in my mind. It must have been a trick of the light, but I could have sworn I'd seen my own face staring back at me.

CHAPTER 2

The distant cry, squealing sound of brakes, tires sliding on asphalt, a sickening crunch and the smell of burning rubber.

I stood and watched in agony, helplessly forced to endure the familiar scene. Every time the same. A dream—no, a nightmare—that would never end. I knew exactly how the next terrible moments would play out. My eyes would be glued to a wrecked car, silent and steaming in the night. A quiet couple dressed in white, like angels, would creep out of the woods and just as quietly back in, holding a tiny squirming bundle. Beyond the bounds of this dream, Lily and Sabastian Stone, childless and wandering, would secretly raise the baby in the sanctuary of their free-spirited world until one day she would remember the horror of this night and know the truth—or partial truth—of her past.

Why does this keep happening? There was a time when I was desperate to know what happened to my birth parents, to know why I was separated from Jonathan and Maggie. To finally understand why I never fit into my own life. I would have given anything to know who I truly was.

But now it was an unending nightmare, playing nightly in the theater of my mind, over and over and over again. Was there something else I was supposed to know about that night? *What is it?* I squeezed my hands into fists and slammed them against my legs. *What is it? How many times do I have to do this?*

No matter how much I willed it to stop, it unfolded in the same heartbreaking sequence. Trapped by the horror of it all, I wished with everything in me that it would change, but knew it never would. My stomach churned; tears streamed down my face. My trembling arms snaked around my body, trying to keep from falling apart, to keep from going insane. It was too much; I had seen it too many times. Overwhelmed with emotion and frustration, I turned my back to the pain.

Ahead, the sinister red glow of a car's taillights split the darkness like two angry eyes. It was stopped in the middle of the road. This, too, was familiar. I'd seen this before, but something made me stop and focus on that detail.

In a few seconds, a figure would step out of the car and start walking my way.

Behind me, a baby cried. Behind me, a pleading whisper slipped off through the trees. Behind me, the two strangers would be stepping out of the woods.

Please...save her. Take her now. GO.

I didn't have to look back to know it was Maggie's jagged, breathy, dying voice begging them to save her child. I had witnessed it unfold hundreds of times, a dream of a memory, but this...this was the part I had been missing. This was what I was meant to see. *Finally.*

I took a step. The car ahead was barely visible in the darkness. Its headlights flickered, and the driver's side door swung open. A figure stepped out slowly. My heart sped up, my pulse thundering in my ears. I fought the urge to run.

The driver reached out and pushed the door closed; there was only silence where there should have been sound. Thick white fog billowed, the car and driver eerie black silhouettes against its fiery glow.

The figure stood motionless for a single beat before moving, stepping with purpose. Behind me, a man was weeping with his face in the dirt, his wife holding a tiny baby in her arms beside him.

The faceless figure continued to approach; in just seconds she would be upon them.

"Hurry! Go now!" I screamed, but my words made no sound. My voice was but a breath.

Frozen in place by helpless panicked anticipation, I watched the figure continue to move closer, its shape about my height, with a small build and curves like...a woman. Her movements were fluid and confident; she didn't hesitate as she walked towards the mangled wreck.

Just steps away, she would soon pass me. In my brain, I knew this was only a dream, but in my heart, I was terrified. That desire to flee was rising; I had to work to push it down. This was important–there was something I needed to know.

Her shoes made crunching sounds on the pavement. I felt my hand move unconsciously up to cover my mouth as she passed, as if she could hear me breathing. She was staring at the wreck, moving cautiously but deliberately towards it, finally close enough that I could make out her features.

She was petite, like me, dressed in black with slick leather pants that hugged her curves, and a cropped black jacket with square shoulders that made her appear capable and dangerous. She was young, maybe even in her early twenties, also like me. Jet black and perfectly straight hair laid flat against her back almost to her waist, trimmed straight across the bottom. Her skin had a rich olive tone, and her figure was slim but strong. I sucked in a silent breath as she stepped past, so close I could smell her perfume. It was earthy and sharp, not at all floral like most women's scents. If I would have reached out, I could have touched her, but I remained frozen where I stood, arms pulled close.

Just as she stepped even with my position, she turned her face towards me, mid stride...as if she could see me there. But that was impossible! *Wasn't it?* We were suspended in space, outside of time, in an unnatural collision of ethereal and corporeal, the union of what was and what used to be.

In that moment, I memorized every detail of her face. The perfectly shaped arch of her dark eyebrows; the tiny scar just above the right one; the slight cleft in the center of her chin, and the bright, wet-looking red color of her lipstick on full hard-set lips. She had terribly intense green eyes that flashed when they met mine. Her likeness was etched permanently in my memory.

There was something behind her eyes. Something...unnatural: a swirling vortex of chaos, confusion, and pain. It was ruined and rotting inside of her.

I could see a reflection of her thoughts inside my own mind; there was only fear and hatred, envy, malice and pride. I tasted them on my tongue, and they were utterly bitter. Surely something so terrible couldn't truly exist, but I heard her breaths, saw the wind blowing her hair, felt the heat from her body. She was very real.

As her lifted foot touched the earth, she was once again looking towards the hissing, broken vehicle at the edge of the road, as if that moment hadn't happened at all. She never looked back.

Lily and Sabastian were gone, which meant I was gone. I wouldn't have been there to remember this. My breaths felt labored and shallow; I struggled to concentrate on the scene that flickered before me, like a television with a loose connection.

How am I seeing this? Is this a dream of a memory...or something else? Could this be yet another nuance of my dreamwalking I didn't know about?

She approached the car, walking around the front to the far side where I had always been too afraid to go. There would be a gruesome sight there that I couldn't possibly bear. From where I stood, I could see her, but not what she could see. Unphased and expressionless, she bent down, reaching out towards something inside. Was she checking to see if my mother was still alive?

"She's not! She's dead, and you probably killed her!" I knew she couldn't hear me, but a dark part of my heart wanted the force of my words to strike her down.

My mouth snapped shut when she jerked her head up, staring directly at me...or rather, through me. Her eyes darted around, scanning the emptiness around us before returning to whatever hideous task to which she'd been set.

With her jaw set tight and eyes narrowed, the woman stood abruptly and circled the car, looking in each of the windows while she kicked glass out of her way with her high heeled black boots. She was searching for something. The hard set of her jaw and quick jerking movement of her body revealed her frustration. My heart sped up again as she walked away from the car to the edge of the woods.

No, no, no, stay away from there. Leave them alone.

Would she go in? Would she find the couple who took the baby? I knew in my head that she wouldn't, but still held the next breath prisoner in my lungs. After a few unbearable minutes of watching her scan the darkness that lay beyond the trees, she finally turned around.

She pulled out a small rectangular phone from her pocket, flipped it open, and held it to her ear. I strained to hear what she was saying, but the sound was muffled and broken, as if I was watching from behind glass. Even though I moved closer, making sure to avoid an accidental glimpse at the horror inside the car, her words were still unintelligible. She waved her hands around dramatically as she spoke, pacing back and forth. Apparently she didn't get the response she wanted, because she slapped the phone closed and shoved it back into her pocket.

I watched her storm back to the mangled car and reach through a broken window, nearly crawling inside. A flurry of curses filled the silence as she brushed broken bits of glass from her hands, then jerked a car seat and a baby's diaper bag out through the window.

Once back at her own car, she threw the two items in the trunk, and with one more long glance back at the wreck, slammed the lid shut. She slid, smooth and snake-like, into the driver's seat, the glowing red eyes of taillights fluttering open as she started the engine.

I suddenly felt a warm breeze encircle me from behind, intimate and comforting. The endless forest of trees that lined both sides of the road began to sway, their leaves rustling like rushing water. The wind carried waves of soft whispered words drifting smoothly into my ears.

Look, it said. *See.*

I narrowed my eyes and focused on the woman's car. It was a black, boxy sedan–too sleek to be cheap, but not bearing the mark of any brand I recognized. Just as it disappeared into the night, I saw the license plate and on it, an unfamiliar symbol. It was a trident without the staff, simple and black against the stark white background.

She was gone; the scene vanished. I stood shivering and alone in the dark.

Strong hands were on my shoulders, the drum of a familiar heartbeat in my ears. I tried to turn, to step, to run. I was trapped. My feet wouldn't move, and my heart raced wildly.

"Andy…Andy!"

It was Will. He was sitting on the edge of the bed, holding me as I thrashed.

I shot up, gasping for air. My flailing hands found his strong arms and clamped on, clinging to the solidness of his frame. I was shaking, completely soaked with sweat, chilled and nauseated.

"Shhh…it's just a dream." He brushed my damp hair back from my face and tucked it behind my ears.

I wrapped my arms around his neck, letting my heart find rhythm with his.

"I'm sorry," I sobbed into his shoulder.

"It's okay." His voice was soft, and I looked into his concerned but tired brown eyes.

How many more nights would we repeat this ritual? How long would he wait–how long until it was one time too many?

"You're okay, I'm here." He dropped his forehead to meet mine and put his hands on the sides of my face, holding it still. "Just breathe."

"I'm so sorry," I cried, trying to take a normal, filling breath. "I don't know how to make them stop."

"Shhh… I know…" His words soothed and calmed me. "I know, baby, it's okay."

He didn't call me that very often, but every time he did, I felt my cheeks grow warm with a blush. Even now, as my body fought against my mind, I felt the heat, and because his hands were still on my face, I knew he felt it too.

"I'm not going anywhere," he said, as if he could read my mind.

After a few minutes, he pulled the quilt from our bed over my shoulders and rubbed my arms as I pulled it tightly around me. When I finally stopped shivering, he slid backwards, leaning against the headboard, fluffing a pillow behind his back.

"Tell me." He yawned, rubbing his eyes as if preparing to be awake for a while.

I wanted this reality we were living to dissolve into a regular happy newlywed life. We should be a couple who dreamed of white picket fences and neighborly barbeques. Real life nightmares and disturbing visions of the past weren't year two marriage trials, which we'd barely just begun; surely those were decade two issues at least. Yet there we sat, my stomach still churning, him fully alert and expectant.

"This time it was different." I searched his eyes. Could he even understand what that meant?

"How?"

"It started the same. That night…I've seen it so many times…over and over, but this time I just couldn't watch it again, so…I turned away." I felt a slight pang of guilt in my admission.

"I guess I hoped it would just be over and I could wake up. But that's when I saw it…someone else was there." My voice was shaky, my words rushed. "I saw…"

"Who was he?" Will sat up straight, leaning closer.

I shifted, lifting myself up until I was on my knees, sitting back on my feet; our bed creaked as I moved. Remembering the disturbing events of tonight's dream made me anxious and restless.

"It wasn't a he, it was a she. A woman, and she was young, maybe mid-twenties? I think…maybe…she caused the accident? I'm not positive, but she was definitely there. She walked past me, Will, and I know it's going to sound crazy, but she looked right at me. I mean, that's impossible, right?"

"Says the woman who walks in dreams."

"I was scared…I'm still scared." I looked down at my fingers twisted together, wishing I hadn't said that out loud.

I didn't like to be scared, and liked admitting it even less.

He didn't respond. I glanced up to catch something flash in his eyes before his expression morphed from concerned to fierce. He was in protector mode; I'd seen it many times before. As he slid forward, his eyes burned into mine, and my heart stopped.

He took my hands in his, stilling their fidgeting and spreading a tranquility throughout my entire body. His eyes remained locked onto mine, shutting out everything else around us.

"I won't let anyone hurt you." His voice was low, almost a growl.

There was no air between us, just the irrevocable pull towards him that I had felt from the very first moment our eyes had met.

"I have to look for her," I whispered almost as an apology. "I have to find her…to make it stop."

He didn't answer. He just held me safely between his hands, trapped by his dark eyes.

"I can't live like this," I pleaded, my voice barely audible. "You have to let me."

I didn't need his permission, but I wanted his understanding.

"I know." He closed his eyes in sad resolve, his words lingering in the vacuum that filled the space between his face and mine.

"Will you help me?"

His eyes flew open. Pain flashed across his face, and his brows drew sharply together. I felt his heart, fierce and forever, torn between protector and partner. He pulled me close and his lips hovered over mine. I held my breath.

"Always." He breathed before kissing me fiercely, stealing the remaining breath from my lungs.

CHAPTER 3

I stood before a great wall, every inch covered with bright, blinking images. It reminded me of the stacked televisions I used to see in shop windows of the little towns I traveled through with my nomadic family. This wasn't Main Street though, and I wasn't watching cartoons or commercials. This was my dreamscape, and I was on a mission. There were hundreds of screens, each with different faces constantly flashing across it. I waved my hand in the air to move the pictures along, searching for one in particular.

Starting the night we returned from our trip to the mountains and for months following, I'd been plagued by the same nightmare, until I saw her. After that, the dreams had stopped, but the search had begun. I desperately wanted to find her. She was, most likely, the one who caused my parents' deaths, and she had definitely been looking for me that night. I just didn't know for what purpose.

Because of Lily and Sabastian, I'd disappeared. I grew up in a strange but loving family, hidden away from the world. But after what happened with Taklos, I knew that I wasn't invisible after all. He had found me; she could too. It seemed like a risk to look for her, but it felt like a bigger risk not to.

There was another reason too, though. This quest brought me a renewed purpose; it filled my nights, and occupied the space where the nightmares had been. If I stopped looking...the space would be empty, and the dreams might return.

Was she even still alive? Was she working alone? She had called someone that night; who was it? What did she want with me, and why did that mean my parents had to die? What about my grandmother, Esther, and my uncle Jacob—were they in danger? There were too many unknowns to leave it up to chance. No. My best bet was to find her first, even if it was just to make sure she wasn't still looking for me.

If I just knew who and where she was, at least I could stay away, and maybe I could finally give Esther the answers she'd been waiting for.

Even though I was technically asleep, I was getting no real rest and it was really starting to show. Will saw it, and I knew his sleep was restless right along with mine. I had to find her soon for both our sakes.

My eyes darted from image to image, looking for the olive skin, dark hair, and unmistakable green eyes I had seen in my dream. Faces ticked endlessly by, and I had to squeeze my lids shut as my eyes started to burn and water. Even in the best of circumstances, with pages of intel, it could take me days to find a target. I had nothing on this woman. No name, no background, nothing. All I had was the image of her face that was burned into my brain. I saw it every time I closed my eyes, as if she were standing right in front of me. That was yet another reason I wanted to find her, to end...whatever this was. Then—maybe I could close my eyes and see nothing there.

If only I could have heard her phone conversation.

I stepped away from the pictures in front of me and took a deep breath, rubbing my eyes, ready to give up, at least for tonight. When I turned back, prepared to swipe everything away, something caught my eye.

"Wait," I said out loud.

I raised both hands and moved them back and forth, as if sifting through a giant deck of cards for just the right one.

"There."

It was her. She was older, but it was definitely her. Those shocking emerald eyes stared back at me from high up on my imagined wall. Everything about her was the same: tiny scar above her eyebrow, little cleft in her chin, even down to her bright red lipstick. My hands were still up; my fingers framed her face, which made her seem even closer. I quickly dropped my arms. I didn't actually expect to find her, and honestly, I didn't know what to do now that I had.

I could try to reach out to her. Would she recognize me? Surely not. How could she? I had been a baby at the time of the crash, and was gone by the time she got to the car.

Finding her image was a small victory, but only gave me one vital bit of information. She was alive. I wouldn't have been able to see this picture if she wasn't; dead people don't dream, and even superpowers have limits. It had been something I considered. The accident had been over twenty years ago; she was a young woman then, but still an adult. She would be in her forties now–maybe fifties? Still young enough to be dangerous. The truth was, if she was alive, she was a threat.

After so many nights of searching, there she was. So close. Maybe I could just slip into her dreams and observe; she didn't even have to know I was there. I'd done that many times before at The Agency. Though I was never very stealthy, I was skilled at blending in.

I paced back and forth in front of her image, chewing on my fingernails and trying to work up the nerve to give it a try.

"Ugh…just do it!"

I squared my shoulders and faced her, making a mental list of all the reasons why this was not a crazy or dangerous idea.

I probably won't even reach her; it's a total long shot. This will take a lot of concentration; I don't think I have it in me, anyway. Five minutes… five minutes and I'm out.

I didn't buy my own lies, but closed my eyes anyway and took deep controlled breaths, centering all of my attention on the image of her face, which I could still see behind my lids. It was very early in the morning, so the odds were in my favor that if she was anywhere in the United States, she was probably asleep. That was another limitation of my ability. Both of us had to be asleep to make a connection.

Several minutes passed. I continued to focus all my energy, all my thoughts, on her image, reaching out into the void to search for her. I felt a familiar shiver run up my spine, meaning I was close.

A bothersome reminder fluttered across my mind, causing a momentary ripple in the thick veil of concentration I'd created. The last time I'd made a connection with someone, it had been with Dovanny

Taklos.

I took another deep breath and blew out slowly through my lips. *Focus, Andy.* I pictured her green eyes, and the wind lifting her dark hair around her face.

The temperature around me dropped suddenly and my eyes flew open. It was dark. The wall of images was gone. I spun around, still only seeing empty blackness, and let out a resigned sigh. I was both disappointed and relieved that it didn't work. Standing there in the cool air waiting to wake up, I prayed for answers. *What is all of this for, Lord? What is it I'm meant to do now? Esther said I would know, but I feel lost...am I...am I just looking for something to obsess about? Is it really just as simple as bad dreams?*

Even though we hadn't officially said it out loud, everything that had happened in the last few months had affected me both emotionally and physically, and not just at night. I knew Will was watching me closely. I'd heard the whispered concerns exchanged between my family; I knew that my skin had been the exact temperature of an icebox, and I was constantly distracted. I was dealing with it, but my poor husband desperately wanted to fix everything. There was just nothing he could do.

This new mission of finding the mystery woman had brought a rush of hope–or perhaps just a different kind of distraction. Will questioned the risk I was taking to keep searching, but he wasn't going to stand in my way. Even he couldn't deny that more information meant a better chance of staying safe. I had to believe that it all meant something. The nightmares and finally the revelation of the one person in all the world who knew what truly happened that night–it had to be for a purpose, so I had to keep going.

I had to know that we were really safe–for good. I had to make it right for Esther. I had to.

And what happens when you're done?

I shook my head, letting that thought fall away. I didn't want to think about who I would be when it was all over. I kept telling myself that was what I wanted, for it to be over; but was that really the truth?

I rubbed my eyes, which were fighting to focus on the nothingness that surrounded me, and decided it really was time to go. I turned around again, trying to find my way out, but there was no light.

Nothing...just darkness. I closed my eyes again, focusing on an exit. When I opened them, it was still dark.

I felt my heart speed up just a little. Something was wrong. I tried to pull up the images from before, and still nothing. I felt a tightness in my throat. What was happening?

Will. No, he wasn't home. He wouldn't be there to wake me if I couldn't get out...maybe this hadn't been such a good idea.

A sudden image flashed across my brain. I couldn't be sure if I was actually seeing it with my eyes or just imagining it.

It was a long hallway lined with endless doors. It was dimly lit by a single row of fluorescent lights that ran down the middle. It had to be real though; I could smell the dampness in the air. The humid moisture of someplace buried pricked my skin. At first, the corridor appeared empty, but one of the farthest lights flickered and I saw her. Just beyond the reach of the light, barely visible, stood a little girl with blond hair. She was dressed in a white gown and stared at me with wide, hopeful eyes. Slowly, she raised a small frail hand, reaching towards me. I couldn't hear her, but her lips formed two words.

"Rescue us."

I gasped, and as soon as the picture formed, it faded away in a cloud of black smoke. I spun around only to find complete darkness yet again. Instinctively, I reached up to touch my necklace. It was warm beneath my fingers but offered little comfort as a terrible thought entered my mind. *You found her.* Water splashed in the distance.

A tiny noise from behind caught my attention and I froze, listening carefully. It had sounded like a whisper. There it was again. And again. More whispers joined in. A chorus of tiny voices swirled all around me, speaking a language I didn't know. The sound was coming from all directions all at once. The voices grew louder; some were deep and feral, others high pitched and shrieking. The goosebumps on my arms grew with the volume. I could hardly breathe; my heart was pounding. The words made no sense, but I knew one thing–they weren't friendly.

The voices drew close...so close, I felt my hair moving with the air, pushed by their breath, back and forth. Around and around they circled, moving ever closer. I fought back against the panic that was rising from a tight knot in my stomach, slowly inching its way up my spine.

I jumped as the cold breath of someone–or something–brushed against my ear. It was asking me a question. When I didn't answer, it asked again. Aggressive and violent.

"I don't understand," I cried, now clutching my necklace with both hands.

"What do you want?" It answered in English, each word drawn out in a hiss.

A different voice from the other side made me jump back in the opposite direction.

"She's ours…" it growled.

"OURS!" A powerful booming voice came from behind, sending me to the ground in a cowering crouch, my arms flying up to cover my head.

As I dropped, I was suddenly ankle deep in water, and it was rising. That was from me; my fear was growing, bringing the level of water with it. I splayed my hands flat on the surface. I could make it rise if I wanted. I could destroy anything around me: everything. A tingle of desire tickled my fingertips and sent ripples out across the surface.

But–unless my destruction was complete–she would know. When she woke, she would know that I, or someone, had been there. If she hadn't been looking for me before, she would start. That was not a mistake I could make, no matter how scared I felt. It took every last bit of courage, but I made the waters vanish, feeling a tiny jolt of power as I controlled them.

"Yesssssssss." A sickly-sweet voice encouraged me. The voices liked my power; they wanted it.

I jerked my hands back, covering my ears as the whispers, wails, and growls continued to swirl. I felt my chest tighten, gasping between terrified sobs that shook my body. My silver lion burned against my chest.

Perfect love casts out fear.

Will. He'd spoken those words to me once when I was scared, too afraid to even step outside the church walls. Paralyzed by the fear of what might be waiting there. As soon as the thought entered my head, the voices all hissed and grew quieter, farther away as if backing up.

The light shines in the darkness, and the darkness has not overcome it.

He'd said that too. They hissed again, howling in pain. The ancient words of God that I'd hidden deep in my heart were hurting them, defending me and pushing back the enemy. I tried to remember another verse…anything…what had I just read that morning…it was in Luke?

Behold, I have given you authority to tread on serpents and scorpions, and over all the power of the enemy, and nothing will injure you.

The voices retreated. I stood up and spun around. *Help me, Lord; help me get out. I need a way out.*

I heard a different sound.

What is that?

The sound of a bell? Something ringing. I turned towards the sound and there in the distance was a light, small but growing–the way out! I sprinted towards it. At my back, I felt the icy words and hissing voices once more.

Over and over they repeated, "She's ours…ours."

I sat straight up, my hands finding the soft fabric of my quilt, which I jerked tightly to my chest. I looked around, frantically searching for Will, still gasping for air. He wasn't there. Where was he? What was that ringing sound?

A movement from my nightstand made me jump. I jerked my head to see what it was. My phone was ringing, and the vibrations were making it dance around on the little wooden table.

I grabbed it and stared at the bright screen. I had a missed call and a couple of text messages from Will. I was still trying to calm myself down, and didn't question why he was calling me so early in the morning.

I slid my thumb across the screen to open my messaging app.

Guess I missed you. Going out again. I'll call when I get in.

Might be late.

I jumped as my phone rang again. Will's name appeared on the screen, and I took a deep breath before answering.

"Hello?"

"Hey, did I wake you up?" His voice was low, heavy with exhaustion.

"Uh…no, I mean…it's okay." Words felt wrong in my mouth, as if my lips and tongue had forgotten how to speak.

"What's wrong?" He was instantly on alert.

"Nothing…I'm fine." I wasn't fine.

"You're lying. What happened?" His words were firm, carrying that tone of authority I recognized from the way he spoke to his team at The Agency, and I held the phone out as if I could see him. What was wrong with him?

"Andy!" he said again when I didn't answer.

"I…I'm okay, really. I was just looking for her… and…" Oops.

"You were looking for…Andy, I thought we agreed you would wait until I got home."

"No, YOU agreed that I would wait until you got home. I never agreed to that," I said defensively. "I'm not one of your subordinates, Will."

He was calling from Colorado, where he'd been helping out with another missing person's case and had been gone for several days. Before he left, he had basically ordered me not to look for her while he was away. I had argued, but he had ended the discussion with a fiery kiss, making my head swim and forget what I was saying, which I still maintained was completely unfair.

I could practically see him running a hand through his hair, his signature move when he was frustrated. Well, he should be frustrated. I wasn't one of his underlings–he couldn't just bark orders and expect unquestioning compliance. I clenched my teeth, entertaining the desire to simply hang up on him.

"You're killing me," he said finally.

My cheeks were flushed from the dream, and also from an embarrassing perturbation at his chastisement. I heard a sad sigh and immediately felt bad for snapping at him when I just really wanted him there with me–desperately.

I should have respected his wishes, even though at the time, I thought it was silly. He was my husband; we had promised to honor and respect each other. He wasn't controlling, and wouldn't have asked without good reason. In truth, after what had just happened, he'd been right.

I could feel his concern, even over the phone, as if it were my own. It was unusually intense. That perception sent a warning shot of ice through my veins. Taklos had been a true empath. Through an unbelievable accident, he gained the ability to influence people simply with his thoughts, but the unintended consequence was disastrous. His empathy became intensified and crippling; he suddenly felt every emotion from every person around him. It was so intense, so painful, that it drove him mad. When I had met Taklos in the dreamscape, he had left a piece of himself with me; what if that had happened again? What if whatever was inside of her head was now inside of mine?

"I'm sorry, Will." I held the phone with two hands as if that would somehow bring him closer.

I listened to him breathe for a few minutes, fighting the urge to tell him to come home. I knew he would be on the next flight if I asked, but he was needed there.

"Why are you calling anyway?" I asked, realizing it was two in the morning where he was.

"You'd asked me earlier to call when I got in and I know it's late, but… I wanted to hear your voice, and then…I just felt like something wasn't right," he said slowly.

"Oh." I remembered my desperate prayer.

"Andy, I know something happened. Please talk to me." His voice was soft now, almost apologetic.

I sighed and decided on an abridged version of events.

"It was dark, and I just felt so trapped."

I didn't mention hearing voices; somehow even in the dream world that didn't seem like a good sign. How could I explain what happened anyway? I didn't even know myself. He didn't say anything for a few minutes, and I knew he was sitting there clenching his jaw with fiery frustration in his eyes.

"I really am sorry," I said. "Forgive me?"

"I'm not mad at you…I just…don't like being gone."

"I know, but they need you. It was creepy, but I'm really okay. I promise not to do anything else until you get back."

He took a deep breath.

"I love you," he whispered.

"I love you, too." I couldn't fight the smile that crept across my lips. "Now…go find the lost things."

"We did…"

I started to celebrate, but something in his tone stopped me.

"Was…was everyone okay?"

"I was too late."

"Oh, Will."

No wonder he had been so on edge. It also wasn't lost on me that he said, "I was too late." He felt responsible, just like me.

"I'm so sorry. I guess it's stupid to ask if you're alright."

"It's not stupid–but…no, I don't guess I am."

"Do you want to talk about it?"

"I just want to be home."

My heart ached for him. He was hurting, broken for a family that was grieving, for his team and for himself. I knew what he was feeling; even though he'd done all he could, it still seemed like it was his fault. I knew, because even though I hadn't done anything but be born…my parents were dead.

They'd called him in because he was the best. He saw things no one else could see; not only the subtle clues that were present, but also the broken pattern of things absent. His talent was wonderful when the job ended with tears of joy, but nights like this–when they were tears of loss–I knew he felt the weight of his gift, and it was heavy.

"I wish...that it was different...that all the lost could be found." His voice broke a little, which broke me a lot.

I held the phone to my ear but buried my face in a pillow. I didn't want him to hear me crying. It was enough for him to deal with his own grief; he didn't need to be worried about mine as well. When I'd managed to pull myself together, I moved my pillow and snuggled under the covers, splaying my hand out across the empty space on the bed where he should be.

"I wish I knew the right words to somehow make it better," I said.

"Knowing you're okay makes it better." Someone spoke in the background, asking Will a question I couldn't make out.

"Yeah," he said to whomever had spoken. "I'll be right there."

"You need to go?"

"Yes." He sounded tired.

"Okay...and Will...I know it hurts. I know your heart is broken, and I love you because of that heart, but I also know you did everything you possibly could; that's who you are. It's who God made you, and...I'm so sorry that this time your gift was used to bring a family closure instead of a reunion. You still did a good thing, even though it doesn't feel like it right now."

He didn't respond for a long minute. Finally I heard him clear his throat before he spoke again.

"I love you, Andy."

"I love you, too."

"I'll be home tomorrow."

Thank you, God.

CHAPTER 4

Will sat across from me at a round table in the little cafe just two blocks from Christ Church. He stared out a massive glass window that overlooked a busy street. It wasn't spring yet, but the sidewalk was already packed with both tourists and locals. It had been a long and unusually cold winter, and everyone was grateful for a few days of warmer temperatures.

Sun poured through the window surrounding us in a halo of light. I wanted its warmth to seep deep into my bones, but I couldn't shake the chill I had felt since the night I'd walked in that disturbing dream. The memory of heinous slithering shadows and formless voices sent a shiver snaking down my spine, raising goosebumps on my skin despite the several layers of clothing I wore. Even my necklace felt like ice, and I tugged on the chain, letting the pendant dangle on the outside of my sweater.

I lifted my steaming hot mocha and drank it down, trying to burn away the freezing hollowness. I had been watching the people and cars moving back and forth. I wondered where they came from, where they were going, what the reason was for their urgency. My eyes tracked the crowd, stopping on every shock of black hair, every petite female, every flash of olive skin.

Could one of them be the woman who was there the night my parents died? Was she out there looking for me like I was looking for her? The people moved too quickly though, and trying to focus on every face as it passed was making my head hurt.

I turned away from the window to find Will watching me intently. I felt my cheeks flush and turned my attention to the remaining puddle of coffee in the bottom of my mug.

He stretched across the table, his hands covering mine which were still wrapped tightly around the white ceramic cup, absorbing its last bits of heat.

"Your hands are frozen," he said.

"You know what they say." I flashed a sly smile. "Cold hands, warm heart."

"Oh, is that what they say?"

"Mmhmm, they sure do."

Our lighthearted moment lingered through the tail end of a second before slipping away. I still hadn't told him everything; he didn't know that I lay awake every night in the dark, listening for any hint of those terrible voices, hoping beyond hope that nothing got left behind. I didn't want to burden him with worries of residual supernatural side effects from a reckless mission he hadn't wanted me to take in the first place. I already felt like I was going crazy; I didn't need confirmation.

"Maybe…" I started to say that maybe we should stop searching, but something stopped me.

His last mission hadn't gone as planned either, and I knew he was still feeling guilty over what he perceived as a failed rescue.

Rescue us.

Why did I keep hearing those words? There was something else I should know. I shook my head in frustration. Who was this woman? At worst she murdered my parents, at best she'd been there and had done nothing to help them. Esther said Maggie had been afraid; that she felt like someone had been following her. That was why she and my father were even on the road that night. They were on their way to stay with Esther. Had it been that woman my mom was running from? But…why?

What did Maggie have that someone would want to destroy?

After finding out she was alive, Will took over trying to locate her. If anyone could find the unfindable, it was him. We had nothing to go on except my description of her and the strange symbol on the license plate.

He'd been buried under a stack of maps, police reports, and lists of data that I couldn't begin to decipher. His eyes were red from hours of staring at a computer screen. He was frustrated by the lack of progress, which was why we had come to the cafe for a much-needed break.

"Maybe what?" Will asked after the deep dive unto my thoughts had left me silent.

"Umm...I was just thinking that maybe I could visit Nadine."

"No way." He sat up stiffly, pulling his hands away and folding his arms over his chest. "Andy, you can't be serious."

"I just..." I caught my head in my hands as it fell forward. "I keep remembering something she said."

"What did she say?"

"In the woods she said, 'I'll find him another one.'" I shrugged and looked up from under the wall of red hair that hung across my face. "I can't help feeling like there's a connection."

He stared at me for a few seconds. His brown eyes sparked with fire as he was, no doubt, remembering that day–the day we met. He'd led the search team that found me confused, terrified, and almost frozen to death in the middle of the woods. The muscles in his jaw clenched; he turned to look out of the window again.

He had been the one to testify against Nadine Greyson, the doctor who had been secretly working with Dovanny Taklos. He had to recount how she had blackmailed poor Nurse Charlotte Phillips into kidnapping me and helping her wipe my memory so that I wouldn't remember Taklos' true plans and agree to continue the assigned mission. He had barely been able to contain his fury when he explained how she had let her jealousy take over, and instead of sticking with Taklos' plan to return me memoryless but unharmed to a hospital, left me drugged in the woods. She had meant for me to die there, and I would have if Will hadn't found me.

"Maybe she knows something."

He took a deep breath and finally looked back at me.

"You know you can't go see her. In person or anywhere else." He leaned forward, lowering his voice to a whisper. "She thinks you're dead, and it needs to stay that way."

He was right. I knew that. If I visited her, even in a dream, that defense of anonymity would be gone.

"I'm sorry I can't give you more to go on."

"What about Esther?" Will said softly.

I looked up at him, confused.

"What?"

"Well, if Greyson knows something, maybe you do, too. Maybe she said or did something while she…" His eyes flashed with something dark, and he shifted uncomfortably in his chair, then cleared his throat. "Maybe Esther can help you remember."

It was my turn to reach for him. He let me peel his tightly clenched fists open and weave my fingers through his.

"Hey." I ducked my head, catching his gaze and drawing it to mine. "I'm okay."

He smiled, but it didn't reach his eyes. Maybe one day we would be more than just okay, but for now, okay was enough. He leaned forward, untangling our fingers, his long arms reaching across the table, hands sliding up to rest on my forearms. I leaned in towards him too and felt the warmth of his touch even through my sweater and the long-sleeved shirt I wore underneath.

"Whenever I think about what she did…" He shook his head, as if chasing away a painful memory. His voice was deep and gravelly. "I just can't think about losing you."

He flicked his eyes up, flames dancing around the edges of his irises, and my breath caught in my throat. We were suddenly alone in the cafe; the bustle of customers, clinking mugs, and hissing machines fell silent. Time stood still and the world dissolved into nothing around us.

The space between us closed in for the length of a long breath, a moment that was only ours, private…intimate. He pulled my hand up, holding it between both of his, and I pushed it forward, my palm settling on the side of his face. He turned his head in, brushing his lips lightly across the tender skin on my wrist, his eyes never leaving mine.

My face felt hot from the bright red blush I knew was spreading across my cheeks. He saw it too, and the corner of his mouth turned up a little, making them flame up again.

The intensity of the moment passed too quickly, and he sat back in his chair, folding his hands casually behind his head. My skin felt cold where his hands had been. He turned his attention towards the activity outside.

"Have you told Esther yet?" he asked, cutting only his eyes towards me. "That you found her?"

"No," I said softly. "She seems…tired."

He nodded. We had both noticed over the last few months that Esther had been slowing down. Even though I hadn't known her long–just over a year, in fact–there had definitely been a change. I couldn't help but wonder if it had anything to do with the night that she had helped me remember what happened to my parents, and a sharp jab of guilt punctured my heart.

I thought this was supposed to stop: the guilt, shame, and sadness. Weren't those things I should give to Jesus and be done with? Maybe I was doing it wrong...

"You should talk to her."

I snapped my head towards him, remembering he was there.

"I know." I joined him in people-watching, picking back up with my secret task of searching faces. "I will."

CHAPTER 5

"Give me your hands, child."

She held her hands out, palms up, open and expectant. After a whispered battle of wills with my husband in the hallway, I'd finally conceded to telling Esther everything–well, almost everything. She insisted on helping, of course.

I moved to let her take my hands but pulled back, cocking my head to the side inquisitively. "Is there something you're not telling me?"

She dropped her hands into her lap. Her expression told me there might be a lot of things she wasn't sharing. Things that were not yet mine to know.

"Are you stalling?" She raised an eyebrow. "I've been around a few years, you know; I recognize a stall tactic when I see it."

"No! I really want to know. Your gift. How does it work?"

I knew she was remembering as I was. The warm October day over a year ago, when I sat in this same creaky wooden chair across from her in her tiny bedroom, just off the long stone hall that ran maze-like under the church. There was something buried deep inside my memory that was so very important, but would never surface on its own. She had held my hands then too. She told me to breathe and to see. I did see.

A tiny sad smile played on her lips, then she looked up as if searching the ceiling for the answer.

"You've read the story of Joseph? The one with the coat?"

"Yes?" I answered cautiously.

"He was a dreamer too, you know." She winked and ran her thumb softly across my cheek. "But when he was taken to Pharaoh and told to interpret his dream, Joseph said 'I cannot. Only God can do that.' That's kind of how it is with me."

"You...have to ask permission?"

"You could put it that way." She laughed. "I'm not like you—you can go walk in the dreams of anyone you want at any time; I can only help if my help is needed, and still, it's not me. I'm just the vessel. I know you understand that."

I did understand. The familiar shiver of icy cold waters rippled across my skin. I'd faced a monster in the deep before, unable to find victory by myself. I knew well the sacrifice and the euphoria of working under a power not your own.

"Why didn't you tell me?" I wasn't mad, just curious.

"I didn't intend to keep it from you. I guess it was just such a treacherous time, and then after that...it didn't seem to matter."

She was right; treacherous was a perfectly accurate word. Once Dovanny Taklos, the presumed terrorist, stepped onto the scene, everything had changed for me. My unique position as an interrogator for the secret government organization known only as The Agency was no longer the ideal combination of purposeful yet hidden. A former target unknowingly leaked knowledge of my existence, and because of his own sordid history, Taklos jumped at the possibility of a partnership. He was the one who had begun to unlock the true extent of my power. Until then, even I didn't know the full capacity of my gift, and I still wasn't sure I'd learned everything. I didn't know much about Esther's, either.

"So, what exactly is your gift?"

"I guess you would say that I help people remember that which was lost," Esther said finally.

"Sort of like Will...but with memories?"

"Has he ever explained it to you—how he can find things no one else can?"

"Yes, he says it's sort of a combination of deciphering patterns and a strong gut feeling that leads him in a particular direction."

She chuckled at my observation. "Hmm. Maybe the gut feeling part."

"Is that why you wrote the book?" I pictured the handwritten journal Will had found on my great-uncle Jubal's houseboat that led him to her in the first place. "The stories of all the Lionhearts?"

"Yes, I suppose so." She closed her eyes. "Some things should never be forgotten."

"I'll never forget the day I met you."

The day I met Esther was both the best and the worst day of my life. I'd finally found a safe place. A funny little village with no connections to the outside world. Taklos couldn't find me there. But Will found something valuable enough to draw me away: a family I didn't even know I was missing. Jubal's story of his late wife, Marie, the journal, and my lion-shaped birthmark led us to the doors of Christ Church and Esther's open arms. From the safety of her embrace, I'd learned of my true lineage. We were descendants of an ancient order filled with women bound into God's service, each one privileged to possess a unique and supernatural talent meant to accomplish God's work on earth as they were directed.

"I'll never forget that either." Her smile was genuine.

"So there's not one big thing, then, that you were meant to do? Like Marie rescuing those school kids?"

"No." Her fingers fluttered to the heart-shaped locket she wore around her neck. I knew there was a faded portrait of my mother, Maggie, and Esther's sister, Marie, inside.

"Courage was no doubt her gift and my sister was still brave, even after she returned from the war, but it was different. She once told me that it hadn't felt like her own feet carrying her towards that building. She said it was as if she were being swept along by a great wave. She had no fear, no urge to look back nor hesitate, and that's why she was able to run into danger when everyone else was running out. It took a lot out of her. She was happy to pay that price and would gladly do it again, but she was definitely a humble woman when she returned."

Ours is a calling that costs. Loving people always costs you something.

Esther had said those words once. Although I thought I'd paid a pretty hefty price already, there was a lingering knot in my stomach hinting that there would be much, much more.

"I guess I thought..." My voice trailed off as I watched my fingers trace the swirling patterns in the wood of my chair.

"That you were done?" she said, drawing my eyes to meet hers. "I understand, Joanna. I know that it weighs heavily on your shoulders. I think that is why God sent that dashing helpmate to you."

She leaned in, nudging my shoulder. I blushed.

"You help people remember things." I reached up to touch the silver lion Esther had made into a necklace for me. It had been Marie's–another of the clues leading me home.

"Yes?'

"Is there any way to–I mean–can you also help someone forget?"

She didn't answer for a long time. She didn't ask what I meant or what I wanted to forget, she only stared at me with wise crystal-blue eyes. If this didn't work, if we learned nothing…there had to be some way for me to move on. If not, I really would go insane.

I knew the pleading face she saw staring back at her was strained with desperation. She seemed to consider her next words carefully.

"The hard things don't always make sense as we are passing through, but we need to trust God to do just that–take us through. The closest I ever felt to Him weren't the times when He took the pain away; they were the times when He carried me through it. Those times should be remembered."

A deep, agonizing grief pulsed from her and hit me hard in the chest, taking my breath for a second. It told me there were more things in Esther's past than I knew–hard, heart-breaking, spirit-crushing things from which she mercifully spared me and kept hidden away so I wouldn't have to bear them, even if just through the reflection of her heart.

"Now, quit stalling and give me your hands."

"There might be nothing to remember."

"Then there's nothing, but we'll still try," she said, her voice firm and powerful. She waved her hands, beckoning me to place mine in hers.

Esther was a woman of quiet strength and when she spoke, people listened.

"Joanna, look at me." I obeyed. "I have known all these years that someone else was there when my Maggie and Jonathan were killed. I've known it in my heart, and I have prayed every day that God would bring to light the truth of what happened that night. Some might think that He was ignoring me these twenty-two years, but I tell you, our God does not delay. When you finally came to me with your dream, I knew it was time. You were given that dream for a reason, and if you feel there might be something we can learn from this woman, Nadine, then we need to trust that instinct."

She held my hands firmly as she spoke and looked into my eyes with such conviction. I felt a surge of resolve and purpose. If nothing else, I wanted to give her answers. She had waited all these years to find out what really happened to her daughter, and more than for myself, I wanted to help her know the truth.

"Close your eyes."

The world grew dark at the shutter of my lids.

"Breathe. Deep and slow…"

I let my lungs pull in great deep breaths.

"Remember, Joanna." Her words sounded far away.

I felt a sharp pinch, then a burning sensation traveled up my arm. I opened my eyes, and was met with a blinding light. I tried to put my hand up to block it, but my arms wouldn't move. Something was restraining them, and I fought against it.

"Stay calm, Joanna. You are safe; listen and see." Esther's voice echoed from somewhere inside my mind. "Breathe…"

I followed her instructions and stopped struggling.

Listen and see. That was the mission. Focus on the mission.

Whatever was traveling through my veins made it hard to focus on anything. My head was swimming, and my vision blurred. It made my heart race. I felt hot, yet very cold at the same time; beads of sweat dripped down my forehead, and shivers raced across my skin. I couldn't remember why I was there. This was different than watching as an observer as I had done when Esther helped me remember the accident. I couldn't step outside of myself this time. Something was wrong.

"Grandma," I said with slurred speech, my eyelids drooping against my will. "I can't…"

I couldn't see her, but I felt the warmth and strength of her hands on mine. Something passed between us and my eyes flew open, everything suddenly clear.

The bright light was coming from a single bulb in a silver bowl-shaped shade that hung from a long wire attached to the ceiling. I was seated in a tall metal chair that was slightly reclined, my hands each bound at the wrists with thick black fabric straps to the curved armrests. I didn't attempt to escape, but took in as much as I could of my surroundings.

The rough grey brick walls of a small windowless room were dotted with a white crystalline substance. Calcium, maybe? The air was musty and stale. This must be a basement.

There were machines on both sides of me, the closest one recording a pulse line picture on the screen. A thin metal pole with a hook at the top held a bag of clear liquid, which was connected by plastic tubing to a needle in my arm. There were little circular patches attached to wires stuck on my temples.

A woman that I recognized instantly as Nadine Greyson sat on a small stool that was pushed up to a metal table just to my right, her fingers flying over the keys of a sleek grey laptop. She was facing me, so I couldn't see what she was typing. She seemed to be intently searching the screen for something, and a wicked smile spread across her lips when she found it.

She clicked a few more keys then sat back, anxiously tapping her teeth with a perfectly manicured nail. When a shrill blip sounded from her computer a few seconds later she leaned forward, statuesque, as she read what appeared. Her fingers furiously clicked across the keyboard once more before she scribbled something onto a small spiral notepad. She pulled her cell phone out of her pocket and checked her notes before punching buttons on the touchscreen.

She scowled at the phone and looked up quickly; her frown grew even deeper as our eyes met.

"Awake still?" she spat, then turned her head and called out, "Phillips!"

I heard the heavy hollow sound of footsteps on stairs, and then a blond woman appeared in the doorway, her face a mix of reluctance and apology. It was my friend Charlotte! Although at the time of this memory, we weren't friends yet—only strangers with an impossible plan and the hope that the other was trustworthy.

"Check this dose. I need her ready for the next round," Nadine ordered.

Charlotte ducked her head in obedience. Her eyes flicked towards mine as she hurried over and started pushing buttons on the machines.

"What if this doesn't work?" she asked, her voice meek and hesitant.

"I have a contingency plan." Nadine looked at me with disgust. "I have to make some phone calls. There's no service down here."

She ripped the top sheet off the notepad and turned sharply, heading out of the door. "She better be ready when I get back," she called over her shoulder.

I ignored Charlotte and focused on the computer screen that Nadine had left open on the table. It was almost turned where I could see, but not enough. I growled quietly in frustration. Now what was I supposed to do?

Charlotte was still busy with the machines. If only I could manipulate this vision like I could with dreams.

I wonder…

With narrowed eyes, I focused on Charlotte, mentally calling her name and imagining her hearing me. She suddenly froze and turned slowly to face me. *It worked!*

"Charlotte," I said forcefully. "Turn the computer this way."

Charlotte's eyes grew wide and she walked over to the laptop, then turned it so I could see the screen. I was disappointed to find only the blank desktop showing, but as I looked closer, there were tabs open along the taskbar at the bottom.

"Open those tabs," I said.

Charlotte robotically reached her hand out and moved her fingers over the touchpad until the pages Nadine had been looking at filled the screen.

A search engine page popped up with white-page listings for hospitals, then a satellite map of a location with lush green topography that I didn't recognize. Finally, Charlotte pulled up a screen with some kind of database. The text was black against a white background, bordered with black and green edges.

"Stop there," I said, and Charlotte obeyed.

The page detailed the results of an inquiry Nadine had made. It was a list of identification numbers, vitals and stats–nothing too detailed, just information like last name, age, and gender. But after each name on the list was a hospital name and location. There was also a little plus sign icon indicating more information was available.

"Charlotte, scroll up on that page."

Charlotte's fingers moved obediently. Search criteria entry boxes at the top of the page revealed the nature of Nadine's inquiry. She had only entered one filter for her search. In the diagnosis request box, two words blinked.

Grandiose Delusions.

What does that even mean? What is she doing?

"Is there anything on that notepad?"

Charlotte picked it up. It was blank; Nadine had taken the page. I felt my lips draw tightly together in disappointment. I stared at the search again. There were hundreds of names on the list; no way for me to memorize them all. I remembered what Will said about his gift, how he could see patterns, and I swept my eyes over the information.

Was there anything in common in all that data?

Ages ranged from teenagers to the elderly, both male and female, varying races, heights, weights. I scanned the diagnosis notes and felt my breath catch as I saw one phrase appear over and over in varying forms.

Over-inflated sense of power.

The sound of footsteps from upstairs drew my attention.

"Minimize the windows and turn the computer back."

Charlotte complied immediately.

She walked back over to the machines and continued what she had been doing as if nothing had happened.

Before Nadine entered the room, Charlotte turned towards me and whispered the phrase that would later restore my memory, "Remember. Fight Taklos, find my son. He's weak in the dreams; you can hurt him there. Remember, Andy…remember."

"That'll be all, I'll take it from here," Nadine said, waving Charlotte away.

Charlotte looked surprised and opened her mouth to speak.

"I said I'll take it from here." Nadine cut her off. Her eyes were focused on mine, but she turned to Charlotte and said sweetly, "I need you to run an errand. I can't finish until you bring me these things."

She handed Charlotte a piece of paper and folded her hands together in front of her, looking satisfied. Charlotte read the list, then looked uncomfortably from Nadine to me.

"Quickly now," Nadine said.

Charlotte hesitated a moment more before disappearing through the door. When we heard the sound of another door closing from upstairs, Nadine pushed a few buttons on the machines and picked up a syringe from a silver tray on a little rolling cart near the wall. She inserted the needle into a port on the IV connected to my arm and pushed in the plunger. Then she took a step towards me, placing her hands on either side of the chair. She leaned close to my face, wearing a smug smile.

"I don't need you anymore, dreamwalker." She was taunting me. "You're someone else's problem now."

I needed more from her. I wasn't sure if the same rules applied, but in the dream world, people couldn't lie.

"Who did you call?" I asked, staring her right in the eyes.

Her expression changed from smug to surprised, but she answered.

"Places where people like you really belong."

"What places?" I demanded. Her face contorted, as if in pain. "Tell me."

Her hand shot out, a folded piece of paper between her fingers.

"Open it."

She resisted but moved her shaking hands to lift the overlapping corners, showing me what was scrawled in black ink.

A list.

"Mental health facilities?"

There were seven locations on her list, angry lines scribbled through four of them. The remaining three were underlined and marked with rough hand-drawn stars and checkmarks.

Under the locations was a phone number, written with a heavy hand and anxiously circled.

"What are you…"

I needed more, but a sudden wave of nausea hit me so hard my vision blurred, and reality rippled. *No, no–there's more; there's got to be more.* I mentally grabbed at the memory, but it flowed through my fingers like water over rocks, fluid and vanishing. In an instant, I was back in Esther's room.

A cold sweat broke out across my forehead, and the room began to spin. I blinked, trying to focus on Esther's face, which though blurry, seemed as ashen as mine felt.

"Paper," I croaked.

Esther handed me the pen and spiral notebook she kept on her bedside table.

My hands were shaking so badly, I could barely hold the pen. Esther covered my hands with hers, steadying them enough to write what I could remember of the phone number. Her hands were still on mine but quickly moved up to my shoulders as I slumped forward into her lap. A heavy dark blanket of fog blocked out the light, pushing me hard towards the floor even though I wasn't moving.

"William! Jacob!"

Hurried footsteps on stone. Creak of oak door. Muffled voices from far away. Darkness.

CHAPTER 6

Cold.

Something icy cooled my forehead. I squinted against the brightness, trying to focus on my surroundings, finally recognizing the tall book-covered walls of the church library. Light cascaded through large stained-glass windows; it pooled warm and colorful on the floor and couch where I rested.

I turned my head, immediately regretting the move. The sharp sting of a splitting headache forced a groan, and I pressed my thumb and middle fingers hard into my temples, trying to suppress the pain.

The cushions on the brown leather couch shifted as someone sat next to me. Although I already knew who it was, I peeked through the barrier my fingers created.

"Hey baby," Will said softly.

I reached out for him, my free hand finding his. He brushed back my hair with his other hand, lifting the wet cloth from my forehead.

"Can you sit up?" he asked.

"Yeah. I think so."

He put his hands under my arms and slid me up without effort, as if lifting a small child. My hands rested on his shoulders.

"Here, Jacob made this for you." He handed me a teacup full of a fragrant green-tinted liquid.

My uncle Jacob made the best tea and was a master of herbal remedies. The smell of peppermint and lemon had an immediate soothing effect as I drew the cup to my lips. There was something else too, a nutty and earthy scent I didn't recognize, smoky and a little spicy.

"What's in it?"

"Um…I think he said it was card-something. Cardamom?"

I breathed in the aroma and sipped it down. It was sweetened with honey and tasted like heaven as it slid down my throat.

"Better?"

"Yeah, thanks." I handed him my empty cup. "So, what happened?"

Will looked me over as he talked, like a doctor examining his patient. His fingers lifted my chin, brushed my cheek, and finally settled on my hands.

"Esther was helping you; do you remember that?"

"Yes."

"I guess it was pretty intense. When you…came out of it, you passed out. Esther called for me, and Jacob and I carried you in here."

"To the library?" I asked, raising an eyebrow.

"I know you like it here." He looked up through his long dark lashes. It seemed like there was something else he wanted to say, but he was quiet.

"I really fainted?" I sank back against the arm of the couch. "That's so embarrassing."

"So…I guess you don't want to know that you threw up on Jacob's shoes too?"

I sat up quickly.

"What?" I was mortified. "No! Are you kidding me?"

"I'm kidding! It was just a little drool; very minimal."

He laughed, catching my wrist as I moved to slug him playfully in the chest.

"Thank you for taking care of me–drool and all." I placed my other hand on his cheek. He hadn't shaved in a few days, and the stubble on his face was scratchy, prickling my thumb as I rubbed his jaw. "I like this; you should keep it."

He covered my hand with his and turned his head to hide a shy smile by placing a soft kiss on my wrist.

When he released my hand, his gaze lingered where his lips had been, eying a raw, red band. *Where did that come from?* He was carefully watching me, his brown eyes dancing around the same unspoken question. Behind their curiosity lay something else–sadness and…regret? He didn't share in my surprise, so he'd obviously already seen it.

"How did this happen?" he asked, swallowing hard as he tenderly held my hand, like a fragile bit of glass that would break at the lightest touch.

"I don't…Oh." I remembered the restraints Nadine had placed on my arms. It wasn't the first time I'd borne physical evidence from a dream–or a memory, or whatever that was. He wouldn't want to hear the answer.

"There was a…a list," I said frantically. I wasn't intentionally trying to change the subject, but that recollection had opened the floodgates for the rest. My hands flew up, thumbs pressed to my temples as I squeezed my eyes shut, trying to create a visual memory. "A list of people and then, um…places. She wrote them down. And a phone number–I couldn't remember all of it."

Now that I'd said it out loud, I felt a sickening sense of loss. It wasn't much–not nearly enough. The familiar prick of salty tears burned behind my eyes and my shoulders sank.

"I think I wrote it down." It felt like an apology.

"You did." Will smiled, that same consistent reassuring smile that eased and comforted. "You did good, Andy."

Good? At best I did okay. A random list of places, some kind of database search for delusional people, and most of a phone number. It was shameful, and my face flamed up with a rush of frustration. What was the point of all of this? It just kept going and going, a ride I couldn't get off of, and it was making me sick. I wrapped my arms around myself, holding together–holding it in.

He looked so calm, so compassionate, and here I was stewing. That felt wrong too. I flipped my fury into mania.

"I don't think I got all the numbers, but we could look it up or something. Just type in what we've got and see what comes up, right? Or just try all the combinations–it's just missing two digits. We should try and call it." I stood up. "Where's your laptop and your phone?"

"Whose number is it?" He gently pulled me back down.

"I don't know." My response was short and my headache returned. I flopped my hands in my lap, palms coming up empty.

I felt Will's hands on my shoulders, "Okay…just tell me what you remember."

I rattled off a quick summary, lightly glossing over the parts where I was restrained and drugged.

"Where's your phone?" I asked again, holding my hand out.

He didn't move. Why wasn't he getting his phone?

"Andy," he said calmly. "I think we should wait."

"What? Why?" We had a lead; what was he talking about?

"First of all, it's not impossible, but two missing digits is a lot of combinations; it'll take some time. And secondly, my phone is not secure. It can be traced."

"Do you have access to a secure line?" I kept trying to get up, and he kept stopping me.

"Yes, but…just hear me out." He held up his hands defensively. "From what you told me, it sounds like Greyson was looking for something or someone specific. I just think we need to know more. If the number belonged to someone with less than honorable intentions and we just go calling them up blindly, it could alert the wrong people."

"What people?"

"I don't know–that's just it. We don't know for sure what the significance is just yet. But that number could be nothing at all, or it could be a one-time use only card. I think we need to find out more before we play it."

Even though he was absolutely right, everything still felt so wrong. I opened my mouth to argue when I heard the creak of the door, and we both looked to see my uncle standing in the doorway.

His eyes met mine and then quickly darted to Will's. The expression on Jacob's face made my heart skip a beat. I looked to Will for an explanation.

"What's wrong?"

He looked up at Jacob, who still stood in the doorway.

"She's awake," Jacob said.

At first, I thought he was talking about me. I cocked my head to the side; Jacob avoided my eyes.

"Will?" I grabbed his forearms, gripping them tightly. I felt my heart rate speed up. Something was wrong.

"We'll be right there," he said, looking over my shoulder at Jacob, who nodded and walked away.

"Will!" I said again, my voice high with panic.

"It's Esther…"

That was all he got out before I leapt up off the couch and flew out the door towards her room, ignoring his calls.

I stopped short just outside of Esther's door. My uncle was already there.

"Jacob," I whispered.

"She's waiting for you." He stepped past and opened the door for me.

I was frozen in the hallway, heart pounding, hot tears stinging my eyes. I felt the gentle pressure of Jacob's hand on my shoulder.

"You should go to her, Andy." He gently nudged me forward.

He was quiet and strong like his mother. He had definitely inherited her humble spirit.

I wanted to be with her, but was afraid of what I'd find, afraid of what I might have done. Had this fruitless endeavor created yet another casualty? After another soft push from Jacob, I stepped into her room. Esther was lying in her bed, covered with quilts and propped up by a fluffy white pillow. Her eyes were closed. I looked back at Jacob, who still stood in the doorway, and he nodded encouragingly. I walked over to her bed and sat on the edge. She slowly opened her eyes, and a sweet smile spread across her lips when she saw me.

"Joanna. How are you, child? You gave me quite a scare."

"I'm okay." My voice was raspy, breaking as I spoke. "How are you?"

She sighed. "I'll be just fine."

She looked tired, but there was something else, too. The strength was gone from her voice. For the first time since I met her, she seemed frail. It *was* my fault. Why did I agree to this? My throat was tight, and I lowered my head, unable to look at her. I felt the pain of my fingernails digging into my palms as I clenched my fists, and hot, salty tears stinging the corners of my eyes.

"Come here, child," she said, her voice just barely a whisper.

I shook my head. *No…I can't control this, and it's dangerous.*

"Come," she repeated. "I need you."

She knew exactly what to say; I immediately scooted closer, and she placed a soft hand on my face.

"No tears now," she said. "You're acting like I'm already in the grave."

I wiped my eyes and nodded, trying to force a smile.

"We should have just let it go." I couldn't look at her. "Everything was fine…we were fine.”

“Nonsense. Joanna. It was not fine. And you’re not fooling anyone. We just need to keep moving forward, fighting the good fight.”

Her characteristic authority was back; it was a relief to hear it.

“Okay,” I said. “I will, but you have to fight with me.”

“As long as I have breath.” She smiled. “Did you remember anything?”

“I think so.” I sat up straight, wiping the remaining moisture from my cheeks with the back of my hand. “Nadine was searching for something and um, made a list of hospitals.”

“See there,” she said.

“It feels like nothing. Not worth…” *Not worth this, not worth anything happening to Esther.* “I just wish I could have heard what that woman was saying on the phone the night of…that night. It seemed important, but I just couldn’t hear it.”

“Maybe I can help.” She pushed herself up.

“No!” I shook my head. “Absolutely not.”

“Joanna…”

“No. I’m serious. You are not doing that again–at least not until you’ve recovered. And it wouldn’t work anyway. I can’t remember it because I wasn’t there.”

We didn’t talk about how I could have dreamed the rest of it, we simply stared defiantly at each other.

“Well, there’s something else you could try,” she said, seeing that I wasn’t going to give in. I narrowed my eyes suspiciously. “Have you ever tried to take someone in a dream with you?”

“No? But still, you’re not…”

“Not me.” She raised her hand, instantly shushing me. “Will.”

Her words didn’t make sense at first, but then I remembered what had happened just hours earlier when I was falling apart under the influence of the vision. I’d felt Esther’s hands, I’d felt something pass from her to me, and my vision was clear.

“Will? Why?”

“Earlier, when you told me about the dream, you said it was like trying to get to something just out of reach, like there was a wall between you and her. It sounds like you need to find a way over. You need a boost.”

“Well, I know he’s good at finding things, but this isn’t anything like that.”

She leaned forward, as if about to tell me a secret.

"He's good at helping you, Joanna."

Esther had given me her strength to continue; that had to be why she was in such a state. Was she suggesting that I could do the same with Will in my own dream? That I could take him with me and his presence would give me the boost–as she called it–that I needed? What would that do to him?

"You're right. I can't help you if it's not something from your own memories. It's something else. Maybe the memory from someone who was there. Maybe it's from her memory?"

"Her memory?" I repeated. "But when I tried to make a connection with her, it was..."

"I don't know how all of these supernatural spiritual matters work." She smiled. "Just that they do."

It had to be from her memory, then; no one else was there–at least, no one who was living. What a terrible thing to know.

"No. I don't want to hurt him." I squeezed my eyes shut, shaking my head against the thought.

"I love you, Joanna. He loves you too. That is a powerful ally. I know that boy would do anything to help you."

I knew it too. He would help me in a heartbeat, give his last breath for even a tiny bit of hope, as I would for him. But I couldn't let him– wouldn't let him. Not yet...if ever. I suddenly felt very overwhelmed. I was still physically exhausted from the intensity of the memory, and I wasn't entirely sure that I wouldn't suffer some kind of strange side effects from the drugs that Nadine had administered, even though it had been in the past. Nothing made sense. My mind wanted to believe it was impossible, but the dull ache from where the needle had punctured my skin and the raw burn on my wrists told me otherwise. Nothing was impossible anymore. When my eyes fell over Esther's sagging shoulders and tired eyes, I knew she was trying to put on a strong face for me, but...

"It's what family does, Joanna. We bear each other's burdens." Esther responded to my unspoken worries.

How much more could they bear before the weight of it crushed them? I remembered her prayer asking God to reveal the truth about what happened that night. He hadn't done that yet. She didn't have her answers. Surely, that meant I had more time.

"I'm going to find her. I'm going to find out what happened," I said passionately, taking her hand. "I promise."

"Don't," she whispered.

"What?"

"Don't promise that, child." She smiled gently. "Not for me. I may not know the answer this side of heaven, and I accept that. You must do the same."

I shook my head. *No. She has to get closure; it has to work out. It just wouldn't be right.* How could she so easily accept never knowing? Her words were so foreign to me, so different from the world I grew up in where everything was about doing what felt right for me. Surely, God wanted her to know. Surely, Esther deserved justice…or was that just what I wanted?

"You must, Joanna," she said again, more forcefully. "Remember, this world is not the end. It's just a tiny dot in the picture of eternity. I know you want answers. So do I, but God doesn't always work according to our schedule."

I finally looked up at her, hiding my internal struggle behind a smile. "I will try."

The soft clicking sound of the door drew my attention. Jacob entered with a tray in his hands.

"Want some tea, Mom?" He placed the tray on the dresser and walked over to the other side of her bed.

"My sweet son," she said. "Thank you."

Jacob unfolded a small lap table and sat it next to his mother on the bed. He handed her a hot cup of tea, which she accepted with shaky hands. I felt a presence behind me and turned to see Will smiling down.

"Take her to rest, son," Esther said to him.

"Yes ma'am." He nodded.

I looked back at her, not wanting to leave.

"I'll be fine. I need to rest now too," she said in response to my concern.

I leaned forward and kissed her gently on the cheek. Will followed close as we left. When we were out of earshot of Esther's room, he reached for my hand, pulling me to a stop.

"Come here." He folded me into his chest where I sobbed until I couldn't stand.

Since the minute we'd met, his arms had been a safe place, the shield behind which I could face the world. I wanted to curl up in their warmth; I wanted to hide there until it all went away. But the danger wasn't something that would fade, for it had already infiltrated the safety of our castle walls—it was embedded inside my head. Poisoning us from the inside out.

I surprised him by pushing away, waving my hands as if fanning away a swarm of gnats.

"I need a...uh, notebook or something. And a pen."

He didn't question my request, but pointed to the stairs and followed me into the kitchen, where I hopped onto a stool at the counter and furiously scribbled down everything I could remember from my trip down memory lane with Nadine. When I dropped the pen, Will took the paper, his brows drawing closer together the more he read. I let my head fall forward onto my arms, suddenly exhausted. I heard the soft shush of the paper as Will put it down, and then felt his warm hands on my shoulders. His thumbs rubbed soothing circles into my muscles, encouraging them to release the knots of tension. I was content to remain under his care for as long as he was willing to provide it.

"I think we should take a trip," he said finally.

I turned my head, peering up at him from under the canopy of my hair. He brushed it back, exposing red, puffy eyes.

"What? Now?"

His hands fell, resting on his hips and he looked down at the floor. His agent stance; he knew something.

"Your mom called while you were talking to Esther."

"Lily? What did she say?" I was suddenly fully alert and sat up straight on the stool, filled with that dreaded anticipation of climbing up to the top of something much too high. "Is my dad okay?"

"Yes. He's fine, but someone claiming to be from The Agency showed up asking about you."

"Why would they do that? I thought my case was closed."

"Matt is the only active agent who knows."

Dr. Matthew Vora was my colleague and Will's classmate from their days at The Academy. He'd been with me on every single one of my missions, including when I had faced Taklos for the first time and the final time. He was there when Will pulled me out of the water. He knew better than anyone what The Agency would do with someone like me, and I knew he would never tell anyone about my new identity.

"No one has been assigned to reopen the case, as far as I know." He didn't want to say what was coming next. "Lily said she had long black hair and very green eyes."

Had Will not reacted quickly and grabbed my shoulders, I would have fallen off the stool.

"Did she hurt them?" It hurt to speak; my throat was so tight.

"No, they're fine. I promise."

"What else? Tell me everything."

"The woman said she was following up because it's been over a year since the search was called off, and your body was never found." His eyes dipped and jaw tensed with his last words, obviously trying to push a terrible memory back into its forgotten place. "She asked a lot of questions about you."

"What kind of questions?"

"Mostly questions they didn't know the answers to. About your job at The Agency, your education, people you might have known outside of work. She wanted to know if they'd heard anything, had any ransom demands, strange phone calls–things like that. Then she asked if they'd heard from me."

"You?" I winced, every word he said was another blow, and I was grateful he was still holding onto me.

"Yes. She somehow knew we were close."

"She's coming…" I couldn't breathe. My hand flew to my throat, clutching at the lion that tingled just below my collarbone.

"Andy."

"She's coming…she knows."

"Calm down, we don't know that. All we know is that she knows about Andromeda Stone, and there's no proof you survived or any traceable connection to you."

I snatched a letter Lily had sent me off the counter and waved it in his face. He caught my wrist and gently took the envelope, placing it back in the basket.

"Lily knows how to be careful; she would never put you in danger."

"Not on purpose."

He parted his lips in protest but stopped.

"What is it?"

"Nothing... I..."

"No, you're remembering something. What is it?"

He looked at me, his brows tipped together questioningly, and I rolled my eyes.

"I took the same Academy classes you did, Will. You looked up and to the left. Now what did you remember?"

"Nothing for certain."

He pulled out his phone and tapped the screen.

"What is it?" I slid to the edge of the stool, looking over his arm.

"An inquiry. I actually thought it was a mistake or maybe the answering service had mixed up accounts. I don't get requests from individuals."

"What did it say?"

"Just a request for a meeting to discuss a missing person. I forgot about it because it was right after..."

His hand moved up, fingers sliding through his hair.

"After what?"

"Colorado." He said it with finality, as if something fell into place, and he reached for Jacob's laptop, which sat closed on the counter.

His fingers flew across the keys, eyes intensely searching and lips turning increasingly downward as he clicked. Both the computer and I jumped when he slammed his fist on the counter before shoving himself away and running both hands through his hair. I reached for the computer, turning it to see what had made him so upset. He'd pulled up the newspaper's website from the town where he'd helped with a search. I scanned an article detailing the search party efforts, including the tragic results, and found a single image at the bottom of the page with a tiny caption. It was a group shot of the search party, looking dejected and tired, but didn't include anyone I recognized–until my eye caught something in the background.

It was Will. My Will. Standing alone under the canopy, the light of a single overhead lantern falling on him like a halo. His head was bowed, hand on his hip, shoulders sagging, and in one hand up by his ear–a cell phone. I traced my finger along the small letters of the caption until I saw his name among those of the search party.

"I told him not to use my name or any picture with me in it." His voice was hard, sharpened with annoyance and frustration.

"Who?"

"The reporter. Mr. Breaking News. He insisted on taking pictures that night, even though we were all at our worst, but I refused to sign the release."

"Do you think someone traced you here?"

"No…not yet."

Will had worked hard to keep his picture and name out of any kind of public forum. He had no internet presence, just a cryptic email under an alias that an old FBI friend helped him set up. All communication he received and requests for assistance came through a third-party answering service; even our cell phones were in Jacob's name. We were practically invisible. I stared at his picture, remembering that night–he'd been so sad.

"You were talking to me." He didn't hear me; he was too busy pacing across the small kitchen.

"Baby, I know you're tired, but I need you to go pack." He turned me to face him, a wild uncharacteristic urgency in his eyes.

"Where are we going?"

"I've got a plan." When I didn't respond, he continued. "I just need to get you someplace safe so I can think."

"We can't just leave Jacob and Esther here. If she finds them…"

"Would you just…" I recoiled at the bite in his tone. He closed his eyes and took a deep breath. "Please, just trust me."

"Okay." I felt small. My hands pulled up defensively; his expression grew pained when he noticed.

He crushed me to him, his strong hand cupping the back of my head.

"I'm sorry." He didn't have to say it, I felt it. A deep, agonizing regret radiated off of him. He was sorry for the harshness, but he was also feeling completely responsible for the situation.

I turned my head up, chin resting on his chest.

"It's not your fault," I said softly. "None of this is your fault."

It's hers. The flashing green eyes of the mystery woman appeared crisp and sharp in my mind. I blinked the image away.

His brown eyes were full of worry; he only allowed the corner of his mouth to turn slightly up in reply.

"I'll go pack."

"Thank you." He pressed his lips to my forehead and released me, disappearing out the kitchen door.

CHAPTER 7

It took me less than thirty minutes to pack and pay one last visit to my grandmother before heading upstairs.

"Have you seen Will?" I asked Jacob, who was busying himself in the kitchen. He was alternating between stirring a large pot of something fragrant and placing plastic wrapped muffins in a large brown paper bag.

"Uh…he needed to run an errand."

Jacob added some spices to the pot and fruit to the bag.

"She keeps telling me she's fine, but how is she really doing?"

"She's still very weak."

I paced back and forth on one side of the kitchen island, nervously devouring a handful of pretzels I'd stolen from the bags Jacob was filling. A war raged in my head: the battle between feeling selfish for wanting answers and feeling responsible for protecting my family, especially after Lily's phone call. Both sides fought with vicious fervor. On which side would Jacob fall?

"If there's any chance I can find out the truth, I feel like we should try." I defended my uncontested decision.

"I understand, Andy. She does too," he said over his shoulder.

"But?"

He stopped stirring and turned around.

"But make sure that you are doing this because God is calling you to and because it's really for the good of our family, not because you think it's what Mom wants."

He turned back around and I lowered my head, frustrated. A few hours ago, I would have doubted the reasons for continuing this pursuit, but now–after she showed up on Lily's doorstep–I couldn't deny the increased urgency.

"How long do you think we have?" I asked him.

He stopped stirring again for a long second, then tapped the spoon on the side of the metal pot and placed it on the spoon rest. There was a sadness in the way his shoulders slumped that broke my heart into a million pieces. Esther had lost so much–almost everyone she loved except for Jacob and now me–but so had he, and now he might lose her, too. He finally turned around to face me.

"We've got time," he said, gently reaching out and pulling me in close for a hug. "She's just a little drained, Andy. She's not dying."

I had really gotten to know my uncle the past year. He had quickly become like a dad to me, a different kind of dad than Sabastian had been. Jacob never had any reservations about offering advice or even calling me out when I was being ridiculous. I respected his opinion and his faith, often going to him with things I didn't understand. He was always patient, helping me work things out and answering my endless questions.

"Oh," Jacob said, releasing me. "This came for you."

He shuffled through a stack of mail on the counter and handed me a small envelope. I recognized the familiar stationary.

"Another letter from Lily," I said, tearing open the small envelope painted with watercolor lilacs and peonies. I expected more details about their recent visitor, but realized she would have sent this letter before the woman showed up.

Jacob poured the soup into a bowl and gathered the bed tray for Esther before disappearing through the doorway. I ran my fingers across Lily's flowery handwriting and lifted the letter to my face, the earthy smell of lavender still lingered on the paper. That scent would always bring back sweet memories for me. It would always be Lily's smell, the mother who raised me as her own, even though I wasn't. There was a time when all I wanted was to get as far away from my parents as possible, but now... now that I knew everything, I missed them.

Andromeda,

I guess I should get used to calling you Joanna, but to me you'll always be my sweet Andromeda Skye. We miss you terribly and are planning a trip to see you and Will soon. Bash had an awful nightmare a few months ago, and he hasn't stopped talking about coming to visit since. Must have been quite the dream; you know how he hates to make plans.

I've been thinking about what you said, about looking to nature to see its creator. The other day, I sat out under the Black Walnut and Silver Maple trees at the edge of the garden. I remembered how you described the intricate workings of their root system and how everything had to work together exactly right for life to be possible. I've always thought of Mother Nature as a great spirit connecting all living things, that all the spirits of all faiths were equally involved in our existence...but now, I'm not sure. Something is so different in you–in a good way. I can't say that I understand, but when I come, can we talk some more?

We do miss you, and I can see that Will makes you so happy, so of course, we are happy too. You deserve all the happiness in the world. We will see you soon.

Peace and love,
Lily

I read her words several times before folding the letter and sliding it back into the matching floral envelope. I'd had several conversations with them about my new faith. They sweetly listened, but never showed any real interest in having a faith of their own. I was encouraged by her openness and desire to know more.

"Everything okay?" Jacob's voice startled me. I hadn't heard him come back into the kitchen.

I stared at the envelope in my hands.

"I don't know how to do this," I said softly, a little surprised at my own admission.

"What do you mean?"

"I just...you and Esther, and even Will, are all like these super Christians. You're so sure of everything, so willing to do whatever is asked of you, to trust God without question, and I'm...I'm just grasping at straws. I'm desperate for answers, for all of us to be safe. I want to keep you with me. I can't even imagine losing any of you now, not after I just found you."

I threw my hands up. "I don't know how to be…this new person."

And I'm angry–why does that woman get to live while my parents didn't? I was too ashamed to say that out loud, though.

He listened as I babbled, his blue eyes steady on mine. That was exactly what he was–steady.

"I guess I need to apologize," he said when I'd finished.

"For what?"

"For giving you the impression that I had it together. I'm a mess, Andy. Anything good you see in me is only Jesus. I'm completely uncertain. I doubt, I fear, and I'm such a…human. I battle against my own nature every day, sometimes every minute."

I stared wide-eyed at him. His words could have come out of my own mouth.

"The only thing I have that you don't…is years. I have the blessing of experience–seeing how God has been faithful to me over and over, even when I failed and was faithless. I know what waits for me when I leave this earth, and it's wonderful; but like you, I don't want to lose my family and also like you, I will fight until my last breath to save them."

"So…it's not completely selfish?"

"Well, I can tell you this truthfully, and not just because I'm your uncle and I love you: there's not many as selfless as you."

I hugged him again and whispered, "Thank you, Uncle Jacob."

After squeezing me tightly, he stepped back and brushed a strand of hair out of my face.

"You remind me *so* much of Maggie." His smile was sweet and sad.

"I wish I could have known her."

"Me too," he said. "One day, you will."

"Will you be safe here?" I picked up my bag and hugged it close to my chest.

"We will be fine. As soon as she's rested, I'm taking her…"

"Don't." I put my hand up and his lips snapped shut. "Don't tell me."

"Okay?"

"I just think it's better, for now, if I don't know. Just in case."

The corner of his mouth twitched into a crooked half smile.

"Funny. Will said the same thing. You can take the girl out of The

Agency..."

I heard a soft cough from behind and turned to see Will's tall figure filling the door frame.

"You ready?"

I thought he was talking to me, but he was looking at Jacob, who bobbed his head in response. Will took my bag, and Jacob replaced the empty spot in my arms with the grocery bag full of snacks. The firm set of Will's jaw let me know he wasn't in the mood to discuss plans. Jacob followed us to the door. I looked around as we stepped out into the cool night air. There were no strange cars in the parking lot, just Jacob's grey SUV and Will's red truck. I looked over my shoulder at him; he nodded towards his truck, then turned and shook Jacob's hand.

"Around back on Columbus," I heard him whisper as Jacob drew him close for a manly one-armed hug.

"See you soon." Jacob nodded. His words carried a weight, as if they meant something more than just a simple farewell.

Will kept his hand on the small of my back as we walked, our bags slung over his shoulder.

"Quit looking around, everything is fine," he whispered into my hair.

"Easy for you to say," I muttered. "I'm bad at covert, if you haven't noticed. Do you really think someone is watching us? Shouldn't Jacob leave now?"

"No. I don't. I'm just erring on the side of caution."

He opened the passenger side door and tossed our bags in the back as I climbed in. Before he shut the door, he rested his hand on my knee. His brown eyes met mine.

"It's going to be okay."

He meant it. I really wanted to believe him. He drove out of the parking lot and turned onto Washington Street.

"I'm sorry," I said after several minutes of squirming.

"For what?"

"For putting you through this last year."

"Andy, what are you talking about?" He leaned forward, looking back and forth before pulling across the next street.

"When we left The Agency, we were running…I kept you in the dark about my plans…it's extremely frustrating. So, I'm sorry."

He reached over and took my hand.

"I won't keep you in the dark long." He tried to hide a smile. "Now, quit moving my mirror. I told you, no one is following us."

I dropped my hand from his rear-view mirror and sat back with a huff. Will headed north for almost twenty minutes. I resisted the urge to ask him where we were going and the similarly irresistible need to continually check the mirrors for a tail. He crossed over Highway 66, and for a quick panicked second, I had the horrible fear that he was headed towards Maryland, to The Agency. His hand was still on mine and he gave it a reassuring squeeze when he felt me tense up.

"Get ready." He turned off the highway and into the Rosslyn Tunnel. "We're going to move fast."

If he was in a hurry, this was not the way to go; the construction–even at night–caused long delays. We could be in this tunnel for ten minutes. Once inside, he turned hard to the right, pulling the truck onto a thin shoulder.

"Let's go." He was already unbuckled and out onto the pavement.

I hesitated but for a second, trying to figure out what we could possibly be doing. I shut my door and turned, surprised to see Jacob standing there, my duffle bag in his hand.

"What's…how did you…"

"C'mon."

I followed him across the lanes to what looked like a classic race car. It was a black two-door Dodge Charger, older model but shiny, near pristine. Its long front end grumbled around the powerful engine. With a hand on my back, Jacob ushered me towards the open passenger side door.

"It's Esther's," he said, as if that would explain anything.

"Thanks Jacob. Be careful and call Matt if you need help." Will took our bags from Jacob.

They moved quickly, exchanging a brief handshake. Jacob wrapped a long arm around my shoulders and gave me a quick squeeze before kissing the top of my head, whispering as Will loaded our bags into the backseat.

"May the Lord bless you and keep you, may He make his face shine upon you and be gracious to you. May the Lord lift his countenance upon you and give you peace."

I couldn't help it; a sharp sting pricked the corner of my eye and I swiped at it with my sleeve. Will saw and a familiar expression passed over his face; it was guilt. I didn't even have to guess, because I had felt it so much myself lately. I didn't know his full plan, but we were running, and he felt like it was his fault that we had to.

Seconds later we were racing out of the tunnel from the same direction we'd come in, and Jacob was in Will's truck, continuing through to the other side.

"He's going to drop my truck in the long-term parking lot at the airport and taxi back to the church. As soon as she's ready, he will take Esther somewhere safe."

"Why couldn't you have just told me this?"

"There wasn't anything to tell until just before we left, and I didn't want to spend time fighting with you about staying to help move Esther."

I shot an offended glance his way, "I wouldn't have…"

He looked at me, his head tipped forward and mouth cocked to the side. Yes, I would have. I huffed, annoyed that he knew me too well.

"Can you at least tell me where we're going?"

"That's still a surprise."

"This seems like a lot of stealth for people who aren't being followed." I rolled my eyes.

"We aren't being followed right now, but we can make sure that doesn't happen in the future."

"Err on the side of caution?"

"Exactly."

That was Will. When it came to me, at least. He would always choose the most cautious route.

"I can't believe this is her car." I explored the interior, touching every button and flipping open every compartment. "Did you know?"

"Not until tonight. Jacob told me when I was trying to figure out how to get us out of the city. She kept it in the underground garage downtown. Apparently, your grandmother was quite the hotrodder back in the seventies."

I ignored his observation and flipped open the glove compartment. It was empty except for an owner's manual and registration papers. I pulled out the manual.

"This is like…an antique, but it's nearly perfect."

I flipped through the crisp pages, amazed.

"She must have never driven it." Will gripped the steering wheel tighter and pressed on the gas, obviously enjoying the way it hugged the curves.

A yellowed paper slipped out from between the pages of the manual and into my lap.

"What's that?" Will glanced my way.

"Looks like the original registration. But–this says it was registered to Anne Abramov. Must be the first owner?"

"Oh." Will reached behind my seat and tossed me a small, rectangular, white box. "Here. I got you a present."

I opened it cautiously.

"New phone?"

"Burner. Jacob has one too, and only he has the number. I just got one for us, so we will have to share for now. Give me yours."

I handed him my phone. He held the wheel with one hand and flicked the back cover off with the other. Without explanation, he pulled out my SIM card and snapped it in half, then tossed the broken card and remaining useless phone out of the window, where it shattered on impact with the road. Out of the back window, I watched the tiny plastic pieces bounce on the asphalt, quickly pulverized under the wheels of the cars behind us. When the last bit of debris was out of sight, I turned around and slouched down in my seat.

"Sorry," Will muttered. The leather of the steering wheel loudly resisted as he tightened his grip.

All of this felt like a dream. Ever since Esther helped me remember my time with Nadine, it was like I hadn't really woken up. The lights of the city whipped past, orange and yellow blurs of light. The loud roar of the Charger's engine drowned out my thoughts and I closed my eyes. I hated all of this. I hated that Will was keeping things from me, even though it was for my own good; I hated that there was still so much about my family I didn't know; and I hated the growing pit in my stomach that warned I might never get the chance to find out.

Will's voice distracted me from the downward spiral my thoughts were taking. I looked over to ask him to repeat what he'd just said and realized he wasn't talking to me.

"Hey Matt, it's Will... Yeah, it's new. Someone has contacted the Stones looking for information about Andy. Have you heard anything about that?"

He hesitated while Matt talked, and then answered a question I didn't hear.

"Woman, mid 40s, dark hair, green eyes; said she was from The Agency."

His expression was more relaxed than before, but his jaw was still tight.

"Yeah, I know. I thought it was closed too. Look, can you check into that for me? See if Greyson has had any visitors or contact with anyone?"

He paused for a moment as Matt replied. Nadine. I could understand why his mind would go directly to her.

"Thanks. Let me know what you find out."

He glanced at me and must have seen the rabbit hole of awful possibilities I was falling into.

"Hey, Matt? I think we might need to get some eyes on the Stones...for safety. Do you have a connection?"

He waited while Matt answered and thanked him again.

After he set his phone down, he reached over the middle console and took my hand. His fingers wove through mine, filling the open places, sealing them up so fear couldn't seep in.

If she found my parents and she found Will, she could find me. And if she found me, she could find Jacob and Esther. Worse, she could use any one of them to make me do whatever she wanted: to steal, kill, or destroy.

Because to save them, I was afraid I would.

"Hey." He shook my hand, which was still clasped in his. "Don't. We will figure it out, okay?"

My head moved up and down in unconscious agreement, but everything inside felt like it was swirling too close to a bottomless drain.

The moon was barely visible above the buildings as we left the city. Will remained quiet. Twangy country tunes from the radio filled the snug interior of Esther's uncharacteristically flashy car, but they did nothing to silence the uncertainty that buzzed uncomfortably between us.

I leaned my head back and rested my tired eyes as the last signs of industry gave way to dark open fields.

CHAPTER 8

The car bumped and jerked as we turned off the highway. My eyes flew open. The moon was high, stars bright. How long had I been asleep?

"Where are you going?"

"I told you, it's a surprise." He smiled.

"This is not the time."

"Trust me."

Why was he smiling like that?

"Will!" I laughed and looked around, trying to figure out where we were.

I saw a familiar site just ahead and looked over at Will with a huge, silly grin on my face. He laughed and shook his head.

We neared the old gas station and I squealed with excitement to see Sarah and Jesse waiting for us in the red ATV their little village used.

"How?"

"I have my ways." He winked.

"Will…"

"I know, I love you too." He reached over and squeezed my hand. "I just thought…since we needed to disappear, what better place?"

I knew exactly what he meant. We both needed this: to see our friends, to let them love us and cover us with prayers, to hide us in the protection of this sacred place.

"No better place in the world."

He had barely shifted into park before I bolted out the door and into Sarah's open arms.

"Andy!" she cried.

"Hi!" I laughed, my heart instantly lighter. Jesse was shaking Will's hand and pointing in admiration to the sleek Charger still rumbling in the parking lot.

"Everyone is waiting to see you. Emily has really outdone herself with the food!" Sarah's eyes were bright even in the dim yellow lights of the gas station.

Will pulled Esther's car behind the building, out of sight of the road in both directions, and after tossing our bags into the bed of the Mule, we all climbed in. I sat next to Sarah as she drove; Jesse and Will stood up in the back, holding onto the roll bars. On the ten-mile ride to the village, we chatted over the roar of the engine, excited to catch up even as our teeth chattered in the chill of the winter air. I filled Sarah in on how Esther and Jacob were doing, and she shared the latest news from the village. Not much had changed except that a new family had moved in, and another had welcomed a new baby.

"You'll love the Calloways," Sarah gushed. "They are so sweet and have been such a fun addition to our family."

It took us about half an hour to reach the village. I expected it to be dark, but was delighted to see that they had lined the main path with tea light candles inside paper bags. It looked beautiful and welcoming, like a holiday. The night air was crisp, the endless winter sky perfectly clear, and in the middle of the village, several people were gathered around the fire pit, working together to build a bonfire. Tiny embers floated up, happily on their way to join the millions of twinkling stars.

Sarah stopped in front of a small cabin to introduce us to the new family. Ben Calloway and his wife Thadie, who was from Natimala, a large South African tribe, were just as lovely as Sarah had described. Ben was originally from California, and they'd met when he'd traveled to her village for work. Their twins, Sipho and Siphiwe, were the most beautiful little boys.

Thadie told me their names meant "a gift" and "we have been given."

I asked her if her name had a special meaning, and Ben answered with a grin as he slid a long arm around his wife's waist.

"It means 'loved one.'"

Sarah and Jesse both groaned, then laughed at Ben's sappiness. Their teasing only encouraged him to pull Thadie closer, placing a sweet kiss on her forehead. After a few more minutes of small talk, we shook hands with the Calloways and headed towards the far edge of the village.

"Didn't I tell you?" Sarah laughed over the roar of the engine.

"You were right, I love them!" I shouted in response.

Sarah pulled up in front of Brian and Emily's house. The first time I'd seen it was from behind half-closed lids, venom from a poisonous snake bite coursing through my veins, as Will rushed me up the stairs surrounded by concerned strangers that were now friends. Just inside would be a small living room, and a wooden chair where I'd sat slumped over and sweating as Jesse, the village's doctor, delivered the terrifying news that I needed more care than he could provide. Brian had been the one to fly down the road with Will in the same ATV to the same gas station where we'd left Esther's car. It had the only phone for miles. Will placed a frantic call to Matt, begging him to bring the anti-venom that would save my life. I still had a set of tiny round scars on my ankle. I'd refused to go to the hospital where Taklos could find me, and Will had refused to let me die. I felt my breath catch in my throat as I was overcome with an intense wave of emotion.

We slowed to a stop and I glanced up at Will, realizing from the tightness in his jaw, those feelings weren't mine–they were his. He looked down at me. A smile teeming with grateful relief spread across his face, and the tension dissipated into the night like the embers of the bonfire.

Emily and Brian came out on the porch when they heard the grumble of the Mule's engine. Brian's arm was tenderly and protectively draped around Emily's shoulders as she turned into him, resting her head on his chest. The light from inside wrapped around their bodies, glowing from behind like a halo, and I felt a flood of euphoria at the perfection of that tiny moment.

As we climbed out of the Mule, they looked at each other with joyful anticipation, and I hurried up the steps into their open arms. I pulled back from their embrace and gasped in delight at the sight of Emily's swollen belly.

"When are you due?" I exclaimed.

"I still have another two and a half months!" Emily laughed, and rubbed her hand affectionately over her stomach. "Although, when it's safe, I'd welcome an early delivery date. It feels like there are five babies in here!"

"Congratulations, you guys. I'm so happy for you." I hugged them again. "I can't believe you didn't tell me!"

"I was hoping you'd come soon, so I could tell you in person." Emily snaked her arm through mine and leaned in, whispering, "I'm so glad you're here. I just wish it was under different circumstances."

Will, Sarah, and Jesse joined us on the porch and exchanged greetings.

"I hope you're hungry! Come on inside; Brian has a fire going in the living room. It's so cozy." Emily tugged on my arm, directing us into the cabin.

Sarah hadn't been exaggerating; Emily had prepared a feast for us. There was a platter of grilled steaks, foil wrapped potatoes hot from the wood stove, broccoli, carrots, homemade bread, and two kinds of pie. We laughed, talked, and ate until we were stuffed.

"Andy, Will told us you guys have a lead on the woman from your dream," Jesse said as we were finishing the last bites of pie from our plates. Since we'd become friends the year before, I'd exchanged letters with Sarah and Emily and had kept them updated on our search.

The laughter died down and everyone grew quiet, waiting for my answer.

"Yes, well maybe," I said slowly, glancing at Will. I wasn't sure how much he had told them.

"Esther helped Andy to remember some more details of what happened to her when Nadine…had her," Will said, his jaw tightening at the last part.

Talking about it made me nervous, but these were our friends. We trusted them, and I wanted to share everything with them. I quickly filled them in on what I had learned from the vision and how it had affected my grandmother.

"It was pretty awful; I didn't realize when it was happening, but I wasn't strong enough to stay focused by myself, so Esther…helped me somehow. I'm not sure exactly how it all works, but it took so much from her, and now I don't know how much time we have left. I don't even know if it's connected to my dream. I know we all want answers, but at what cost?" I found myself rambling. "There's more."

As I continued the account of the disturbing phone call from Lily, the concerned faces of our friends stared back at me.

"You're sure no legitimate agent would be looking into this, right?" Brian asked.

"I've called Matt to check, but yeah," Will answered.

"I guess it wouldn't be strange for her to ask about your past. Maybe she's trying to find out if there's someone you'd be hiding with." Emily looked to Brian as she spoke, as if asking for affirmation for her theory.

"She asked if Andy had ever been institutionalized, as in a mental health facility."

My head snapped towards Will.

"What?" I almost hissed at him. Why wouldn't he have told me that?

"You said in your letter that you saw a symbol on the car from your dream." Jesse leaned forward, hands folded in front of him, oblivious to the questioning daggers I was flinging at Will. "Can you draw it?"

I nodded. He reached over to a nearby table, grabbed a pencil and small square notepad, and passed them to me. Everyone leaned in as I drew the symbol, and Jesse sat back hard in his chair when I turned it to face him.

"Andy, I think it's more than answers you're looking for," he said after a few seconds of silence.

"What do you mean?"

"Well, if what you saw in the vision of this Nadine woman is what I think it is–it sounds like there might be more lives at stake."

Rescue us. The memory of that split-second vision flashed across my mind.

"I wondered about that too," Sarah said. "When you were talking about what you saw on the computer."

"I think we should ask Ben," Jesse said to Sarah, who nodded emphatically in agreement.

"Wait...what's Ben got to do with it?" I felt an uncomfortable knot forming in my stomach; I was back at the top of a coaster track, the seconds before we would tip and freefall down the other side. "I thought he was an engineer?"

Jesse and Sarah exchanged a glance, I looked over at Will. He was staring down at his hands, which were clasped tightly together. We were balanced so precariously–any second we would go over.

"Ben used to work as an engineer, but he also volunteered with an anti-trafficking organization when he traveled to Africa."

"I don't understand." No one heard me.

"I wish we had a printout or something from that database." Sarah leaned closer to Jesse. "Or even the list of places she was interested in."

"I…I guess I forgot my notes." When I thought about it, I didn't remember seeing them on the counter when I was in the kitchen with Jacob. Maybe he had accidentally thrown them away.

"Here."

All eyes turned to Will. His voice was strange–dark and gravelly. Something awful and sour crept up my throat. He moved slowly as he pulled a folded paper from his pocket and tossed it onto the table.

No one moved; we simply watched as the paper slid, coming to rest in the center of the rustic wooden table we all surrounded.

"It's Andy's notes…from her vision," he explained, refusing to meet my eyes.

Still no one spoke or moved. There was a near visible cloud of apprehension that crept up from the floor, enveloping us with its chilled humidity. Why were my notes bothering him so much?

"I've been trying to decipher the meaning." Will's words were soft, barely audible. "To figure out what she was doing."

Slowly, Jesse reached out, drew the paper towards himself, and flattened it. We watched in silence, everyone frozen as he read. He leaned towards his wife, showing her the contents. Jesse and Sarah were the resident doctor and nurse of the village. If anyone could make sense of my notes, or what I saw in the vision, it would be them.

"Jesse." Sarah reached out and placed her hand on Jesse's. "Go get Ben."

Jesse rose without speaking; my eyes followed as he hurried out the door. He took all of the air with him as he left, and my chest ached for its return.

"Are you saying that she was, what…trafficking people?" Emily whispered to Sarah, one hand unconsciously moving to protectively cover her belly, the other reaching for Brian.

The three of them leaned in, engaging in a soft discussion, using words that turned to jumbled mush in my ears. I was watching them from the outside but unable to participate, like a scene inside a snow globe.

Will's head rested in his hands, his fingers woven through his messy dark hair.

"Can you please tell me what's going on?" I said finally, standing quickly enough to startle everyone except Will, who raised his head slowly, unphased.

"What does this mean?" I pushed my finger down onto the symbol I'd drawn.

"It's the Greek letter psi." Will's answer drew everyone's eyes like a magnet. That wasn't his complete answer, though. He knew something, something he didn't want to know. He also looked very tired.

"But—what's the significance? Why would this be on someone's car?"

Sarah reached across the table and picked up the little pad, holding it up for everyone to see.

"It is the Greek letter psi, among other things," she answered. "But it's also the symbol for psychology."

"Are you thinking the woman is a doctor? A psychologist?" Brian asked, taking the pad from Sarah and examining it closely, as if the answers were hidden somewhere in my doodle.

"Maybe." Sarah stood up, her fingers pulling on her bottom lip as she paced. "But maybe that's the connection you're sensing, Andy?"

Brian picked up my notes and read over them. "What are delusions of grandiosity?"

"It's when you think you have superpowers," Jesse answered clinically, entering from the back, breathless and with a wide-eyed Ben Calloway in tow.

I felt everyone's eyes on me, and my face flushed with heat. Ben offered an apologetic smile as he took my notes from Brian. Jesse stood shoulder to shoulder with him, pointing at a few things I'd written.

"You said this woman was a doctor?" Ben's black eyes swept across the table, unsure of who specifically he was asking, finally settling on me when I nodded.

"You wrote here that the background was green and black. I believe she was accessing a medical database through a back channel," he explained.

"What is that?" Brian asked.

"Doctors enter patient information into their local system; only the doctor or doctors responsible for that patient have access—privacy laws and all that. Now, there is a national database that only select individuals would have access to; it's highly classified. Well, there are those who find doctors or nurses, or medical transcribers who are willing to sell that patient data. And there are countless hackers who can just go in and steal it."

"For what purpose, though?" Brian asked.

"For all kinds of things," Ben said. "Just as a horrid example, with access to a national database, you can have your pick of organs–you'd even know the blood type and medical history of the victim. You can find a doctor skilled enough to do the surgery, and with the right set of filters, you could even find a doctor with just enough misconduct to be easily persuaded. You wouldn't believe the things that are bought and sold on the darkest of the dark web. The least of which being kidneys and livers."

The group recoiled collectively, horrified and disgusted.

"So, there's a back-channel database out there with all the patient information from all the doctors?" Brian asked.

"Yes. Being a doctor, she would know how to interpret the information, and being a criminal…"

"She would have known where to find it." Jesse finished Ben's sentence. "She made a list of hospitals from that search."

"She was looking for more people like Andy," Emily whispered to Brian, her hand fluttering to her mouth as if it were too dreadful to even speak.

"I've been thinking that, too." Will finally spoke up. "It seemed like the only explanation as to why Nadine would have risked letting Andy go. She thought she could get a replacement."

It clicked. The search criteria, the list of hospitals, the sick reptilian smile on her face. *Places where people like you belong.*

"Makes perfect sense," I said, searching the faces around the table for…something. "Where else would you find someone like me but the psych ward? I mean…you'd have to be crazy, right?"

How many times had I thought that myself. Their expressions ranged from shock, to confusion, to pity. And then there was outright disgust etched across Will's face. I knew it wasn't directed at me, but that didn't make me feel any better.

We were flying downhill at full speed now, no breaks. I felt a cold spike of adrenaline shoot up my spine, and rubbed the goose bumps that formed on my arms. If Sarah was right, and this woman was doing the same thing as Nadine, she was dealing in priceless currency–buying and selling human beings like property. Searching for valuable assets hidden among the sick, abused, and insane.

Trafficking, human bondage and slavery–was one of the darkest parts of human history and in most parts of the world, including the United States, it was still a disgusting and common practice. The image of Nadine's smug smile flashed across my mind.

If Nadine had let me go, someone else had to take my place. The imaginary ride I couldn't escape was still racing downward, but had now plunged into total and endless darkness. The little girl in the hallway appeared in my mind, her pleading words echoing through my brain.

Rescue us.

"Andy?" Sarah whispered, touching my arm. "Are you okay?"

"I think I need some air," I said, standing quickly. "Excuse me."

As I hurried out, I saw Will rise to follow me. Sarah placed a gentle hand on his arm and shook her head, silently telling him to let me go.

CHAPTER 9

I hurried outside into the cool night air, sickened by the theory we'd formed, and feeling even more frustrated than before for overlooking the obvious. Suddenly, I couldn't get far enough away from where the horrible truth still hung in the air, thick and suffocating. I stumbled down the steps of the cabin and onto a gravel path that wound throughout the village. The trail stopped just outside of the village center, where families were already enjoying the bonfire.

Children laughed and danced to the sound of someone playing a guitar. Couples snuggled close on large log benches surrounding the fire in a circle. It reminded me of those precious innocent nights from my childhood among the caravans: close community and worry-free moments. Long before I knew of the evils that preyed on the innocent and unsuspecting.

There was joy and singing all around–it reached my ears but didn't permeate my heart. They were right in front of me, but might as well have been a million miles away. My eyes settled on the bobbing heads of Ben and Thadie's boys, their dark hair and chocolate skin tinted red by the light of the bonfire.

They held hands and skipped in a circle while chanting a happy song in Thadie's native tongue.

The thought of someone taking them from their parents, trading them like property, was too much. I wrapped my arms around my stomach and tried to hold myself together. Well over a year had passed since that incident with Nadine. What if she'd found someone before Will had found me? What if the woman from my dream was doing the same thing? If she'd just started when my parents died, that was twenty-two years ago. What if she had people right now, afraid and abused? Would we be too late? What if we couldn't find them?

My stomach churned, over-filled with anger and helplessness. I put my hand out to brace myself against the wall of a nearby cabin and fought back against the nausea, which was threatening to send back up everything I'd just eaten.

"Andy?"

It was Emily. I'd been so distracted by the turmoil in my gut, I didn't hear her walk up. She carried two blankets, one of which she held out for me. When I didn't accept, she shook it out and draped it over my shoulders. She then wrapped the other around herself.

"Come sit with me." She took my hand. "Oh, you're freezing!"

I let her pull me closer to the fire and onto a bench that was unoccupied. She sat close, and with the corner of the blanket in her hand, put her arm around my shoulders so that her blanket was wrapped around the both of us. Even under the cover of both quilts, I shivered. There weren't enough layers on the planet to chase away the cold of this reality.

"That was pretty intense, but you know that no one thinks you're crazy, right?" she asked, her breath making clouds in the air as she spoke.

"No," I replied honestly. "I don't even know if I believe that myself, Emily."

She didn't answer, but I felt her arm tighten around me.

"We're just two people. What can we do against such evil? I mean..." My voice cracked. "What if we are too late?"

"Do you believe what your grandmother said?" she finally asked. "That you would only learn something from that vision if you were supposed to?"

"Yes."

"Then you have a part to play still," she said gently. "If you believe

Esther, then you have to believe the implications."

"Why though? I mean, Will I understand. But why would God choose *me* for this? I'm not a soldier, or a detective or a doctor. I'm just…"

"Andy, you've already played such a huge part, and you don't even realize it."

"What do you mean?"

"Nadine was going to go search out another person, right? But Will found you. She meant for you to die, but you didn't. Just by living, you stopped her plan. Who knows how many were spared simply because you didn't give up? And you can't give up now."

Emily shifted, taking my frozen hands in hers. She lowered her head, forcing my eyes up.

"God almost always uses the least likely, the weakest, the least qualified to accomplish His plans, so when it's all said and done, there will be no doubt about who He truly is. It's not about us—it's about Him."

"But how will I know what to do? Where do we even begin?"

"Remember what you know to be true…and you'll know. God promises to help us when we are in trouble, and He always keeps His promises." Her voice was soft but strong and full of conviction. She truly believed the words she was speaking.

"We will help you, too." Sarah's voice startled me.

I looked up to see my friends. Sarah sank down next to me, sandwiching me between her and Emily. I felt Jesse's strong hands on my shoulders from where he stood behind us and Brian moved around the bench, dropping to one knee in front of us. They'd formed a protective barrier, sealing me safely inside.

"And you'll be covered in prayer. Every day, every hour," Sarah said. "Starting right now."

I was washed in warm words of confirmation from my friends as they agreed with her and began to whisper prayers of protection, comfort and strength. One by one they prayed for Will and me. I had never experienced anything like that before. I couldn't understand it, but I felt a peace flow over me. It started in my heart and overflowed outward into my body, slowly filling up every cracked and empty part until I felt a renewed strength and burst of courage. My eyes settled on Siphiwe and Sipho, and I was surprised to find them standing still while everyone around them was swaying and dancing to the music. They were holding hands and facing us, simply standing there. Their intense black eyes met mine, then gentle, innocent smiles spread across their lips.

The anger, doubt, and helplessness didn't completely disappear, but its thirst for control was quenched for now.

I let the prayers of my friends settle over me like a cloak, and when we left, I would wear them as armor. They would cover and protect; they would serve as weapons against the enemy and as light in dark places.

Long ago, on a bridge overlooking a river of deep dark waters, I decided once and for all that I was willing to go whatever distance necessary. Finding out there were more than answers at stake had humbled and changed my perspective, upgraded the urgency of the mission. I knew that Will and I weren't enough in ourselves, but in that moment, I was reminded: we weren't alone. Emily's wise understanding had brought such hope, that though we lacked resources, numbers, and physical strength…it might just be enough to simply refuse to give up.

CHAPTER 10

I returned to find Will and Ben hunched over my notes and several notebooks Ben had brought from his house, pointing and discussing in hushed voices.

"Well that's what they do," Ben explained to Will. "They gaslight their victims–make them think it's their own fault, they deserve it, there's no way out, or no one will want them. In this case, they could be making them think they're crazy. It's a great ruse; you basically convince the family to hand them over, no one is looking for them… It's the perfect con."

When he saw me, Will snatched the page up and asked Ben to meet him outside.

"What's going on?" I asked.

"Just trying to figure it out." He smiled and answered quickly. Too quickly.

I opened my mouth to question him further, but he cut me off.

"You look tired. Go on to bed. I'll be there in a few minutes."

He placed a quick obligatory kiss on my forehead and walked out before I had a chance to argue. He was keeping something back; then again, so was I.

The worst thing in the world for Will was the thought of me being in danger, so I decided to show him and his strange short behavior some grace.

The truth was, I was tired. More than tired. I was completely exhausted from the hours-long emotional roller coaster ride, and said a quick goodnight to my friends. But despite the peace I'd felt earlier, my sleep was restless. When I woke for the fifth time, Will had finally appeared, lying on top of the covers still fully dressed but breathing the deep heavy breaths of sleep.

I slipped out of the guest room in Emily and Brian's cabin and made my way to their cozy living room. After adding another log to the still-burning fire, I snuggled up on their small couch with a blanket and a hot cup of tea.

I watched the flames dance and flicker, hoping it would lull me to sleep. A small click from the master bedroom alerted me to Emily's presence. She headed towards her bathroom then joined me on the couch when she was done.

"Ahh…nothing like a baby sitting on your bladder." She laughed.

"Do you think it will be a boy or a girl?"

"I think a boy, but you just never know. There's so many old wives' tales about how to tell. I guess we won't really know until he's here."

"Do you have names picked out?"

"Um…I think we've decided on Elijah for a boy and Abigail if it's a girl."

"Those are both beautiful."

We sat in silence for a few minutes.

"I feel like there's something you aren't telling us," Emily finally said.

She was watching me with gentle, encouraging eyes. Emily saw things no one else did. There was no use denying it; I knew exactly what she was talking about. I hadn't even told Will. I looked back at the fire and chewed my bottom lip, trying to decide if I could put into words what I was hiding. I'd been playing with my necklace and touched the lion to my lips, its silver finish cool on my skin.

"You're safe here, Andy. You know that, right?"

I knew. This was the place I had always felt the safest. This village had saved my life in more than one way. When we arrived, Taklos had been searching for me in my dreams. I hadn't slept in days, and his growing presence in my mind was taking its toll. I had been in bad shape before getting bitten by the snake. He needed electricity to power his reach, and there was none within miles.

This hidden place, secluded from the world and all its distractions, had been the only place I could find real rest.

Emily was patient and didn't nag or try to persuade me. She simply waited until I was ready. I took a deep breath and closed my eyes.

"I told you that I found her?" I said, keeping my eyes closed. "The woman that was there the night my parents…"

"Yes," she said, mercifully not making me finish.

"I told you that I reached out, but nothing was there." When I opened my eyes, she was watching me expectantly. "That's not exactly true."

"You saw something?"

"I heard something."

I told her everything. I told her about the disappearing image of the little girl, her silent plea, and the strange voices that seemed to back away when I remembered the scriptures. She listened quietly.

"Now do you think I'm crazy?" I whispered.

"No, Andy, not at all." She pulled me close.

"Sometimes I feel crazy," I said into her shoulder.

"You're not, I promise. Why don't you throw another log on the fire; I want to show you something." She pushed herself to the edge of the couch and laughed through a groan as she struggled to get up. "Whew! That keeps getting harder."

"Aren't you tired? I don't want to keep you up."

"Don't be silly; this little one would keep me up anyway with all the kicking," she said, giving me a playful shove. "Now, go on."

I agreed and went over to stoke the fire while she walked to her bookshelf. We met back on her sofa; she held something old and tattered in her lap. When she moved her hands, I saw it was a Bible. I looked up at her questioningly.

"Listen to this, and I think you'll understand what's going on." She flipped through the worn pages. "This is from Ephesians, chapter six, verse twelve. 'For we wrestle not against flesh and blood, but against principalities, against powers, against the rulers of the darkness of this world, against spiritual wickedness in high places.'"

Spiritual wickedness in high places.

She ran her slender fingers tenderly across the page and looked up at my confused face.

"You know better than anyone, there is more to this world than what we can see," she said. "I believe what you experienced was spiritual. I think you did make contact. If it's true that she's involved in some kind of...trafficking, there's definitely some evil forces at play here too. You said a person can't lie in dreams. I think you heard the true voices in her head, whatever she has allowed to take root there and in her heart."

"You mean, like...demons or something?"

She shrugged, "Yeah, or something. Definitely something evil, because it retreated at the word of God."

"So...you're saying they–whatever they are–they're afraid of God?"

"That's exactly what I'm saying," she said passionately. "It doesn't take brute force or physical weapons to fight these battles, it takes spiritual strength that comes from faith in a very, very powerful God. *He* is greater; *His Word* is greater than anything...anything...in this world, even the hidden things."

Her words were so full of truth, I knew in my heart I needed to listen. I needed to heed her wisdom and commit every word to memory. These moments with Emily would be crucial. I stared down at the small leather-bound book in her lap. I'd known it all along–war was coming, and the powerful ancient words on its yellowed pages were my true line of defense.

"Tell me more."

We spent the next hour poring over every verse and chapter that she could remember.

"How do you know all of this?" I asked after she finally closed her Bible.

"My dad," she said with a sigh and a smile that told me she was remembering something precious. "He and my mom–well all of us, I guess–were missionaries in Africa."

"Really?"

"Yeah, I was actually born there, delivered by a Natimalan midwife. We lived there until I was ten. In fact, Thadie Calloway is from one of the areas my father visited. The culture was so rich and wonderful. I loved the people, but there were other forces at work there as well. You can't imagine the things we saw. In some parts of the country where we served, there were all kinds of demonic worship practices. When we were scared, my dad would remind us of all the things I just shared with you."

"So how did you end up here?"

"When we moved back to the States, my dad pastored a small church in Vermont. We faced a different kind of evil there, much more subtle and crafty. The idea of being your own god, worshipping oneself. In some ways, it was a harder mission field. There was a retreat we would attend each year just for pastors in the northeast US and their families. That's where I met Brian when we were teenagers. He was just a few years older and worked at the camp as a counselor for the little kids. I'd see him every year, and always looked forward to that week."

She blushed a little when she talked about Brian. I could certainly relate to that.

"Vermont, though? It seems a long way from here," I said.

"Our church was in the middle of nowhere; no cell service or anything. When it grew in membership, we moved closer to the city and I started to have some strange symptoms. I'd get dizzy, have unexplained headaches and nausea. Finally, we discovered I was electrosensitive. We'd always lived far away from cities, and I never had severe symptoms like that. So when Brian and I got married, we started researching and found this place."

"It's like a sanctuary," I said, smiling.

"It really is, in a lot of ways. You know Brian has pastored our little church since we moved here, and I can't think of a better place to raise our baby. I know it's a different life than most people live, but it's perfect for us and we have plenty of chances to minister to the hurting." She tucked her hair behind her ear and let her head rest on her arm.

"Well, you certainly ministered to me." I smiled. "How did the Calloways end up here too?"

"You know Ben was an engineer and was working to build bridges near Thadie's village. That's how they met. There's quite a bit of conflict in that area, some political unrest, I think. Things were pretty scary for them for a while. When he left with Thadie and the boys to the States, they were searching for a place that would be safe and that reminded her of her home. My dad was one of the few people she knew here, and he told her about this place."

"I can see why she would love it here."

Emily smiled softly and sighed.

"You must be so tired; thank you, Emily...for everything," I said, hugging her once more.

"Of course," she said softly. "Goodnight, Andy."

She shuffled off towards the restroom one more time, and then disappeared into her bedroom.

My own restlessness had ceased for the most part, and Will and I had a long day ahead of us tomorrow. After making sure the screen covered the fireplace, I tiptoed back to the spare room. I snuggled up next to Will, who had finally made his way under the covers. He mumbled a few unintelligible words before folding me into his arms.

Exhaustion won over worry. I finally drifted off, unable to settle the question of whether Emily's lesson about invisible battles was comforting or terrifying.

CHAPTER 11

"I can't believe Will let me sleep that long!"
Emily and Brian were sitting at the table in their small kitchen when I padded in, still rubbing the sleep from my eyes, even though I'd already dressed and freshened up in the bathroom.

"Where is he?" I looked out of the window over the sink.

When they didn't answer right away, I turned, and the expressions on their faces made my blood run cold.

"Where is he?" I asked again, my hands gripping the counter behind me so hard that it hurt. I'd been here before–in this very house in fact–waking to find Will gone. Once again, I was unable to tell if I was awake or dreaming; questioning my sanity had become an everyday occurrence, and not a routine I wanted to keep.

Brian stood and walked towards me. He reached out, but I shrunk away.

"Andy, come sit down." He was too calm.

"I don't want to sit down. Where is Will?"

He sighed, glanced at Emily, and reached for something on the table.

He hesitated, then offered it to me. In his hand was a plain white envelope, which I accepted with shaking fingers.

Written across the front in black ink was my name, in Will's handwriting. I didn't have to open it to know what it said.

"How long has he been gone?"

"Aren't you going to read it?" Brian asked.

"No." I snapped, the envelope crunching as I squeezed my hand closed around it. "How long?"

"Jesse just got back from dropping him at the station." It was Emily who answered, shrugging when Brian shot her a questioning glance.

I stormed off to the bedroom, slung my clothes in the bag and was on my way to Jesse's cabin within three minutes.

"Andy!" Brian called as I left. "Don't you even want to hear his side?"

"NO!" I yelled, not looking back.

Less than two minutes after that, Jesse was behind the wheel of the Mule again and I sat next to him, steaming. He'd been reluctant to comply with my request for a ride to the gas station, arguing that Will was long gone and I "should really just read his letter." After a serious threat of stealing the Mule and driving myself, leaving him with a very long walk to retrieve it, he conceded.

As the noisy ATV bumped along down the dirt road, I tried to form coherent thoughts and calm myself down, but the reasonableness required to do so was beyond my capability. I was irritated with my friends for going along with whatever plan Will had sprung upon them, but my quarrel wasn't with them.

"Andy...I really think you ought to let me explain."

I glared at Jesse, my arms folded tightly across my chest.

"If you must, but it's not going to change anything."

"Last night Ben and Will went over your notes. Ben has been on the inside of missions like this."

"And."

"And it's dangerous. You have no idea who to trust. The network is extensive and widespread. After the visit to your parents and the connection with Nadine, there's a very good chance she's still looking for you–a very good chance there are others in her grasp right now."

"So why in the world would he go off alone?"

"Because he's trying to protect you, don't you see? It could go south so fast. One minute you'd be with him, and the next gone. She could have you locked away and transferred from hospital to hospital with no record. You're safe here with us. Honestly, he's safer too."

I didn't understand what he meant by that last part, but he was right; I was safe there. Just a day before I might have agreed to stay if he'd asked me to, but more than his suffocating need to protect me, it was the fact that he didn't give me a choice that made me so angry. There were so many things in my life I didn't choose. I didn't choose to have my parents killed and my childhood with them stripped away; I didn't choose to have Dovanny Taklos come into my life and turn it upside down; I didn't choose to have these nightmares that started a second major life-altering upheaval. I wasn't angry about these things–I accepted them–but still, if there was a choice to be made, I wanted a chance to make it.

"He loves you. He agonized over this."

"Yeah, well, he should have agonized a little more."

Jesse didn't try to talk to me again. He was a doctor; he knew when he'd lost a patient. When we arrived at the gas station, I was further annoyed to see that Will hadn't come to his senses and returned.

Without a word, I jumped out of the Mule and walked straight towards the payphone. It struck me as I picked up the receiver that the last time this phone had been used was probably when Will had made a desperate call to Matt. I shoved a few coins into the slot and punched in the number to the burner phone.

He didn't pick up. A generic robotic voicemail greeting answered instead. I waited for the beep and spoke through my teeth.

"Will Carter, you turn around and come back here this minute. I am headed for the highway and either you use those powers of yours to find me, or I'm sticking my thumb out and getting in the first car that stops."

I slammed the receiver back in place and jerked my duffle bag out of the back of the Mule. It was a good hike to the highway from the gas station if I stuck to the paved road, but only a little over a mile if I cut through the woods. If Will had stopped right when I called and headed back, it would be at least an hour before he reached me. Still, I opted for the woods.

"Andy!" Jesse called as I huffed across the road and into the brush.

"Don't bother, Jesse."

He jogged to my side.

"Why don't you at least let me drive you to the highway, and we will wait there for him."

"No thanks."

I kept walking. I knew I was being irrational, and I really needed to calm down. I needed lungsful of fresh air, the closeness of nature, of creation. I needed my heart to pump oxygen to my brain so I could think clearly. My mouth was dangerously close to uttering some harsh words I'd surely regret.

"Then…I'm coming with you."

"Suit yourself."

Jesse followed silently, only stopping when we heard the distant ringing of the payphone.

"Andy…don't you…"

"Nope."

I heard him sigh and hurry to catch up with my hurried pace. We marched through the woods in silence, making good time. I heard the rush of cars flying by long before we reached the edge and broke through the tree line. A tiny sting of reluctance shot up my spine before stepping into the tall grass just beyond the woods. *It would serve him right if I got bit by another snake.* I smirked at my childish thought, but hurried towards the freshly mowed area closer to the road. Jesse stayed close as I turned to follow the highway south.

We'd walked less than five minutes before I heard the squeal of tires making a quick U-turn behind me. *Hmm, he either broke the sound barrier down the highway, or he was already on his way back.* Despite the overwhelming desire to turn and look, I refused and kept walking. The black Charger sped up beside me and jerked quickly off the highway just ahead, flinging grass and dirt as he skidded to a stop.

"Thanks for the ride, Jesse," I said nonchalantly, continuing my approach to the car.

"Uh…you're welcome?"

"Want a lift back to the gas station?"

"No. I think I'll walk."

He followed me to the car and watched in disbelief as I chucked my duffle bag into the back seat after jerking open the passenger side door.

He peered around me, making eye contact with Will, who shrugged apologetically.

To Jesse's surprise, I reached out and pulled him in close for a firm hug.

"Please tell them thank you for everything, and that I'm sorry for leaving without saying goodbye."

Jesse nodded, speechless as I released him and climbed into the car.

"You're sure you don't want a ride back?" I asked.

"Yeah...yeah, I'm quite sure." Jesse backed away slowly.

I didn't blame him. I wouldn't have wanted to be in that car with us either.

"Thanks again," I said before slamming the door.

With a heavy sigh, Will pulled off the shoulder and back onto the highway.

"And..."

"Don't." I snatched the unopened envelope from my pocket and flung it on the console between us. "Don't ever do that to me again. You don't get to leave me. You don't get to decide what's too dangerous. You just don't get to make these decisions for me. We do that together. I go where you go."

The burn of tears singed my lids and I looked away. He'd witnessed more sobbing breakdowns than any husband deserved, but this time...I just couldn't stand it. This was the first time he was the cause.

He didn't answer for a long time. For miles and miles, we rode in silence. I didn't ask where he was headed. I didn't demand a response or explanation. I just sat. I didn't even know what I wanted him to say, so I was satisfied with the quiet.

As the minutes clicked by, my heart started to soften, to empathize. He was just as lost as I, just as torn. Desperate to protect and to prevent. His heart ached at the thought of leaving me, but couldn't continue to beat at the idea of someone trading me like property, of the idea of someone drugging me in an asylum or any of the unthinkable things to which Ben had alluded. I felt his vulnerability, his desperation, and I finally understood. He couldn't make any other choice.

Lives were in danger; I was in danger, so for him, giving up was out of the question, but my presence meant his attention was split. Constantly having to be on guard was a distraction.

Distractions meant mistakes. Mistakes meant death. The only way for him...was on his own. Jesse's explanation finally made sense. If I was safe, even if I wasn't with him, he was safe. I didn't agree, but I understood.

I shot a glance his way. His expression was pained, his brows drawn together, and I realized what he was doing. He couldn't explain with words why he'd done what he'd done, and knew I wouldn't have listened if he tried, so he was allowing himself to feel all of these emotions deeply, knowing that I would feel them too. It was hurting him to do this, to fully embrace his fear and get to the root of his actions, but he loved me enough to endure it. Even in his faults he was heroic.

I felt a release in my spirit. My shoulders, which had been tight and stiff, began to relax and my breathing slowed. I still didn't have any words for him, but my anger was quenched. I hated being mad at him; it felt wrong in every way, like I was out of sync with myself.

"I panicked." His simple two-word response was a perfect explanation for his actions. "But Andy...sometimes you just have to trust me."

The blur of green out of my window reminded me of the first time we met. I'd watched trees blur by then too and I'd trusted him–from the very beginning, though I wouldn't admit it for a long time.

"I know." I finally responded. "Just...don't ever do that again."

"You either."

"Okay."

"I was coming back."

"I know."

I didn't turn away from the window but offered my hand, hiding a small smile when his warm fingers wove through mine. His touch had always been a balm to my restless heart; even now, though we were still at odds, I only wanted to be near him. Things weren't fixed, but they were no longer broken either.

"You know." His expression was very serious. "You're beautiful when you're ang–"

"Don't you dare." I turned away quickly, smothering a laugh with the back of my hand, while attempting to jerk my other hand free from his. He held tight, and I didn't resist further.

"Will, where are we going?" Highway signs indicated we were nearing Richmond.

"South."

"South?"

"Yes."

"Are you saying that to torture me or because you have no idea what you're doing?"

"No...I have an idea. I can't put it into words. I just know."

"Of course." Sometimes Will's super-intuition was downright

annoying.

We'd just pulled off the highway to get gas when the phone buzzed in the cup holder, and he released my hand to pick it up.

"Carter," he said.

Hearing him say that made me smile. I knew it was out of habit; even though he was no longer officially an Agent, he still maintained many of his agenty mannerisms.

"Hey Matt." I sat up, watching him. "Yeah, just a minute, I'm parking now."

He pulled around to the back of the gas station and stepped out of the car. I followed, standing in the crook of my open door. He listened as Matt talked for several minutes. He ran his hand through his hair and took a deep breath, the color draining from his face. This couldn't be good.

"How? No one believes that, do they? Well, what about visitors? Yes, sounds like the same woman. What about exterior cams, can we get a hold of that footage?"

He placed his hand on his hip, his stance reminding me, once again, very much of the Agent Carter I had first met just a year and a half before.

"We really need to find out how she got in, and how she even knew where to find Greyson in the first place... Yes, that's what I'm worried about too... I know, but I'm working with limited information."

Will listened as Matt spoke again.

"Okay. Thanks, Matt... Yeah, I don't know...after this, we might need to rethink things."

Will glanced up at me watching him. He flashed what he meant to be a reassuring smile, but there was something uncertain behind his eyes. He turned and walked away from the car towards the building, keeping his back to me. I leaned against the car, my arms draped over the low roof.

"Yes, I have it." His voice was quiet. He looked at me over his shoulder then turned back quickly towards the building again. "Thanks for your help, Matt. Let me know if you learn anything else."

He slid his phone into his back pocket, hooking a thumb in his front belt loop. I watched him leaning against the corner of the gas station store like a model in a magazine ad, his muscular arm stretched up above his head, staring off across the empty back parking lot to the busy highway in the distance. I wondered what Matt had said that he didn't want me to know, and just how bad this new intel would be.

I wasn't even within twenty feet of him, and I could feel the tension radiating off his shoulders. Maybe I should have stayed in the village, out of the way. Now I was making him divide his attention, simply because I couldn't stand watching from the sidelines?

How many more times could we survive this before he would be done? Just how many more times would "I love you" be enough to cover what we were going through? Would he get tired of the sleepless nights and the nightmares? Would his patience for situations over which he had no control run out? Would our relationship be one of the casualties of this mission? Seconds before, I was furious with him, and now...now I was just desperate to keep him.

I knew Will was different, but I'd seen so many families fall apart growing up. When the relationship stopped being easy or fun, people would just walk away, touting a change in heart's desires as their reasoning, as if that were an unquestionable explanation. They fell in and out of love as easily as dead leaves were picked off branches by a winter wind. Even though we had a solid foundation, it was hard to put those fears–that insecurity–to rest.

As if pulled by an invisible magnet, I crossed the distance between us and slid my arms around his waist from behind, resting my cheek against his back. He didn't move his left arm from the wall but slid his right hand up and over mine. His stomach was firm and strong beneath my hands, but there was tenderness in the way his thumb unconsciously rubbed gentle circles on the skin of my wrist. I loved that about him. He was as solid and immovable as a hundred-year-old oak, but sweetly protective and soft like the willow branches I hid under one scorching southern summer in Georgia.

"What did Matt say?" I asked.

He took a deep breath before answering.

"He was able to check the visitor logs where Greyson is being held, and she did receive a visitor that matches your dream woman's description. She identified herself as Greyson's attorney."

"When?"

"A few months ago. Around Thanksgiving."

Just a month after my dreams started. He was holding back; I could still feel the tension he was trying to hide, protecting me, even if it was from himself. He cleared his throat and explained more.

"Not just anyone can walk in there. They would have verified that information, so either she is skilled in falsifying documents, or connected to someone who is. We don't know how she found Greyson in the first place though, and that worries me," he continued, his voice trailing off as if he were talking to himself.

"Do you think this woman knows someone at The Agency?"

I really wished we knew her name.

"I don't know how else to explain it," he said. "It would have to be someone who was involved in your case at some level; someone who knows you and Greyson."

I could feel him mentally scrolling through the list of everyone at The Agency connected to my case, systematically assessing and eliminating. He knew every detail since he had been the one assigned to my protection after finding me in the woods.

"That could be so many people," I said. "Would they really have to have known about me, though?"

"What do you mean?"

"Well, she didn't show up at my parents' house until after she visited Nadine. So...theoretically, Nadine could have been the one who told her about me. Maybe she caught wind of what Nadine was doing–what she'd been looking for–and was simply curious. Nadine had access to my file; she knows more about me than anyone. And Lily and Bash were listed as my next of kin."

"Bash?"

"Oh...yeah." I laughed softly. "I used to call him that when I was little. Lily still does."

"Hmm. I bet you were cute...a little redheaded firecracker," he said, walking me backwards towards the car. He sat on the hood, one foot on the bumper and one on the ground. I stood between his knees, his hands resting casually on my waist, mine loose on his shoulders.

"We still don't know how she found Greyson, though."

I shrugged. "How confidential was Nadine's trial; who was there?"

Whenever I mentioned her name, he cut his eyes away quickly. I knew he didn't like thinking about her after what she'd done to me, but I couldn't help but wonder if there was something more he wasn't telling me. I didn't press. I didn't want to risk him pressing back.

"It was closed, obviously, no media. She was a contracted civilian, so she did have civilian representation. I was there, then there was Matt, Charlotte, and General Williams. The only other people were The Agency prosecutor and the judge. They never disclosed the location of her transfer."

"Could it have been her attorney?"

"He didn't even know her location. If she had requested a visit with him, he would have been contacted, but she didn't, and Matt said no one had been to see her since she was sentenced."

"Until..."

"Right...until."

"So what do we do now?" I asked.

He picked up my hands, his thumb grazing the white gold band that encircled my ring finger.

"Andy," he finally said. "I think it's time we try something else."

I felt my body stiffen.

"What do you mean?"

"I think I should go in with you–to your dream."

"How did...what are you talking about?"

"Esther told me. There's something else there you need to know. She knew you would never ask me to do it, but that it could be an option if we ever got..."

"No."

"Andy." He pulled me close, locking his hands together behind my back.

"I can't," I said softly.

"I know you're afraid..."

"It's not that." I pushed against his chest, but his arms remained firmly around me. "I'm not afraid."

"Then what is it?"

"First of all, I've never done that before; it might not even be possible."

"And?"

"And...and I can't bring you into this...this world of nightmares and exhausting, never-ending replays of death." I threw my hands up over my face. "It's too much to ask...of anyone."

What if you hate me for it? What if I lose you to it?

He sighed and let his arms drop. I was throwing him for a loop. He'd tried to leave me out of it, and I was the one forcing myself back in. Now, when he was actually asking to work together, I was pulling back.

He shook his head and let it fall forward as I stepped back. I held my breath. He finally looked up. I knew what he saw when he looked at me.

He saw firm defiance in my eyes, and I saw sparks in his. He stood, towering over me like a giant, his hands finding their way back to his hips.

"Joanna Marie Carter, you listen to me. When are you going to get it through your head?" He lowered his head a little to catch and hold my narrowed eyes, repeating the words I'd just said to him. "I go where you go."

"You just tried to leave me behind!" I threw my hands up.

"I already told you I was coming back. We both know that was never going to work. I was…I don't know, scared, I guess. It was stupid."

"But look what happened to Esther."

"Look what's happening to you," he said, reaching out and taking my frozen hands in his.

"This is different."

"How? Tell me, Andy, how is this any different?"

"It just is. I can't, Will. What if…"

I couldn't say it, but it hurt my heart to even think about what my life would be like if there was no Will Carter. I thought somewhere in my mind I heard the *click, click, click* of our coaster cart nearing the top of the incline, turning my stomach into a knotted mess.

"I'm not afraid." He slid his hands up, holding me by my upper arms.

"I know that. I just…you don't understand…" I couldn't look at him.

"Don't you trust me? I thought we had settled this…"

"Of course…it's not like that."

"Do you not think I'm strong enough?"

"No! I know you are strong." I pulled away, stepping back.

"Then what? Talk to me."

"I'm trying!" Now it was my turn to run my hands through my hair.

He didn't answer; he just folded his arms across his chest. Long, tumultuous minutes passed, yet he waited. Finally, I sucked in a deep breath and looked him straight in the eye.

"Will. It has nothing to do with your strength. This is nothing like anything you've done before. It takes something from you and leaves something else behind. It's me, and maybe I'm just being selfish, but I love you–who you are, exactly how you are. I don't want you to be like me. What if it's too much, what if you hate me, and…"

"I, what…fall out of love with you?"

I looked down and shrugged. That was part of it…most of it. I heard him sigh as I stared at a loose piece of concrete and nudged it with the toe of my shoe.

I felt his finger under my chin, lifting my head and forcing my eyes to meet his.

"I never fell *in* love with you," he said, smiling sympathetically at the look of pure horror that his words brought out on my face. "I *chose* to love you. I wake up every day and keep choosing to love you. It's not some arbitrary thing that I have no control over. It's a choice. And I promised that I would choose to love you every day of your life–nightmares and all."

The all too familiar tightness of emotion crept up my throat. His words were sincere and he meant every one. I felt the same way. Falling in and out of love was not something we were capable of, because this wasn't an involuntary emotion. It was entirely intentional. He held my face tenderly, my cheeks flaming up between his hands.

"We made a promise, Andy, to God and to each other. I promised to love you more than myself. Even when it's scary or hard, even when it hurts, even if it kills me. Even when I'm an overprotective idiot, even if you're stubborn and threaten to hitchhike down the highway. I intend to keep that promise," he said, his voice barely a whisper. "We made another promise, too. To follow the call, to stay the course. We have to keep that promise. If we can do something and we don't, baby, if anything can break us–that will be it. Neither of us can live with that."

Standing in the empty back parking lot of a tiny gas station in the middle of nowhere, I finally understood completely. The love we chose was the strongest kind. It came with security and strength, because it wasn't selfish; it wasn't forced. It was formed of free will–chosen. I could trust him with everything, because he wasn't a slave to his emotions–he was making deliberate decisions. He loved me enough to call me out when I was being selfish, too.

The harsh truth of his challenge sunk in. Answer the call. Stay the course. Keep the promise. I stared him down. He stared back, unwavering.

"UGH!" I threw my hands up and broke away from his hold.

"What?" he said, half laughing, and half confused.

"You! You're so…good!" I slumped back against the rough brick wall like a pouty teenager. "Even when you leave me and go off to save the world on your own!"

He laughed, reached over and grabbed my hand, pulling me back up into his arms.

"I love that you won't let me." He laughed into my hair.

"There you go again," I said sarcastically, making him laugh even harder.

"I'm sorry," he flashed that crooked smile that made me blush. "I'll try to be less…good."

"Okay, Mr. Perfect." I leaned back, his arms still around me, and rolled my eyes at him.

He laughed again, hugging me close. I loved his laugh; it was a deep and joyful sound I didn't hear often enough. I laughed with him, letting my head fall against his chest as it shook with his chuckles.

He brushed my hair back and kissed me softly on the forehead before he wiped his eyes with the back of his hand. The sun was directly behind him, peeking out around his sides and forming a glowing halo. He certainly was beautiful. He was handsome, of course, but his heart, honest and courageous–that was truly beautiful.

"What?" he said, catching his breath and wiping his eyes again.

I couldn't help it. I launched myself towards him, grabbed his face with both hands, pushed up on my tiptoes and planted a long kiss right on his lips. I took him by surprise, but he quickly recovered, his hands sliding to firmly grasp my waist, pulling me closer and eagerly kissing me back.

"So…you've forgiven me then?"

"Almost." I kissed him again.

"Are you trying to distract me?" he asked, keeping his mouth close to mine.

"Of course not."

"Then what was that for?"

"For being perfect," I smiled, kissing him yet again and drawing a low growl from his throat.

"Mmmm Mrs. Carter, you're pretty perfect yourself." He winked, then cut his eyes to something over my shoulder. "We better get going before that police officer comes to see what's going on over here."

I felt a shot of adrenaline zip up my spine and scrambled away from him. However, when I scanned the parking lot, frantic and embarrassed, I found it deserted. I shot him a look of feigned offense, which quickly faded at the sight of his mischievous smirk.

I giggled, playfully punching him on the shoulder as he walked to the passenger side, taking the handle and pulling the door open for me. I stepped off the curb and moved to get in the car. He stopped me with two strong hands on my shoulders.

"What?" My hand fluttered to my mouth, trying to hide a ridiculous grin.

"I meant it. I want to go in with you, Andy," he said, suddenly serious. "I think we both know this is no longer a fact-finding trip. This is a rescue mission."

Rescue us.

I didn't answer right away. His words hung in the silence of the cool afternoon, an invisible challenge between us.

"Okay," I said.

He stared at me for a few seconds, his expression unreadable.

"Okay," he said, satisfied. "But not on the road." He moved so I could get in the car and walked around to the driver's side.

"What do you mean?" I clicked my seatbelt into place.

"I'm too distracted, constantly looking over my shoulder. In order to do this, I assume we have to be asleep, yes?" He turned the key and the Charger's engine roared to life.

"Yes, that's generally how dreams work."

"Well, Dr. Freud, we need some place quiet…away. But I want to keep moving."

He turned onto the service road and pointed the car towards the highway.

"Do you want to go back to the no-zone?" I couldn't figure out what he needed. "Where *were* you going?"

He shifted, reaching into his back pocket and pulling out a folded paper. It was my notes. I unfolded it, reading cryptic words in my own handwriting.

"I was going down the list." He turned onto the interstate. "No, even at the village, we will be standing still. I think it's time we call your uncle."

"Jacob?"

"No," he said, tossing me the phone. "Jubal."

CHAPTER 12

"Andy! Yur looking more and more like yur momma every time I see ya."

"Hi, Uncle Jubal," I said, melting into his warm embrace.

"Can't say how nice it is to see ya again." Jubal leaned back, examining my face for a long moment, then shook his head as if in disbelief.

"I've missed you too."

"Yur car'll be safe and sound there in Henry's shop. My nephew's a good fella."

"Thank you for coming to get us." I took his offered hand and stepped onto the rocking deck.

"Oh, think nuthin' of it. I wasn't but a few miles upriver, believe it or not. I was supposed to meet a friend on down-aways, but I's havin' trouble gettin' on my way, now I guess we know why."

We'd stopped just outside of Richmond and had been surprised when Jubal said he would meet us in an hour.

After greeting Will with a handshake, he shuffled into the cabin of his houseboat and we followed, our bags slung over Will's shoulder. When he moved to dump them onto the couch, Jubal waved his hands around emphatically.

"No, no no, you youngin's are taking the bedroom. That old couch is no place for newlyweds."

"Oh no, we couldn't," Will said.

I walked through the cabin, down a narrow hallway to the helm, leaving them to politely argue about sleeping arrangements. The small helm room was just as I remembered: rows of tiny lights, switches, and knobs on a square panel next to the large steering wheel. Jubal's rickety stool, its blue vinyl seat covering cracked and worn from use, sat empty in front, ready for its captain. The lingering smell of grease and gasoline filled the air.

Rolls of maps were neatly stored in a tall wicker basket in the corner, and on the wall that separated the helm from the cabin was a small bulletin board littered with receipts, boat maintenance documents, and lists in Jubal's shaky handwriting. On top of all of it though, as if given a place of honor, was a small rectangular card, secured with a clear plastic pushpin. It was our wedding invitation–a simple white card with navy writing. I ran my fingers over the text, its raised ink bumpy under my touch. We'd just celebrated our first anniversary a few months ago, just before Christmas.

My eyes traveled from the cursive script to my fingers that hovered on top, tracing each curved letter. A golden beam of evening sun fell on the small heart-shaped diamond of my engagement ring. I would never forget the day Will gave it to me.

"Come walk with me?" he had said, his hand outstretched and open, waiting for mine. I eyed him suspiciously but took his hand anyway.

It was a Monday; exactly six weeks since I had died. Well, since Andromeda Stone had died. Technically, I was a ghost. After Will pulled me from the river, Matt had brought me to my grandmother, and that's where I had been ever since. Deep down I knew I was hiding, but wouldn't admit it. I hadn't left the church, not even to walk the grounds.

I'd certainly covered every square inch of the sanctuary, kitchen, library, and maze of underground hallways, but for some reason, I couldn't bring myself to step out of the door.

After a short inquisition into the tragic disappearance of Agent Stone and the trials, Will had resigned from The Agency and moved into an apartment just a block away to continue his work in a freelance capacity.

He'd just returned from a trip that morning, still excited from the high of helping–that time a happy success.

He led me down the narrow stone hallway and upstairs, where the sounds of the organ were echoing off high stone ceilings. I thought it unusual to hear that on a Monday; Cynthia, the church organist, usually rehearsed on Wednesdays.

He looked back and smiled as we walked through the doors to the open sanctuary. I narrowed my eyes and tried to hide a smile, wondering what he was up to.

I immediately recognized the tune as we stepped inside. Since coming to know my new family, I had spent many hours in that very room. My favorite hymn had become *Be Thou My Vision*. The words spoke directly to my heart and resounded deep within me; I was constantly humming or singing it, even plunking out the melody on the piano when no one was looking.

Will led us to the front row where we sat, hand in hand, listening as Cynthia gracefully moved her fingers across the keys, sending the deep tones of the hymn in waves down the steps from the altar. She played all four verses, then smoothly transitioned into *It Is Well,* another of my favorites.

"Andy." Will's voice was soft on my ear.

I didn't realize it, but I had closed my eyes, simply swimming in the music. I felt my ears burn from a blush and looked up at him through my lashes.

"Do you know what's special about this spot?" he asked, sliding his arm behind me on the pew.

"No, what?"

"This is where you told me everything that happened with Esther. Where you told me that you had prayed to God and He had saved you." He was close. I knew he could hear my heart's thunderous beat inside my chest.

"Do you remember?" He tucked a loose strand of my hair behind my ear, his fingers brushing gently along my jaw, sending cool tingles across my skin.

"I remember," I whispered.

The music had stopped. I glanced over; Cynthia had quietly slipped out.

Will reached under the wooden pew and pulled out a box. It was wrapped in shiny white paper and a thick purple satin ribbon fashioned into a loose bow. I looked up at him with wide eyes.

"What is this?"

"Don't open it yet." He smiled.

"What's going on?" I narrowed my eyes suspiciously.

"C'mon." He stood and held out his hand again, which I quickly accepted.

He led me across the front of the church, past the rows of empty pews, towards the side door. I hesitated as we approached. He felt my resistance and stopped.

"Will..." I stuttered. "I can't."

He turned, then took both of my hands in his.

"I know you're scared, and that's okay. No one would blame you for staying in here forever after all that's happened." He stepped closer, sliding his hands up to my shoulders. "But perfect love casts out all fear. You have that perfect love now, God's perfect love; it's your new name and your new life."

I could barely breathe. I recognized the verse he was paraphrasing, but I was so unsure of what waited for me out there. I was safe in these walls, where I lived my ghost life.

He gently tipped my chin up with one hand and kissed me softly.

"This place is more than a sanctuary. It's been a place of healing for you, I know that, and I'm so grateful for it. But you're hiding in here now."

I wanted to be offended by his words, but I couldn't be offended by the truth. His voice was low and soft, and his lips brushed my forehead as he spoke. His words fell over me like warm rain, seeping through the cracks in my armour.

"I will go where you go, and I will stay where you stay; but I hope you will come with me into the light. You've been freed from darkness, Andy; don't hide from the light."

With those words he stepped away, letting his hands drop, then turned, opened the door, and walked outside. Light from the bright afternoon sun flooded through the opening, creating an arch that peaked at the toe of my tennis shoes. I stared down at it, desperately desiring to bathe in that warm golden pool, but scared to step in.

"You're the bravest person I know, Andy. I know you can do this," he said, drawing my gaze from the floor to his warm brown eyes. "I'll be on the bench."

He turned and walked away.

I stood there for what felt like hours, but in reality, it was probably just a single minute. Will was right. There was nothing supernatural about this building, but I did find refuge and healing there. I had desperately needed that before; now, I was just hiding. I was safe inside these walls, where no one would see me, and I was surrounded by nothing but hymns and books. It wasn't a bad place to be, but I knew God hadn't called me to hide. This place and this time had given me life, yet there was still life to be lived outside that door. I was no longer of that world, but I had to walk in it. I couldn't remain a ghost, as one dead.

I looked down again at the patch of sunlight and took a step forward. Nothing terrible happened. The next step was easier. Soon I was through the door, in the bright light of day, and onto the garden pathway. A crispness in the air hinted that winter was near, but the liquid gold of late afternoon sun poured through the trees and onto my skin. Everything was alive and suddenly vibrant, like I was stepping through time, from a monochrome world into techno-color.

The trees were on fire with the brilliant hues of fall. Bright red, orange, and yellow patches dotted the grounds; I wanted to kick myself for almost missing this sight.

I turned a corner and there he was, beaming from where he sat on the bench. The tiniest look of relief passed over his face before he stood and greeted me with a bear hug.

"I knew you could do it," he said into my hair, still holding me tightly.

"Thank you," I whispered back.

He let me go and motioned for me to sit.

"You can open that now." He pointed to the package I was still holding.

"Okay," I said with a nervous laugh.

I slowly untied the ribbon and pulled back the paper, revealing a simple brown cardboard box. I looked up at him curiously as an adorable boyish grin spread wide across his face.

"Go on."

Inside the box was a Bible with a leather cover that was the most beautiful shade of sable brown.

"Oh, Will..."

I didn't have my own Bible yet. I'd pored over all the different versions in the church library, but didn't have one of my very own. I flipped open the cover and saw it was the book of Revelation; it was upside down.

"Turn it over." I heard him say.

I obeyed and my breath caught as I read the name embossed on the cover.

Joanna Adley Carter.

I looked up and gasped to find him kneeling in front of me with a small blue velvet box in his hand.

"When I pulled you out of the river and thought you were gone, it destroyed me. I felt like I had been ripped apart from the inside out. But when you opened your eyes, I knew that I had to keep you with me forever. I want to love you, protect you, and serve by your side for the rest of my life. Joanna Marie Adley...Andy...will you marry me?"

My eyes filled with tears that I fought to contain. I'm sure my mouth was gaping wide open in disbelief. Marry him? He wanted me to be his wife–to belong to him forever?

The tears escaped and poured down my face; I couldn't find the words to speak. He reached up, wiping my cheek with his thumb. I threw my arms around his neck and pulled him towards me with such force that he had to put his hands on the bench on either side to keep from falling over.

"Is that a yes?" He laughed.

"Yes!" I said, before any self-doubt crept in.

"Andy?" It was Will's present voice.

"Yes." I turned and blinked back the threat of more tears.

He leaned into the helm room, looking around as if in a museum before letting his brown eyes fall on mine.

"I lost. We will be staying in the honeymoon suite." He stepped fully into the room. "You okay?"

"Yeah." I sucked in a deep breath. "Just...memories."

"Mmm," he said, running his hand along the control board. "This boat holds a lot of them."

He was right. We'd spent not even two full days with Jubal on his floating homestead, but it had been a safe place for us when we desperately needed one. A place where I'd finally accepted my growing feelings for Will and took another step towards trusting him. I didn't know it at the time, but it had also been where I'd met the first member of my new family.

"Why here?"

He looked up and I watched the confusion meld into understanding. He shrugged.

"I know I'm asking a lot of you, and it will ask a lot of me too," he said.

I folded my arms, defensive against the impossible supernatural feat I was still reluctant to attempt. He stepped forward, rubbing his hands on my arms.

"I needed a place where I could…where we both could rest. On the road, there's just too many unknowns, too many possibilities. Even though we'll be heading the wrong direction, here we can keep moving and be safe. I can be fully present."

My eyes flicked back and forth between his, searching for a chink in his armor but finding none. His resolve was set. His expression suddenly lightened into a grin and he stepped back.

"Now, the captain is requesting our presence at dinner, madame." Will bent in a dramatic bow and held out his hand.

I giggled despite myself, took his hand, and followed him back to the cabin where my sweet great-uncle was placing the last of the dishes on the table.

CHAPTER 13

"Are you ready?" he asked.

"No," I said honestly. "Not at all."

"You can do this." His hand found mine, sending a rush of warmth through me. "We can do this."

I was hoping logistics would solve my problem for me, but bringing Will into my own dreamscape hadn't been nearly as difficult as I thought. Especially after the intentionally filling dinner Jubal had made, the blazing heat of his bedroom, and the rhythmic cradlesque rocking of the house boat. I'd never slept so soundly in my life. The deepness made it a snap.

After our intense truck stop conversation, I'd been reluctant but willing. Now, as we stood together in the dark, just steps from my familiar nightmare, the doubt returned. I was back on the roller coaster, zooming downward with my heart in my throat and stomach in knots. I could still feel the light rocking of Jubal's boat even there, and thought about just sabotaging the whole mission–except I knew how dangerous that lie between us would be.

I completely trusted Will; it was myself I didn't trust. I knew I would be drawing from his strength, just as I had from Esther–but intentionally this time. The memory of her lying in bed, weak and tired, flashed in my mind. My hand fluttered to my necklace and I squeezed the lion pendant between my fingers. What if I couldn't control what happened in there? What if something went wrong? What if the woman showing up at my parents' door was just a coincidence, and we spent all our time and energy chasing shadows? What if…

"Andy." Will's voice halted the assault of apprehension. "Stop."

I shot a harsh look his way, prepared to defend my worries, ignoring the fact that he seemed to be able to read my mind. He was staring at something above me. Of course. He was seeing the images of my thoughts, flashing insolently above my head. It was unnerving to have someone walk in my dream the way I had walked in so many others'. Regardless, these were legitimate concerns.

"Maybe we should wait until…"

"Stop." He dropped two strong hands on my shoulders. He spoke with an authority that I both admired and found incredibly annoying. "You're spiraling."

"Will," I sighed, resting my forehead on his chest. "I know we agreed to do this, but…I just really don't want to hurt you."

He pushed me back, moving his hands to cup my face, forcing my eyes to meet his. His face was flushed, and flames flicked at the edges of his dark brown irises. My breath, on its way out of my lungs, retreated back inside.

"How many times have I had to step back and watch you walk into the fire, out of the safety of my world and into yours where I can't reach you? Do you have any idea how hard that is? Every night when you close your eyes, all I can do is pray that you're going to open them again in the morning. Every time you wake up screaming, I beg God to forgive the anger in my heart, but I am also just so thankful that you're still with me."

His words sliced through my heart, sending the burn of emotion up my throat. I had no idea he felt this way. All this time I had been so focused on my own battles, my fight. I had been totally oblivious of the war he was fighting. He had no control, no way to help me in my world.

No wonder he was so protective in his. As much as we both trusted the Lord and believed He was the God who breathed life into the universe, our weak human hearts still ached for control. Will pressed his lips to my forehead.

"For once, Andy…baby, please let me walk into the fire with you." His voice cracked a little, and I broke.

"Okay…okay. I'm sorry. I didn't realize." My fists twisted around the fabric of his t-shirt, urging him near. I pushed up onto my tiptoes and crushed my lips to his. His fingers wove into my hair, cupping the back of my head and pulling me ever closer. He tasted like summer, like sunshine and beaches and all the warm things.

"Thank you," he whispered against my lips, sending flames across my skin.

I stepped back, shooting him a sly smile.

"You know, it's really not fair when you do that." I looked ahead into the darkness.

"Do what?"

"You know what. When you call me that, it makes me want to agree to anything." I should have kept my mouth shut, because a wickedly handsome grin spread across his face.

"Oh, really?" He teasingly drew out the last word.

"Yeah, Romeo–remember the first time? I was trying to die, and then you went and said that," I said with a laugh.

"Well, I'd say I'm sorry, but…" He shrugged.

"You're not."

"No, not at all."

"Well, for the record…it's an unfair advantage."

"Noted," he said, his tone official. "Now, quit stalling."

I huffed and reached for his hand. With one last glance between us, we stepped forward into the darkness.

"Whoa," I heard Will gasp.

I knew he had felt that same little stomach flip as I had. As quick as it took us to blink, the scene appeared. I looked up at him, allowing myself a fraction of a second to enjoy his wonder, but that feeling disappeared as soon as my eyes traveled past him to an empty stretch of dark country road.

There was nothing there. I was standing in the middle of the road as always. It was the same length of cracked pavement, the same dark empty woods–but there was no car, no smell of burning rubber, and no haunting sounds. The night was clear and completely silent. I spun around; still nothing.

"What is it?" Will asked, watching me with concern.

"Something is wrong," I said. "This is different."

"Is different bad?"

"Almost always."

"Andy," Will's voice was edged with caution. "Whose dream are we in?"

"Mine...I think." It had to be; there was no one else there.

A distant sound drew both our gazes.

"What is that?" he asked, looking back at me.

"I don't know."

From far off, the tiny orbs of headlights appeared over a hill. The little golden pair dipped in and out of sight as the car they belonged to traveled over uneven terrain. I was frozen, staring as twin lights bobbed ever closer.

"Andy," I heard Will's voice, but it didn't register as something I needed to respond to.

I was filled with terrible anticipation, mesmerized by the unfamiliar sight and once again teetering precariously at the top of some dangerous precipice, lingering breathlessly in the seconds before plunging down the other side.

"Andy," he said again, more forcefully. I still didn't move–couldn't move.

He looked back and forth between the approaching lights and my frozen expression.

"Andy!" He grabbed my arm and jerked me towards him, walking us backwards, off the road to the safety of the shoulder.

My back was to his chest, his arm across my shoulders, keeping me close. My heart began to pound, matching his beat for beat. I didn't want to see what was about to happen, but I couldn't look away.

"Look," he said, dipping his head to whisper in my ear.

My disobedient eyes followed the length of his arm and beyond in the direction he pointed, but what I saw there didn't make any sense. Just to our right, off to the side and hidden by the trees, was a dark colored boxy sedan. I thought I recognized it. It didn't appear to be running; all of the lights were off, but in that position, if it pulled forward, it would move right into the path of the car that was approaching.

My stomach tightened painfully with a sickening feeling of dread.

There was someone else here; there always had been. The headlights grew bigger and closer, and I heard the click and gentle purr of an engine. The car in the woods had been started. It wouldn't be visible to anyone driving on the road because of the thickness of the woods and its headlights were off.

"Will?" My voice was strained, and his name came out as plea. The earth tipped forward, sending my brain reeling and my body felt weightlessly lifted as if the ground suddenly fell away. With nothing left to cling to, I grabbed hold of the only solid thing: Will. My fingers dug into his arm, which rested securely across my chest. He remained an anchor, keeping us from floating away on waves of heartbreak.

I could feel his heart pounding against my back through his shirt, and his body was as tense as mine. *I don't want to see this...I don't want to know.* His grip tightened. We clung to each other, desperate to stop whatever was about to happen; both knowing we couldn't, because it had already transpired.

It seemed to unfold both all of a sudden and in slow motion at the same time. My brain registered what was going to happen a split second before it did. The car hidden in the woods shot out into the road in front of the other car, causing the driver to swerve and slam on his brakes. As they fought against friction, trying and failing to regain a grip on the road, a sickening screech of tires on asphalt filled the space around us. It sliced painfully through the silence of the night, and my hands shot up to cover my ears. I squeezed my eyes shut.

"No!" My scream flew over and above the horrific scene playing out in front of us, never reaching any other ears but mine and Will's.

My voice cut through the frozen moment, bouncing back and hitting me from all sides, like I was hearing the word and its echo at the same time. It was an impossible mystery, but I knew then that it was the same cry I'd heard all those times when I'd entered a dream...as if I'd always been there.

Will pulled me in, spun us around and shielded me with his body. He held my head to his chest, one of his hands covering mine, which was still clamped hard over my ears, trying to keep out the sounds of what was happening just a few feet from us. His other arm was wrapped tightly around my waist. I knew he was watching, because he jerked and tensed at the horror unfolding in front of him. He was witnessing what I couldn't bear to see.

I tried to focus only on the sounds of my own ragged breaths and his heartbeat, blocking out the rest, but some of the noise still reached my ears. It was so heartbreakingly familiar, and I finally knew the source of those cloaked sounds that I had heard every time I entered my dreamscape.

This moment…this was the origin. Although now it was so clear, my mind couldn't accept that I had been here before, not just as an infant in my real life, but here, in a dream with Will, locked in the safety of his arms. The sound was too familiar, exactly as I'd heard it all those times, hindered from fully reaching me because of his shelter. Time didn't exist here: neither moving forward nor back, events occurring in a non-linear, incurved, and divergent order. All of this knowledge was absorbed and dissolved in the same breath, gone before it could be understood.

Will's grip loosened, and I knew that it was over. I moved my hands and looked over my shoulder to see the same horrific scene I had witnessed so many times and I relaxed, simply because from there I knew what to expect. With this realization, a disturbing chill crawled up my spine. The expression on Will's face was exactly what I imagined my own looked like: a mix of shock, horror, and hopeless despair. His eyes were shiny with unshed tears as he looked down at me.

"I'm so sorry, Andy." His voice was shaking and his breaths heavy.

I was sorry, too. I was so very sorry he had to witness all of this, and worse, what was to come. My heart ached with sorrow. No one should have such terrible images forever burned into their mind. My eyes searched his for signs of regret–was this too much? Did he wish he hadn't agreed to it?

"Even if we don't learn anything new." He answered my unspoken question.

It struck me then, just how profound his sacrifice was. He was willing to share in my pain; he was willing to experience this haunted ride, to be jerked around every curve, flung down every bottomless drop, even if it was for nothing. Even if it was just so that I wouldn't have to go alone. Now it was there in his beautiful mind, forever a scar where before there was none. It shouldn't have been…none of this should be.

In addition to incredible sadness, something else began to grow inside. It was just a tiny little seed, but it settled into the pit of my stomach. I'd felt it before, always ignoring it until it was gone. It was more than anger, something unnamed and wildly raw. I knew for sure now that this woman was a murderer. She was a heartless, remorseless killer.

I didn't ignore it this time, but instead buried it under a secret protective layer of shame. I didn't want to pull any more from Will than I had to, so I needed to stay focused–we didn't have much time.

The eerie silence following the crash cocooned us, humid and heavy, sucking the air out of our lungs. I turned to fully face the scene. Will still held me close, my body moved only by the rise and fall of his chest pressed against my back. He dropped his arms, wove his fingers through mine, and we watched in silence, neither of us willing to risk letting go.

The trees began to sway, moved by a strange and unseen force. I didn't move from the safety of Will's presence but looked around, trying to figure out the source, since I didn't feel any wind. My eyes settled on the overturned car in front of me on the road. I knew whatever was causing this windless wave was just on the other side.

I heard a weak whisper and closed my eyes. I'd never ventured that far, never able to face what was hidden by the broken wall of metal and glass. But now, it was time. Drawing from Will's strength, I focused on the raspy words.

In my head a new scene began to materialize. A young woman's face slowly evolved from obscurity to clarity. Her features were familiar, and familial. It was Maggie, my mother. I could see her as if I were right there in the car with her. I had been with her, when I was very small. I was very small now. My infant eyes couldn't see far, but I could see Maggie, and I could feel her. I felt everything she was feeling. She was hurt, badly hurt. She was afraid, but even more than that, she was determined.

All around us was broken glass, tiny little squares that twinkled in the moonlight. It was painful for her, but she stretched a shaking hand towards the night. Her weak fingers moved. The nearest branches soon mirrored, swaying back and forth, creating a soft sound.

"Help her." Her prayer was urgent, desperate. "Send...help."

The words slipped out across her fingers and were carried deep into the woods by the smooth dance of the trees. A supernatural distress call.

She kept her hand outstretched but turned her head back towards me. Her other arm was pinned by the seat of the car which had been twisted from its place by the force of the crash, leaving only her hand free. It was close to me, open and her fingers curved, as if she were holding an invisible ball in her palm. Her eyes traveled past her hand and settled on mine. I'd been crying, but stopped when our gazes met. I saw my own tiny hand reach out, only able to touch the tip of her finger. Something passed between us. All of her, everything from before she even existed, dissolved into my tiny finger with a spark.

I gasped and felt Will's grip tighten, but I kept my focus and watched in awe. My tiny body was still strapped securely into a car seat, its belts snugly holding me in place. She looked around and my eyes followed to see what her eyes saw. All around, suspended in the air, were hundreds of tiny chips of glass, shards of metal, and razor-sharp pieces of plastic. She was holding them back by some unseen force, but she was weakening.

"Hold on, sweetheart. Oh, please hurry," she whispered, pleading with an invisible someone.

I watched as she desperately looked around the wreckage. An agonizing cry escaped her lips as her eyes settled on what she was searching for, the near lifeless body of her husband, my father, half hidden under the wreckage. He stirred at the sound of her cry and she gasped in hope.

"Jonathan!" Her voice was barely audible. Her lungs, crushed under the weight of the seats, struggled to take in air.

"Maggie...the baby," his voice was just as soft.

"I'm trying...I can't hold it much longer."

"I love you, Mag...always and forever."

He had no strength left. He groaned, and through sheer willpower, pulled his arm free and grabbed onto her, giving her the very last of himself.

"I love you too," she cried, hot tears pouring from her eyes which struggled to remain open. She was fading, but his touch gave her just enough to stay awake and hold back the debris that was threatening to hurt their baby.

He didn't answer.

"Johnny..."

He was gone, and any minute she would be, too.

Something stirred in the woods. She cut her eyes hopefully towards the sound. I watched as what looked like angels approached. A man and woman, both dressed in white, crept closer and the man knelt, peering into the car. He gasped when he saw her, and his hand flew to his lips.

"Please...please save her," she whispered. "Don't let them find her."

"Hold on," he said, sliding back as if to get up. "We will get help."

He stopped when she begged him again and looked back at her hand, which was shaking uncontrollably.

I saw Sabastian reach into the car and carefully unlatch me from the car seat. His hands were shaking as he held me. He looked up desperately at Lily, who bent down and folded me securely into her arms, her face low enough to see Maggie's.

Their eyes met for just a second, and what passed between them was a silent promise, a last wish, and a beautiful act of love, acknowledged only by an almost unnoticeable tip of Lily's head.

I felt Lily's warm breath as she softly kissed my face and for the first time my nose filled with the calming earthy scent of lavender. As Lily backed away, I saw Maggie's face. Her eyes, the same ocean blue as mine locked onto me. Her lips moved.

"I love you, Joanna," she mouthed, soundlessly. "Be brave."

There was no fear in her; she was fierce even then as the last of her life slipped away. A soft smile spread across her beautiful lips before her eyes fluttered closed. I knew when she opened them next, she would see the glory of heaven. Sabastian fell face first into the dirt and wept. The baby in Lily's arms began to cry.

My eyes flew open and at the same time, overcome with the utterly beautiful despair of what I'd witnessed, my knees gave out. Will's hands were quick to tighten around me, holding me up as I sagged in his arms. I struggled to take in a normal breath.

"I saw…" I gasped. "I saw…everything."

He didn't answer; he was staring at the couple disappearing into the woods. I heard his breaths, heavy with emotion, from behind me. I gasped for air through silent sobs. I wanted to fall on the ground and weep as Sabastian had done, to bury my face in the dirt and heap ashes on my head, but there was still something else we were there to do. Maggie had been strong and brave, her last words telling me to do that same. I wondered why I had never seen all of this before, but the presence of Will's warm hands answered my question. I couldn't have seen it before; he had to be there. He had to be the solid thing that would hold me up when the world beneath fell away.

"She's coming," I said, my breath ragged.

"C'mon." He stepped towards the road but hesitated when he felt me resist. "Andy?"

I had seen this over and over again. I knew what was coming but I was scared this time, more than ever before.

"We don't have to do this now." His resolve was wavering under the intensity. "We can try again."

Be brave.

No, we had to do this now. Everything I would learn tonight was important and essential. I couldn't put it together yet, but I knew that I was getting some of the final pieces of the puzzle, and I had to continue. He'd been the one insisting before, but now that we were actually here, in the middle of a literal nightmare, his desire to protect me was taking over. He was brave and he was strong, but his first instinct was to get me out of there. I was his weakness. It was my turn to be solid.

"No," I said. "We have to stay."

My mind was willing, but my body frozen.

"But…I need your help," I said.

He stepped up behind me once again, his hands on my arms. I felt the heat of his breath on my neck, his heartbeat in sync with mine, and he led us closer to the wreckage. The mysterious woman had already reached the car and circled around, looking into the windows. She stood off by the shoulder of the road, peering carefully into the woods with narrowed eyes.

"How are you seeing this?" Will asked.

I pointed into the woods. In the darkness, deep in the trees, a tiny white spot was barely visible.

"Is that…"

"Sabastian."

"He stayed?" Will said with wonder. "How did you know?"

"I figured it out after…the first time I saw her."

"So, are we in your dream now…or his?"

"Both." I breathed. "Maybe hers, too."

"I didn't know you could do that."

"Me neither." It wasn't without effort, though. It was how I'd seen the empty road and the cause of the accident. I had to have been in her dream then. She was the only one there. My heart raced at the possible return of dark, uninvited intruders.

Focus, Andy. Stay focused.

She turned, facing us, and pulled out the small phone I had seen before.

"This is it," I said. "Are you ready?"

"Yes." There was no doubt in his voice.

"Give me your hands."

He slid his hands down my arms and interlocked his fingers with mine once again. I steadied myself and closed my eyes, dragging deep, intentional lungsful of air and focusing on the image of the dark-haired woman. A tingling sensation buzzed across my skin where it touched his.

"Will…"

"Do it, Andy."

He squeezed his hands over mine. I heard him gasp and a rush of adrenaline filled my head with a euphoric lightness. I clenched my jaw, opened my eyes and blocked out everything else except for her moving lips.

"Marco, It's Elena," she said. Her voice was velvety smooth even though she sounded annoyed. "The mark is dead, and the child is gone."

I tried to memorize everything about her and commit her words to memory. She had a slight Italian accent and didn't look around as she talked. She seemed confident no one would be coming any time soon. Marco must have asked her a question because she spat hatefully back into the phone.

"I mean the child is not here… Yes! I did exactly what I was supposed to, but there was an accident, and don't worry, I didn't scratch his precious car…. No, don't bother, there's nothing you can do…it's too late. She must have…I don't know."

She hesitated and cast a quick glance over her shoulder at the broken car to her left.

"Look, I tracked this woman down without so much as a name; that has to count for something. Just send the sweeper," she ordered, and paused for a few seconds while Marco talked. "I will find her! It's a baby, Marco–she couldn't have just walked off. Maybe we can salvage something out of this. He should have never given up on Meraki. So far none of these marks have been anything of value… Yes, I know other than the one the project hasn't been successful either, but what is it they say about omelets? Besides, I'm sick of running all over the country every time something strange shows up. There has to be an easier way. I told you this could end badly… Yeah, I know, well, one day maybe it will be my call… Just get someone here to clean up this mess."

She slapped the phone shut and shoved it into her pocket. We watched as she grabbed the diaper bag and car seat from the car and tossed them in her trunk. When she started the engine, a small light flickered over the license plate and I recognized the familiar boot shaped outline of Louisiana. She drove off into the darkness; it was finally over. Still reeling from the high, I turned around to face Will.

He looked a little green.

"Will?" My hands grasped at him, searching. "Are you alright?"

"Yeah," he said weakly. "I'm just a little...I feel a little sick."

"Time to go." I wrapped my arm around his waist, and he leaned on my shoulder. I searched for a way out.

As we headed towards the tiny orb of light that would lead us out of the dream, I cast one more glance over my shoulder at the wrecked car. I knew this was the last time I would see this image, and felt a strange mix of relief and regret. It was traumatic and horrific, but it was the closest I would ever get in this life to knowing them, and Elena was the reason why. I mentally patted that little seed of anger I'd buried earlier.

"Will?" I shook him by the shoulders. "Will."

He sat up quickly, causing me to jump back. He looked at me with wide eyes and immediately leapt off the bed, running down the tiny hallway to the bathroom. I grimaced at the sound of him retching and headed towards the open door to help him recover.

CHAPTER 14

The sky was a majestic pallet of brilliant pink and orange hues when I slipped quietly out of the cabin, pulling a quilt tighter around my shoulders. We'd meant to get an early start, but after last night's dream, I let Will sleep in. It had taken quite a toll on him, and he had been up sick most of the night. I stayed up with him, like he'd done for me so many times, and apologized over and over for the hell I had put him through.

"I can't deal with your guilt right now, Andy," he'd said through dry heaves. I held a cold washcloth on the back of his neck. "I told you I was in, and I meant it."

His words stung. I realized just how much he'd been carrying me, since the very first time he reached out and touched my frozen hand in the woods. I sat back on my heels, hit hard by the truth. This was the first time he'd ever let his guard down enough for me to see just how much I'd allowed him to bear.

"Okay." It was all I could say.

I pushed aside the desire to further apologize and took care of him until he finally fell asleep on the couch in the early hours of the morning. We'd convinced Jubal to go back to his bedroom, since Will was needing quick access to the bathroom.

I sipped a steaming hot coffee from one of Jubal's chipped mugs and curled up in one of his deck chairs, tucking the quilt into any open space until there were no more passages for the chilly morning air to sneak in. I replayed the events of the dream in my mind over and over, unsure what to think of what we learned. We had names—well, first names anyway—and the shape of a state on a license plate. It also confirmed what we had suspected all along: that the accident was no accident.

I told you this could end badly. Her cryptic words echoed in my ears. Had she meant for my parents to die…or had there been another planned outcome?

It was almost too terrible to think. She referred to my mother as the mark, not me. Maggie had been the target after all, or both of us. Elena said something about it not being her call and made sure to mention she hadn't scratched "his" car. Someone else was calling the shots.

Esther never mentioned Maggie having a gift. She most certainly did, although I wasn't sure what exactly it was. Just after the crash, she was keeping the glass and debris from hurting me, and she was somehow affecting the wind and trees.

I shifted uncomfortably, thinking of that horrible experience with Taklos where my fear almost killed us both. I had used my own hands to control the waters then, and felt a rush that scared me more than Taklos did. I'd felt a rush last night too—but pushed that memory far away into the recesses of my mind.

Under the quilt, I clasped Will's phone against my chest. I knew I should call Esther and share what we had learned, but I was hesitant. How could I put into words what we'd seen? How could I tell a mother the details of how her daughter had died? It was too much.

There was also the matter of my little anger seed that I was keeping well cultivated. My hand unconsciously settled on my stomach. Esther would be so disappointed if she knew. I covered it with more imaginary soil. Maybe if I just buried it deep enough, it would go away.

I took a deep breath, settled against the high wooden back of the chair, and watched the sun creep ever upward over the trees. My heart ached, broken for my grandmother, for my mother and father, for myself. It was shattered into a million tiny pieces for Lily and Sabastian; the image of him prostrate and grieving would forever be burned into my memory.

Lily's letter came to mind. That's what had caused me to put it together; her mention of his uncharacteristic plan to visit after a bad dream. I wished they had a phone so I could call and apologize for making him relive that night again. Though I'd finally convinced them to find a place to settle down permanently, they still shied away from most modern conveniences, preferring to remain "off-grid." When we needed to get in touch, their neighbor was kind enough to lend her phone. I'd have to relay a message through Jacob. It wasn't safe for them to have contact with us. The consequences of this search, however unintended, were reaching much too far.

And Will. My sweet husband was now yet another eyewitness to the horror we all shared. I wished I knew the point of all this heartache and death. I trusted that God had a plan, I really did; but it was something I had to continually remind myself of.

I closed my eyes and silently poured out my heart in prayer. Esther said that He was the God who hears, that He would always be listening and be my help in times of doubt and trouble. This was certainly one of those times. I ended my prayer with a simple request: *Just give me my next step, please.*

The phone vibrated in my hand, and Esther's number flashed across the screen. So much for not telling her. I took a deep breath and held the phone to my ear.

"Hello?"

"Joanna?"

"Hi. How are you feeling?"

"I am much better, feeling very strong today. How are you, child?" Her voice did sound stronger and I smiled.

"I'm good. Will had a rough night, though."

"What happened?"

"He went with me…into the dream." I curled my fingers tighter around my coffee cup, letting its warmth seep into my frozen bones.

"What did you learn?" She sounded eager.

I took another deep breath and shared the night's events. My voice cracked as I told her about Maggie saving me and her last words to Jonathan. I felt my throat tighten when I said I knew for certain it wasn't an accident. My stomach twisted when I described the woman who murdered my family, and her callous conversation with someone named

Marco. She listened without comment. By the time I finished, I had to wrap my arms around myself to keep all the broken pieces together.

"It was the same woman who went to see Lily and Sabastian, I'm sure of it." I finished.

"Thank you, child," she said finally, her voice hoarse.

"I'm so sorry."

"None of that now. My Maggie was brave and true to the end. I am proud of her...and her daughter," she said softly.

"Grandma, especially after this...I know she is somehow connected to Nadine–to what she was doing. I just know it. She is finding people like us and taking them, hiding them in mental institutions, maybe? I don't know why... Well, I can imagine why," I said, feeling a headache begin to form behind my eyes. "I mean...could that be true?"

"Yes. I think you're right," she said, a strange certainty in her tone.

"I don't know how she's finding them, or what she's doing with them, but I'm sure it's not good."

I squeezed my thumb and middle finger against my temples, trying to keep the growing migraine at bay.

"I don't know what to do," I said, confessing again my uncertainty. Maybe someone would have the answer. "Even if we find her, who would believe us? Who would help? I feel like I'm just wandering around in the dark."

I was doing it again; what had Will called it–spiraling? I heard her take a deep breath.

"I could give you a sermon if that's what you're looking for, and tell you story after story of ordinary people doing extraordinary things, but you already know them: David, Daniel, a young girl named Mary, a simple fisherman named Peter. You know them. They are your kinsman in Christ–their faith is a legacy to strengthen us, examples for us to follow."

"I don't feel much like them at all," I said, squeezing my eyes shut and suddenly feeling incredibly inadequate.

"Maybe they lived thousands of years ago, and hundreds of years apart from each other, but they all had two things in common. First, they were just regular, broken, unworthy people, and second, they believed God when He told them something," she said in that familiar knowing way. "It's hard when you don't know the way to go. I feel frustrated too; I really do."

Rescue us.

He did tell me. He'd been telling me for months. Rescue who, though? How many could she have taken in twenty years? How wide did this network reach?

"You don't have to know all the details. In the dark of night, it only takes a single tiny flame to light the way." Though her voice was barely a whisper, it bore all the strength of our ancient and powerful lineage. "But Joanna, when He calls, you must answer. You must."

"I will," I answered, equally as soft.

"I know you will. And I know you had hoped your work was finished. These last few months have taken so much from you. We see it, your Uncle Jacob and me. We see how hard it is for you to keep going, but don't give up yet. You know more than anyone what it's like to fight with strength that's not your own."

"I feel guilty for not wanting to keep going," I said, my eyes squeezed shut. *And I'm so angry.*

"It's okay to not want to. I'm proud of you for doing it anyway. I will forever be grateful to you for giving me those precious few moments with my Maggie. I know it tore you apart to see, but I feel like I got to have her back even if just briefly."

Her last words undid me. Hot tears streamed from under my closed lids, and my shoulders shook with silent sobs. I wanted to thank her too, for being my family, for pouring into me all the love and instruction that she had these past months. I never thought I'd find a place where I truly belonged, and because of her, I had. I was too overcome to speak, though.

She waited silently for me to pull myself together. I took a few deep breaths and wiped my face dry with my sleeve.

"Tell me you're safe," I said, clearing the giant lump of emotion from my throat.

"Yes, child. We are safe."

I wanted to know where she was. I wanted to call Matt and have him send the full force of The Agency to stand guard outside of her door. But it was better that she stay hidden.

"I should go check on Will."

"That's good. He will need you. They seem strong, these men of ours, but the strength that a woman carries in her soul is unmatched by the most powerful man…except Jesus."

I laughed at the comical way she added on that last part. "That was very profound."

"Maybe I'm a prophet." Esther laughed.

"Oh, there was never any doubt of that." I enjoyed the lightness of our banter. "Did you have to take care of my grandfather?"

I immediately regretted asking when she didn't answer right away.

"I tried."

"We don't have to talk about it."

"I'll tell you about him sometime. I'm the memory keeper, after all, and it's good to remember...even the hard things. How else would we learn? I will say, I'm relieved to know that you won't have the same troubles; you and Will are equally yoked."

"Um...should I know what that means?"

"It just means you are both followers of Christ, equally, and your life is in balance with your beliefs."

"So, he wasn't a believer then?"

"Oh, he had beliefs–strong ones–but his heart was deceived, and loyalties misplaced. In the end, he made a choice, and chose the world over us. I wish..." She took a deep breath, letting it out slowly, blowing long forgotten memories out with it. "Ahh, never mind. A story for a different day."

I couldn't imagine anyone knowing Esther and not being transformed simply by observing her faith. Maybe she wasn't always the unshakeable pillar she was now. Maybe there was hope for me yet and like Jacob said– I needed the gift of experience. I was about to say good-bye when I remembered Maggie's outstretched hand.

"Maggie was like us, wasn't she? What was her gift?"

"Honestly, I'm not sure," Esther said. "For most of her life, there was no sign that she was a part of the sisterhood. I was relieved, actually. It's an honor, and I would have been overjoyed to have her among us, but there is risk, and I was just as happy that she would be safe. The first sign I saw of anything different was just before you were born."

"What do you mean?"

"I went to stay with her during the weeks before, just to help around the house and let her rest. It had been raining so much, but we finally had a break in the weather, and we decided to go for a walk. We were walking along the sidewalk downtown. Some men were hanging an awning and it slipped. It would have fallen right on us, but Maggie put her hands out and it just...stopped, and fell the other way."

"Did anyone see?" I asked.

"There were people everywhere! Anyone could have seen. I don't think many people did, because it happened so quickly. We never talked much about it. Maggie just said she felt her hands suddenly tingling, and then it stopped just as suddenly. You were born the next morning."

I considered her story for a few minutes.

"Did I...was this because of me?"

"What? No, how could you think that?"

"She never showed a sign of having a special gift until I came along. She was taking me to safety when she was killed."

"Joanna, enough." Her authoritative tone was back. "That reasoning is a complete stretch. I could take responsibility as well, if we follow your logic. You're giving yourself far too much credit. The only person responsible for what happened to our Maggie is this Elena woman, and whoever she was working for. Even if they didn't mean for her to die, their actions caused it."

"Okay...okay. You're right." *She needs to pay.* I hushed my thoughts.

"I know what you're feeling. I have felt it myself. I desperately want my daughter back. I want what happened to be changed, and it hurts so much that blaming myself actually feels better than accepting the truth. Sometimes I think she would still be here if I'd just stayed longer, or went to see her instead of her trying to come to me, but those what-ifs will only drive you mad."

A tiny laugh escaped my lips.

"You always seem to know the right thing to say. How did you get to be so wise?"

"Oh, a lot of living and countless cups of tea." Her tone was light again, and there was a refreshing playfulness to her words. "There's not much that can't be solved over a nice hot cup of tea."

We talked a few minutes more about what Jacob made for breakfast, and I recounted Jubal's story about his recent trip up the Rappahannock. I wanted to linger there, to remain in the simple moment where we were just a grandmother and granddaughter enjoying a pleasant conversation.

It passed too quickly. After saying our final goodbyes, I stood on the deck, watching the smooth running waters of the James, an occasional ring of ripples coursing out from the center as a fish broke the surface to feast on an unsuspecting insect. Years upon years of history flowed between its shores and it was fitting that we'd stepped back in time, even if just in a dream, while it carried us toward the future.

The mechanical churn of an engine starting up broke my trance, and the boat lurched forward. I took one more longing glance at the peaceful river we were leaving behind before trudging back inside.

Chapter 15

Will was sitting on the edge of the couch pulling on his shoes when I walked in.

"Hey," he said with a smile. "Where have you been?"

"Outside. I made coffee."

He looked better; less green but still pale, and there was exhaustion in his eyes. I swallowed a mouthful of regret and poured coffee into another mug for him, setting it and the cell phone on Jubal's little table. He finished lacing up his boot and watched me as I gathered quilts and pillows, meticulously folding and stacking.

Suddenly, I felt embarrassed, as if I were standing there naked and exposed. The night before had been the most raw and vulnerable moment of my life and I really just wanted to hide.

"Andy," he said finally.

"I talked to Esther," I said without turning around.

"Oh?"

"Mhmm. I told her everything."

"How was that?"

"It was hard, but she was gracious, of course."

I moved about the room, dancing around his unspoken questions and continuing to talk so he didn't have the opportunity to voice them. He walked over to the table and took a sip of his coffee, but I could still feel his eyes watching me and it made my insides squirm.

"Andy?"

"Have you heard anything else from Matt?" I retreated into the bathroom, searching for a purpose, and grabbed my toothbrush.

I glanced up at his reflection in the mirror. His brows furrowed and I gave him a quick smile before going to work brushing my teeth. I doubted my ability to convince him to drop it, but it couldn't hurt to try.

He watched me for a few more seconds then sighed. "No, not yet."

I left the toothpaste out for him but packed the rest of our toiletries. Soft footsteps on the cabin's wooden floor signaled his approach and I avoided his eyes as he came up behind me. His warm hands rested heavily on my shoulders, but I kept my gaze focused on the little blue case I was mindlessly organizing.

"You can look at me, you know." He gently squeezed my shoulders, encouraging but not forcing.

"I know." My voice was soft.

"Andy," he said firmly. "I'm fine."

I cocked my head to the side and finally looked up at the reflection of his face in the mirror. When our eyes met, he read my expression with perfect understanding. It was much easier to bear someone else's burden than watch them bear mine.

"I know," he said. "I know, okay?"

"You don't regret going?"

He turned me around and pulled me into an embrace that smothered any remaining insecurity.

"I know how hard that was for you." I felt his breath hot on the top of my head. "Thank you for letting me be there. And no–I don't regret it."

"It was hard for you, too." I let my head rest on his chest, comforted by the deep consistent thump of his heart.

"Ehh, I've had worse." He shrugged, diffusing the tension of the moment.

I breathed out an amused sigh and wrapped my arms around his waist. We stood, silently swaying in time to the movement of the boat.

"I don't know what to do next," I said after a long moment. I think I'd said that to everyone now, *and I'm so angry.*

That stubborn thought kept popping up; why couldn't I get rid of it?

He didn't respond. Maybe we could just stay here on the water, in this space between worlds–moving, but not traveling. Maybe if we just held on long enough, locked in this silent safe place, it would all just disappear. I squeezed my arms and held on as tightly as I could. He held me just as tightly. I could tell he was hoping for the same miracle.

The light ping of an incoming text message from Will's phone broke our trance. He loosened his grip and looked down at me.

"I don't know what to do next either. We'll just keep going until God tells us otherwise. But hey, we have more information than we did before. Today we have two names; yesterday we had none. So, let's be happy about that, yeah?"

"Yeah," I said, pushing myself up on my tiptoes and kissing him softly.

"I love you." It sounded like a question.

"I love you," I answered with certainty.

He planted a quick kiss on my forehead and walked to the table where the phone was pinging again. I finished packing our toiletry bag and watched him in the mirror. He read the text message and glanced up at me before raising the phone to his ear.

"Hey, Matt. Got your message. You found something?"

His back was to me so I couldn't see his expression, but he stood motionless as he listened.

"So, not much then. Well, whoever it is, they're playing their cards carefully. What about the database? Anything on that?"

Will turned, motioning with his arm for me to join him as he placed the phone on the table and slid into one of the creaky wooden chairs.

"Hold on Matt, Andy's here too." He touched the speakerphone button when I took the chair across from him.

"Hey, Andy." Matt's familiar deep voice sent a wave of warm comfort through my veins.

"Hi, Matt. Thanks for helping us."

"Of course! Wish I could do more. So I was saying that I looked into the search Greyson was performing, and found something unusual. I obviously don't have the same access she had without going through illegally, which might alert the wrong people. So I don't have specifics, but there was a spike in the number of reported diagnoses starting almost immediately after Greyson received that visit. They aren't big numbers, but it's not a very common occurrence so it only takes a few to show an increase."

"So, you think...what do you think?" I couldn't put it together.

"I think that after visiting Greyson, the theory that people like you exist was renewed. I think Greyson told her everything, and she's doing two things: looking for you specifically, and looking for people like you."

"Looking for people like me how?"

"She's probably doing exactly what Greyson did, searching the database and having patients transferred as well as being liberal with that diagnosis. She's either a medical professional herself, or working with one."

"After Andy's dream last night–I think that's what she's been doing all along." Will's eyes held mine as he talked.

"Is there anything you can tell us about that spike? Anything we can use to try and find her? I know Nadine had her list, but this... Elena could be anywhere...or everywhere." I stared at the phone, wishing Matt would crawl out of the screen and be present with us.

"Actually, yes," he said. We heard the rustle of papers. "I can see regional activity as part of environmental tracking and treatment specialization, and it looks like the concentration of patient intake is in.... Louisiana."

A shock of ice shot up my spine, the hair on the back of my neck standing at full attention. Will looked as if he felt the same.

"Isn't that where..."

"Yes." Will's answer was a sword, cutting off Matt's question. The muscles in his jaw tightened and he stared out of the window, his eyes searching for something they couldn't seem to find. "We're going to run down the list," he said finally.

"You won't be able to find out anything specific about patients, but you can ask about the diagnosis. I could make calls for you."

"No, I don't want to draw attention to what we're doing; we still don't know who at The Agency leaked Greyson's location. If you get too close, it might tip them off. We need to find her, find out exactly what she's doing, and then call in the calvary. It has to be a surprise, or we risk her disappearing and moving whoever she's got. I know you'd be careful, but we just don't know how much clearance and access they have; they might be watching you now."

Watching Matt? I reached out and grabbed Will's hand.

"Matt." My throat was suddenly so dry, I could hardly speak. "You haven't spoken to…" I didn't want to say Jacob's name; what if someone was listening?

"No, don't worry. This line is secure. Everyone is safe."

"What about Nadine? When she took you and found me…" I couldn't say; I couldn't say their names or mention the church. I felt that familiar desire to run, to jump up from the table and take off. Will's other hand covered mine, anchoring me to my seat.

The memory of Matt's blank stare and Nadine's confident smile flashed in my mind. She'd tracked him down after he'd left us in Alexandria. I'd just met my grandmother and uncle for the first time and was standing alone in the parking lot of the church when Nadine showed up, an entranced Matt in tow, compelled by Taklos to do whatever she said.

"Andy," Matt's voice was calm. "Greyson didn't know."

"But you were there, Matt…"

"She never asked me why you were there," he said. "She didn't know."

She didn't know. My lungs released the breath they held hostage; Will squeezed my hand.

"Everyone is safe," Matt repeated.

I zoned out, missing the specifics of their goodbyes. My chest ached from the remaining tension. Even though Matt assured me my family was safe, I couldn't shake the worry of what-ifs. Someone was still inside The Agency who betrayed us, who knew about me and who knew this Elena. There was no evidence to suggest that she knew that I was the baby she'd lost so many years ago, but how long until she figured it out?

Over twenty years ago she knew about my mother somehow, and just over one year ago someone else knew about me: Dovanny Taklos.

"What are you thinking?" Will was sitting back in his chair, arms crossed over his chest, watching me as if I were a fascinating alien creature.

"They're connected."

"Who? Greyson and Elena?"

"No…Elena and Taklos."

He leaned forward, resting his arms on the table, his posture demanding more.

"What if…what if Elena was Plan B?"

"How so?"

"Taklos hatched this elaborate scheme, right, to get to me? He wanted my abilities. Elena wants people with abilities."

"Yes?" Will said, his brows drawing together. He looked like he was trying to guess where I was going with this.

"She was working for someone. What if Taklos wasn't the boss, like we thought, oh...oh...OH!"

"What?" he laughed.

"What if he's working for someone too? What if it's the same someone who Elena is working for? When he failed, she went to finish the job."

When I finally stopped talking and looked back at Will, I found him staring at me with a strange look on his face.

"Why are you looking at me like that?" I asked.

"Just watching you work." He shrugged. "It's fascinating."

I slugged him hard on the shoulder. He grabbed his shoulder and pretended to be hurt, causing me to slug him again.

"No, seriously though," he said, still smiling. "You could be right. If that's the case, whoever it is, they are well protected; important enough for even Taklos to protect. We went through every known contact of his and Greyson's. He was questioned–thoroughly. He never revealed another partner or employer. We just have to figure out who it could be."

"How, though? We can't get to him."

"Well, I hate to say it, but you knew him best."

I pushed back from the table and stood, pacing across the room for a few minutes before sinking down onto the couch. He was right. I did know him–probably better than anyone. It wasn't something I wanted to do, but I tried to remember everything Taklos had ever said. Will sat quietly, watching me. I closed my eyes and took long, deep breaths like Esther had taught me. I could almost feel her hands on mine, gently coaxing forward into light the things forgotten in darkness. It was like she was there. *Listen and See.*

I thought back to the first time I interrogated him, picturing his thin, skeletal figure. I had originally been sent in to obtain intel on a potential terrorist attack, of which Taklos was the suspected mastermind. It quickly became clear that the whole attack was simply a ruse to get Taklos into the facility and me into his mind. He had been overly obvious with his movements about the country to purposefully draw attention to himself.

The brief I'd studied explained a little about his past, his associates, and the accident in a Russian lab that led to his heightened ability of persuasion.

He didn't want to talk about that.

Who could it be? Could I already know? My hand made its way down to my necklace, and I rubbed the lion pendant between my fingers as I searched my memory. Maybe he had let something slip; I just needed to remember. *Focus...*

Remember...

"There is this one thing," I said finally.

"What?" Will asked, standing.

"I don't know that it's anything."

"Andy...spit it out." He rolled his eyes.

"Goncharov. He was one of the scientists in the lab when Taklos was hurt. The only one to escape. He was the one I was supposed to ask about in the original interrogation. I think his first name was Otis."

"I thought Taklos said he was dead?"

"He did...sort of. I saw an image of a burning house. He never actually said the words 'he's dead.' He can't lie in the dream, but that doesn't mean he has to be completely truthful, either. Maybe I took that for granted."

I stood too, uncomfortable with the memory of those terrifying encounters with Dovanny Taklos, and wondering why the thought of Otis Goncharov stirred such anxiety inside of me. When my eyes finally met Will's, he wore that same strange expression again. The corner of his mouth turned up into a crooked smile.

"He's the only loose end I can think of." I shrugged. "Maybe he was a silent partner? Maybe he works for the same person? Maybe he's nothing."

In two broad steps, he crossed the room and towered over me. I looked up and was captured by those deep chocolate brown eyes that had melted my heart from the first. A spark burned behind them now; he slipped a warm hand along the side of my face, drawing me close and placing his lips on mine.

Once again, we flew, a throng of emotions passing between us. It was desperate yet sweet, both taking and giving. It fed a deep hunger we'd both been suffering from. It was hope, but in the back of my mind I heard the faint ominous click, click, click of the climb before the fall.

He pulled away far too soon, and I groaned. He smiled.

"Well done, Nancy Drew." He tucked a loose strand of my hair behind my ear.

"It's just a guess." I tried not to get my hopes up too much; we still didn't know what it would mean even if I was right.

"It's a good guess," he said brightly over his shoulder.

"Now we have two impossible people to find. Why are you so happy?" I laughed. He looked almost giddy.

"Because now we have a connection, and that…I can work with."

He was gone in an instant, disappearing through the door to the helm where Jubal was plotting our course.

It took me a minute, but I realized what he meant. It was his specialty. Finding the lost things. Over the last few months, he had told me several times that he felt like a failure for not being able to find this mysterious woman, although it was a near impossible task, considering we had zero information on her. This was a new challenge, a second chance for him. I walked down the hall and peered through the window to the helm. An overpowering sense of déjà vu filled my mind seeing him standing there with Jubal: maps spread across the control board, the two of them pointing and discussing the best course.

Was this how we would live our lives? On constant repeat, condemned to ride the same ride over and over? I prayed that this would be the last; that when we pulled into the gate this time, we could finally step off.

CHAPTER 16

I stood over the small sink in Jubal's kitchen, handing him the last of the plates I'd just rinsed. He dried it with a clean but well-worn dish towel and placed it on top of the stack in the cabinet. We'd worked in silence, both pretending not to listen while Will manned the helm and called in every favor he had to find intel on Otis Goncharov. He joked that watching me work was fascinating, but watching him was something truly amazing. It wasn't just about finding people lost in the woods; he knew just who to call and what to ask for. He was like a machine. I'd always wondered how his gift worked; he was remarkable.

"Come sit with an old man, will ya?" Jubal's warm hand lightly touched my shoulder.

I looked into his soft grey eyes, my brain taking seconds too long to interpret sounds into words.

"Sure." I'd been far away, blinking hard as I returned.

His feet made shushing sounds on the hardwood floor as he shuffled over to the table. I followed and sank into the chair he'd pulled out for me.

"Thank you, kind sir," I joked.

To my surprise, he didn't take the chair across from me, but instead walked over to the tiny bookshelf that stood against one side of his couch and drew something from it.

He joined me and placed a brown leather journal on the table, his hands lingering on top, as if he were reluctant to let it go. On the side, a faded image embossed in gold caught my eye. It was a lioness, reared and ready for battle–the twin to my pendant, which tingled against my skin.

"Did you know I was the first besides yur momma and daddy to hold you when you was born?"

"You were there?" If my fists hadn't been under my chin, my jaw would have hit the table.

"'Course, I was," he said, running his fingers along the edge of the book. Much as it had the last time I sat at this table with him, the evening sun cut through the glass in golden rays, specks of dust floating around him like tiny fairies. He laughed at some memory I couldn't share. "Boy, was Marie ever jealous, too."

"Esther said that after my parents died, it was as if I never existed."

"She's right. One reason why I didn't tell the whole story last time you was here. I can't even explain the mess we was in. Me and my Marie, even Esther n' yur Uncle Jacob…we all thought we'd gone plum crazy. One minute we was celebratin', holdin' a sweet new baby girl, and the next, our whole world was gone: no Maggie, no Jonathan…no baby. Didn't make no sense–and no one believed our story."

I moved my hands, weaving my fingers together; I needed something to hold onto.

"But you was never forgotten, Joanna Marie, not for one single minute, ya' hear?"

Jubal stretched one hand across the table, reaching for me. I let him take my hand, his wrinkled age-spotted skin feathery soft against my palm. We'd been here before, he and I, talking of lost love. I didn't know he was family at the time, but looking back–I should have.

"There wasn't one single day when yur family wasn't searchin', wasn't prayin', wasn't hopin' you'd find yur way back home. Pleadin' that all we'd lost would be returned."

My heart clenched so tightly I thought it might burst. All the time lost was unbearable, all the missed moments, the years that had slipped away. Taken. Stolen from all of us. It hurt too much, and that little angry seed pushed up through its cover, resilient and strong.

"I hate that my Marie lived out her last days still wantin', but that's just what I see with my own earthy eyes. Vision's not so good, ya know. Truth is, she's forever rejoicin' with the Savior, and wants for nuthin'."

"I really wish I could have known her." My fingers found Marie's pendant under my shirt and held tight through the fabric.

"I know you do." Jubal released my hand and sat back. "When you lose your beloved, the world seems awful lonely, awful dark an' empty. Our sin's got the whole world upside down–fairness and goodness right near gone–things just ain't as they should be. Can stir up a good bit of anger inside a man."

"Rightly so," I muttered.

"Can't say I hadn't felt the same. Can't say how many times I pleaded with Jesus to take me on home. Lord, I miss my girl so much." He stopped, choked on the words, one of his trembling hands meeting the other in front of his mouth.

I couldn't move, couldn't speak or breathe. His grief was paralyzing, the agony of his broken heart filling every atom between us and tearing my own into shreds.

"I couldn't understand why He'd let me go on livin', when all I had in the world was gone. Couldn't figure why this old heart just kept on beatin'."

He cast his watery eyes down to the journal, its leather cover softened from use and edges worn smooth. His gaze caressed the edges, lingering along the spine and pages as if they were a precious treasure. I followed suit, wondering what memories he was reliving. He lifted his face, his eyes catching mine.

"Then one night a little red-haired girl stumbled onto my boat."

I pressed my hand over my lips, capturing a sob.

"And I got to be the first to hold you again."

My sob broke free, along with a waterfall of salty tears. Jubal let me cry, waiting patient and calm until I pulled myself together enough to hear what he had to say next.

"Don't let it harden you, Joanna. The wrongness of this world–it's broken and hurtin'. But don't you give up. We never know why the Lord chooses to let us keep on when we just want to go on home."

He slid the book towards me.

"This belongs to you."

It felt too sacred to touch, too precious to accept. I shook my head.

"I can't." My voice was barely my own.

"I see her." He pushed the journal further towards me. "When I look at you, in yur eyes…I see that girl that jumped. The fearless one."

He'd told me of how he met Marie, when they were young. He'd seen her from far off, jumping without pause off the top of a waterfall into a lake below, coming up laughing. He'd fallen in love with her then, her heart the bravest he'd ever known.

"That's not me; it can't be. I'm terrified."

"Courage idn't bein' without fear. Courage is bein' so filled up with fear you think yur gonna burst and goin' on anyway. That's what I see."

"But I always run."

"No shame in runnin', so long as it's in the right direction."

He pushed himself up from the table with a groan, and softly patted my shoulder as he passed.

"That's yurs. Yur history. Sometimes when the future is shakin', yur past can give you somethin' solid to stand on."

He left, the journal still untouched on the table in front of me. I could hear the deep hum of Will's voice from the helm as he talked, still searching for a lead on either of our targets.

As if trying to see through the cover, my eyes crossed from staring at the journal. Finally, I pulled my hands out of my lap and rubbed them together before reaching out.

I ran my thumb along the spine, feeling the strong curved lines of the animal pressed deep into the brown leather. I lifted it gingerly and flipped through. Page after page was filled with Esther's delicate script, a detailed record of the most important secrets of our family. The stories of each Lionheart Woman. As I watched the pages fall, my head filled with echoes of soft voices that were strangely familiar. I had never met their owners, but I knew them. I thought I felt my lion pendant buzz against my skin, but I figured it was the soft vibration of the boat coasting along the river.

My hand stopped on one page; I recognized the name at the top. *Liza.* It was the name Will had seen, the name that led him to my ancestor, Miriam Eliza Yerik. Her nickname was Liza, and she had been a schoolteacher during the Civil War. That search would eventually lead him to Esther, Liza's granddaughter.

I reached out and touched the page where Esther had written Liza's name in thick black ink. As my fingers made contact with the paper, I felt a strange tingle and jerked my hand back. I looked up quickly; Will was now outside, and Jubal silently steered us upstream from the helm. I was alone.

I looked back at the journal and could have sworn I saw the words on the page waver, as if looking at the book underwater. Once again, I touched her name. Then as clear as the room in front of me, I saw her.

Liza appeared on a dusty cobblestone street, carriages and horses passing her on either side. She stood motionless, staring at me. Wispy tendrils of curly auburn hair that had escaped her bonnet floated around her face. Her gloved hands were clasped gently in front of her; her posture was tall and strong, unnerved by the chaos around her. A knowing smile spread across her lips, and she opened her mouth to speak.

"Joanna," she said.

The sound of her voice came from all directions at once and I gasped, pushing myself back from the table as the journal dropped onto its wooden surface with a clap.

"Andy?" Will appeared, walking through the fog that had been her image. "Hey...you okay? You look like you've seen a ghost."

"What? No, I...I think I'm just tired."

The journal lay closed on the table, a slip of paper sticking just barely out of the top. I pulled it out and saw one word written in an unfamiliar handwriting.

Remember, it said.

Was there more to this little book than history? Will was talking, so I tried to focus.

"...will check with Port Authority and see if anything comes across on arrivals. If there's no airline record, maybe he came over on a ship. Andy, are you sure you're alright?"

I sat up straight, pulling the journal out of sight into my lap.

"Yes, sorry. What else did you find out?"

"Paul will run a cross check on the names Elena and Marco with locations in Louisiana or the surrounding states and any association with mental health facilities."

"Who's Paul?"

"FBI friend–owes me a favor."

"Hmm, must be some favor. I guess he didn't find anything on Goncharov yet?"

"No, nothing as far as flights around the time we think Taklos came over, but we knew it was a longshot. He wouldn't be likely to use his real name."

His real name. For some reason, those words clicked in my mind. *Why is that important?*

"Do you think we could somehow get our hands on Taklos' file? The real file, not the one I was given with the one paragraph of intel?" I asked.

"What are you thinking?" Will was already pulling his phone out again.

"I just...I don't know. Maybe there's something. Do you think it's possible to get it?"

"Maybe. Jake is running the division now," he said before tapping a number into his phone.

Jake Thompson was one of Will's closest co-workers from The Agency. He had been the only one Will trusted to head my security detail in his absence. I had overheard him warn Will that The Agency suspected him in my abduction, which was ridiculous, of course.

"Can we trust him?" I whispered as he held the ringing phone up to his ear.

He gave me a soft smile and said, "Don't worry."

"Thompson." The cabin was quiet enough I could hear Jake's voice.

"Hey, it's Carter."

"Will Carter! Where've you been man, it's been a long time!" Jake's tone was light and joking.

"Yeah, I know, how's it going over there?"

"Oh, you know, the same. Always a bad guy to chase, always some bureaucrat with his khakis in a bunch slowing us down. Where are you working now?"

"I'm doing some consultant work. In fact, that's why I'm calling. There's been a connection to Taklos in my case."

"Taklos? Really? What's the case?"

"I can't really say, it's..."

"Classified...gotcha. How can I help? You know if that guy is even still breathing, he isn't getting out anytime this century, and I certainly can't get in to question him."

"I'm pretty sure it's just a matter of some paths crossing, but I was hoping to get my hands on his intel file. There were a few contacts I needed to cross check and eliminate."

"Case file, huh?" Jake paused; I could tell he was thinking it over.

"Let me see what I can do."

"I really appreciate that. You can play the interagency cooperation card."

"What agency am I cooperating with?"

"Like I said..." Will glanced at me and winked.

"Classified, I know. Well, I can't make any promises, but I'll give it a shot."

"Thanks, Jake."

"Any time..." Jake sounded like he wanted to say something else. "Are you doing okay?"

I knew why he was asking. As far as everyone but our closest friends and family knew, Will had watched me die almost a year ago. Jake knew that Will cared for the late Agent Stone.

"Yeah, I'm good. Some days are better than others."

That was certainly true.

"I'll get back with you as soon as I can on that file–and don't be a stranger," Jake's tone was genuine and compassionate. "You know there's a place for you here if you ever want to come back."

"I know. Thanks again."

After the call was safely disconnected, I reached for Will's hand.

"I hope he can help us." I searched his face for signs of how he was feeling.

It had been hard for him to leave the work he loved at The Agency, but it had been his decision, not mine. I wondered if talking to Jake had made him regret that choice.

"Me too." He raised my hand to his lips and kissed the back of it.

"He doesn't know you got married?" I lifted a curious eyebrow.

"One less thing to explain." He shrugged.

During the remaining hours of our trip, he fielded calls from Paul and surprisingly, Jake. We were both shocked when he said he would be sending over the file as soon as Will was ready.

For the second time, I said a sad goodbye to my great uncle and stepped off his boat into unknown territory. This time it was onto a deserted city dock instead of the wooded shore of a nature preserve.

"Thank you, Jubal–for everything."

"As long as this old heart keeps beatin'." Jubal gave me a cryptic wink before shaking Will's hand.

After a short taxi ride and yet another favor from one of Will's contacts, we were traveling down a dark highway in a car rented under the creative alias of Mr. Smith.

It was nearly ten when we decided to stop and chose a small inn on the outskirts of Knoxville.

"Did you find what you were looking for in his file?" Will asked after I'd stared at the file Jake had faxed for well over an hour.

"No, not really. I don't know what exactly I'm looking for. I thought maybe there was a connection to his family, but the file doesn't list any parents, and only says he was raised in a boy's home." I yawned, stretching out my arms over my head.

"I'm about to fall asleep. How about some coffee?" Will said, heading towards the door. "Will you be okay here?"

The feeling that we were dangerously close to something evil hadn't left us; I knew he was being overly cautious, but I wasn't offended in the least.

"I'll be fine," I said reassuringly.

"Lock the deadbolt," he said over his shoulder, then disappeared through the door.

After the lock was secured, I returned to my spot on the paper-covered bed. A careless step caused my backpack to topple over and Esther's journal to slide out onto the floor. I stared at it for a few seconds before picking it up. My fingers gently turned the worn pages, stopping at the story marked with Liza's name. I could hear Esther's voice in my head as I read her words and smiled at the comforting peace it brought.

CHAPTER 17

*M*iriam Eliza Yerik was not a woman of striking beauty nor the quickest of wit; her singing voice was average, and she had no wealth to speak of. She wasn't a particularly gifted pianist, did not show promise in constructing elegant garments, and due to her employment as a simple schoolteacher, she would never be fully accepted by the refined ladies that lived in the well-kept manses of town. Any of these qualities would have made her noticeable in her time. Instead, she was reserved, humble, and meek. Other than a brief encounter with a handsome Confederate soldier named Tom who happened near her cottage one early spring morning, Liza knew nothing of romance or courtship.

Liza's story is not one of danger nor intrigue; hers is an unsung, seemingly unimportant chapter in the history of the Lionheart women, yet it is worthy of record, as are all of God's merciful works.

Liza lived almost invisibly, passing unseen throughout her life. She would sometimes spend an entire afternoon in town, picking up sundries at the general store, dropping off a parcel at the post, or shopping for thread at the tailor's store, and not exchange pleasantries with a single person aside from the shopkeepers and postmaster.

She would sweep silently along the dusty streets in her soft grey fustian dress adorned with a wide white collar and simple eyelet. Nothing stood out about Liza Yerik other than her vibrant auburn curls, which were usually pinned and concealed beneath a wide-brimmed black bonnet.

All of Liza's incredible qualities were hidden on the inside, and aside from her mother, Amelia, she had never dared share them with another living soul. The secret inner workings of Liza's talent, if made public, would have surely led her straight to the hangman's noose. When Liza Yerik looked into the eyes of another, she would know the innermost truth in their mind. It wasn't a phenomenon that happened with every contact—only when Liza would deeply concentrate long enough—but her sharp mind was quick, and it took her just seconds to reach that level of focus.

It was not as if Liza could read minds; she was not a fortune teller nor magician as some claimed to be. What she saw was more of a reflection, an echo of feelings that Liza could interpret, as if she were seeing through clouded glass. She could discern instantly if the person was honest or deceitful.

In her time, knowledge of Liza's gifts would have branded her a witch, someone to be feared and driven from society. She was not a witch, though, and never served anyone but the Lord. Her mother had shared stories of the great heroes of old, ancient champions with supernatural strength, deep spiritual understanding, and unbelievable victory in battle.

Liza never felt a connection to that heritage. She didn't see herself as brave, nor cunning. She was simply able to see the truth when others could not. Her life was peaceful and quiet. She was content in her service, her humble occupation, and meager compensation.

Liza's home was nestled deep in the woods surrounding the Rappahannock River. The war had been ravaging the surrounding cities, and almost every man in the country was enlisted to serve. Her own father and brothers were just such men. Liza and the women of the town were doing their best to continue on in their absence, but the winter of 1862 had been near unbearable; the war had arrived on their doorsteps. No one was spared the horrors of battle, and Liza worked tirelessly to comfort her students as so many suffered incredible losses, living in a constant state of fear and uncertainty.

Liza's gift had kept her out of trouble on more than one occasion.

When a lost or deserting soldier had shown up at her door, she was easily able to determine if it was safe to help.

One particular autumn evening, Liza and her mother heard a knock on the door. Amelia answered to find a man slumped against the door frame, and a small boy cowering behind him. The injured man fell to the floor, and the women carried him inside to tend to his wounds. They worked silently, only exchanging worried glances as Liza peeled back the man's shirt to find he'd been shot. Amelia swept the crying toddler into her arms. He was scared, but unharmed. The man uttered just three words before he slipped off into an eternal sleep.

"Save the boy."

Liza and Amelia buried the man and cared for the boy in the following days, as Liza had found his concern for the boy in the few moments before his death to be sincere. She convinced Amelia to not yet go to the authorities. The boy was not much more than a toddler and unable to speak. The women took to calling him Michael after Liza's eldest brother, who had been killed in battle just a few months prior.

Soon after that awful night, Liza learned through a letter from her aunt that the children of both Union and Confederate officers and important government officials were being taken; held as leverage to sway their decisions in battle and legislation. Evil was far-reaching, and no one was safe. The entire family of one important senator was killed in their home; the body of his youngest son was never recovered. Soon after, the senator himself was also found murdered in his office. Liza knew of the man; he and his family had passed through her city several years before, and he was an honest, God-fearing servant of the people.

The senator's son wouldn't have been born when they'd visited, but Michael's white blond hair and startling blue eyes reminded Liza very much of the senator. Liza suspected the boy was his missing son, John, and set out to locate his next of kin. She left the child with her mother, scraped up what remained of her meager savings, and traveled to Washington, seeking information. Upon reaching the city, she quickly met the minister of the senator's church, who had displayed an ambrotype of the family in memorial. She was not surprised to see Michael's round face in the image, seated on the lap of his beautiful mother.

She discovered the deceased senator had only one living relative, a cousin, who was a commander in the Union Army. She presented herself as a potential tutor for the children of the wealthy supporters and patrons of the war in order to gain audience with the commander.

Although most thought him a civilized and compassionate man, Liza found only deceit and ill-intent behind his eyes. The more she researched, the more she discovered that turned her heart as cold as ice. The commander was full of corruption to the highest degree and carried allegiance to neither the Union nor Confederate states. He had no children nor wife that he claimed, but Liza had seen greed, lust, and wrath in his heart. She knew that the boy could never go to this man, even if he was his only living family. She trusted in her gift, knowing it was given to her from God for His purposes, and she hurried home.

Liza raised the boy as her own, and even though it was assumed the child was an orphaned relative, Liza still silently and gracefully endured the accusations and whispers from the townspeople, as she was unmarried. Liza grew very ill when Michael was a young man. She passed away quietly and without ceremony. Michael John Yerik, had flourished under Liza's care, and after her death became a minister of the church in Fredericksburg, going on to lead a traveling revival throughout the eastern states with his wife Abigail and daughters, Esther and Marie. He spoke with a sacred reverence of his mother, crediting her with teaching him the most essential foundations of his faith. He wrote in his final letter to his daughters that it was his greatest desire, as was his mother's before him, that his children grow to love the Lord above all else and serve Him alone, loving His people before themselves. Liza never got to see the fruits of her labor in raising young Michael, but because of her quiet bravery, many souls were saved.

CHAPTER 18

I shared Liza's story when Will returned empty-handed and with disappointing news of a broken coffee maker. We both sat silently for a few minutes, taking in the unsung heroine that was Eliza Yerik.

"So, it passed through Michael, even though he wasn't blood related."

"I don't understand," I said. "What does that mean?"

"Well," Will said thoughtfully. "It makes sense, like how God adopts us, you know?"

When my expression explained that I didn't know, he continued.

"Jesus is God, but also the son of God. God is the king and so therefore, His son, Jesus, inherits the kingdom. We, being fully adopted into the family of God through faith in Jesus, are also fully sharing in that inheritance, just like Liza and Michael."

"So, Michael became a part of the bloodline as if he were born into it? It's not really a bloodline but...a faithline."

"Exactly. At least, that's how I see it."

"Hmm."

I chewed on his words for a while. God loved us, truly loved us. He had always wanted to be with us, but it was our own selfishness and pride that separated us from Him. Even so, He made a way. He willingly sent Himself to earth to live as one of us, and to ultimately pay, through his death, a debt we couldn't. Though we could never deserve it, we get to share in everything He has. And as the only human to ever live a perfect sinless life, Jesus was the only one who could pay it–the only one worthy. That's what His love made us: worthy. Esther was wrong. Liza's story wasn't unimportant. It was possibly the most important.

There were other stories in that journal. What else would I find if I kept reading?

"What are you thinking?" Will finally asked. He sat on the bed, facing me, his hand resting on my knee.

"It's odd that my mother could…move things…or hold them back. I don't know how to describe it exactly, but it's similar to what I can do in a dream. And then there's Liza's ability to know a person's intent."

"Can you do that too?"

"I think so. Looking back, I can see it. I remember knowing I could trust someone or having a very strong feeling that I couldn't. Like when I met you, I just…knew you were good and honest."

He smiled shyly.

"And Nadine…I just felt like she was a snake from the beginning," I said. "Maybe I should have paid more attention to that."

His brows drew together.

"What is it?" I asked.

"If you have what Liza had, and you can tell if someone is trustworthy…" he hesitated.

"Yeah?"

"Why did it take you so long to trust me?" He looked me right in the eye, allowing no escape.

I had to force the break and looked down. His hand was still on my knee and I traced the outline of his fingers.

"Honestly, I don't think it was that I didn't trust you. I think it was more that I didn't want to admit it," I said. "I trust you now, though."

"Well, I hope so." Smiling, he took a deep breath and thankfully didn't press the issue. "So, do you think that these things are passed down, like inherited traits?"

I shrugged. "Maybe."

"I wonder what else you can do."

I looked at him, searching his face, trying to discern what he was thinking. "Does it scare you?"

"Are you asking if I'm scared of you?"

I shrugged again, looking down at our fingers now woven together. With the emotional turmoil that I'd been experiencing lately, I was a little scared of myself.

"Come here," he said, his voice low. He leaned towards me, his hand cupping my face, just below my ear. I let him pull me closer, my heart speeding up. "I'm not afraid of you, Andy. The only thing I've ever been afraid of...is losing you."

His deep dark brown eyes burned, and my breath caught in my throat. He was letting me see all of him–exposing his fears, raw and unfettered– but I was holding back. Would he truly feel the same if he knew? If he knew of the venom I tasted every time I thought about Elena and what she had done, the violent thoughts I'd entertained–would he fear me then?

I curled my fists into his shirt, pulling him closer, holding on with everything that was in me to the goodness that was Will Carter. There was desperation on my lips when they connected with his, and from the way his arms locked around me, I knew he felt it, too. We melted together, holding to each other like deep roots cling to the earth in a storm. I prayed we were rooted deeply enough to weather this.

While we found solace in each other, our rest was anything but peaceful. We both tossed and turned and ended up only falling asleep after blankly staring at reruns of old TV shows for several hours. I woke the next morning to find Will hunched over a stack of papers at the little round table by the window. I slid out of bed and padded over to him, wrapping my arms around his shoulders and resting my chin on the top of his head.

"Anything groundbreaking?"

"I'm just mapping our route. Look at this."

I moved around to his side. He pushed his chair back and pulled me into his lap, smoothing the map so I could see the whole state. There were three red dots, forming the three vertices of a triangle.

"New Orleans?"

"Right in the middle."

Sure enough, though the three places on Nadine's list were in different cities, they formed a perfect triangle around the crescent city.

"I guess we're heading to New Orleans."

"Just in time for Mardi Gras." He slid his arms around my waist, hugging me close.

"Well, at least we'll eat good." I patted his hand, tapping out of the cage of his arms. "Guess we should get going. It's a long drive."

Nine long hours later, we wove through downtown New Orleans, marveling at the juxtaposition of streets lined with well-kept and updated townhouses on one side and run-down Creole cottages on the other. Artists, musicians, and street performers were winding down their acts for the day even though the streets were crowded with tourists seeking the vibrant and often dangerous nightlife.

Decorations of purple, green, and gold adorned every shop window, and the streets were already littered with colorful bits of confetti and discarded red plastic cups.

"There it is," Will said, pointing to a long two-story townhouse style building made of red brick. The ornate black railings of the upstairs balconies were draped with lush green ivy and free-standing fan-like ferns in oversized pots.

"Really? It's beautiful." I felt a little silly being so excited about our accommodations, seeing as we were on a mission to track down a possible murderer and human trafficker. Will must have pulled some serious strings to find an open room this close to the parade route a few days before Mardi Gras.

We were able to find a guarded parking lot just a block past the inn and checked in under the new and equally less creative aliases of Mr. and Mrs. Jones.

It was too late to visit the first facility on our list, so Will spent the evening reading every bit of information he could find on the web that mentioned it. Grumbling about outdated websites, he finally joined me on the balcony when the live music from a nearby restaurant crept through the open French doors.

"I wish we were here under different circumstances," he said, echoing my earlier thought.

"Does this place ever sleep?"

"That's New York. This…" He put his hands on the rail on either side of me, pressed his cheek against mine and spoke slowly, drawing out his words in a southern accent. "This is the Big Easy, baby."

I shivered at the bass of his voice and blew out an amused breath. He took my hands and wrapped his arms around me, bringing mine along. As we swayed slowly to the music, I closed my eyes, letting the sounds of a vibrant living city fill my ears.

Somewhere out there, beyond all the music and partying, a black-haired predator was stalking the innocent and frail; even the warmth of Will's arms couldn't chase the chill that seeped into my bones as we stood in the dead center of her hunting grounds.

That night, my sleep was plagued with shapeless shadows that crept ominously around the edges of my dreams. Even Will's steady heartbeat wasn't loud enough to drown out the whispers that taunted from just beyond what I could see.

Morning didn't bring answers, but it at least brought light and the distracting hum of city life.

"I'll go grab us some breakfast if you want," I said, waving my hand over his computer like a magician. "So, you can do your thing."

He'd been up before me, once again hunched over his computer, searching and plotting, making lists and drawing lines between scribbles.

He looked up, surprised, like he'd forgotten I was there, and blinked a few times before his brows drew together in the middle. I knew he was mentally running through all the possible scenarios of what could happen to me. I ruffled his hair and kissed him quickly on the cheek.

"I'll be fine. That cafe with the beignets is right across the street."

He frowned, but acquiesced anyway.

A few minutes later, I walked out of the double glass doors of the inn into the cool humid air of a New Orleans winter. As I crossed the street, I glanced back to see Will on the balcony of our room, leaning over the black curved metal rail, watching me. I waved and rolled my eyes, mouthing "I'm fine" at him.

He shook his head, smiling that crooked smile that made my cheeks burn, but turned and walked back in through the French doors. He had work to do, and I was starving. The cafe was busy with tourists, a long line already forming at the counter. I found an empty table outside and sat down, waiting for the line to dissipate.

Someone had left a newspaper, so I picked it up, meaning to flip to the comics, but something else caught my eye. It was a short article on the bottom of the front page, giving updates on a missing person's case.

The teenaged son of a well-known businessman in Baton Rouge had been on a weekend mission trip with his youth group to continue cleanup and rebuilding efforts from a devastating hurricane that happened over a decade before, but still continued to affect the area.

The boy, Chase Goodman, disappeared from his dorm room, seemingly without a trace. He had just recently been given a prestigious award for a persuasive essay on religious freedom in foreign countries, and was the leader of a growing teen activist group supporting religious refugees. Chase had been planning to visit Africa on an extended mission trip in a few months. It was still assumed he was a runaway as there were no signs of a struggle, and none of his roommates reported seeing anyone the night he vanished.

There was a heartbreaking quote from his father, insisting that his son would have never abandoned his family in such a way. Chase had been missing for over two weeks, and the article detailed the police's efforts to begin searching waterways. The chances of a happy ending seemed slim.

Chase's young face in the form of a school picture smiled up at me from the paper. It was a black and white image, but I could tell he had light colored eyes and probably dirty blond or light brown hair. His cheeks were round, making him appear younger than sixteen as the article described.

A mysterious trail of heat flamed up my spine when I looked at him, but the sudden sweet sound of a zydeco street musician drew my attention away from the paper, and I looked up to see the line had all but disappeared. I tucked the paper under my arm, planning to read it again later.

"Hungry?" I gently kicked the inn room door closed behind me.

"I'm always hungry." Will smiled from his place at the table and clicked the cover of his laptop closed.

"Do we have a plan?" I pulled a to-go cup of coffee from the drink carrier and brought it over to him along with a white paper bag full of hot beignets.

"Plan is a generous term for what I've got." He sat back, stretching his long arms out behind his head.

"That's pretty much how I go through life, so…" I joked.

"I'm aware," he said sarcastically through a mouthful of beignet, white powdered sugar falling onto his navy-blue t-shirt.

I laughed and tossed him a napkin. The mattress springs creaked as I plopped down with my own bag and devoured a pastry, licking my fingers before picking up another.

"Think we can just walk up to the door and start asking questions?" I asked.

Will had turned when I started to talk, and nearly choked when he saw me shove an entire beignet into my mouth.

"Whaa…" I said, my mouth full.

He was laughing so hard he could hardly catch his breath, which made me laugh too, and then choke as I inhaled the sugar. I covered my mouth with my hand and ended up with sticky white powder all over my face as it shot out of my mouth through my fingers. I finally finished chewing through the laughter, and Will wiped his eyes with the back of his hand.

"Ahh, Andy, you've never been more beautiful," he said, shaking his head.

"Oh yeah…just gorgeous." I laughed, heading to the bathroom to wash my face.

When I was finished, I leaned against the bathroom door, my arms folded. He had turned back to the desk and was sliding all of his maps and lists into a folder. I held my clothes and towel, prepared to get ready for our fact-finding mission, but an uncomfortable uneasiness settled over my shoulders, anchoring me in place.

Our little room was a bubble, safe and isolated. The minute we stepped out of that door–there was no turning back, not that there had been before, but this felt like the final point after which it was a straight shot to the end. Whatever end that might be.

"I'll get the car. Meet you outside in fifteen, or do you need more time?" His eyes darted to the towel draped over my arm.

"No," I said with forced confidence. "I'll be ready."

CHAPTER 19

"There it is." I pointed past Will, drawing his eyes to a green and white sign directing us to Boutte. "How do you say it?"

"Boo-tay," Will said, stretching out the words. "According to the internet, anyway."

"Ahh, Louisiana," I sighed. "I can always count on you."

The first two stops had been a bust. The first, in Mandeville, was no longer offering inpatient services due to funding cuts. The second office had undergone a sudden change just after Thanksgiving, and now only served geriatric patients. Even though it was an interesting coincidence that both places had major changes in clientele at almost the exact same time, it didn't get us any closer to Elena.

A sudden winter thunderstorm had popped up as we left our second stop in a small town named Violet, leaving us soaked with icy cold rain water and another dead end.

I had let my head drop back against the seat as my cheeks burned. "This is like a wild goose chase–we're getting nowhere. That whole thing,

Esther helping me remember, could have been for nothing!"

Will glanced my way as he drove, his expression reassuring. "No, not for nothing. It's a puzzle. We just don't have all the pieces yet. We've still got one more stop."

The windshield wipers groaned against the strain of their work as we were pelted with a torrent of water.

His hand found mine and he sucked in a breath. "Geez, Andy, your hands are like ice."

My heart felt like ice, too. The image of the little blond girl kept floating through my mind like a ghost. She was out there somewhere, waiting for us–waiting to be rescued–and I couldn't understand why God would allow the delay.

The storm had passed by the time we reached Metairie, the sky a strange mixture of storm clouds and sunshine, meeting tumultuously together over the city. The road to Boutte was mostly interstate, but the directions then surprisingly led us to a subdivision.

"Is this right?" Will asked, turning down yet another residential street.

The neighborhood was older, established homes of varying degrees of update on either side of a tree-lined street. On his next left turn, we exchanged a questioning glance. The left side of the street was consistently dotted with simple wood framed homes, but on the right stretched an open field, surrounded by a high chain link fence.

We pulled up to the gate. The guard shack was unoccupied, and the gate chained shut. Will pulled to the side of the road leading up to the facility and got out, walking cautiously to the fence.

Yards ahead, where a large brick structure should have been, was nothing but the burned shell of a building. I felt my jaw tighten and my ears burn.

"I can't believe this," I said under my breath, my fingers curling around the cold metal of the fence links.

Will looked over his shoulder before kicking loose a piece of fence. The metal made a loud clicking sound that echoed in waves down the length of the fence. I scanned the row of houses behind us as he pulled back on the loosened section, seeing no movement other than the slight wave of a curtain in the front window of a blue house on the corner. He crawled through the opening and held the fence back as I followed. We walked towards the rubble, which was only marked off-limits by a single ragged strip of yellow caution tape. He slid smoothly under the tape and stepped through the blackened doorway. There was exposed wood, charred from fire, and piles of broken cement everywhere.

"I guess this wasn't on their website." I stepped over a twisted metal support beam.

"No." His short answer revealed more than he intended.

"What do you think happened?"

"See over there?" He was pointing to what was left of a corner.

"What is that?"

He stepped gingerly over the debris and pointed out a large black ring burned onto the brick, the inside of which seemed untouched.

"This must have been where the source was."

"The source of what?"

"The explosion."

"So…this was arson?"

"I would say so, yes." He pulled his phone out of his pocket and tapped the screen, scowling at what came up.

"What?" I asked.

He walked back over to me and handed me his phone. It was open to a newspaper article. I scanned it quickly and looked up, confused.

"This says it was an electrical fire–an accident?"

"Sound familiar?"

I looked around again. It did sound a little too familiar, too many "accidents."

"Did you notice the date of the fire?" he asked.

I swiped my finger across the screen, opening it to the article again. Will moved closer and pointed to the date.

"But that's over a year ago."

"You don't recognize that date?"

I looked again and shook my head. He stared at me for a long second, his expression blank as if he were somewhere else.

"That's the day after I pulled you out of the river."

The day after I'd faced Taklos on a broken bridge, and the day after Nadine Greyson had been arrested for her part in my abduction.

He walked a few steps further as I read the rest of the article, my hand fluttering to my lips at the description of the damage.

"Will…" I gasped. "They…they all died."

He turned to respond, but a groaning sound from above drew our eyes upward. Before my brain could even register the danger, Will had already launched himself towards me.

He shoved me forcefully back and up against the one wall that was still fully standing just as a giant overhead support beam that had been teetering against a crumbling column crashed down right where I had been standing.

Will's hands slammed against the bricks on either side of me. My arms instinctively flew up around my head and I curled into his chest. The beam knocked over one of the few remaining interior walls. A large section fell forward and landed across his back, pushing him forward, his arms straining to keep his body and the wall from crushing me. The wall broke to pieces on impact, and a cloud of dust and debris rose up around him as his body remained a protective shield around mine. I could hear him breathing heavily, coughing as the dust settled.

"You okay?" His voice was gravely and low.

I lowered my hands, finding his face seriously close. His dark brown eyes searched mine.

I swallowed hard and nodded, my hands finding their way to his chest. "Yeah. Are you?"

He winced as he pushed himself away, then turned his arms over, checking for injuries. The skin on his palms and forearms was raw and small cuts ran across the flesh, bleeding just a little. He shook his hands and looked around. "I'm fine."

"Turn around." I ordered, twisting him with my hands on his waist.

He turned and I lifted his shirt to assess the damage. His back was red and scraped, but otherwise looked okay; nothing seemed broken, anyway. I was certain we would see a big ugly bruise later, but thankful I didn't see anything worse.

"Are you sure you're okay?" I asked.

"I'm fine. Let's go. This whole place could come down any second." He pulled me through the doorway and back out onto the unkempt lawn. I could see the wheels turning in his mind as he looked over the remains of the building from the outside.

His hand was tightly clasped around mine, even though I was sure it was hurting him. He was focused on what was left of the site, but I became acutely aware of our surroundings. A grey truck slowed as it passed. A dark-haired driver on his cell phone curiously looked our way before speeding up and going on. Almost all the residents had now appeared on their porches, pointing at the small cloud of dust that rose from the building. I looked back at Will and found him staring down the street in the direction the grey truck had gone.

"What is it?" I asked.

"I don't know," he said robotically.

"Let's go before someone calls the police." I tugged on his arm, standing on my tiptoes to see the blue house where the curtains had moved. It was still dark inside, and no one had come out, even though I was sure someone was home.

I didn't believe his claim that he was fine, and I also didn't want to draw any more unnecessary attention. All these eyes focused on us made me nervous. I was used to anonymity; it was safe and allowed me a certain amount of freedom. A chill crept up my spine, and even though the post-storm sunshine had warmed the air considerably, I shivered. Something was off, and it wasn't just the incredibly infuriating disappointment I felt about our wasted day.

"Ya'll alright?"

I'd just opened my door when a white-haired man struggling to hold back a wiggling terrier called to us from the sidewalk.

"Yes, sir, thank you." Will's expression immediately brightened and without missing a beat he said, "It was a close call. Name's Smith—structural engineer with Amcorp Industries."

Will stepped forward, offering his hand to the man, who accepted with a smile.

"I'd appreciate you not telling my boss that we neglected our hard hats."

The man snorted before being jerked forward by a leash attached to a harness on this hyper little dog. "Pleased to meet you, Mr. Smith. I'm Hardy."

"This is my colleague, Ms. Jones," Will motioned towards me, and I waved at the smiling Hardy but stayed close to the car. "Do you know much about this place?"

"Oh yeah. Lived here my whole life, walk Trudy by here every day. So sad about the fire—tragic." He shook his head and pulled Trudy close, scooping her up into his arms while she fought to escape by attacking him with her wet nose.

"It really was a terrible accident," Will said, cocking his head to the side when Hardy chuffed skeptically. "You don't think it was an accident?"

"I'm not one for conspiracy theories, but there's been weird goings' on at that place for as long as I can remember."

Will shoved his hands in his pockets and leaned toward Hardy, silently encouraging him to continue.

"In fact, the night of that fire…" Hardy looked around as if checking to see if anyone was listening. "I saw one of them small buses pull up in here and cart off a whole load of patients."

"Really?" Will sounded fascinated.

"Sure did. More'n once, too. Now buses and vans were always coming and going, but I thought this one strange because it came right smack in the middle of the night. I know, because Trudy here had just had some surgery and her medicine was making her need to go out all night long and I saw that van loaded up and leaving each time. Driver looked none too pleased about it, either."

"That is strange. You got a good look at the driver then?"

"Oh yeah–dark haired fella. Glasses and sort of scruffy looking."

"Hmm…I wonder where they were taking them?"

"Oh, I saw it–bus said Central New Orleans Behavioral Health Hospital. Had a big fleur de lis on the side. Hospital needs to do some updating if you ask me; it was so faded, I almost couldn't read it."

"I guess they got lucky then."

"I don't know if going from one hell hole to another is lucky, but I guess it's better than getting blown up."

I covered my mouth, hiding the shock at Hardy's blunt statement. He shook Will's hand again and they walked together the remaining steps to our car.

"You know, it's funny," Hardy said as he stooped to set Trudy back down on the sidewalk. "You're not the first I've met looking for the skinny on that place."

"You get a lot of curious folks stopping by?"

"No, actually. Since it's not out on the main roads, not many people know it was even here. But not long before the fire, I was out walking Trudy, like I always do, and a snooty blond woman came by. Driving real slow in a bright red sports car, so naturally me and Trudy asked her if she needed help. She wanted to know about this place–said she was doing some kind of research, asked if anything strange ever happened. Said she was meeting with one of the docs. I had some stories to tell, but she got a phone call and waved me off. Guess she should've stuck around. Wasn't but 'bout a week or two later the whole neighborhood heard a big bang, and came out to find the whole place on fire."

"So, you heard an explosion?"

Hardy's mouth snapped shut and his cheeks turned a deep crimson. Then he looked over both shoulders and turned quickly back around when the curtains in the front window of the blue house shifted again.

"I...I can't be sure. They said it was a fire–an accident; I'm sure that's what it was."

Trudy jerked hard on her leash, Hardy had to step backwards to keep from falling over.

"Guess she's ready to go. Nice to meet you both."

We waved and both slid silently into the car, stunned and confused by Hardy's revelation then sudden suspicious retraction. In the distance, the dark clouds overtook the sun, bringing the promise of another storm.

"Is our next stop Central New Orleans Behavioral Health Hospital?"

Will held his phone, scrolling with his thumbs.

"I don't think so."

"Why?"

"Because according to everywhere I'm looking, it doesn't exist."

CHAPTER 20

Will was quiet on the way back to the inn. I was, too. I was worried about him, frustrated at the dead ends and cryptic clues we kept running into, and increasingly uneasy about our whole mission. We had all these little bits of information that we had gone through extensive and costly lengths to acquire, but they were leading us exactly nowhere.

"Andy?"

Will's warm hand on mine drew me back from the dark place my mind was wandering. He smiled softly as my gaze slowly drifted his way.

"You okay?"

"Fine," I said quickly. "Um…kind of hungry."

"You can talk to me, you know. I'm frustrated, too."

He squeezed my hand. I pulled it away, reaching to adjust the heater. His brows dipped together, and his lips turned down.

"Isn't it supposed to be the wife asking the husband to talk about his feelings?" I scoffed.

He sighed. "Yeah, I guess it is."

We sat quietly for a few more minutes.

"I am frustrated," I said finally, looking down at my hands. "Every time I think we are onto something…"

"Dead end. I know," he said.

I was surprised by his admission. But he was there, too. He was with me, struggling, fighting right by my side, getting crushed by buildings, and I was wallowing alone in my frustrations.

"I'm sorry," I whispered.

"Yeah, me too."

"What for?" I asked, confused.

"I should have never gone into that building today, much less let you go in. You could have been killed. It was…it was really stupid." He shook his head and leaned forward, his forearms on the steering wheel. I noticed he winced as he moved.

I stared at him. So, that's what was off. He'd pulled an Andy and put curiosity before caution.

"You couldn't have known…"

"That's just it; I didn't know, and I walked right in." He sat back. His knuckles were white from their tight grip on the steering wheel. "I want to find her–to find something so badly, I'm taking risks and getting careless."

I didn't know what to say, but my mind was racing, assaulted with turmoil. This was exactly what I was afraid of. We'd played this game of tug of war for weeks, each of us taking turns rushing forward and then pulling back. Now he was second guessing our mission. We couldn't give up now, but he was right about one thing–it was dead end after dead end.

"I'm not giving up yet," I snapped, my harsh comment more for myself than Will.

"I didn't say we should." Will's hand was heavy on my shoulder–too heavy–and I leaned away.

"Then what are you saying?" My hands found my forehead, rubbing hard in an attempt to smooth the wrinkles my scrunched expression formed.

"Just that…we should be more careful," he growled.

I grumbled something vaguely resembling an agreement.

I was still shaken from our near-death experience, missing Esther, unreasonably disturbed by a wispy curtain and a random grey truck, and so confused as to what we were even doing here. More than anything, I was so…angry. I wanted to see Elena brought to justice, I wanted to see her locked up forever–or worse. Despite my efforts, the fury continued to grow, and that didn't fit at all with who I was supposed to be.

Where was all the grace and mercy? Where was the patience and faithfulness? Suddenly, the cab of that truck was a coffin, and I couldn't breathe.

"Can we stop there?" I said, pointing to a small deli just ahead.

"Sure," Will said flatly.

"I'm just…really hungry."

"Well, Mrs. Carter, we can't have that." He smiled, but it didn't reach his eyes.

As soon as he parked, I threw open the door and climbed out into the cool air, which was even more humid after the earlier storm. I took deep breaths until Will was next to me on the sidewalk.

"Ready?" he said.

"Yes, I'm starving." I forced a smile.

"Yeah, I'm getting that. Have you ever had a muffuletta?" He offered his arm.

I took it and with wide eyes replied, "No, but that sounds delicious."

"You say that about everything."

"I like food." I shrugged. "All kinds."

"I'm getting that, too." He laughed and squeezed my arm, pulling me closer to his side.

The tension between us seemed to have lifted for the moment and we were back to being Mr. and Mrs. Carter, young newlywed couple, instead of ex-agents Will and Andy, supernatural crime fighters.

We grabbed two muffulettas for dinner and headed back to the inn. I sent him on ahead to the room while I went to the front desk to extend our stay one more night.

He was sitting at the little round table in our room, unpacking the delicious smelling foil-wrapped sandwiches when I walked in. The air was hot, steam still spilling out of the bathroom door, and his wet hair looked black.

"How's your back?" I asked.

"Bruised already, but otherwise okay, I think."

I glared at him skeptically, and he shrugged, his words muffled by the huge bite of sandwich he'd just taken, "Ady, I fie, weally."

I smothered a laugh and grabbed my own dinner, plopping down onto the bed, peeling back the foil and marveling at the thick layers of ham, turkey and salami smooshed between two slices of toasted bread and slathered with a fragrant olive relish.

I turned it around several times, trying to figure out how exactly to eat the giant sandwich.

"So, I know you said it was arson," I said. "Do you think that the building was destroyed deliberately…somehow in connection with Nadine?"

"It is an awfully suspicious coincidence."

"Maybe someone could get in to talk to her? Maybe Matt could…"

"Andy." He put his food on the table, his back to me. A coldness in his tone moved across the room and crept up the leg that I'd let dangle over the side of the bed. I tucked it up underneath me. "There's something I need to tell you."

He took a deep breath and stood, crossing the room to stand in front of me. Suddenly, I wanted to crawl away from him, but I forced myself to stay still. He crossed his arms and looked down at the floor. When he looked back up, his expression was unreadable.

"Greyson is dead," he said softly.

Good. I was shocked at my initial response, and quickly looked down at the food in my lap. Immediately following was a crashing wave of very deep sadness. I was quite sure Nadine had never come to know Christ, and now it was too late for her. I was afraid to open my mouth, because I didn't know which half of my heart might come out.

"Andy, did you hear me?"

"How long have you known?"

"Since the gas station…when I talked to Matt."

"What happened?" I picked at the seeds on my bread.

"Uh, well, they said it was an accident." He sank slowly onto the bed, keeping his distance.

Another accident. I glanced at him. He was leaning forward, his elbows on his knees, his chin propped up on his folded hands. The weight of this secret had been hard for him to bear, even if just for a day, and I could see that he was tired from carrying it.

"You think it was something else?"

He took a deep breath. "I find it a little suspicious."

"Yeah, me too. When did she…when did it happen?"

"About two hours after her lawyer visited," he said, cutting his eyes up towards me. "The lawyer with long black hair."

"That's a lot suspicious. Could she have done something to Nadine?"

"No one saw anything."

"How did she… um…"

"Apparently she had some kind of allergic reaction? No one knew of any pre-existing condition or food allergy; there was nothing in her file or in her medical records. She was found unresponsive in her cell just after lunch. They couldn't revive her."

We looked at each other for several seconds.

"Why didn't you tell me?" I already knew why; he was, and would always be, a protector. My protector.

He shrugged, still resting his chin on his fists. "I didn't think it was the right time."

"Were you ever going to?"

"Of course." His tone was strained, and he looked at me like he couldn't believe I would ask that.

"Is there anything else you haven't told me?"

"Andy," he said softly, looking at me with pleading eyes. "I'm sorry."

He leaned over and reached for me. I didn't want to be touched; it felt wrong. Everything was wrong. Somehow Elena had crawled out of my dream and poisoned everything in my waking life.

"Um…I'm going to take a shower," I said, sliding off the bed, avoiding his touch. As I started to close the door to the bathroom, I saw his head tip forward, his hands sliding through his hair. I couldn't leave him like that, and spoke over my shoulder. "I understand why you did it. I'm not mad. Let's call it a night…I know you're tired."

I couldn't be mad; he didn't tell me about Nadine for the same reason I wasn't telling him about the darkness creeping up inside. We wanted to spare each other. We bore the burdens so the other didn't have to; that was a good thing. Right?

I took my time in the shower, scrubbing every inch of my skin. No matter how much I washed, I still felt dirty, covered in a sticky film of suspicion and unease. When I came out of the bathroom, wrapped in a fluffy bathrobe and followed by a cloud of steam, he was back at the computer. The newspaper I'd picked up at the cafe that morning was spread out on the bed.

"Did you read this article? About the missing boy?" I asked, drying my hair with a white towel.

"Yes. Do you think it's related?" he asked, watching me carefully.

"I don't know; there's something about it." I was captivated by the image of the boy's smiling face. "Maybe nothing."

"If I've learned anything with you, it's never nothing." Will smiled softly, watching me for a few long seconds. "Andy, do you want to talk about Nadine?"

"Not particularly." I answered quickly, noticing that was the first time he had called her by her first name. He started to say something, but I smiled sweetly and sashayed over to him, hushing him with a kiss on the cheek. "Have you seen my pajama pants?"

He nodded towards the other chair, where my plaid flannel pants hung over the back. I turned to go, stopped short by his arms locking around me. "You can see I'm trying, right? Do you forgive me?" His voice was soft, his eyes pleading.

"There's nothing to forgive. You did what you thought was best. You wanted me to trust you, and I do." For the first time, I was uncomfortable in the cage of his arms. Everything about how I was feeling lately was uncomfortable.

His eyes narrowed, as if he didn't quite believe my response. I looked up coyly through my lashes.

"You know it's really not fair that you can feel what I'm feeling, but I'm in the dark about what's going on inside of you."

"Whatever do you mean? I'm an open book." I made my eyes wide and innocent.

He dropped his arms. I snatched up my clothes and hurried back into the privacy of the bathroom, where his suspicious eyes couldn't see. I stared at my reflection in the mirror. The girl staring back was strong, but a fire burned behind her eyes; a growing fury brought a blush to her cheeks and neck. I split my wet hair and pulled the two halves to the front, attempting to hide the redness on my skin. I should feel badly that Nadine was dead, and I did, but a bigger part of me felt angrier that yet another life had been ruined because of this Elena woman. I should weep for Nadine's lost soul; I should hope that, somehow, she repented and believed before her death; but no tears came. My compassion was eclipsed by a terrible thirst for justice–or was it revenge?

What is wrong with you? I asked the girl in the mirror. She didn't answer. I made a note to deal with her later. Right now, we needed to keep moving forward before someone else got hurt...or killed.

CHAPTER 21

I had never been one to have vivid dreams when I slept, which seemed strange, given that a big part of what made me...me was centered around dreams. But unless I was dreamwalking, my sleep was peaceful and uneventful. The exception, of course, being the last several months, when almost every night had held either nightmares or visions of the past. So when I found myself standing in an endless empty field basking in the sun, I was very confused.

Had I stumbled into someone's dream? I looked around. It really was quite lovely and felt oddly familiar. Had I been here before? The grass was dry and tall. Its soft, wispy tops brushed my outstretched palms as I walked. In the distance, tall blue mountains rose up against the sky, their tops spattered with snow. A gentle breeze floated across the plain, directing the grass in a silent dance.

It was quiet and warm. I closed my eyes, took in a long, slow, deep breath, and turned my face towards the sun. If I were going to have a dream, this was pretty close to perfect. I enjoyed the sun's warmth on my skin for a while before I got the feeling that I wasn't alone.

Sure enough, a young woman stood next to me. I wasn't startled, though. I felt like I knew her, even though I was sure I'd never seen her before. She was facing the mountains like me, gazing at them with a perfectly contented smile.

"It's beautiful," she said.

"Yes, it is." I couldn't take my eyes off of her. She was definitely someone I knew, but who?

We stood in silence for another minute.

"I don't have long, Joanna," she said, still looking off into the distance.

"Where are you going?"

She closed her eyes and took a deep breath. A glorious smile spread across her lips as she said, "Home."

"Where do you live?"

She laughed softly and as she turned to look at me, her blue eyes met mine and I gasped.

"Esther?"

She was young–younger than me–but I was sure it was her. The breeze gently lifted the strands of her strawberry-blond hair that danced slowly around her face. Her skin was smooth and soft, her eyes bright. She stood tall and strong, her back no longer crooked from the weight of age and time. She was so perfectly healthy and beautiful.

Her eyes sparkled with some knowledge that I couldn't know, and I felt my lips curling up into a smile to match hers.

"This is a dream…right?" I asked.

"Yes and no." Her voice rang clear, like a bell.

I couldn't help but marvel at her; she exuded such peace and joy. Something passed across my mind.

"Wait," I said, my smile fading. "What do you mean you're going home?"

She reached out and took my hands. Hers were so warm, I was instantly calmed.

"Joanna, you must listen." She looked and sounded different, but she spoke with the same authority that I had grown to know. "I have to tell you something now."

I felt a terrible lump rise in my throat. Deep down, I knew what she was going to say.

"No, I don't want to hear this," I said, pulling away.

Her grip on my hands was firm, and her eyes held mine intently.

"Listen now, child. You must continue on. You must keep running the race. I have lived a wonderful life, full of love and purpose. I made my own choices, and I have no regrets."

"But I didn't finish yet, you don't have answers. This just can't be…it's not…"

"Don't." She pointed a straight finger in my face, immediately silencing my argument. Her eyes burned with the fire of fierce conviction. "Don't you dare say that it's not fair. We have been given more grace and more mercy than we could ever imagine–and we deserve none of it. Fair would be a lifetime of misery as payment for our selfishness and pride."

I huffed and turned away, but she tugged on my hand, pulling me back. When her other hand settled softly on my cheek, gently tuning my face towards hers, the fire was gone, and a genuinely grateful smile spread across her lips.

"But look at what I've been given instead. Having you in my life, even for this brief time; knowing what happened to you, that you were safe, you were loved…that's what I had always hoped to learn. That is what I begged for all these years, and not only did I get to know, but I got to look into your eyes, hold you in my arms, and share the precious truth of our calling with you. I even got to see you fall in love and get married! But above all of these wonderful things, I got to see you become new; see you accept God's gift of grace and forgiveness. I got to know that we would be together forever. There's nothing more precious to me than that."

"But…I'm not ready. I still need you." I knew my resistance wasn't going to change anything, but I wasn't giving up without a fight.

"I know you think that is true…"

"It is true!" I jerked my hand from hers and walked away. My breaths were heavy, and I felt my face flush hot with anger. "How is this right? How could this be the way it ends? How!"

She patiently watched me stomp and rant, her face bearing a kind and understanding smile. I finally turned around again to face her.

"I just thought we would have more time," I whispered.

She nodded; her young eyes held all the wisdom of her earthly age.

"Who do you say that God is, Joanna?"

"What?"

"It's a simple question. Who is He, truly?"

"I… He's…" I stumbled over my words. Why couldn't I answer? I closed my eyes and let her question sink deep into my heart. If I was dreaming, I knew I couldn't lie, so whatever I said next would be the truth. Hundreds of words swirled around in my mind. He is the Creator, Father, and Friend. He is Savior, Messiah, King. The beginning of all things. All knowing. Loving, yet just. Merciful and kind. Compassionate and holy. Finally, at the root of it all, I settled on one single word.

"Sovereign," I said. "God is sovereign."

I opened my eyes to see her nodding at me.

"So you know that whatever He chooses, ordains, or allows is perfectly within His right to do? He cannot choose wrong, because He is the very definition of right."

I nodded in agreement.

"Let me ask you one more thing," she said. "Do you trust Him to keep His promises?"

I opened my mouth to speak but stopped. It seemed like an easy answer, but I felt an incredible weight in her words. She wasn't asking for the answer I carried around in my head; she was asking for the truth that I held secretly and protected deep down in my heart. Did I truly trust that God would keep His promises? Would He do what He said?

"I want to say yes," I said. That was the honest answer. It hurt, and hot tears filled up my eyes.

I felt her hands on the sides of my face, pulling my downcast eyes up to meet hers.

"Keep going," she said, emphasizing each word. "You have had to face more tests of your faith in just the last few months than most people face in an entire lifetime, and each time you have held onto the truth. It is there, inside of you. He will keep every promise, Joanna. Keep saying it until you believe it."

"Why do you have to go? I don't understand." I placed my hands over hers, which were still warm on my cheeks.

"You don't have to understand. Some things we learn over time, and some we never know this side of heaven. It's not for us to know. God's love is a mystery so big we can't even begin to comprehend its depth."

"I know, but I'm still afraid." I tipped my head forward until our foreheads touched. I knew she was leaving soon; I just wanted to hold on a little longer. This was what I would miss the most: her unfailing faith and her consistent wisdom.

I would miss the undeniable familiarity and connection of true family.

"Remember," she said softly, "Even when you don't understand, even when the answer is no, even when you hear no answer at all... just...remember what is true."

I couldn't answer, so I just nodded. I felt her strong arms around me, pulling me in close. Even now, she was instructing, guiding, and urging me ever forward.

"I'm going to miss you," I sobbed into her shoulder.

"It won't be long, child," she said softly. "This life is but a moment."

She pulled back and put her hands on my shoulders.

"There's something else," she said, suddenly very serious. "There is a great darkness ahead. You mustn't let it overcome you. Trust in what you know to be true, and remember the power that is in His name."

There were so many questions I wanted to ask. What darkness? What did that mean? How was I supposed to fight it? What if the darkness was me?

"What if I can't?"

"He can," she said fiercely. "It's always been Him...always Jesus. You can't give up. You must continue. Fight. Trust and obey. Remember, more than even our sacrifice, He wants our obedience. All things...through Him."

In my head, I knew all the reasons why she was right, but my heart doubted. What if we just walked away, returned home to the safety of friends and family? Maybe we could just call Matt and have The Agency take care of everything. She must have read the uncertainty in my eyes, because she squeezed my arms once more.

"It's not about you," she said, looking over my shoulder. "But it can only be you."

I turned to see what she was looking at, but there was nothing there except the wide sunlit prairie that ended at the foot of the mountains.

"What's going to happen?"

She shifted her eyes back to meet mine.

"I can't tell the future," she answered with a laugh. "I just know you are the one God chose for this purpose."

The breeze we'd been enjoying picked up strength. She smiled and took in an excited breath, making her shoulders rise and fall dramatically.

"It's time."

I felt like I should be sad, but she looked so happy.

"Is this what happens?" I asked. "I mean, is this what our new bodies will be like?"

She looked down at herself, held her hands out in a shrug and laughed. "Maybe…it's your dream."

"Yes and no?" I repeated what she had said earlier with a smirk.

The breeze became a wind, the waist-high grass bending and swaying under its force. Esther looked off towards the mountains, then back at me with a smile. She winked knowingly and started to walk towards the rising hills. The wind picked up even more, shushing and hushing across the open field. She turned one last time and waved.

I raised my hand to wave back when I heard a voice from behind me. It was so close, I turned to see who was there, but there was no one. When I turned around again, she was gone. I was sure it was her voice I had heard just then, speaking a single word.

"Remember."

I sat up quickly and found myself out of breath. The field was gone, the mountain was gone, Esther was gone.

Esther was gone.

I was in our room at the inn. It was dark.

Esther.

The red numbers on the alarm clock told me it was four in the morning. Tuesday.

I reached out and found the space next to me on the bed empty. My eyes searched the room, settling on Will's silhouette. He was standing by the window, his shape bathed in moonlight. One hand rested on his hip and the other held his cell phone to his ear. His head hung low and even though I couldn't see his face, I could tell something was wrong. He ran his hand through his hair.

"Okay…yeah," he said. "We'll see you soon."

He looked down at his phone for a second before turning, looking surprised and sad to see me sitting up, staring back at him. His eyes dropped to the floor.

"She's not gone," I said, my throat tightening against the truth I fought to accept.

He walked over and sat on the bed next to me. I pulled the covers up tight around my chest and leaned away, wanting him to say it wasn't true.

"She's not gone…it was just a dream."

"Andy." His voice broke. "I'm so sorry."

It wasn't just a dream. Esther was gone.

"Did she get to them? Did she…" I grabbed his arms, my fingers gripping until they were white. He shook his head, not understanding.

"Was it Elena?" My voice was squeaky, tight and strained against the words I didn't want to say.

Visible comprehension passed over his face and he peeled my fingers from his arms, drawing my hands up together in his.

"No." He spoke with certainty. "Jacob said she was at peace…she wasn't suffering or in pain. She just…slipped away."

She's gone. How could she be gone? I wasn't finished. I was supposed to have more time. It was my fault. I killed her.

No.

It was Elena. I didn't care what he said; Elena killed her. That woman was a murderer. She killed my parents, she stole my family, my childhood, and now because of her, Esther was dead too.

Lord… I started to pray, but stopped. I couldn't, even in my mind, I couldn't. I cuddled my little seed of anger, caressed it, watered it with disdain and tenderly put it back in its hiding place.

"…memorial service when we are ready. He said there was no rush, since she had asked to be cremated." Will had been talking.

"Okay," I replied.

He looked at me, his brows knitted together. He thought I was in shock; I could feel it. If he looked much longer or deeper, he might see the truth. I pushed myself forward and into his lap. He wrapped his arms around me. He was preparing himself, waiting for me to fall apart, and I could have right then. I could have let out all the sadness and anger I'd been feeling, but I didn't. I let his arms hold me together and used his strength to push it all back down.

"Poor Jacob," I whispered.

"We can head back first thing in the morning." He buried his face in my hair.

"No, we have to keep going," I said plainly.

He didn't answer, but I could feel his confusion.

"I saw her."

"What?" He pulled back, searching my face. I know he was expecting to see tears, but my eyes were dry.

"Esther…I saw her in my dream tonight," I explained as his hands moved up to hold me by my arms. "She told me she was going home."

He didn't reply, but there was sadness in his eyes.

"I guess she was telling me goodbye."

"I…don't know what to say," he whispered. "Did she say anything else?"

"She said to keep going…to finish it."

I wasn't ready to tell him everything, especially the part about the mysterious darkness. I was afraid he would see what I was thinking, that he would see the growing rage inside. I would deal with that later; right now, I needed it to keep me focused. Besides, he loved her too; he was also grieving. It wouldn't be fair to dump that on him tonight. His sad eyes searched mine. I saw that he wanted to be helpful, to do something, but he didn't know what.

So I let him hold me again, my head resting against his chest, the familiar thump of his heart beating a calming rhythm in my ears. Eventually, I fell asleep again with a vague memory of him covering me with the blanket and for the second time that night, my mind was filled with vivid dreams. Only this time I was a little girl again at a carnival, taking my first ever roller coaster ride. Something went terribly wrong, and the track only ever went down, never up or around curves…only further and further down. All I wanted to do was to get off.

CHAPTER 22

W hen I woke, Will was gone. Boxy numbers on the alarm clock read seven thirty. Night was over; a yellow blaze of morning sun turned the sheer white panels on the French doors to fire. The dream that had begun so beautifully had turned into yet another nightmare, one from which I was more than relieved to wake. It was just another normal day–well, sort of normal–as the sounds of a gathering crowd floated up to our room, reaching me even through the closed doors leading to the balcony. It was Fat Tuesday. Mardi Gras. Will's coat and car keys were still where he'd left them yesterday; he must have gone to the lobby. I got up, took my clothes, and headed to the bathroom, envisioning an intriguing day of parades and celebration. A soft knock on the door interrupted the blissful daydream.

"Andy?" Will's muffled voice said from behind the door. "You want some coffee?"

"Yes, please!" I called over the sound of the running water, and flung my hair back as it fell into the sink.

He was sitting at the little round table by the window when I came out of the bathroom.

"Thanks." I took the cup of steaming brown liquid he offered. He pulled me into his lap and brushed the wet tips of my hair back off my shoulders.

"Hey," he said, pulling at a string on the sleeve of my shirt. "Are you okay?"

All possible chances of normalcy drowned in the wake of his innocent question. It wasn't a dream.

Esther was truly gone–and with her, the privilege of mourning. Every ounce of grief was tucked away, divided up and stowed in little hidden compartments marked for later use. When I shifted, Will tensed, preparing for an onslaught of emotion. He expected me to fall apart. I would have expected the same, but necessity won out over the frivolity of anguish. There was no time for that; we had a job to do. God had called me into service–given me this gift, this talent, and a mission to complete.

But Will was waiting, his expectant arms ready to field whatever amount of heartbreak was to come. As much as I needed to focus on my job, he needed to do his as well, and his current assignment was that of comforter, bearer of feelings.

"I miss her already."

It was the most I could allow.

"It's okay to grieve, you know," he said. "We can take time. We can even go back home."

I shot up, needing to escape that treasonous suggestion as quickly as possible. My sudden exit caused him to pull his hands back, and when I turned to face him, they were still in the air as if he were a suspect ordered to freeze. His shocked expression deposited a heavy lump of discomfort in my stomach. *Keep it together, Andy.*

"I know." I leaned over and kissed him. "But she wanted us to keep going. I just feel like that's what we should do."

"Okaaaay," he said, but it sounded more like a question.

I finished getting dressed, uncomfortable under the scrutiny of his stare. Out of habit, I reached for my necklace, my searching fingers coming up empty. A flash of panic quickly vanished; I'd taken it off in Knoxville. There was no good explanation, but it had felt heavy, and I needed relief from its weight. I ran my fingers over a soft baby blue cloth at the bottom of my toiletry bag. The silver chain with Marie's lion pendant was safely wrapped inside.

I hadn't been able to put it back on; it was a constant aching reminder of another Andy, the one full of mercy and grace. There was no reconciling that girl with the one staring back at me in the mirror.

She was strange, but she wasn't a stranger–I'd seen her before. Once. Her hard, vengeful eyes had stared back at me from deep in the woods surrounding Samantha Prescott's peaceful hidden church. She'd been stalking me for months and finally caught up, slipping with stealth through a window that I'd left open. The woods. Nothing good ever happened in the woods.

"What is it?" Will leaned against the door frame, arms folded.

I stared back at him for a long minute.

"I just wonder…why Nadine left me alive. She meant for me to die, so why didn't she…" I shook my head, the rest of that question a choking cube of ice lodged in my throat.

He reached out and I let him pull me back into the room where he slowly sank into a chair. He ran his hands down both of my arms until they reached my hands. I felt that familiar electric tingle on my skin when his thumb skimmed across the top of my left hand, stopping when it reached my wedding ring.

"Thank God she didn't." He lifted my hand and gently brushed his lips across the little band encircling my ring finger.

"I've always just thought of her as pure evil, but even though she hated me, she couldn't kill me–not outright anyway." I was dangerously close to revealing too much about my own heart.

"It's one thing to hate someone and want them dead, and an entirely different thing to actually do it, although it's not any different in God's eyes." He looked up, his head tipped knowingly to the side. Did he know?

"Do you think there was ever any hope for Nadine?" I searched his eyes, trying to feel what he was feeling. He worried–and he carried a burdensome load of guilt, though I couldn't discern the cause.

"Nadine Greyson made her choice," he said finally. "She could have turned everything around at any time. She chose not to. There's always a choice."

"But…what if she didn't know?" I whispered, remembering how lost I'd been before Esther told me the truth. It was too late for Nadine now.

"She did." He bobbed his head to catch my eyes. "Andy, look at me. She knew. I made sure."

"You did? When?"

"During the trial." His fingers twisted the ring gently around on my finger. "I sent the chaplain to see her."

"Why didn't you tell me?"

"I don't know, I guess I just wanted to forget the whole thing. It didn't matter, anyway. She sent him away."

I didn't have a response. What could anyone say to that knowledge? *There's always a choice.* Nadine had deliberately chosen to ignore the gift of grace. He chose to show her mercy, even though I could tell by the fire that burned behind his eyes when her name was mentioned that he hated everything she'd done.

"There you go again," I said with a breathy laugh. "Being Mr. Perfect."

He didn't smile; in fact, he winced like my words had hurt.

"Don't paint me as a saint, Andy. I sent the chaplain because I couldn't face her myself, and I did it because I thought maybe she would be more cooperative. I thought that if by some impossible chance she ever got out– if she was a believer–she wouldn't come looking for you."

He lowered his head, resting his crown against my stomach, and slid his hands up to hold my waist. I was floored by his confession.

"I'm not proud of it." His voice was soft, contrite and repentant. "Maybe that's the real reason I didn't tell you."

This was the most honest conversation we'd had in a long time. It was the perfect opportunity for me to share my own secrets, to meet him there in the intimate, humble place of confession. But he clung to me, broken, hurting, and vulnerable. He had been my solid thing so many times, reassuring and strong; it was time to return the favor.

I sank to my knees, causing him to sit back in surprise, unable to hide the evidence of lingering soreness as he moved. I rested my arms on his knees, taking his hands.

"Maybe your motives weren't perfect. Maybe they were even selfish, but deep down, you knew she needed grace, and you offered that to her. God promised to forgive us when we ask. When you believed and accepted His Son, He did that for you, covering everything, past, present and future. He'll forgive you this, too. You can't bear that burden or think your reasoning affected her choice in any way. That would be arrogant, after all. It's God's salvation to offer, not ours. He alone bears the consequences–good or bad–for the choices people make. And it was…her choice. Hers alone."

His eyes finally met mine, deep, chocolate brown eyes that were so honest. My lips, pressed together in an attempt to hinder my own confession, parted, but the buzz of his phone interrupted our intimate moment.

"Thank you," he whispered, standing.

"You're still ahead." I shrugged. In our game of saving each other, he was definitely winning. I tapped my finger playfully on his chin as he raised his phone to his ear.

"Carter."

It was Paul with an update. He was still working on the passenger lists from Port Authority and Immigration. The crosscheck containing the names Elena and Marco didn't turn up any useful leads.

"Can you add anything with Central New Orleans Behavioral Health to the search parameters? Just see what comes up?" Will asked.

After ending the call, Will went down to the lobby to check out. Our encounter at the burned hospital and Hardy's tip had him spooked. He wanted to keep moving.

I had just finished packing my bag when the room phone rang. I figured it was Will, telling me he was ready with the car.

"Hey, I'm not quite…"

"Ms. Jones?" A man interrupted, keeping his voice hushed and disguised.

"I think you have the wrong room."

"Isn't this the Ms. Jones who was snooping around the hospital yesterday? Or should I say Ms. Stone?"

I almost threw the phone down, but the door clicked open as Will walked in and I froze.

"We're all checked out–just need to return the key. There's already a huge crowd out there. We should get going."

"Do not react," the man instructed.

My first thought was that it was Hardy, but this voice was not his. It belonged to someone younger, someone less gruff but much more sinister.

I turned away from Will, who thankfully disappeared behind a closed bathroom door.

"Who is this?" I hissed.

"Someone who can help you find what you're looking for."

"I…I don't know what you're talking about."

"I don't have time for games. Come outside–alone. You have five minutes."

I looked over my shoulder. Will was still in the bathroom.

"I can't…"

"Figure it out." The man sounded annoyed. "Or else."

Will stepped out of the bathroom, his back still to me as he packed. A tiny red dot appeared on his shirt, bright and bouncing and right on target to pierce straight through his heart.

"Five minutes," the man repeated.

"Okay." I held my breath, the hand that held the receiver shaking as I spoke. "Okay, I will."

The red light disappeared and a final hollow click echoed in my ear. I watched my trembling hand lower the receiver back onto the cradle, requiring the help of my other to get it into place.

"Who was that?"

I jumped at Will's question.

"Front desk." My mouth was dry; it hurt my throat to talk. "Um, they want to give us a coupon for our next visit."

"Oh?"

"Yeah, I'll go get it. Meet you at the car?"

I hurried to the door, avoiding his gaze.

"Give me just a minute. I'm almost ready," he said.

My hand was already on the door handle. I felt the prickling sting of a cool sweat across my forehead. The distant sound of a marching band wafted up from below. It's quick tempo matching that of my pounding heart.

"It's okay, don't rush. I'd like to get a glimpse of the parade anyway."

Please don't argue.

I pulled the door open, but he was there in an instant, his hand holding it closed. I clenched my teeth; two minutes had already passed.

"What is going on, really?" He towered beside me, imposing.

"Nothing… I…"

"You're acting strange."

So, that's how I'd have to play it–I'd fake a fight. My eyes were daggers; I launched a deadly and unexpected assault.

"How exactly am I supposed to act, Will? My grandmother just died, probably because she was trying to help me find some kind of serial killer that may or may not be involved in human trafficking and blowing up a bunch of people. We have meaningless clues that keep leading to dead ends. I am stressed. I'm upset, and I need some space–so will you please move?"

The knife plunged deep and he recoiled. Victory was easy–too easy–and it felt terrible. Maybe it wasn't so fake. I hated the injured look on his face, and I hated even more that I'd been the one to put it there, but it was better than a bullet hole in his chest, and he wasn't blocking the door anymore. Another minute had passed.

I dashed down the hall towards the stairs, risking a glance back at our room. He lingered in the open doorway, a mix of shock and suspicion painted across his face.

I slid down the stairs by the rails, almost falling on my face in the rush. The metal exit door collided noisily with the outer wall as I burst through, searching the alley for the mystery caller. Somewhere inside, I was aware of how foolish and reckless it was to continue on this course. But the image of that tiny red laser light on Will's back was all the motivation I needed to ignore warning and reason. The alley was empty. Was I too late? I ran toward the front of the building and looked up, searching the balcony until I found our room. The glass windows were still intact. I let out a breath, a rush of relief quelling the nausea in my stomach.

The street ahead was full of parade watchers. A giant float decorated with colorful paper rolled slowly by, its riders tossing beads, candy, and plastic doubloons at the cheering crowd. Masked faces drew close, sending spike after spike of alarm through me with each surge. A crowd of bodies with unidentifiable faces closed in around me, urging me unwillingly away from the sidewalk and into their midst. Behind elaborately decorated masks, wild eyes and wide smiling mouths bounced in rhythm on all sides. Flashes of purple, green, and gold sparkled in the sun, baubles and beads raining from above as greedy hands snatched them from the sky. This was a mistake–all wrong.

The chaos and disorder, though meant to be enjoyable, was nothing but upsetting for me. I spun, trying to find an exit, a path back to the safety of the sidewalk, but the pulsing crowd swept me further into its depths. A warm hand slid into mine and my eyes closed briefly in relief before turning to face Will and beg forgiveness for my outburst.

But I was jerked sharply backwards, landing hard against the solid frame of someone tall. Someone who was not Will. He spun me to face him, his features, unlike most of the others, completely veiled by a dark blue and terrifyingly expressionless mask. Nearly black irises captured me from behind the emotionless veil, the only human feature visible as his head and body were fully covered with a cloak of rich navy velvet.

Even his hands, one of which painfully gripped my arm, forcing my trembling body to his chest, were covered with matching navy gloves.

"Scream and someone dies." He jerked me closer, the same voice from the phone hissing in my ear.

Before he finished speaking my heart had taken off, pounding hard against my ribs and sending a shot of fiery adrenaline through my limbs. Run! I wanted nothing more than to run, but the hard round barrel of a gun digging into my side kept me frozen in place. Happy, unsuspecting people packed tighter in on all sides, not one of them aware of the threat just inches from their jubilee. I prayed, for their own safety, that they remained blissfully ignorant. His piercing black eyes demanded obedience, even more than the weapon, and he kept them centered on mine as we moved out of the crowd into the privacy of the alley. When we stepped free of the mob and were semi-hidden in the narrowness of the space between buildings, he spun me again, my back pressing hard against the rock of his chest. He kept his weapon low but moved his hand upwards, long, thin fingers working their way up to my neck.

I tried to bring my racing thoughts under control and ignore my brain's chastisement of such rash and foolish behavior. He could drag me down this alley and into a waiting vehicle in seconds, and I needed to keep that from happening.

"You said you could help." My voice was strained, my dry throat working hard to form words.

"She's going to do it again."

"Do what?" I grunted as he pushed the weapon harder, metal grating painfully against my bones.

"You were there! You know what—unless she finds what she's looking for, she'll try to kill them all."

"What is she looking for?"

He leaned close, the heat from his body radiating against me. He smelled sterile, like rubbing alcohol and bleach. He was close, too close. His hand was still at the base of my neck, unmoving.

"You." He breathed. "She wants you."

I had so many questions. He had the perfect opportunity to take me, but he didn't. I wanted to turn around and remove his mask: to see his face, look in his eyes, and gauge his intentions. He could have been lying. Maybe she even sent him to trick me, to get me alone. I couldn't be sure, but one thing was clear–this man knew Elena.

"I know you're thinking you can catch her, but you won't. She will never stop until she gets what she wants."

"Why not just take me to her?" It was risky to tempt him, but if he was talking, he wasn't leaving.

He jerked his hand away from my sternum and closed his fingers instead around the soft flesh of my upper arm, pulling me further back into the shadows. My questions were frustrating him; he seemed confused, scrambled, as if he were two people trying to operate the same piece of machinery.

"You have to go to her. Just you."

"I don't understand." That's what I was trying to do: to go to her!

I was angering him. It was dangerous–I knew that–but I needed time. He wouldn't just say exactly he wanted from me, and everything I felt from him was in pieces, clashing like a piano that was out of tune.

"I'm giving you a chance to save your husband." An unexpected tenderness rode in on the back of his words.

My husband. My eyes shot up. I felt him before I saw him. Across the street, Will's dark head was bobbing above the crowd, searching. He was anxious, a building frustration forcing his hands up and through his hair.

I watched him, but as if from some other realm, hidden behind a veil that kept us invisible. So, that was it. This man wasn't offering a way to stop Elena or bring her to justice. He was delivering the verdict, telling me the only way to quell her appetite…to keep her from devouring another throng of innocent people…to save Will…was to give her the one meal she truly desired. A sacrificial lamb, savory and filled with delectable supernatural flavor. Me.

Will's frantic searching stilled. He became the only stationary thing in a rippling sea of movement and chaos. I watched his chest rise and fall as he took deep, controlled breaths and systematically scanned the crowd, the street, the buildings. His eyes would find us in seconds. There was no time for the rest of my questions, so I chose the most important, the only one that truly mattered.

"Where?"

"Mercy down…" He tensed, growling in frustration; he must have seen Will too. "I will contact you. When I do, get rid of him and say nothing of this!"

"Wait…" *Mercy down*? What does that mean?

"Nothing–or next time, his chance is gone."

He shoved me hard into the crowd. I flew directly into the arms of a sweaty shirtless man with a neck full of plastic beads. He laughed and came at me with half open eyes and breath that smelled like a brewery.

"Hey, sweetheart! You wanna party?" His slurred words slid over my ears as his arm snaked around my waist, his slimy fingers finding the flesh beneath my shirt. I cringed, squirming to get away.

Suddenly, he flew backwards, hitting the pavement hard, the drink in his red plastic cup splashing on the ground. Unphased, he rolled over and kept laughing as his friends tried unsuccessfully to drag him to his feet.

Will loomed on the sidewalk, the fire in his eyes hot enough to force everyone around to give him a wide berth. His fists were clenched, knuckles white and the muscles in his forearms bulging as he flexed. I looked back into the alley, but it was vacant.

Will stepped towards the drunk man, who was still trying to get up, and I launched myself between them, pushing back with my hands on his chest. It didn't faze him; he kept moving.

"No! Will! Don't!" He plowed forward unfettered, dragging me with him, as if I were nothing but a wisp of wind. "Will, look at me."

He froze; his eyes, dark and furious, slowly shifted to mine and for the first time, I was afraid of what I saw there. Instinctively, I shrunk away, but he snatched my hand, regret carving a path across his features. People were watching, too many eyes intruding on our private world. Despite my reservations, I pulled him away from the crowd, into the same alley where I'd just been accosted by the mysterious informant.

"What is wrong with you?" I yelled over the noise of the festivities, which had resumed as if we'd never been there.

"Me?" He threw his hands up and glared at me like I'd just asked him the most ridiculous question. "Do you even realize…"

He shook his head, unable to finish. His whole body was twitching and both hands dove, fingers first, through his hair, clamping together behind his head as if he were trying to restrain himself.

"Andy, what are you even doing out here?"

I was about to tell him what happened; it was screaming inside, demanding to be released. I could still feel the hands of the man from the alley, painful and pleading. My skin burned where they'd touched, ached where he'd squeezed, and I feared it would be so forever, unless…

I grabbed Will's shirt, jerking him towards me. My hands slid up to his neck, my fingers red against his flesh, bringing him close. My lips pressed against his, begging for a new memory, for anything to replace the thoughts that kept my insides twisted in knots. He returned my kiss, equally as desperate, his hands hungrily closing in around my waist, but then his touch grew too anxious and burned just as hot as the one I was trying to forget.

A ball of fire unfurled in my stomach, spreading its blazing tendrils like a plague throughout each nerve until every cell was infected and scorched by its heat. *No, this isn't helping—this is worse.*

He wrapped his arm around my waist, lifting me and walking us backwards until my back made contact with the rough bricks of the inn's wall. My feet touched the ground again as he moved his hands to grip my arms. His fingers wound too tightly, pressing into the bruised grooves my attacker had left behind. There was no tenderness exchanged between us—only want—only the desperate desire to quench pain's unrelenting thirst. But the sorrow, the anxious uncertainty, and chaotic confusion we shared couldn't be eased, even by the comfort of each other. Like a bandaid over a gaping wound, it only served to worsen our condition. We needed something more, something beyond the depths of human ability.

This was wrong; this wasn't love between us. It was fire and ice, it was grief and passion and fear. It was a fight, and we were both losing.

"Stop."

I wasn't talking to him but without warning, he dropped his hands, as if a switch were flipped, and stumbled back, leaving me cold and breathless. I slapped away a single angry tear from my cheek.

He was a statue, his expression devoid of emotion. I turned away, defensively folding my arms across my chest.

"Andy." My name was strained on his tongue, agony in his voice. "What are we doing here?"

A stabbing pain attacked my stomach, and I squeezed my arms tighter.

"Please, let's go home," he pleaded.

"I can't," I whispered. "Not yet."

She's going to do it again. The man's cryptic warning was still fresh in my mind, along with vivid images of the charred remains of a hospital now only occupied by the ghosts of murdered residents.

"Why?" He didn't approach, scared to touch me.

I couldn't tell him the truth. I wanted to, but I could still see the red dot from a laser site dancing across his back, just as clear as it had been in our room. I tightened my grip around my stomach even more, wishing to fold in on myself until I disappeared altogether. Will's pained and confused expression added to the weight of this impossible situation and I turned away, unable to bear it. I fished around for some distraction, some reason to stay.

"Isn't Paul sending a list? We need to…"

"We can do that from anywhere."

"What if something else comes up? We should be here."

I paced the alley, terrified he'd finally force his hand and drag me away.

"Don't you still think she's here somewhere? Can't you just…feel it?"

He didn't answer. I stopped, facing off with him in the private cove of a dirty alleyway where, around us, all manner of debauchery marched in mocking circles.

"If we don't find anything by this weekend, we can go back. Just a few more days, please?"

"Fine." His eyes were uncertain, but his tone was relenting.

I'd won the battle, but my victory felt empty, triumph diluted by secrets and deceit. I prayed the promised intel would come soon. All the plates I was spinning, precariously balanced on the unstable sticks of my sanity, were growing in number. They were dangerously close to crashing down around me, shattering my already broken life into an irreparable heap.

CHAPTER 23

Any attempts to convince Will to stay at the inn were in vain; my reasoning was weak and drew too much suspicion. If the man from the alley found me once, surely he could again. I prayed our move wouldn't anger him and cause him to withdraw his promise of information.

I made excuse after excuse for not leaving the room once we settled in the new hotel. My behavior was already erratic and unpredictable, and even though it felt like a dirty betrayal, I continued to use Esther's death as explanation for my actions. My greatest weapon, however, became affection, which I wielded unrelentingly, pressing upon him freely when he attempted to question my decisions, and punishing him mercilessly by withholding otherwise. Each pass by a mirror further reflected my slow descent into dark poisonous waters, ruinous and without a measure of depth.

But it didn't matter. The decision had been made mere seconds after the man from the alley presented his ultimatum. Turn myself over to Elena, or lose Will and who knows how many others.

There was only that. Only getting to her without sacrificing anyone else–although from the darkening crease on his brow, I knew there was one more casualty of her wrath. His heart would be broken, but his life would be spared. I tried to make peace with that compromise.

Wednesday, Will went to City Hall to put in a request for records of businesses matching any name close to the one we were searching for and I waited for a phone call–or any kind of contact–that never came.

Thursday, we changed hotels again, and Will went to pick up the results from his query. When his search resulted in yet another dead end, he tried to convince me once more to go home.

"Just a few more days," I said softly, running my hand down his arm, fingertips barely touching his skin.

He turned away, subtly rubbing his arm where I'd touched him and nodded without looking at me.

By Saturday, Will's suspicion had brimmed to the point of overflow; I had to do something resembling normalcy. While he was in the shower, I hurried to the lobby and left instructions with the desk clerk in case the mystery man called. When I returned with a decoy soda and news that I wanted to go with him, he visibly relaxed.

"You know, you're right. I've been cooped up in here and it's not doing any good. I know I've been on edge the last few days; take me to lunch?"

The hopefulness in his response sent a dagger of treachery into my gut. As if to seal any chance of redemption, I also suggested a picnic and walk through the park, sneaking a call to the hotel while he went inside the restaurant. No messages yet.

Encouraged by my emergence from hibernation, his enthusiasm for our mission was renewed. We visited the library, searching the archives and microfiche. I took the chance to secretly search for any places containing the name Mercy, but came up empty. After several hours, I desperately wanted to steal away and check in with the hotel again.

"I'm going to take a break." I stood behind Will's chair and wrapped my arms around his shoulders.

"Alright. I'm almost done here."

He shifted forward, intently searching the article he'd scrolled to. His phone was on the desk beside him. I leaned around the other side, and he turned, placing a soft kiss on the cheek I offered.

"See you in a minute." I smiled and walked away, his phone in my pocket.

As soon as I stepped outside, I called the hotel and asked the clerk if there were any messages. She said no. I pushed the end call button a little too hard and the phone clattered to the ground.

"Oh! There it is." Will jogged down the steps to meet me.

"Yeah, I uh…was going to call Jacob, but I'll do it later. Find anything?" The lies flowed easily now, as water over smoothed rocks, their resistance worn by time and use.

"No." He didn't elaborate.

It was Saturday evening. Will had promised to stay until the weekend. Tomorrow it would be over, and I wouldn't be able to convince him to wait any longer. We both agreed there were people in danger, but we had no evidence, no suspects, and no victims. Every time I remembered that, the little seed of anger sprouted up just a bit more. It had now been four days and the man from the alley had yet to make any contact. I had to face the possibility that it was just another false hope–that she was toying with me, sending him to scare us away. Any reasonable person would have taken the visit at face value and given his warning due respect, but I was far beyond reason's reach.

Once back at the hotel, instead of obsessing over a message I would obviously never receive–just another in a long line of meaningless messages–I spent the evening furiously searching the list Paul had finally sent, hoping beyond hope there would be something there. Going home felt like failure, and ever since that phone call, I kept seeing phantom laser lights on everyone and everything. I couldn't live the rest of my life this way, looking over my shoulder, waiting for the other shoe to drop.

I couldn't stand to even consider it.

Will stepped out several times to make or receive phone calls, but I barely noticed. There had to be something we missed, some bit of information that would lead us to Elena. I had moved from the table to the bed, and eventually from the bed to the floor as I laid out page after page, trying to find something–anything.

On my fifth time through the passenger list, I had an epiphany. I launched myself across the floor to Taklos' file that Jake had sent over. We had printed out all the documents in the hotel's lobby office in Knoxville. I tore into the folder and flipped quickly through pages until I found what I was looking for.

On the page detailing the little information available on Dovanny Taklos' childhood, one paragraph listed his home as Municipal

Orphanage, but only until he was six. I scoured the rest of the pages, finding some photocopies of official looking Russian documents. Hidden on the margin of page two was a handwritten note in Russian. I'd been given a crash course in the language in preparation for my mission with Taklos and was able to decipher one phrase.

"Released to custody of O. Kusnetsov - Aug 4, 1994."

The scribble was followed by some more Russian words I didn't know how to translate. With that paper clenched in my hand, I crawled across the floor to the pages with lists of passengers. I ran my finger down the columns until I found the one I was looking for. On page three, halfway down, my finger stopped on the name Oatis Kusnetsov, who entered the country weeks before Taklos under a medical visa.

"Hey, Will! Look at this!" I called, turning around. He wasn't in the room. I pulled myself up off the floor and groaned. My body was stiff from hunching over the pages all evening. I looked through the curtains onto the walkway outside of our room, but didn't find him out there either.

I picked up the hotel phone, and paced back and forth across the floor, chewing on my fingernails. He didn't answer. I aggressively punched his number again. It rang once before he answered.

"Andy?" It sounded like he was driving.

"Where are you?" I asked, my tone accusatory and harsh.

"I went to get dinner. Don't you remember?" he answered, sounding defensive.

No. I didn't remember.

"I asked you what you wanted; you said, 'surprise me,'" he continued.

I didn't remember any of this.

"Andy, I really think…"

"No. I remember. I'm sorry…I just…um, I'm just tired." I stuttered through another lie.

I heard him take a long deep breath.

"I'm on my way back." His voice was hard, edged with some emotion that I couldn't place.

When Will stepped through the door, he stopped short and his eyes scanned the room, taking in the sea of papers I'd spread out. There was no amusement in his expression as he placed a large brown paper bag on the round table by the window.

I'd already forgotten about our phone conversation.

"You've been busy," he said.

"Look…look at this!" I shoved the two papers with matching names towards him.

He took a long time to read each one. I dug into the bag of food and was already stuffing a handful of french fries in my mouth when I pulled out a pamphlet that was hiding between two stacks of napkins. It was a colorful brochure showcasing the newly remodeled downtown hospital, MMH.

"What's this?"

"It was stuck under my windshield wiper. I guess they're advertising." Will barely glanced up from the papers.

"Well?" I said, my mouth full.

"Looks like you found something."

"Right?" I said excitedly. "I think that could be Goncharov, like an alias–the first name is similar."

"Okay…well, we can look into it tomorrow," he said, sitting down.

I swallowed the fries and sank into a chair across from him. "Isn't there someone you can call tonight?"

"Andy, it's almost ten o'clock…on a Saturday night." He put the two pages together and laid them on the table.

I sat up tall in the chair and looked out the window. He was right; it was dark outside.

"You've been staring at those pages for hours, and a computer screen for hours before that," he said softly, lowering his eyes. "Have you talked to Jacob yet?"

I looked from the window towards him. His head was down, but his eyes cut up to meet mine. He held my gaze for a few seconds before I shrugged and started unpacking the rest of our dinner.

"Um…no, I guess I wanted to have some good news to give him before I called." I handed him a Styrofoam take-out tray.

"I'm sure he wants to hear from you, regardless of the updates," he said, tearing open a plastic cutlery package and holding it out for me.

"I'll call him tomorrow."

"Tomorrow is Sunday." He poked at his food with his own plastic fork. Then when I stared blankly, he said, "I think we should go to church."

I opened the to-go container filled with creamy crawfish etouffee over rice, and looked up at him, prepared to cover my hesitation with excitement about the food. His expression was firm; there was no use discussing it.

I suddenly felt ashamed that I'd even considered arguing over attending church.

"Sure," I said, giving him an agreeable smile.

I felt his eyes as I turned my attention back to my dinner and with my first bite, swallowed down the aggravation at being constantly watched like a side show act at the carnival. I was pretty hungry, and it was delicious even with the extra side of annoyance I didn't order. After we finished our meal with an obvious and uncomfortable lack of conversation, Will went down to the lobby and returned with a white foam cup, which he presented like a peace offering.

"What is this?" I asked, accepting his gift.

"Tea–chamomile."

"You know about tea now?" I was suspicious but breathed in the soothing floral aroma.

"I learned a few things from your uncle." He started gathering up all the papers I'd spread over almost every surface of our small hotel room. As he turned, I noticed the hospital pamphlet sticking out of his back pocket. "Drink up; it'll help you sleep."

Although I doubted its effectiveness, I humored him. Will mentioned that I had been talking in my restless sleep, but I wasn't making sense. In truth, my waking thoughts weren't making much sense either. Who were we even searching for? Elena, Goncharov, Kusnetsov, or someone else entirely? Maybe the man who'd grabbed and threatened me in the alley? I just wanted to find someone, anyone to take responsibility for all this pain. Surely, we would come across some kind of a solid lead to find Elena and turn her into the proper authorities, whoever they were. If we couldn't...well, I had been forming a plan for that too. Once she was taken care of, then I would sleep.

As I sipped, we watched the news. There were several stories about local politicians, a weather report indicating rain in Sunday's forecast, and in the world news report, there was an update on the volatile situation in Sudan.

A pretty blonde reporter wearing a bright blue suit spoke in a professional tone from behind the news desk.

"Leaders from the International Summit are still attempting to resolve the matter of President Deng's proposed ban on foreign aid from religious organizations. John Robins, founder of the Christian organization *Mercy*

Calls, was scheduled to speak last week on behalf of the over two-hundred missionaries and ministry workers currently serving in Sudan.

"However, Robins' trip was suddenly cancelled when his six-year-old daughter went missing from their Texas home. Robins has not spoken to reporters or released a statement as to any plans to attend the summit.

"If Deng is successful with his proposal, all religious aid workers will be forced to vacate the country immediately or face imprisonment. Robins' appeal was an anticipated event, and it is unclear whether summit leadership will postpone their decision.

"In other parts of Africa, a series of viral outbreaks have raised concern with the World Health Organization. Travel advisories have been issued to Zambia and South Africa."

"I think I'm going to take a shower," I said, after the political commentary portion of the news began. I never did enjoy listening to people argue.

"Okay." Will smiled weakly. He looked like he wanted to reach for me, but he didn't.

I hated this thing that stood between us. It was made of invisible stones, expertly laid. A wall that kept growing, pushing us further apart. I knew if I looked down at my hands, I would see them building it, brick by brick.

I escaped to the bathroom. The steaming water was refreshing and relaxing enough that I thought I might actually have a chance of falling asleep. As I turned the faucet off, I heard Will's muffled voice through the door.

I wrapped myself in a towel and cracked the door quietly. He held his phone and tossed a bottle of painkillers into his duffle bag.

"Jacob…" he said. "I think we have a problem."

CHAPTER 24

"A ndy." Will sat on the edge of the bed, unbuttoning the blue oxford shirt he'd worn to church.

I looked at his reflection in the mirror as I brushed out the curls in my hair.

"We need to talk."

"About what?"

"There's something wrong."

I hurried to slip a baggy sweatshirt over my head and turned around to face him, my voice edged with concern, "Are you okay? Is it your back?"

"It's not about me." He stared down at his open hands.

I knew then what was coming. Heat flashed up my neck and spread across my cheeks. I saw its rosy trail as I spun back around and mentally ran through a list of possible ways to avoid this conversation.

"Are you hungry?" I glanced up hopefully. "We can talk over lunch."

"Andy," he chastised me softly.

I tried honesty. "I don't want to do this right now."

He stood up. "Well, I don't either."

"Then let's not!"

I flashed a flirtatious smile and started towards him.

"Stop doing that," he said forcefully, putting his hand out. I froze. He saw my confused expression. "Stop using that to avoid talking to me. It's not playing fair. I love you, and we have got to talk about what is going on with you."

"There's nothing going on. I'm fine." I held my hands up.

"Baby, you are not fine." He cocked his head to the side.

I hated it, but that word that usually made my heart skip a beat now just made me mad.

"Why do you think there's something wrong with me?"

"Because…you're just not you, Andy. You don't cry anymore." He lowered his head when he said it, as if it hurt him to admit. "Not even when Esther died."

I huffed and folded my arms defiantly. "So, because I don't break down at every little thing now, there's something wrong? Is it because you're afraid I won't depend on you so much anymore?"

"Every little thing? Can you even hear yourself? And don't try to make this about me. This is one hundred percent about you, and you know it."

"Oh, please," I said sarcastically under my breath. I blinked; there was no burning of salt from tears, and my throat wasn't tight from swallowing back the emotion. There was nothing but the comfortable easiness of rage.

"Where's your necklace?"

"What necklace?"

He threw his hands up. "What necklace? Your lion necklace. You've only worn it every single day since Esther gave it to you. You didn't think I would notice?"

"It's a necklace, Will. It's not like I threw my wedding ring away," I snapped.

"You might as well have." I don't think he meant for me to hear, but I did.

"Now who's not playing fair."

"Look, I don't want to do this without you, but right now, I feel like you are long gone." He stepped back and sank onto the bed, his head dropping into his hands. "I'm trying to help you."

"You're always trying to protect me from everything! It's not cute anymore!"

"I said 'help you,' and I'm not trying to be cute." Will ran a hand through his hair.

I turned away. Seeing him like that made me feel too guilty. I rested both palms on the countertop and stared at my reflection again. The girl in the mirror was hard; her eyes sparked with fire, her jaw set tight, and lips drawn in a sharp straight line.

I flicked my eyes to Will, watching as he picked up his phone, looked at the screen, and put it back down.

"Jacob is here," he spoke as matter-of-factly as if he were giving a weather report.

"What?" I turned around sharply. "Why?"

"I called him." He shrugged, looking so defeated, so lost.

"Why would you do that?"

"Because I don't know what else to do." The emphasis he placed on each word exaggerated his desperation.

"What is this–an intervention?" I spat. "He's just lost his mom, Will; he's dealing with that."

"Yes, Andy, I know that. And he's dealing with it by himself, because we are here, and not there with him." His words cut deep. They burned my ears and echoed eerily in my mind.

"He's coming to take you home." There was nothing but resolve in his tone as he moved towards the door. I could hear Jacob's footsteps on the walkway outside.

"Why, Will? Why now?" I hated the whine in my voice. "I am doing everything I can to…why are you doing this?"

He stopped, his hand on the doorknob. He looked over his shoulder, but not directly at me.

"Because I need to make sure you're not going to…" He stopped and took a deep breath. "The mission–we need to focus on the mission. I know you're willing to sacrifice, but what God wants more than our sacrifice is our obedience."

Esther had spoken those same words. He couldn't have known that. Everyone kept saying these spiritual things to me that I didn't understand.

"What are you talking about?" I had thought of nothing but the mission this whole time. My heart started to race. How could he do this? I had to see this through–I had to make sure she was brought to justice somehow. He couldn't make me leave now.

"I told you…you talk in your sleep."

What? What was that supposed to mean? I looked around, but there was no way out. I was trapped. He did this on purpose; he planned it. I had never felt this way before, but in that moment, I was furious with my husband. I wanted to hurt him.

"I will never forgive you for this," I hissed, regretting it before I even finished.

His shoulders sagged. Will opened the door, and Jacob's silhouette appeared in the doorway. They exchanged a quick glance and Jacob stepped inside.

"I'm not leaving," I said defiantly, before either of them could speak.

They looked at each other again. Will walked towards me. I backed as far as I could into the corner. I knew the fury written all over my face equally matched the pain in his. He wrapped his arms around me, and my body went stiff. I didn't relax into his embrace, even though there was nothing threatening about him.

"I won't force you," he whispered. "Please, talk to Jacob…please."

For the first time in a long while, I felt my heart clench in agony. His words were so heavy, and I could feel his hurt as if it were my own. My arms longed to wrap themselves around him, but I kept them still. He held me for a few more seconds, kissed my forehead, and stepped away. He didn't look back as he walked towards the door, only stopping to place a heavy hand on Jacob's shoulder.

"I'll be on the balcony," he said to Jacob, who nodded without taking his eyes off of me. Then he was gone, taking all of the air in the room with him. I knew we'd just crossed over the peak. My stomach clenched in preparation for the plummet.

Jacob stood silently for several minutes.

"I don't know why he called you all the way down here. I'm fine," I said, throwing up my hands and finally ending our unspoken showdown.

"I've never known you to be a liar, Andy." His words stung.

"I'm not…you know what, fine. Let's get this over with." I marched across the room and plopped down into one of the uncomfortable square framed chairs by the window.

"I think you should come back with me," Jacob said, still standing.

"And I think I should not." I spoke with such finality, my tone so sarcastic, I even surprised myself.

He stared at me, unphased.

"You're a fighter, Andy, but I'm not your enemy."

I squared my jaw, choosing to ignore the truth he spoke. My eyes told him I wasn't giving in. I knew I'd face obstacles trying to do what was right, but I never imagined those would include my own family.

"Alright." He lowered himself into the chair across the table from me. "Then we are going to have a tough conversation right now."

My cheeks flushed again. Somewhere inside, the knowledge that I was acting like a rebellious teenager existed, but it was buried so far under my self-righteousness that it was easy to ignore. Jacob sat up straight and folded his hands together on the shiny varnished tabletop.

"You listen to me, Joanna." He sounded so much like his mother, I had to look up at the ceiling to stomach it. "I get it. You are angry, and you have every right to be, but this is more than that. You're letting that anger take over, and it's going to destroy you."

"I'm not angry. I just want to do what we came to do." I slouched back in the chair.

"It's okay to be angry," he said softly.

Not this angry.

I shot a harsh glance his way. "I know it is, but I'm not."

"Seriously, Andy…" he started.

"Okay…fine. I'm angry, is that what you want me to say? I'm furious. Filled with rage! There, I said it." I threw my hands up and glared out of the window. That was the first truthful thing I'd said all day. I could see Will's shadow on the balcony. *I miss him.*

"It's not a sin to be angry, you know," he said softly. "Even Jesus felt it. Injustice should result in righteous anger."

His words were surprising. Surely, what I felt was wrong; I'd known that, but just couldn't stop myself from reveling in it.

"It's what you do with that anger that matters. Jesus was righteously angry because the people were defiling the temple, the place where they were supposed to be worshipping God. He was completely justified in his emotions and His reaction, for that matter, because He is God. Feelings aren't wrong or sinful; they just are. But we can't be ruled by them. How we respond to them is our choice, and that's where we get into trouble."

I listened without responding. I wanted it to be true.

"But you are more than just angry. You've got to know that. That is why Will called me. He loves you, and so do I. We cannot let you continue on this way."

"What does it matter? As long as the job gets done."

Something flashed across his face; his patient resolve wavered, and his cheeks grew red.

"Because if you met her right now, right this minute–you would kill her, and you'd never find true answers, or anyone she might be hurting." He was harsh, spitting his words at me like bullets. "You're willing to sacrifice them and yourself for revenge. That's why it matters."

"How could you say that?"

"I didn't say it–you did. In your sleep. We know, Andy…we know what you're planning to do. If you don't find her, you're going into the dream, and you're going to take her out. Tell me I'm wrong."

Will's words suddenly made sense. I opened my mouth to disagree, but I couldn't. There was no defense against the truth. I had been planning just that. If we couldn't find her, I was going to end it.

"You might want vengeance," he said. "Most would even say you deserve it, but it's not yours to have. It's God's and His alone."

"Then why would He give me this ability if I'm not meant to use it?"

"He might have given you the ability, but everyone has the ability to kill; they don't need some supernatural power to do it. But He also gave you–and everyone else–a choice, because that's what true love is: a choice."

"What do you want from me?" I couldn't stay seated any longer and shot up, the chair falling backwards behind me.

"Talk to me, for starters," he said softly, unphased by my actions. "Just tell me the truth."

I stared at him. He was kind. Even now, when I was so hateful and rude, he was nothing but kind. How was that possible?

"Andy, you've had to mature so quickly. So much has happened in just a few months, and there's no way we could have prepared you for all this. I'm so sorry. God chose you for this mission, but somewhere along the way, the mission got lost." He lowered his head.

"Well, I wish He didn't choose me," I said, my voice high.

"I know; I wish the same. I wish you didn't have to be the one, but I know that God loves you. He does." Jacob leaned forward.

"Then why…" I realized I was loud and stopped. I didn't want Will to hear. I was inches from my breaking point, and I didn't want him to see me shatter. "What happened to her?"

It took him a second to process my question.

"She just… died."

"But she was better. When I talked to her, she sounded better." It was silly to argue; nothing would change the fact that she was gone. "Was it…

was it because I made you take her somewhere else?"

"She was weak, but the move didn't affect her."

"The move didn't–but something else did?"

"No. I didn't mean it that way. Nothing out of the ordinary happened except–"

He stopped; his brows drew together as if he were remembering something for the first time.

"Except what?"

"No…it's nothing."

"Talking goes both ways, Jacob." Resolved, I folded my arms and stared him down with raised brows.

When he saw I wasn't giving in, he sighed.

"I'm not sure. After she talked to you that last time, she was happy, really happy. Then a little while later, so just kind of…zoned out? It was just for a few minutes. I don't even know why I thought of it, but that had nothing to do with you."

No. No, it couldn't be. A little while after I talked with her, I was on Jubal's boat. I was remembering.

"Why would she do that? I didn't ask her to do that!" My hands flew to my chest, holding my bones together as they tried to split apart and spill my heart out onto the floor. We were zooming downhill fast…too fast. No air…couldn't breathe…

"What are you talking about?" Jacob moved slowly around the table, approaching with his hands outstretched, reaching for me.

I skirted away from him, my eyes wide and frantic like a cornered animal. Something wild bubbled up inside, something explosive and poisonous.

"It was me! She was helping me! I felt her–I was trying to remember and I felt her there! Jacob…why did she do that? Why did she have to go? Why?"

I made my own choices and I have no regrets. That's what she said. *Well, you chose wrong, Esther!*

"I don't know. We might never know, but I believe Paul when he said that all things work together for the good of those who love God and who are called according to His purpose. But you also have to understand, His ways…"

I crossed the remaining inches to that edge I'd been avoiding and was instantly over, screaming at him with every manner of raw animal fury that had been building up. I didn't care what came out, I didn't care who heard, I didn't care about anything but releasing the pressure of a thousand bricks stacked on my chest.

"Good! How is any of this for my good or anyone's good? My parents are dead, my grandmother is dead, a whole hospital full of people–dead. Even Nadine is dead. Innocent people are being taken, and she's doing who knows what with them! How is any of that good?"

He stared at the feral thing before him with an unreadable expression. I'd rather it was anger or exasperation, but it looked a lot like compassion.

"You didn't let me finish. You're hearing, but you're not listening. It's not good. No one is saying that what is happening is good. Here's what you need to understand." His voice grew in strength and volume as he continued. "His ways are not our ways and His thoughts are not our thoughts. You're making judgements based on what *you* think should happen or how *you* think life should be. But His ways are so much higher, you can't even begin to understand. You think you know better than the God who spoke the universe into being? Who do you think you are?"

I threw my hands up in frustration.

"You say you believe in God, that you love Him. If that's true, then you have to trust Him to keep His promises. If we trust Him, truly trust Him, then we can remain in Him and all things *will* work together for our good–either now or eventually, even the terrible choices of other people. We have to remain, Andy, and believe that He will make all things right in the end."

"How can you ask me not to do something, when I'm probably the only one who can?"

"I'm not asking you to do nothing." His tone was steady and gentle. "We can't see the whole picture; we only see a tiny part. You're hearing the words, but you don't understand the meaning."

Remember.

Esther's words echoed in my mind. I shook my head, fighting against the truth he was telling me. I remembered Esther's hands holding that tapestry, showing me the indistinguishable mass of threads that made up the back. She had turned it over to reveal a beautifully created picture made from the same thread, and reminded me that while we are living in the midst of the messy backside, the Creator alone knew the masterpiece that would be on the front when it was finished.

"You have to let it go, Andy," Jacob pleaded. "You might have the power to avenge, but that doesn't mean you should. You can be angry, but you cannot let that control you. Hating her is the same as if you murder her yourself. Don't you see? It'll destroy every good thing."

"*She* destroyed my family, she destroyed…everything! She deserves every bit of what she gets!" I spoke through clenched teeth.

"Maybe she does, but then again so do I and so do you." He reached out for me again, but let his hand drop as I pulled away. "You need mercy just as much as she does."

Mercy and grace. Those were the words Sarah had spoken to me, the words that I had used to overcome Taklos. Surely he was as evil as Elena, and yet I hadn't hated him. Why was she so different?

"Are you saying I should just let her go?"

"No, of course not."

"Then what, Jacob? Just tell me what I'm supposed to do?" I begged.

"We rescue." His words slapped me in the face so hard that I stepped back.

"Rescue her too?"

"If that's what we're called to do, then yes." Then to make any further argument pointless, he said, "It's not about us, Andy. It's not about you, or me, or Will, or even Elena. It's only ever been about God and His plan. *He* is sovereign. *He* is completely in control, and because we love Him, we obey. It's not ever been about who we are, but who He is. It's our job to overcome evil with good, not the other way around. Remember, Joanna, please remember."

Remember.

"This hate you're carrying around–it's stealing your joy and the joy from everyone else, from their sacrifice. You don't think your mother would have chosen the same path to save you? Maggie would have died a thousand times to save you, to make a way for you to save others!"

Now his voice was loud.

His words smashed straight through that wall I had put up.

"Stop," I said softly.

He didn't stop. He stood up, towering over me.

"And Esther! She spent twenty-two years waiting, Andy! Waiting for you, waiting to help you find the truth. Do you even know how happy that made her? You would take that from her?"

I covered my ears. "Stop!"

He stepped close and grabbed my wrists, pulling my hands away from my head. His grip was firm, but it didn't hurt.

"No! You need to hear this. If you're going to let it take you, then you need to know who is going down with you."

"Stop it!"

"Maggie, Jonathan, Esther. All of them would willingly and joyfully give their lives again and again to save you, to save those people, to answer the call. How dare you diminish that with some selfish quest for revenge!"

I sank to the floor, my arms stretched up, wrists still in his grasp. I felt the first fiery prick of tears at the corners of my eyes.

"Jacob…please," I pleaded.

"I lost *my* sister and *my* mother too! And now I'm about to lose you. You'd take the last family I have left away from me? And what about Will? Do you even care about what's going to happen to him?" He let go of my arms, and they dropped heavily to the floor in front of me.

"Of course I do," I cried.

"You think Elena is destroying your family? She doesn't have to– you're doing a pretty good job of that yourself. You're so intent on destroying yourself, fine! But go ahead and dig two graves, because where you go, Will goes! How are you any different from her, then?"

That was it; I was undone. My forehead hit the carpet with a thump, and the wall crumbled; every last brick dissolved into smoke and ash. The angry seed I'd been nurturing shriveled up and broke apart. It wasn't completely gone, but it was dry and dying. An ugly guttural cry escaped my lips. Air rushed in, but my broken lungs refused to allow entry. I was falling…falling forever.

Through my breathless sobs, I heard the door open and then felt warm hands on my shoulders. A familiar heartbeat echoed in my empty chest. Without looking, I knew Will was on his knees in front of me, solid, strong, and waiting as I bottomed out from the downward descent.

He cupped my face in his hands as my eyes frantically searched his for relief from the crushing weight of my betrayal.

"Breathe, Andy."

With his words, my lungs opened, giving permission for air to enter. I reached for him with leaden hands and he folded me easily up into his ready arms.

"I'm sorry!" I cried into his shoulder. My tears left dark circles on his shirt. "I'm so sorry."

"I know, baby, I know." He pulled me tight against his chest, the warmth of his skin spreading life into all the dead places.

I put my hands on his shoulders and pushed him back. "I'm so angry, Will. I hate her." My last words came out as a sob. In desperation, I looked up at Jacob, who dropped to his knees beside us. "I don't know how to get rid of it!"

Will brushed my wet hair out of my face. "Keep talking, Andy."

"She took everything. She took my mom and dad. Jacob's family…our family! It's not fair; I didn't even get to know them. I had to watch them die over and over again because of her." There was no air–no movement in my lungs and a searing, pulsing sting shot up my spine into my brain.

I was small again, trapped in a metal cart that slid along rickety rails. This was the jerking part–the part where you get painfully slammed into the sides if there isn't someone there to cushion the impact. It wasn't Bash and Lily though, it was Jacob and Will. They were there on either side, taking the hits, absorbing the blows as the ride went on and on.

"Keep going, Andy," Jacob said, his hand rubbing circles on my shoulder.

"She took my life! Why does she get to live when they're dead? She took my grandmother. I barely got to know her, and she's gone. They're all gone… and… and…"

"And what…"

"It hurts," I said, barely able to speak the words.

My head dropped forward, resting against Will's chest. I fell apart in his hands and he moved them around, picking up all the pieces, putting them all back into place.

"Don't let her take you too, Andy. You can be angry. What she's done is unthinkable, and God will have justice, but don't be another of her victims," Jacob said, his hand still rubbing soothing circles on my back as my body shook with great heavy sobs. "Let God transform and renew your mind. Let Him have His vengeance."

"Forgive me…please forgive me," I begged both of them and God, although I doubted anyone but the Lord could translate the sounds I made into words.

They waited patiently as I cried. On the floor of that hotel room, I repented, confessing my hatred and asking God to take it, to help me let it go. Slowly, ever so slowly, the Lord swept away the ashes of my crushed spirit.

He mixed them with my tears of confession and molded them into something beautiful—something new. I sobbed until there were no tears left to cry and my head pounded so violently that my hands were balled up in fists at my temples, holding my skull to keep it from bursting apart. But it made sense that it would hurt to purge my heart from all the vileness I'd been storing. I welcomed the pain; it was a reminder that God loved me enough not to leave me to drown in my anger.

"Let's get her up." Jacob's voice was somewhere far away.

Will's hands slid under my arms and he lifted me like a child. He put one arm under my knees and carried me the few steps to the bed.

"Here, Andy." Jacob handed me a glass of water and a small capsule. "It's just an aspirin. You should sleep."

I took the medicine and swallowed it down before covering my swollen face with my arm. I felt the bed move as Will sat next to me. He ran his fingers through my hair, brushing it back from my face and neck.

"Put this on her wrists," Jacob said. "It's lavender."

I felt Will's thumbs, massaging circles of earthy-smelling oil onto my skin.

"I'll be right back." Will's lips were pressed against my temple.

"I know it's not over, but I'm proud of you, Andy. I love you," I heard Jacob say from across the room.

The two men stepped out the door. I could hear the low rumble of their voices just outside but couldn't make out what they were saying. I was exhausted, so very tired of the adrenaline from the never-ending up and down, side to side, glide into the gate only to start again. I just wanted to be done: to get off this roller coaster and leave it behind, never to ride again.

The calming sweet smell of lavender filled my nose. Its effects were working quickly, and I was thankful that sleep was near.

Lord...please forgive me. Help me not to hate her.

I wanted to pray more. I hadn't talked to God in so long, but a heavy black wave of sleep came and quickly swept me away.

CHAPTER 25

My rest wasn't dreamless, but it was peaceful. Until it wasn't. The familiar image of the little girl in white hovered over the waters of my dream world, flickering and staticky. She remained as she had before, simply standing in a dirty hallway, alone.

Something shifted behind her in the dark and I saw it approaching slowly with ghostly shadow hands and long-reaching fingers.

"RUN!" My words were breath, silent and unmoving. I tried to get to her, but my legs wouldn't budge because they had no form–only vapor. All efforts were futile, visibly slipping through my fingers like sand. I watched it pour, funneled through the slimming curved shape of an hourglass, pulling me with it. I fought and kicked, trying to swim out, and woke just before my head disappeared beneath the surface.

The room was bright, sunlight instead of sand pouring in through the light-colored curtains. The clock read 1:00, and I thought perhaps I was still dreaming until I realized it was 1:00 pm. I'd slept for almost twenty-four hours!

Sitting up, I looked around the room and found it empty. There was a note on top of my Bible, which still lay on the nightstand where I'd left it after church. It was from Will, letting me know he and Jacob would be in the lobby. Next to the note was a white envelope. I lifted the flap; my lion necklace was inside. As I tilted it, the silver pendant and chain slid out into my open palm. I stared at it for a minute, rubbing my thumb over the smooth figure of the lioness. She was strong and beautifully fierce. The emerald embedded at the tip of her tail seemed to glow as always. My fingers traveled up to my neck, to the place where she belonged, unsure if I was ready to put her back just yet.

I laid the necklace across my Bible, my fingers lingering to trace the script Will had embossed on its cover. *Joanna Adley Carter*. I noticed a small slip of white paper sticking out of the top of its silver-edged pages, and opened the book to the page it marked.

The paper slipped out, falling to the floor. I picked it up and read another note in my uncle's handwriting.

Andy,
Before you do anything else, read these words out loud, and listen to God's truth.
  Lamentations 3:19-24.

  I love you,
  Jacob

I turned to the book of Lamentations. Admittedly, I hadn't spent much time there; its name didn't sound very uplifting. Although it felt strange to read out loud sitting alone in a hotel room, after a deep breath, I did it anyway.

"I remember my affliction and my wandering,
The bitterness and the gall.
I well remember them,
And my soul is downcast within me.
Yet this I call to mind,
And therefore, I have hope;
Because of the Lord's great love, we are not consumed,
For his compassions never fail,
They are new every morning;
Great is your faithfulness.
I say to myself, 'The Lord is my portion;
therefore I will wait for him.'"

An emotional breath hitched in my throat, and as ancient truth filled my ears, a renewed strength filled my heart. The verses had awoken a ravenous hunger within and I devoured the rest of the chapter. As my mind absorbed verse after verse of hope, conviction, repentance, and forgiveness, I was reminded that while I had ignored Him for a time, God had not abandoned me. Justice was His alone to exact, and no longer my responsibility. I was free–finally free–from that burden.

I reconciled this chapter with the new covenant of grace that Jesus established. There would be a reckoning for the evils of man, and mercifully–for my own sake–grace to the sinner who had come to know the Savior. I held my Bible on my lap, silently staring at the words. A thickness filled the room, pressing in around me, healing, embracing, and comforting. I was not alone. I closed my eyes; a peace that I couldn't understand calmed my aching heart. There was still turmoil, uncertainty and trouble, but it was subsiding enough to allow me to step into the next moment, and then the next…and the next.

I don't know how long I sat there suspended in time and space, but eventually my eyes fluttered open, surprised to find myself still in the hotel room, even though I don't know where else I expected to be. I closed my Bible and placed it gently back on the nightstand, knowing it was time to leave this room and join my waiting family.

I took my time getting dressed, feeling foolish and embarrassed about my behavior the night before. Jacob and Will had done what was necessary, and I had just experienced a supernatural encounter with the Holy Spirit, yet my heart was still troubled. I still struggled to keep the anger away. I spoke directly to it in the mirror.

"You can't control me," I warned. "I won't let you. WE won't let you."

I picked up my necklace that I'd laid across the counter and fastened it around my neck. I knew there was nothing magical about it. It was only silver and stone, but that same strange tingle I experienced when I touched Liza's name in the journal buzzed against my skin. It felt right, back in its place, a symbol of the lineage to which I belonged. I smiled, thanking God for that little reminder that He was my Father, and I, the daughter of the King. I took a long, deep breath before leaving to meet my boys in the lobby.

We talked for a long while, each expressing forgiveness, grace, and thankfulness for the other, then finally found laughter again over the pizza Jacob had ordered. He went to the lobby's kitchenette for coffee, and Will stepped outside when Paul's number flashed across his phone's screen.

"I'm sorry I didn't come home," I said when Jacob returned.

"Me too," he said. "I've missed you both…it's been hard."

His words hurt, but I appreciated that about Jacob. He'd never been afraid to tell me the truth.

"Do you still think I should leave?" I picked at a piece of crust on my plate.

I heard him take a slow, deliberate breath. Without lifting my head, I cut my eyes up to see his face. He regarded me carefully for a minute.

"I'll leave that up to you," he said finally. "I think what you're doing here is important. I think Mom would have wanted you to finish what you've started. She would say that the dead can wait; it's the living that need you now."

I stared at him, sensing there was more. "But?"

"But I can't read your mind. I don't expect that everything you've been dealing with is suddenly healed in one night. Can you keep it together?"

I wanted to answer right away but paused, truly considering his question.

"I think so."

"Then stay," he said, casually picking up his cup. "Finish it."

That was another thing I appreciated about Jacob. He had more confidence in me than I had in myself. I knew that Will still wanted me to go home; I could feel it in the hesitant way he had hugged me when I joined them earlier. Will would always default to protector, but Jacob had lived his whole life with a fierce warrior for a mother. He had grown up hearing the stories of our family, and was no stranger to watching her run headfirst into the darkness to bring light, even in her everyday life.

Will would always be my safe place, my steady, solid thing. He would go to the ends of the earth to save me; he would always protect me. Even when I threw it in his face yesterday in a selfish rage, I held onto that constant.

Jacob was my family, the closest I would ever get to knowing my biological parents. He would always tell me the truth, even when it hurt. He trusted me to do the things I didn't think I could. If I needed to go into battle, Will would be the one holding my shield and Jacob would be the one handing me the sword on my way out the door.

I thanked God endlessly for both of them.

"What will you do?" I asked Jacob.

"I think I'll stick around for a few days." He took a sip of coffee and leaned back in his chair. "There's really nothing for me to do back at home. I've taken care of things for now. Mr. Jenkins is handling the grounds and church duties, and offered to do that for as long as I needed."

"Good," I said, causing him to glance sideways at me. "I'm glad you're here."

"You're not mad at me?" His mouth turned up at one corner.

I laughed softly, watching Will through the large sliding glass doors as he paced across the parking lot, still on the phone. "No, how could I be? You did what was necessary."

"So will you."

My eyes darted back to him. For the first time in a full day, I thought of the man from the alley and his message. *She wants you. Only you.*

Jacob was relaxed in his chair, looking out the window. I hoped he was right but didn't get to dwell on the uncertainty long, because Will came back into the lobby.

"Well?" I asked expectantly.

Will exchanged a look with Jacob, who gave him an approving nod.

"I think we've got something." He slid back into his chair at the table and leaned in close, causing us to do the same. "Paul got a hit on that phone number from Nadine."

"Where?" Jacob asked, and we both sat up attentively.

"It pinged off the cell tower downtown," Will said. "There's only one hospital in that range–Mercy Memorial."

Recognition sent an anticipatory chill up my spine. He'd told me! In the alley, he'd said it–or started to.

"Mercy Memorial?" Jacob repeated. "Is that a hospital?"

"Yes. The new name anyway–it used to be New Orleans Medical Center. And look at this."

Will pulled several papers from his back pocket, one being the pamphlet I'd seen before. When he unfolded it, the inside cover revealed the hospital's new full name. MMH was Mercy Memorial Hospital. He also pressed open a lined paper torn from a spiral notebook where he'd written a long list. On each line he'd scribbled the name of a doctor's office or medical treatment facility and in the middle of the page, Mercy Memorial was one of the few underlined places.

No wonder I couldn't find it anywhere; it was too new.

I felt a warm rush of heat on my cheeks. I thought he had abandoned the search, entertaining a traitorous idea that he quit caring and was only going through the motions to humor me until he could convince me to go home. But he hadn't. All this time, he'd still been looking.

"I was so close. Paul said it took him a while to follow the breadcrumbs; none of the combinations except one led to anything, and it was a burner phone. Long story short–it led to the original Central New Orleans Behavioral Health. The name has changed six times over the last decade. It was continually disappearing and reappearing under new names and management, and in new locations. Until last year, it was closed due to funding cuts."

"Let me guess." I tried to sound casual, as if I didn't have the inside track. "In November, they suddenly got a generous grant fully funding the entire operation?"

Will faked surprise. "You must be psychic. And Tuesday, the phone was turned back on; GPS tracked to Mercy Memorial. I also asked Matt to look into it, and see if anything stands out to him as unusual."

"You mean like are they creating a secret army of superheroes in the basement?" I fell against the back of the chair and he shrugged. Tuesday– the day I received the cryptic phone call. So that was the answer; she was there. Now I just had to figure out a way in. *Be patient, Andy. You've got one shot–don't blow it.*

"We could go check it out," Will said, then held up his hand as if stopping whatever thought he assumed I was having. "From the outside."

"What if you make contact with an employee–get a man on the inside?" Jacob leaned forward, looking very serious. "Want me to pose as an orderly?"

Man on the inside. Maybe we already had one.

"Not a bad idea." Will rubbed his hand along his chin, then when my mouth fell open, he clarified. "Not Jacob being an orderly, but getting a man on the inside. Although, it would take some time."

Time we didn't have; my dream the night before and alley man's warning made that perfectly clear.

"I could get in easily." I almost forgot they were there until I looked up and saw them staring at me. I shrugged. "All I'd have to do is tell the truth."

"Well, that's not happening, so forget it." Will threw his napkin onto the plate as if that were the end of any discussion. His phone buzzed, halting our audible argument for the moment. We stared at each other across the table, engaged in a silent battle of wills. His gaze never wavered even as he touched the green blinking circle to accept the call and turned the speakerphone on.

"Carter."

"Hey, it's Paul again." A deep, friendly voice greeted us.

"Whatcha got?" His dark brow shot up, daring me to look away.

"Yeah, that name, Kusnetsov? Where did you find it?" Paul asked, his tone hesitant.

"Uhh...it's connected to another case I was working on."

"You think it's connected to your current case too?"

We called an understood truce and he looked down at the phone, turning down the volume so only the three of us could hear and only if we leaned in closely.

"Maybe. Did you find something?"

"I don't know what you're working on, but I'd be careful. This Kusnetsov, if it's the same guy, is on about ten different government watchlists. He's connected."

"How did he get into the country?" Will asked.

"Well, once I dug a little bit, I discovered that he has several aliases, and each one is being watched by a different organization in a different country. Any one name might not have kept him from the country, but all together–it's a different story."

"Interesting," Will said, deep in thought. "Did you find any connection to that name I gave you earlier, Elena, or Dovanny Taklos?"

"Uh...hold on." We heard the sound of clicking as he typed. "Elena... Elena...hmm, there is something here in a bank record. A large payment to an E. Cordova from one of the aliases."

"What's the date on that?"

"Looks liiiike...November twelve."

Will and I looked at each other; I felt the color drain from my face. That was the day after Elena visited the prison. The day after Nadine died.

"Can you track the receiving account, get a full name or address?"

"I think so," Paul said. We heard the clicking of keys. "Well...maybe. This routing number isn't in the States. Hold on, this might take me a minute."

None of us moved, imprisoned by the suspense Paul's search had created.

"Okay, I'm in. Elena Cordova. Address is a PO Box."

"Recent purchase?"

Keys clicked. "You know, I am so not authorized to do this."

"I guess I'll owe you now."

"Nah, you're still ahead." Paul snorted and we heard more clicking. Will shot me a 'don't ask' glance when I raised an eyebrow at him. "Here it is. Last purchase was two weeks ago to a place called Nexgen Pharmaceuticals."

"I wonder what she ordered?"

"Hold on…" More clicking. "I'm tracking the invoice number. Looks like she ordered a boat load of something called Clozaphinol… delivered…Monday. What's Clozaphinol?"

"No idea," Will said, rubbing his hand across his forehead, smoothing out the wrinkles etched deep by worry. "Anything else?"

"Not really. All the other purchases look pretty normal; this chick likes to shop–expensive tastes, too. There are pretty regular deposits to someone named Marco Dominguez."

"Marco?" I mouthed.

"Does that account have an address?" Will asked.

Click, click. "One fifteen Rockingham Ave. New Orleans. Oh! Dr. Dominguez. He has a medical license on record."

"Thanks, Paul."

"Carter…what are you into? Do you need backup–we've got guys down there, you know," Paul said softly. Will quickly picked up his phone, turning off the speaker.

"I'm not sure just yet, but I'll let you know," Will said into the mouthpiece before saying a short goodbye.

"What's the plan?" Jacob asked after Will had shoved his phone back into his pocket. I held my breath. Maybe this would all fall into place.

"I think the hospital is the priority, but I'd like to check out Marco's place too."

"Well, I can do that." We both turned to Jacob and he shrugged. "What? I don't have anything else to do."

"I don't know…" I squirmed.

"You're not the only one who can be stealthy." Jacob smiled.

"First of all, I'm not stealthy–at all–and secondly, I'm not sure it's worth the risk."

I wasn't comfortable with the idea at all, but at least he'd be far away from the hospital–and Elena.

"I'll call you when I get there," Jacob continued, convincingly. "You can tell me what to look for. I'll just...drive by. Slowly."

"Fine." I relented. The danger was relatively low. It was broad daylight, and if he stayed in his car, he'd be fine. Right?

"This is strictly recon," Will said, tipping his head forward and glaring at both of us. "Understood? No one takes unnecessary risks."

Jacob and I both blinked innocently at him. "Of course," I said.

Will shook his head like a dad about to take two unruly children to dinner at a fancy restaurant.

"I'm going to regret this," he muttered as the three of us walked through the sliding glass lobby doors.

CHAPTER 26

Mercy Memorial was a typical looking city hospital. Newly painted, light colored brick exterior, rows upon rows of windows, and a large divided parking lot. Pristine blue and white signs directed us to a side entrance for access to the individual offices. Central New Orleans Behavioral Health wasn't specifically listed, but one side had a generic arrow indicating behavioral health services were inside.

Will parked in the lot closest to the side entrance, taking a spot near the back and in between two other cars so as not to stand out. We squinted against the sunlight and watched through open windows as typical hospital activity moved in and out. I didn't want to appear too eager, so I bided my time, praying for an opportunity.

"Carter?" I hadn't heard his phone buzz. "Hey, Jacob."

He set the phone on the dash and turned on the speaker. "What do you see?"

"Looks like a house. Like a regular residential house, I mean. No cars in the driveway." I heard a click and a hum–maybe the window being rolled down. "Doesn't look like anyone is home."

"You should go," I said.

"I'll park a few houses down, go on stakeout."

"I meant you should leave. That's not funny, Jacob!"

"I know, Andy. I'm just going to watch, okay...wait." The sound of an engine revving came over the speaker. "There's a cellar...that's unusual for New Orleans, isn't it?"

"Time to go..." I said.

"I'm going to check it out."

"What?" I grabbed for the phone as if I could reach through and shake him. "No...Will?" I looked to him for backup.

"Check your surroundings first, Jacob."

Traitor!

"Got it. There's an alley behind this street; it looks like I can go in from the back and stay hidden by his fence."

My heart was pounding. I was the one that was supposed to take the risks, not Jacob. I held my breath. He stayed on the phone as he drove around to the alley and, at Will's instruction, parked three houses down.

"I can't believe you," I hissed, jerking my hand away as Will reached for it.

"He's fine," Will whispered.

"Andy, I'm fine." Jacob echoed Will's assurance. "It's open."

"Jacob, don't go in."

He just kept ignoring me. My fingers ached from being twisted together so tightly, but it was the only thing I could control at the moment. I heard the creak of rusty hinges and the soft thud of a wooden door falling back.

"It's dark." Jacob said. "I'm going to take...loo...ound."

"Jacob, you're breaking up." Will said.

"No...ng...ere...o far."

"Jacob!"

No answer.

"Jacob!" I abandoned my plan to infiltrate the hospital and waved my hands frantically. "Start the car. We have to go get him."

Will was already fumbling with the key, but stopped and was eerily still.

"What are you doing? Go!"

"Shh." His hand suddenly on my arm wasn't meant to comfort but to silence.

He was staring out of the front window. What was more important than Jacob possibly being murdered at that very moment?

A man approached. He was dressed casually in a grey button-down and matching tie, a messenger bag hung over his shoulder and a phone was pressed to his ear. He was talking, distracted and serious–no hint of pleasure in his conversation. His curly black hair was purposefully messy, perfectly complimenting his black framed glasses and a few days of stubble on his jaw. I knew his face.

Will's gaze turned to the vehicle next to us. It was a small grey pickup. My hand flew to my mouth. I'd seen that truck before, too. Outside the burned hospital!

Without warning, Will grabbed me, hauled me over the center console and put his lips on mine, his hands on the side of my face, covering it. I gasped, but our kiss was institutional, lacking passion of any kind, purely a ruse to hide our identities.

Will held me in place, his lips moving slowly over mine as we listened to the sound of footsteps on concrete. They stopped just outside his window.

"Well, I could if you wouldn't keep calling me back in for every nutjob that shows up. I haven't been home in three days."

A car door opened, then closed again.

"Whatever, I'll get it done just…handle your part."

Footsteps again, moving away. Will turned his head and mine, blocking any possible view of our faces. He slid his hands through my hair and stole a glance into my terrified eyes before kissing me again. My hands found his shirt, twisting into the fabric, letting him know I was about to explode.

"Stay calm." He breathed into my mouth. "He'll be okay."

The truck roared to life and quickly pulled out of the parking lot. When I fell breathlessly back into my seat, he was already dialing Jacob's number again. No answer.

"Will, I've seen that man before."

"I know." He dialed another number.

"Paul," he said quickly, the phone tucked between his shoulder and ear, and his hand on the car key. "I need the vehicle registered to Marco Dominguez…yes, rush please…mmhmm…what color?"

He didn't have to share Paul's answer; his paled skin gave me all the information I needed. That couldn't be the same Marco that Elena was talking to in my dream–this man was only in his late thirties at the oldest. It didn't matter, though. Jacob was all that mattered.

"Call him back," I said, my voice tight and strained.

"He's not answering." Will looked around, as if searching for something he'd lost. He slammed his fist into the steering wheel.

"Andy…" He took a deep breath, looking up at me with pleading eyes. "I…can you please stay here?"

He looked torn, and I could feel his uncertainty. It was rigid, uncomfortable, and spanned the distance between us like a tightrope. He wanted to keep me close, but also safely away at the same time. He stared down at the phone in his hand, then held it out for me to take. When I didn't, he tossed it and the car keys across the seat into my lap.

"If I'm not back in fifteen minutes, call Matt and then Paul. They will know what to do."

"What are you going to do?"

"I'm going to get that doctor back."

"No, Will…"

"Andy, please. I'm trying to do the right thing here." His eyes were burning, conflict etched deeply into his drawn brow. "Please. Trust me."

His phone buzzed and he answered without looking, "Jacob! Oh Matt, listen I need to call you ba– Can it wait, we found the hospital. Jacob's in trouble and I need to get inside."

"I should do it," I said, snatching the phone from Will's hand and turning on the speaker. This was it. The opportunity I'd prayed for, now even more urgently. "The doctor just left and we need him to come back. Tell him, Matt. I have the best chance. I told you, I just have to tell the truth."

Matt was silent for two beats too long.

"She's right." Matt's voice was low, carrying the sound of sad truth. Will looked like we'd betrayed him. "Don't overdo it, Andy. And Will– don't let them give her any medication. Tell them she's already under care and you're on vacation, that she's having a manic episode, a break from reality. Give them my number for medications."

"No…I…no…" He shook his head.

I placed my hand over his. "Trust, remember?"

His brown eyes flicked back and forth between mine, the muscles in his jaw tightening against his resistance.

"Alright," he said finally.

"No medications, okay? And you can take her out of there at any time. They won't try to keep you unless you pose a danger to yourself or others, and even then–just be careful."

I was already out of the car, trying not to run into the building. I turned off the speakerphone and held it to my ear.

"Thanks Matt."

"Andy, wait," he said. "There's something you need to know. I checked more into that diagnosis and found an alarming number of deaths from a drug used to treat it. They all traced back to Louisiana, to those hospitals on your list."

I glanced over my shoulder. Will was still at the car, but moving quickly to join me. "Which drug?"

"Clozophinol."

Will was at my side.

"Be careful," Matt said again, this time his warning pregnant with hesitation.

When I handed Will his phone again, he tapped a few times on the screen.

"Yes, I'd like to report suspicious activity at my neighbor's house. One fifteen Rockingham Avenue…I saw a strange car in the alley and a man snooping around the outside. Okay, thank you."

"You called the cops?"

"I'd rather him be arrested than dead."

Everything inside begged to run–to keep running until all of this was a distant memory. But that would keep me running forever, and so despite the overwhelming need for self-preservation I headed directly towards the thing I feared the most. All the blood rushed from my head and I felt my knees fall out from under me. Will caught me under my arms. The extreme anxiety pulsing off of him eclipsed only by my own.

"I swear, Andy, you're killing me," he whispered. "Can no one in your family stay out of trouble for five minutes?"

We walked through a completely normal looking glass door into a completely normal looking waiting room.

CHAPTER 27

"**D**o it," I said through my teeth, pushing Will towards the receptionist's window, where a smiling blond sat reclined in her chair and chatted casually on the phone until she saw us.

She sat up quickly and slid back the glass window, a bright flash of red spreading across her cheeks. "Hi. Do you have an appointment?"

I stood behind Will, my hands on his back, pushing him towards her.

"No, ma'am, but my wife needs to see the doctor." He pointed towards the row of chairs lining the wall opposite of the receptionist. "Why don't you go sit down, babe."

I chose the chair closest to him and wrapped my arms around my waist, rocking slightly. *Don't overdo it, Andy.* It wasn't an act though; I was about to fall apart if I didn't hear from Jacob or see Marco walk back through that door in the next few seconds.

"We are on vacation, and my wife has some…problems. She's on a treatment plan but her grandmother died recently, and I think she's having some sort of episode. I don't know, uh…a break from reality? She just really needs to see the doctor; can she see the doctor?"

She peered around him and looked me over. "Can I speak with her?"

"Sweetheart?" Will tenderly touched my shoulder.

I took my turn in front of the window.

"Hi, my name is Patricia. What's your name?"

"Andy." Keep to the truth; that's the in.

"Andy, can you tell me what's going on?"

I looked at Will, as if asking if she was trustworthy–although I was the better judge. He nodded encouragingly.

"There's a bad woman who is trying to find people like me."

"What kind of person are you?"

"I am part of a secret society. We're warriors for God. We all have different abilities. My grandmother helped people remember things, and I can talk to you in your dreams. I can even move things there, like water...and I can see what you're thinking. She's after me and others. I need...I need to save them."

It sounded completely insane as I said it and I waited for her to pick up the phone, but she didn't.

"Thank you so much for sharing that with me, Andy. That must be very frightening." She just smiled at us. "The doctor has already left for the day, but I can make you an appointment for the first thing in the morning. You said she is already receiving treatment?"

Will nodded, looking as dumbfounded as I felt. What was happening? Was she really turning me away?

"I'd be happy to put in a call to her physician and request a prescription for the evening."

"No," Will said awkwardly. "That's okay...I'll call him."

He took a few steps, expecting me to follow. She slid the window closed. I just walked in there and told this woman that I was a dreamwalking superhero on a mission from God and she didn't even seem to care. Was this a joke? Did Patricia really not realize how dangerous I was? *A danger to myself and others.*

I let my head fall dramatically into my hands and spoke just loud enough for her to hear. "She's going to make me kill her."

I heard the smooth sound of a glass window sliding open. "What was that?"

"She's going to make me kill her."

Will heard this time and snapped his head around, his face pale with alarm.

"You know what, I think we should get you in today. I'm going to page the doctor." Patricia did an excellent job of hiding her concern behind a disarming smile. She passed Will a clipboard through the window. "Can you fill out these forms, and a nurse will be with you in just a minute."

"What are you doing?" Will hissed as we walked back to the chairs.

"Telling the truth."

"That's not funny, Andy. Let's just go."

"No." I stared at him defiantly. "Not until he comes back, not until Jacob is safe. I'll watch out the window. The second I see his truck, we can go."

"Andy?" A short brunette in light blue scrubs was waiting at an open door to the left of Patricia's window.

"I haven't finished the forms," Will said, standing.

"That's okay, I'm just going to take her vitals. She will be right back." She pushed the door open wider and motioned for me to follow. "I'll even leave the door open so you can see her."

Will remained standing, his hand holding the clipboard in a tight fist. His other hand moved, slowly inching towards his waistband where I knew his gun was tucked. A long intentional stare into the nurse's eyes relieved any distrust. She was honest and kind. I slid my hand down his arm, stopping him from reaching his weapon and bringing his attention back to me.

"It's okay." I nodded, sending silent assurance. "The doctor isn't here yet."

His eyes never left me as I met the nurse at the door.

"Andy? My name is Debra. It's nice to meet you."

Debra's round face lit up as she smiled, and I could only find one word to describe her–nice. Her bright hazel eyes reminded me of Samantha Prescott's. It seemed like a lifetime ago that I sat with Sam in the little church in the woods. I'd seen a scary side of myself that day. This morning I was sure that side was gone, extinguished by repentance and grace, but now the icy chill that snaked its way up my spine made me question that. As I stepped over the threshold into the hallway, I wondered if Nadine was right–if this really was where someone like me belonged.

"This way, honey." Debra's hand was warm on my shoulder.

She was gentle, chatting about cheery things while she took my blood pressure and counted my pulse. She winked as I stepped onto the scale.

"How long you been married, honey?"

"A little over a year." I met Will's eyes from where he paced in the waiting room, flicking his gaze between me and the window that faced the parking lot.

"He loves you," she whispered. "That's clear as day."

"He does." I smiled. Maybe we'd be okay. Dr. Marco would be back any second and we could sprint out the door, meet up with Jacob, and call in the cavalry to shut this place down. I hadn't seen her, but could feel the sliminess of Elena Cordova all over. It blew through the vents and dripped down the walls like an invisible toxin. Although Debra and Patricia both seemed like legitimate health care workers, and good ones at that, I was confused as to what scheme Elena was running.

Debra handed me a small clear plastic cup. "We need a sample, and then you're all done."

"A sample?"

"Restroom is right there."

Oh. A sample. I looked at Will, who shook his head–definitely not on board with losing sight of me. It's a bathroom; what could possibly happen in a bathroom?

As I closed the door, I saw Patricia standing next to Will, pointing to something on one of the forms, and heard Debra being paged over an intercom. The lock clicked into place and I turned around. A cold hand clamped over my mouth, and I was standing face to face with Elena Cordova.

"Hello, Andromeda."

I gasped and reached for the doorknob, which was pushing hard against my back, but she grabbed my wrist and twisted, my cry muffled under her hand.

"Don't you dare," she hissed. "Marco is waiting just outside that door. One wrong move from you, and your boyfriend is history. Are we clear?"

I nodded and squeezed my eyes closed. They watered from the pain as she continued to keep my arm bent in the most unnatural position. She jerked me forward and pushed me towards the other side of the bathroom, where she punched in a code on a small keypad.

The wall opened up, revealing another hallway identical to the one from where I'd entered.

The man from the parking lot leaned against the wall, his arms crossed over his chest. He looked bored. And tired. And not where she said he would be. I jerked away from her.

"Will!" I screamed. "Run! Will!"

Marco's arm was instantly across my neck, cutting off my scream and forcing me to a quick stop. My feet flew out from under me. He hauled me up and I kicked, trying to find my footing.

"Get her under control," Elena said as casually as if she'd said "Good morning." She continued down the empty hallway as I continued my struggle with Marco.

He didn't put up with my resistance for long but squeezed his thumb and forefinger hard into my neck. I managed to squeak out a small cry before blackness closed in from the outside of my vision.

When I came to, I was gagged and slumped over the arm of a chair in what looked like an office. I tried to move, but realized my hands were fastened with thick nylon straps to its wooden arms. An identical chair was next to mine and both were positioned in front of a large dark mahogany desk, clear except for a sleek silver computer monitor, wireless keyboard, and office phone. Seated behind the desk in a tall, cushioned leather chair, Elena swiveled slowly back and forth, her hands folded together under her chin, and her eerie green eyes trained on mine.

Something about the way the corner of her red lips pulled up into a victorious half-smile made me want to throw up. I narrowed my eyes, silently challenging her, which only made her smile grow bigger. She said nothing, just continued her slow, methodical sway.

I let my eyes wander, searching for clues as to my location and a possible exit should I get the chance. Behind her desk and chair the wall was split at the middle, the top part being a large pane of frosted glass lit from behind. On the left side, an open door revealed crisp white walls lined with counters, and I heard the electrical hum of machinery. It looked a lot like Matt's lab at The Agency.

Her office was spacious, sparsely furnished, and incredibly tidy. The only cluttered surface was a floor-to-ceiling bookshelf behind me, which I had to crane my neck to see.

"You like?" she asked, continuing to ignore my glare. "It's quite the collection. It's taken me almost forty years and over a million dollars to amass."

I tried to keep eye contact with her, letting her know I wasn't afraid, but that was a lie. I was terrified, and the way her green eyes slid over my face made me want to cry.

"It's always an exciting day when I get to add another unique item."

She winked and pushed herself up from her chair to answer the phone, which chirped twice.

"Yes?" she said sweetly.

"Oh…Miss. Cordova." I recognized Patricia's voice. "Um, Mr. Carter would like to see his wife, he's very agi…"

"That's fine, Patricia. Send him back."

"Oh…okay."

With her pinky, she pushed a few buttons and picked up the receiver. "You're up."

She hung up, raised her eyebrows, and took a deep breath, excited anticipation making her expression bright. "Well, here we go."

To my surprise, she left.

Jesus, I know you can hear me. We need help; please, Lord. Send help.

I counted one hundred and sixty-two seconds before I heard soft voices outside.

"She's in there?"

Will!

"Yes, sir. The doctor is– Sir, you can't have a gun in here!"

"Then call the police," he growled.

I held my breath; he was just on the other side of the door. I looked around; no sign of Elena or Marco, but why? Why would they leave me and let him come get me? It didn't make sense. That's when I saw him.

Marco. Or rather the shadow of Marco.

Just inside the door to the lab. If he hadn't moved, he'd have remained invisible. Will wouldn't know he was there!

The handle to Elena's office door turned slowly and the door cracked open. I saw the barrel of Will's gun, then his long arm, then finally his brown eyes falling wide and serious on mine. I shook my head and screamed muffled unintelligible warnings.

Will swept his weapon back and forth, peeking quickly behind the door and leaning to peer under Elena's desk. Then he laid his gun in my lap and began frantically ripping the restraints loose. When one hand was free, I tore at the tape covering my mouth, ignoring the searing sting as I pulled it free.

"It's a trap!" I said before getting the tape all the way off.

I heard a soft pop as the second strap hit the floor. Will grabbed his gun off my lap and spun around, stumbling backwards and trying to raise his weapon with a shaky arm. I scrambled out of the chair and hid behind him, my hands on his sides. I saw Marco standing in the doorway to the lab with a weapon of his own. Will stumbled again and sucked in a sharp breath when I squeezed my hands on his waist. I looked down, horrified at the dark red stain spreading quickly under my fingers.

As he sank to the floor, I followed, looking up at Marco for an explanation which I found in the form of a silencer screwed on to the barrel of his gun. He grumbled something about telling me to get rid of him before loading the weapon again. Nothing made sense. Marco's words, the fact that Will was not fighting back, nothing.

"Will...get up," I begged, reaching for him, my hands grabbing at his shirt. "Please, get up."

"Run Andy," Will grunted. He finally raised a trembling arm and fired at Marco, hitting and shattering the glass window instead. Marco never flinched. I heard another soft pop and Will jerked his hand back, his gun skittering across the floor.

Marco was on us in less than a second, kicking Will's gun further away and pointing his weapon at my husband's head.

"NO!" I screamed, throwing myself over him and into the line of fire.

Will weakly tried to push me away, his face nearly colorless.

"Run...Andy...run," he said over and over.

"Phone," Marco ordered.

I was still protectively hovering over Will. Marco leaned closer, pushing the barrel of his gun hard against my head.

"Give me his phone," he said, his voice hushed and harsh. And familiar. I'd heard that husky whisper before, but couldn't put a memory together in the chaos of panic swirling in my brain.

I reached under Will, who groaned when I moved him. I fished his phone out of his back pocket and gave it to Marco.

Marco lowered his weapon and stepped aside as the office door opened again and Elena entered with an empty wheelchair. I ignored them and frantically tore at Will's clothes, which were now soaked with his blood. I ripped off my jacket, balling it up and covering the growing stain on his left side.

"Will!" I screamed. I looked up at the stoic expression of the man standing over us, tears streaming down my face. "Please, let me call for help."

There was no response; his demeanor was emotionless and cold. I searched his face for any kind of compassion, but he looked away, refusing to meet my eyes.

"Marco, finish it." Elena said.

He raised his arm, pointing the gun at Will's head.

"NO!" I flung myself over him again, squeezing my eyes closed and waiting for the fiery burn of a bullet.

"He'll be dead in a few minutes. These bullets are laced with tranqs–no need to waste another." Marco's miraculous words surprised me, and I looked up at him, but his eyes shifted away again.

"Fine," Elena sighed. "Get the van, and make sure that nurse doesn't call the police."

I watched in shock as Marco tossed Will's cell phone onto the ground and stomped on it with his foot. It exploded into tiny worthless bits of plastic and metal, which he left scattered on the floor as he walked away without looking back.

"Was that really necessary?" Elena called after him, shaking a shard of plastic off her boot.

I felt beads of sweat form on my forehead, and my stomach cramped with desperation. He was dying. He was laying there dying, and they didn't care. This was a trap, and we walked right into it. At least Jacob was safe, and he knew where we were. Maybe if I could just stall her, he would bring help. I looked around for something–anything.

"Please, let me call someone for him…please."

She laughed and shook her head as if I had just told the most ridiculous joke, then jerked the office phone so hard the cord popped free from the wall. She sighed and said, "We must get going now."

"Please, I'll go with you, just let me help him," I begged.

"No…Andy," I heard Will gasp, grabbing my hand. I turned my attention back to him.

"Oh, you'll go with me regardless," Elena spat and turned away.

Oh God…please…please, I prayed. Will's eyes fluttered shut and his hand slipped away from mine.

CHAPTER 28

"Will!" I begged. "Please...please don't go."

I held the jacket tight against his side. It was already dark with his blood. His breaths were short and jagged, and when he coughed, bright red droplets dripped from the corner of his mouth.

"No!" I cried and prayed out loud, "Oh God, please, save him, please."

"Your god isn't listening." Her voice slid over my head, dripping like venom into my ears, down into my stomach, where a tiny remnant of rage sprouted back up. Even after hearing all of Jacob's truth, the lie that I needed that anger for strength remained. It did feel like God wasn't listening, like He'd turned away and left us alone to die.

"Andy..." Will's voice was barely a whisper. I looked down at his face, where his head was cradled in my lap, and breathed a great sigh of relief that he was still alive.

"Will, I'm sorry, I'm so sorry. I don't know what to do. Tell me what to do," I sobbed, my lungs tightening with helplessness. He'd said those same words to me once. Were we doomed to live this awful cycle over and over?

I could feel him slipping away as each beat of his heart pumped more of his blood out of the wound in his side. The rage sprout grew its first leaves.

"Listen to me," he said.

I leaned in close.

"She's a liar; God will always hear you."

"Please hold on. I need you." My tears dripped onto his forehead and I pulled him closer. "I need you."

I looked up and around the room in panic. There had to be something I could do. There was nothing–no way to call for help, not that she would let me. He was going to die on that dirty tile floor, and there was nothing I could do to stop it. That angry sprout shot up and became a healthy thick vine that stretched out its sticky tendrils and wrapped them around my heart. At that moment, I hated Elena Cordova more than ever. Venomous black poison flowed out of the vine and seeped into every cell. It burned from the inside out, worming its way through ventricles, igniting each nerve. My thundering heart pushed it through my veins, where it soon poured out of my eyes, as thick and destructive as lava.

In the corner I saw her shelf, every inch covered with antiques and collectables. On the bottom, behind a first edition of *The Catcher in the Rye,* carefully stored in a glass case, was a long, shiny, and very sharp looking dagger. A dark and desperate thought entered my mind. I didn't need to be asleep to take her out. That pulsing vine pumped surge after surge of adrenaline. I tasted the bitterness on my tongue and savored it. I set my jaw tight in determination. Focused on the blade that was held in place only by a small wooden easel, I shifted Will's body in order to crawl towards it. I banked on her underestimation of just how vengeful and enraged I was. It was just a few inches away. If she didn't notice me grab it, I could...

A sudden pressure on my hand stopped me. I looked down and Will's eyes were wide, those deep brown eyes that could see right through me. He knew exactly what I was planning, and that I was just angry enough to do it.

"No..." he croaked. "Don't."

I have to save you. That's what I meant to say, but what I said was, "I have to stop her. She has to pay." I would make sure she did.

"Not you...it can't be you." He coughed. Little drops of his blood splattered on my shirt.

I ground my teeth together. I was consumed with fury, and yet restrained by the pleading in his eyes. I let out a cry so feral it was almost a roar, and slammed my fists hard on the floor. Pain shot up through my arms, but it didn't matter.

I wanted to pound them again and again until my skin split open and my bones broke.

"Andy, baby, please."

My name, weak on his lips, quieted the rage long enough for me to pull him to my chest, trying to let my heart beat for his, like he had done for me once. He had said those words to me before, when I was giving up, on the cold bank of the Occoquan River. He'd begged me to live then, and now he was begging me to live again.

His mouth was next to my ear, and I could hear his shallow breaths, the drug laced bullet rendering him almost motionless. I screamed and sobbed, taking in great gasping breaths of helplessness and brokenness. I was angry with him for stopping me, and yet loving him so much for that at the same time. Here he was saving my life even as he was losing his.

"My pocket," he whispered. I drew back and searched his brown eyes for an explanation. There was something there that hadn't been there before. It was a little spark, a tiny sliver of fire; it was hope. That was enough for me.

I glanced over my shoulder. Elena was on the other side of the broken glass window, filling her leather duffle with clinking glass vials, clearly confident I wouldn't be attempting to escape. I wrapped my arms around him, lifting my body to hide what my hands were doing. I reached into his pocket and pulled out a flat little rectangle about the size of a business card, but it was thick and plastic. Pressed into its surface was a strange symbol. I could barely make it out, but it looked like some kind of dog.

"What is this?"

He raised his hand and pushed my fingers closed around the little black card.

"Tracker. Lift the end…push the button. Keep it with you. She's going to take you, but they'll be able to find you. Hide it."

"Who?"

He jerked then, his face contorted with pain.

"Agency," he said through gritted teeth, "Keep it, promise me."

"No…" I sobbed.

"Andy…promise me." He shoved my hand towards my chest, his eyes pleading with mine. "Please."

It wasn't hope for us that I'd seen in his eyes. It was his hope for me.

"Promise," he said desperately, squeezing my hand so hard it hurt.

"I promise."

"I love you." Why did his words feel like goodbye?

"Time to go." I felt Elena's claw-like hands on my shoulders, jerking me back.

"NO!" I screamed, fighting against her.

She continued to pull me away from Will. I flailed and kicked at her, breaking away and crawling back to him.

She stumbled backwards, but quickly recovered. Lurching back towards me, she grabbed my hair and pulled my head back to show me the gun in her hand, its barrel fitted with the same silencing device as Marco's. I didn't care if she shot me; I was ready to fight her until my last breath. She didn't point it at me, though. A sickeningly evil smile spread across her lips and she turned the weapon instead towards Will. She knew I wouldn't risk his life further. That vine of rage clenched tightly around my heart now fully entwined with each nerve, each vein. I made a secret vow—if he died, either she or I would too, but he wouldn't go alone. She met my fiery glare with one equally as hideous.

"Now," she ordered. "Get up."

I looked back at Will. His eyes met mine for a split second and then fluttered closed. I prayed that he could read my thoughts, but he was fading quickly. As much as I wanted to exact revenge on her, I wanted him to live more.

I had one chance to save him. I launched myself over him and just before she jerked me back again, I whispered in his ear.

"Please live."

She kept her gun trained on him as she pulled me up, and I stumbled backwards towards the wheelchair she was pointing to with a long-manicured finger.

"Sit," she ordered, and walked around to the back, never lowering her weapon. "Strap your arms in."

I obeyed, sobbing as I fastened one wrist to the chair and then the other, using my teeth to pull the cuff tight. She pushed the chair into the hall and I looked back. He was still...too still.

Please let them hurry, Lord. He has to live.

Under his hip, tucked between his belt and jeans where she couldn't see, a tiny red light was blinking.

He hadn't activated it before, because he knew it was the very last resort. He was willing to die so that I could have a chance to live, but I was willing to do the same, so I had broken my promise.

Will reminded me that God was always listening. Despite the vicious war raging inside, I still believed and prayed He would hear my cries for help. I was still alive so God wasn't done with me yet, and I trusted that Will would be okay. He had to be. I knew as long as his heart beat in his chest, he would do whatever it took to find me. He finds the lost things. I just had to hold on a little longer.

Elena rolled me down a maze of hallways and out a sliding glass door into the fading evening light. Her hand remained wrapped around the hilt of her gun, which she pressed hard against my back, hidden from anyone passing by. I searched the doors we passed, looking for any clues as to where other patients could be.

Marco was waiting in a short white bus equipped with a wheelchair lift. It bore the same name and faded fleur de lis symbol that Hardy had described. He'd said the man driving had dark hair and glasses, just like Marco. Had he taken the patients out before the fire? Why would he do that and still be working for her now? How could he have existed when I was a baby and yet be so young? Was he a trick—meant to confuse and disorient? If so, it was working.

"Get rid of him, and go ahead and finish off the rest. I've got what I need now."

A flash of surprise slipped across his face, and Marco's brows drew together for a fraction of a second. He looked towards the building, his eyes bouncing off a small window just above the ground. A basement? The window was covered from the inside with what looked like paint, light escaping through the thin spots. I thought I saw something move on the other side.

Finish off the rest? *She's going to do it again—she's getting rid of the evidence.* I jerked against my restraints, but they held. There was nothing I could do. *It's all up to you, Lord. I have nothing.*

I stared down at my hands, covered with Will's blood which had already dried up, and with it any hope of victory. At least she didn't allow me to wallow in despair long—a sharp prick of a needle in my neck followed by the slow burn of some drug being pushed into my veins brought a quick and welcomed sleep.

CHAPTER 29

Someone was dragging me, strong hands firmly fixed under my arms. I tried to move my legs, to get my feet under me and stand, but they wouldn't move. Was it dark, or were my eyes closed?

"Just pick her up!" A forceful female voice with an Italian accent echoed off walls I couldn't see.

The hands slid around my waist and I was quickly lifted. I turned my head and tried to get my brain to focus on something, anything.

Doors. There were a lot of doors. Long fluorescent lights hung overhead, but the hallway was still dark.

I've been here before.

"Where…" I tried to speak, but my mouth felt numb and swollen.

The man carrying me glanced down and back up quickly. He remained expressionless as he toted my limp body. He was tall and slim but muscular. It didn't seem to strain him to haul my hundred-ten-pound frame. He had short black hair and rich, ebony skin. When he looked at me, his irises were almost black, but they weren't cold. They were the warm black of midnight swim in summer.

He looked like someone I knew, but not as they were; rather as they would be.

"Here," the woman said.

I knew that voice. *How do I know that voice?*

Elena. Elena killed Will.

I screamed as it all came suddenly flooding back. The sound echoed off the hard stone walls of the hallway. The man stopped suddenly and looked down in a panic, trying not to drop me as I thrashed.

"What did you do?" she hissed.

"Nothing. I have done nothing," he said, his voice deep and heavily accented. He sounded South African.

I cried and flailed in his arms, tired angry sobs shaking my body uncontrollably.

"What is wrong, Omncane?" he asked frantically, then looked up desperately at Elena. "What is wrong with her?"

"Oh, stop fussing, Themba," Elena said without looking at him as she dug through a brown leather satchel.

The man named Themba pulled me slightly closer, protectively.

Even in my hysteria, I knew that tiny gesture was important. It was so slight, Elena didn't notice.

"What are you doing?" he asked.

"Shutting her up," Elena answered just before I felt a sharp sting on my arm. "And you will do well to remember your place."

Immediately, a fresh warm wave of drowsiness flooded through me. It draped a heavy blanket of numbness over the awful pain, making me forget who I was longing for, and stealing the little strength that remained in my limbs.

Themba looked down at me apologetically as my eyes closed once again.

"I am sorry, Omncane," he whispered.

I heard the metal-on-metal sound of a heavy door being opened.

"Put her there."

The world fell away as Themba bent over, and I heard the gritty squeak of springs as he laid me on a thin mattress.

"Will she be okay?" His warm hand lingered on my arm.

"She will be fine. Now go, there is much to do," Elana snapped, sounding annoyed at his concern.

I heard the same scraping metal sound once again and then silence. Sleep was coming. I didn't fight it. I prayed that when I woke, somehow this would have all been a terrible dream. Or maybe I would just sleep forever.

As I lay on the bed longing for escape, my thoughts muddled and swimming, a flickering image floated peacefully across my memory. It was Esther, and she was reading to me. She sat on the bench in the garden of Christ Church, and I at her feet. It was spring, the sweet smell of hyacinth filled the air.

"David was lost, you see, child. He was scared and alone in the desert, pursued by the enemy."

She read from Psalms, the sixty-third chapter. When she got to verse five, she stopped and leaned in close.

"Now, listen Joanna–this is important. You will need to remember what I'm about to read and understand that the love of God was more meaningful to David than life."

She looked down at me over the well-worn pages of her Bible to make sure I was paying attention. When satisfied, she continued.

"My soul shall be satisfied as with marrow and fatness; and my mouth shall praise thee with joyful lips: When I remember thee upon my bed, and meditate on thee in the night watches. Because thou hast been my help, therefore in the shadow of thy wings will I rejoice. My soul followeth hard after thee; thy right hand upholdeth me. But those that seek my soul, to destroy it, shall go into the lower parts of the earth..."

She'd kept reading, but the memory faded and so did I, humming a broken melody of praise through my dry and parched throat just as David had centuries ago. The God he had praised in the darkest of his nights was the same God that was with me. I didn't know where I was, what was going to happen, even if I'd live to see the next day. I only knew one thing, and let that be the prayer that kept my heart from breaking in two.

I know you're here.

"I knew you'd come."

I opened my eyes to see the rounded face of a little girl.

How long had I been asleep? Maybe I still was.

"Are you the angel I saw in my dream?"

Her words didn't make sense. I rubbed my eyes, groggy from whatever Elena had given me. Through squinted lids, I peered at the little girl that sat cross-legged on a cot next to mine.

It was her. The girl I'd seen in Elena's mind, just before I heard the terrible haunting voices. The same little girl who kept whispering the plea to rescue. She had the same dirty blond hair, the same sad eyes. She was even wearing the same white gown.

I reached out and touched her hair, just to make sure she was real. Her smile looked out of place on such a thin, gaunt face. The dark circles under her young eyes reminded me of the tired girl I once saw in the mirror back on my great-uncle Jubal's houseboat. She was a girl in need of saving.

"Where am I?" I croaked.

"In the sleeping room."

"No…I mean, where is this place?"

"I don't know." Her voice was small, just like the rest of her. "I prayed. I asked God to send an angel to rescue us."

"I'm not an angel." I tried to sit up, saddened to find myself still in this awful reality.

The room spun, and I slid back down onto the mattress. The little girl laid down too, her face even with mine, her brown eyes staring expectantly. They were as warm and honest as Will's.

Will. I felt a sharp pain in my heart and winced.

"Are you hurt?" she asked.

"I have a broken heart," I whispered. I thought I should be crying or angry, but I felt very much removed from myself.

"My momma had a broken heart," she said. "That's why she had to go see Jesus, so He could fix it."

I reached over and brushed a strand of her hair behind her ear. She knew. She knew what it felt like.

"My momma had to go see Jesus too," I said slowly. My words felt thick in my mouth.

"Did God send you to take us home?" There was such hope in her eyes.

I didn't know what to say, so I told her the truth. "I don't know."

Her face fell. It wasn't the answer she was looking for.

"What's your name?" I tried to distract her from her disappointment.

"Amy," she said brightly, hope renewed. "Amy Jean Robins."

Robins? Why do I know that name?

"Nice to meet you, Amy Jean Robins. My name is Joanna, but my friends call me Andy."

"Andy is a funny nickname for Joanna," she said with a giggle.

"It is, isn't it?" I smiled weakly.

She reached out and took my hand.

"I prayed for you, Andy," she said. "I saw you in my dream."

"I saw you, too."

She didn't say anything, just squeezed my hand and smiled. I wanted to ask her so many questions, but my eyelids were too heavy, being pulled down like shades by the weight of whatever drug was still coursing through my body. I had no idea how long its effects would last. Honestly, I wanted to give in to the sleep that was threatening to take over. If I were unconscious, I wouldn't have to think about Will. I wouldn't have to relive every one of our last seconds together, or drive myself insane wondering if they got to him in time. I wouldn't have to think about trying to live the rest of my life without him if they hadn't. I wouldn't have to consider just how short the rest of my life might be.

I didn't have to wait long. A thick dark cloud filled my brain and just before I slipped off, I whispered, "Keep praying, Amy."

My sleep was plagued with jumbled, confused images and bits of dreams. I was continually rising and falling, strapped tight into a rickety metal cart. I heard a familiar click, click, click. Then the high-pitched scream of brakes, and the sounds of people screaming and laughing at the same time. When I was up high, I could see for miles–across fields and even over mountains. In the distance, tiny golden embers from the village bonfire rose up to heaven. My fingers spanned the distance, attempting to touch them, but they were always just out of reach. The bright eyes of Ben and Thadie's boys stared from the darkness at the edges of my dream. Their little hands stretched out towards me. Siphiwe opened his mouth to speak.

"Themba," he said, his little voice not more than a whisper.

The word floated slowly between us. I could see it swishing back and forth in the air like a feather.

"Andy." There was another tiny voice. "Andy, wake up, please."

I forced my eyes to open. Amy was kneeling on the floor next to my cot, her small hands folded nervously together as if in prayer.

"You were sleeping for so long," she said, worry etched all over her young face.

"I'm sorry." I tried to smile. "Are you okay?"

She nodded. She wasn't okay. None of this was okay.

I sat up slowly, still a little woozy. I looked down, fighting off a wave of nausea at the sight of the dark brown stain on my shirt.

A large lump formed in my throat as I stared at it, praying that wouldn't be the only part of Will I'd ever see again.

Amy's icy fingers on my arm mercifully pulled me away from the edge of a bottomless pit and I took a good look at my surroundings for the first time since the man Elena called Themba had carried me in. *Themba.* The boys had spoken his name…why?

The room had bright white-tiled walls and a similar white-tiled floor. It was empty except for our two cots and a small tiled half-wall providing what I guess one could call privacy for a bathroom area. The door to the hallway looked like it was made of solid steel and had only a thin slit of a window near the top. There was a small panel to the side with a button and keypad that looked like some kind of intercom. Were we still at the hospital? No…she put me on a bus; we were somewhere else, but I had no idea where.

I walked slowly along the walls, running my fingers across the tile, looking for any kind of weakness. The room was clean, obviously cared for by someone.

"Amy, does anyone come in here…to clean or anything?"

"Themba does," she said.

I looked at her. She'd moved back to her cot and was absentmindedly pulling at the hem of her gown.

"Do you like Themba?"

She shrugged. "He's quiet mostly." Then she smiled as if remembering something. "He brings me cookies sometimes, though."

"How long have you been here?"

"I don't know." She looked up at me. "What day is it?"

"Monday, February 25th."

"It was my birthday," she said sadly.

I sat next to her, brushing her hair back off her shoulder. "When is your birthday?"

"January number fourteen."

I felt my hand flutter to my lips. Six weeks? She had been here for six weeks?

"Can you tell me what happened?" I asked, hoping that talking about it wouldn't upset her. "You don't have to if you don't want to."

She stared at her gown for a few seconds and then looked up at me, resolved. "It's okay. I can tell you."

I lifted my hands when she moved suddenly, unsure of what she was doing. She tucked her legs up underneath her and wiggled down to lay her head on my lap. I hesitated, then let one hand rest on her shoulder and the other brush through her hair lightly with my fingers. Other than the kids I grew up with in the camps, I didn't have much experience with children, but I could feel her loneliness rolling off in crashing waves. She missed her family terribly and she was scared.

"It was my birthday," she said again, her voice soft. "Daddy was at work, on a faraway trip, but he promised to take me for ice cream when he got home. I stay at Miles' house when Daddy is on trips. He's my best friend next door. He's got a puppy. Miles told his momma my daddy was home, 'cuz our car was there, so I went home. I thought he had come to surprise me. Only Daddy wasn't there; it was that lady. She said that I was supposed to go with her, and she'd take me to my daddy; he was waiting for me. I didn't believe her though, Andy, I didn't. Me and Daddy have a secret password; Daddy said not to go with nobody unless they knew our secret password, and she didn't know it."

A single tear rolled down her cheek, and I wiped it with my thumb. I barely knew this child, but something deep inside ignited at the confusion and desperation that filled her brown eyes. I pushed my lips together, keeping the R-rated words I wanted to shout in response to Elena's deceit away from Amy's innocent ears.

"I tried to run away and back to Miles' house, but she got me. She didn't take me to my daddy, she took me here."

"I'm so sorry, Amy."

"Do you think my daddy is looking for me?"

Compassion suppressed the fire and I pulled her close.

"Oh, of course he is. I'm sure he hasn't stopped looking for you."

"Do you think he will be mad at me?" She turned in my lap and looked up at me with wide, worried eyes. "He's got a real important job. He won't want to leave it."

"No, honey." I choked back tears. "No, I'm sure nothing is more important to your daddy than finding you. He's going to tell you how brave you are when you see him."

Esther...I suddenly missed my grandmother so much I couldn't breathe. Amy missed her daddy like that. I knew then that I would do everything I could to get this little girl back to her family.

Revenge was nothing; it was selfish and useless–a waste of precious energy. Only the rescue was worthy of effort.

I looked around again. There had to be something I could do. Maybe I could reach Matt in a dream, tell him…what? I didn't have any idea where we were. This building might be in another state, for all I knew. I let my head fall back, and stared at the ceiling. It was white too, covered with textured ceiling tiles, but something out of place caught my attention. Tucked in the very corner of the room by the ceiling was a small black circle. A camera. We were being watched.

I leaned over, letting my hair fall around my face.

"Amy, I'm going to try and get you home to your daddy, but I'll need your help. Just nod okay, don't answer out loud. Can you help me?"

She nodded the tiniest of nods and my heart clenched painfully when a hopeful smile spread across her lips. We spent the next few hours whispering back and forth, Amy doing her best to answer all my questions. We thumb wrestled and played rock, paper, scissors over and over. I knew the camera was watching, so we kept our backs to that corner and tried to look as though we were simply playing.

So far, I'd learned that there were at least two other people there. Amy didn't know much about them other than there was a girl and a boy. The boy was older, a teenager she thought. She said the little girl looked like Themba and called him "Ubaba."

She could never see the sky from anywhere in the building and there were no windows, so I assumed we were underground somewhere. The only other grownups she had seen were Elena, Themba, and the mean-guy, who I knew was Marco. Elena made sure the children were fed and clean, but they were always kept separate. Only Themba came to visit and play with them. I wondered why she'd put Amy with me. I wondered why Amy was there in the first place.

"Amy," I asked, twisting strands of her hair into a braid. "Is there something…special you can do? Something maybe no one else can do?"

"I can cross my eyes like this," she said, turning her head and giving me a funny look.

"No, silly, not like that." I wasn't sure how to word my question. "You know how you saw me in your dream?"

"Yeah."

"Well, I have a secret to tell you." Her eyes grew wide and she leaned back so I could whisper in her ear. "I can visit people…in their dreams."

"Wow!" she said, a huge grin falling across her lips.

"Can you…do anything like that? Maybe something different?" I asked.

She tapped a small finger on her chin for a minute. "Daddy says I have a superpower."

"What is it?"

"He says I bring peace." She giggled. "Like he does for his job."

"What's your daddy's job?"

"He helps people. He even goes long ways away sometimes to help people."

"Amy…is your daddy's name John?" I asked, remembering the news broadcast I'd watched in the hotel room.

She turned to face me, her eyes bright. "You know him?"

"No, but I've heard of him and how he was working very hard to help people. He's a good man."

"Daddy says Jesus called him to Africa." She wrinkled her nose. "Have you heard of Africa?"

"I have." I smiled at her innocence.

"Do you think maybe I can ask Jesus to call Daddy again? To tell him to come get me? He can take you home too, Andy, there's lots of room in his car."

"I definitely think you can do that. Jesus hears our prayers. I'll pray too." I pulled her close, wrapping my arms around her tiny frame.

"Okay." She snuggled into my arms. "That's better than…"

"Than what?"

Amy curled her arms into her chest protectively. "Promise you won't be mad?"

"I promise."

"That lady told me that there were more people like you and they were in trouble and I should ask you where they were so she could help them. She said 'cuz I was so smart, I was the only one who could do it. She said she would take me home to daddy if I did. But I don't like her, Andy. She's bad and I don't think she wants to help people at all."

Amy sat up, her brown eyes pleading for understanding, wisdom beyond her years deepening their color. So that was why Amy was my roommate. Clever, Elena…very clever.

"Well, she was right about one thing. You are smart, Amy." I tapped my finger lightly on the tip of her nose. "She is bad, but you know what? God is good and He's on our side."

A giant smile spread wide across Amy's face. She stuck up her pinky and when I didn't move, she grabbed my hand and peeled my pinky finger up like hers. She hooked hers in mine and shook our hands.

"Pinky promise we win."

I smiled but didn't answer. I couldn't promise that. I made my own pinky promise though. I would fight. Until death stole the last breath from my lungs and silenced the very last beat of my heart, I would fight for Amy, and for whoever else was with us there waiting for rescue.

"Polka-dot peanut butter," Amy whispered.

I leaned back, looking at her for clarification.

"It's the password. Tell Jesus to say it when He calls Daddy, so Daddy knows it's okay."

"Polka-dot peanut butter," I repeated with a serious nod.

"Did I help you, Andy?" she asked, reaching up and twisting her little fingers into my hair.

"You sure did, Amy. You helped me so much."

Her face was buried in my shoulder and I was thankful she couldn't see the tears that were running down my cheeks. As I held her, she became very still, her breaths heavy and deep. Soon she was asleep, and I wondered if it was nighttime. I watched the soft rise and fall of her shoulders and decided that her dad was right. Amy did bring peace. It might not have been a superpower, but it was her gift.

If Amy didn't have a supernatural ability like me, maybe I was wrong about what Elena's true motives were. Kidnapping Amy was keeping her dad in the States instead of in Africa and speaking to the summit. Could it be political?

Amy said there was a teenage boy there, that he had blond hair with blue eyes, same as the boy from the paper. He had ties to Africa, too. Was it him? What could she possibly want with him? If I didn't get out of here soon.... I shook my head and wished Amy did have a superpower and that it was melting steel with lasers from her eyes.

"Hmm," I said out loud.

Maggie had held back the glass and debris from the crash, keeping me safe. I had already toyed with the idea that our gifts were passed down when I'd read my great-great-grandmother Liza's story. I thought I had some of Maggie's ability in my dreams, but what about when I was awake?

I stared at the door, clenched my fists, and focused all my energy on the large steel barrier. Nothing happened. I let out the breath I'd been holding and rolled my eyes. What had I been expecting to happen—the door to fly off its hinges in a cloud of smoke? Maybe I needed to focus on something smaller. My eyes settled on the hinges. Once again, I balled up my hands and stared, focusing all my thoughts and intention. I concentrated so hard and so long that my hands began to shake. Still, nothing happened. I sighed in frustrated disappointment. Maybe I didn't inherit Maggie's gift after all.

Amy was sleeping soundly in my lap, and I let my hand rest on her shoulder. As I looked down, I noticed my wedding ring was gone. Without moving Amy, I felt around on the mattress.

Had it fallen off? I wiggled out from under Amy and covered her with the grey blanket Themba had brought while I was sleeping. I stood up and patted my pockets, then knelt and searched the floor under the cot.

It wasn't anywhere. I reached up and touched my neck. My lion necklace was gone, too.

I walked over to the bathroom area, looking all around the sink and mirror. They weren't there, either. Elena must have taken them. I put my hands on either side of the small porcelain sink and stared at myself in the mirror.

Focus on the mission, Andy. The mission is what matters. Work the problem; what can you do?

Nothing. I could do nothing. I was trapped with Amy in this stupid "sleeping room."

I stepped back suddenly, my eyes falling onto the sleeping girl on my cot. We were in the sleeping room! I could sleep. I could dream! I headed towards Amy's empty cot and flopped down. I was about to pull her pillow over my eyes to block out the light when a loud bang made me jump.

I dashed to Amy's side, protectively covering her with my arm as the large metal door slowly slid open.

CHAPTER 30

ny hope of finding help in a dream was lost when Elena marched into the room. She carried a tray of food and wore a smug smile on her face.

"Hello Andromeda," she said, dropping the tray onto the empty cot. It was filled with sandwiches, a bunch of grapes, and bags of chips.

"I see you've made a friend."

I had to pinch my bottom lip between my teeth to keep from smarting off about how my "friend" was far smarter than she assumed.

I narrowed my eyes at her. "What do you want?"

She sighed and clasped her hands together in front of her, smiling as if I'd just asked her for her Christmas wish list. "Oh, so many things. Where should I start?"

"Start with what you did with my rings and necklace?"

"You won't be needing those anymore. I got rid of them for you."

I met her mocking expression with defiance.

"What are you doing with these kids?"

She laughed. She wouldn't be offering me much information. I would have to go about this another way. She was dressed stylishly in tight black jeans and wore a cream-colored blouse under a black leather jacket. Her black high-heeled ankle boots clicked across the tile floor as she walked.

She didn't look much different than she had in my dreams, other than the fact that she was twenty years older. Her hair was still shiny and fell straight down her back, but its black color was now streaked with silver. Her makeup was perfect, complete with bright red lipstick. She obviously spent a lot of time on her appearance. If she wouldn't talk about her plans, maybe she would talk about herself.

"I guess you've been one step ahead of us this whole time."

"You could say that," she said with a cocky smirk.

"So, how do you even know who I am?"

"I was looking for you." She swirled her hand around in my direction. "Well, your...type. But you can thank that dreadful woman, Nadine, for the introduction. She was pretty clever, that one. She even set up a meeting with me, pretending to be doing research or something. She never showed though. I found out later she came all the way to the hospital, but never got out of the car. I couldn't have given her what she wanted anyway, but she sure had something I wanted."

"She didn't?" That surprised me. Elena plopped down onto the cot with the trays. That surprised me too.

"No. But the description of her 'patient' was intriguing. It took me a while to track her down, but once I did, she wasted no time in telling me about you—Andromeda Stone, the girl who can walk in dreams. I'd actually begun to doubt people like you truly existed. She said you were dead, but when she told me about mister tall, dark, and handsome who was just soooo in love, I thought maybe you'd faked it. Guess I was right, huh? Your parents, the hippie ones...they're cute. Lucky for them, they don't know much."

It was painful to keep up this charade. Hearing her mention Lily and Sabastian almost sent me over the edge, but she was talking, so I kept my cool.

"Why did you kill her?"

She shrugged and reached across the cot, pinching a bunch of grapes from the stem.

"Loose end." She popped a grape in her mouth.

Well, that was one question answered. She just admitted to murder. Was I a loose end too?

"Why? Did she know who you were?"

"She said she didn't, but you know these criminal types." She leaned close, like she was going to tell me a secret, and whispered. "You just can't trust 'em."

"You're pretty smart."

"Whatever." She shrugged again and flipped her long hair over her shoulder. "Your trail went cold untilll...until one night, I had a strange dream."

I felt my eyes grow wide. I had dreamed of her; she'd walked past me and looked right into my eyes. At least, I thought it was my dream, mine and Sabastian's. Could it have been hers too?

"I hadn't thought of that night in so many years. I was young then; it was one of my first...anyway."

First what? Jobs? Or had it just been for fun? I gripped the mattress, and she smiled as her eyes fell on my hands. Amy was still sleeping behind me, or I would have launched myself at her.

"I always wondered what happened to that baby." She narrowed her eyes. "The one that got away."

"You killed my parents."

She tossed another grape in her mouth. "Yeah...sorry about that. Guess Daddy was a jumpy driver, huh?"

Her tone was laced with sarcasm and vile, disgusting disregard.

"You did alright though," she said. "Got yourself a nice government job."

"Are there a lot of people looking for..."

"Freaks like you?" She interrupted. "Ehh...I watch the chat rooms on the dark web and most of the people in those groups are a joke; sickos who believe in real life vampires and stuff like that, but I've learned that's where the real monsters like to hide, mixed right in with the fake ones."

"Which one are you?" I asked, immediately regretting tempting her anger.

She simply smiled though, and shrugged like she didn't care. But her apathy was a mask, and a thin one at that. She kept trying to make me feel unimportant–a freak, as she'd said. But it was all false. She'd spent two decades seeking me out, and now, she was negotiating. Keeping the apparent value low so as not to drive up the cost.

"What do you mean you were looking for me?" I asked. "How did you know I even existed?"

"It's my job to know things. I already told you, I'm a collector."

"Your job? Who's your boss?"

She waved a finger back and forth. Got it, that topic was off limits.

"You're not a doctor?"

"Of course not," she said, scoffing at the idea. "I'm merely a consultant. I just have to find an administrator with...questionable morals and the need for a nice big bonus check, and boom...I'm in."

"Then what? You gather up a bunch of people who think they have superpowers and hope they're for real?"

"It's not so far-fetched, is it? Didn't sweet nurse Patricia think you belonged with us?"

"How would you know, though? That they're not just...sick." I shook my head. How many times had I thought I was crazy myself? I knew well that horrible confusion of knowing that something isn't right in your mind but being unable to discern reality from fantasy. It was awful.

"I find that under duress, a person shows their true colors."

Except for the soft whisper of Amy's breaths, the room was silent. Under duress. She meant torture–of one kind or another. Show me your powers or else. At least I knew what was coming.

"Have you found anyone else...like me?"

She cocked her head to the side, her narrowed eyes asking the same question of me.

"No."

"What happens to them? All the ones you've...collected?"

"As a collector, I find a lot of things. Some are valuable, but that's rare. Some aren't of use to me, but might be to someone else, or at least to their family. So, that's always helpful in the funding department. Most of what I find is useless though–to me and everyone else. It takes up space, and eventually, I have to throw it out."

"You're saying you force people to pay you to let their sick family member go?"

"That would be horrid, Andromeda. I transfer them to the very best care facilities in the nation–for a very nominal fee. I'm doing them a service."

I wanted to scream. She was talking about people–broken and hurting people–living, breathing people.

She all but admitted to selling them or holding them hostage if they were lucky enough to have a family who cared. But the rest...the ones who were alone. She could have done anything, transferred them, turned them out on the street, anything! But she killed them. At least–she thought she did. I prayed the buses of people Hardy saw were spared, but there was no denying her intent. I squeezed my jaw so tight it hurt. *Keep her talking, Andy. Maybe she'll make a mistake.*

"You knew we were here. How?"

"Well, after my little visit to Nadine, I *was* looking for you specifically, and once I saw you in that dream, I knew you were looking for me too. Since you were technically dead, I tried tracking down your boyfriend. He's no dummy, I'll give you that. I was running out of ideas. Then, strangely enough, I had that same dream again. Because of what Nadine told me, I knew what you were doing. I knew it was only a matter of time until you found me, so I just had to sit back…and wait."

"You've been watching us since we got here?"

"I've got eyes everywhere." She fanned her fingers and waved her hands mysteriously. "I sent Marco, and when he saw you talking to that old man, I knew it wouldn't be long until you stumbled on good ole' Mercy Memorial. I watched you walk right up to the door."

She spoke so nonchalantly, as if none of this mattered. "You aren't very stealthy, you know."

I wanted to ask her about Marco; how was he so young? It couldn't possibly be the same man that she'd called on the phone the night she caused my parents' accident. Her words that night played over and over in my mind. She didn't mean to kill them. Maybe there was some kind of humanity left in her, although as I studied her, I couldn't see it. I needed to keep her talking. I was just buying time, but it was the only plan I had.

"You set it all up? You knew we were coming; you made sure our search ended here?" She played us, and we picked up every crumb she laid out. "The burner phone–you turned it back on?"

"Yep," she said happily as she put the last grape in her mouth. "If you found the old hospital, then you'd have known Nadine went there and that she'd called me, although I can't quite figure out how." She leaned forward, fascinated, as if we were girlfriends sharing secrets. "Tell me, how'd you do it–since she's dead–how did you know?"

There was no way I was going to tell her about my vision of Nadine. I could imagine her eyes lighting up with new possibilities.

When I didn't respond, she leaned back on her elbows, her lip pushed out in faked sadness. "That's really too bad about Prince Charming."

She was so confident and prideful. Perhaps that would be her downfall.

She had also become suspiciously forthcoming. It was unnerving. I figured she had no plans of ever letting me go, so why not just tell me everything? Although, she hadn't *really* told me anything I couldn't have guessed myself. What was her endgame?

"So, you're what–going to sell me to the highest bidder?"

"Oh no, you're all mine," she said, laughing. I wanted to slap that smug smile right off her face. "My prize."

Taklos had used those same words. Things hadn't worked out so well for him. Did her boss approve of this? Was he even aware of it?

"I won't work for you," I said through my teeth.

"Hmm." She wasn't concerned. "Well, we'll see about that, Andromeda."

That's not my name. I almost said it out loud. She had to know that; she knew I was the baby from the crash that she caused.

A flicker of emotion passed across her face. Why did she want me to be Andromeda so badly? Why did that matter? She'd not mentioned Esther or Jacob at all. *I tracked her down without so much as a name.* Isn't that what she'd said? Maybe she didn't know. But it didn't make sense. Esther and Jubal both had said that after the crash, it was as though the baby never existed, that I was never born. If it wasn't Elena...then who? She'd checked for life that night, but I never saw her look for a wallet or purse. Somehow–she never knew our names.

It wasn't somehow though, was it? It was by the grace of God. Even in the midst of such horror, He made a way.

And He could do it again. I narrowed my eyes defiantly.

She'd taken my wedding ring and necklace. She was erasing my life...and all the better that she did.

My original plan to simply eliminate her once I got to sleep was more and more appealing. Maybe that was the way. She was close enough that I could find her in seconds. Jacob and Will had both begged me not to even think of it, but what choice did I have now? If it came to Elena or Amy... Amy would win. A pinky promise saw to that.

She seemed to have all the power–always one step ahead–but I wasn't worried. She had to sleep sometime. I still had a card to play in this game. I looked her over, studying her carefully, feeling that same sickening disgust as when she'd first appeared in the hospital, but there was something else, too. She was evil, pure and uncut. Just looking at her made my skin crawl. Taklos had been evil too, but his hate was forged from pain. Was it the same for her? I remembered what had happened when I tried to sneak into her dream the first time. Were those voices in there now, speaking to her? How awful her existence must be. Jacob's reminder that we all need God's grace slipped through my mind.

If I had the chance, would I show her grace? Honestly, I wasn't sure.

"Why are you like this?" I asked without thinking. "Who made you this way?"

Her jaw tensed and her eyes turned even colder than they already were. She stood, clasped her hands behind her back, and stepped towards me. I remained on the cot, protecting Amy, who hadn't stirred.

Elena bent, her eerie green eyes staring direct and menacingly into mine. She quickly jerked her hand around and slapped a metal handcuff that I didn't even know she had on my wrist. She yanked the other end of the cuff hard, pulling me off the bed and onto the floor, making me yelp as the metal bit into my skin. She dragged me over to the other cot by the wall. I struggled, trying to get up, but she hooked the open cuff to the cot rail. The bed didn't move, and I quickly realized it was bolted to the floor. I flopped around, pulling against my restraints as she stood over me, sinister and satisfied.

"No one made me. I made myself!" she spat. She reared back and kicked; the sharp toe of her boot made damaging contact with my ribs. I felt a snap inside and cried out, but put a hand over my mouth. I didn't want Amy to wake up and see this or worse, fall victim to her wrath.

"I do what I want. I take what I want. I get what I want," she said, kicking me hard between each sentence. I had to stop her, or she was going to break more bones and maybe even kill me.

"You'll do what I want too," she said, swinging her foot back to kick me again. This time I leaned into her instead of turning away and wrapped my free arm around her leg. Her eyes grew wide and she stumbled backwards, falling hard to the floor, landing on her elbows. The restraints kept me from crawling to her, so I jerked her towards me.

Every move was torture and my body screamed, agonizing spears of pain shooting through my side. But she slid easily across the slick tile floor as I pulled, powered by nothing more than adrenaline and self-preservation. I shifted up to my knees, crawling over and straddling her. She fought, spitting curses and threats.

"Get off of me!" The piercing screech of her voice echoed off the tile walls.

I only had one hand to truly fight her with, but managed to get her flipped so I could wrap my legs around her from behind and hook my free arm across her neck. I grabbed the bed rail with my cuffed hand and pulled, giving myself leverage, and squeezed. I wasn't trying to kill her; I just needed her to pass out so I could get the keys and get Amy out of here. She kicked her feet and clawed at my arm with her nails, drawing blood. I didn't let go. I used every bit of strength I had to keep my arm in place.

She kept struggling and just as she started to slow her defense, a sharp prick followed by a slow burn weakened the leg that was wrapped around her waist. I gasped, trying to keep my hold, but my muscles suddenly stopped obeying and relaxed against my will. She pushed away and scrambled to her feet, hurling more curses before she pulled her hand back and slapped me hard across the face. My body was limp, unable to react, even though I tasted the coppery bite of blood on my tongue. She bent and snatched an emptied syringe off the floor, then threw it against the wall behind my head. Bits of broken glass rained down into my hair as it shattered. I slumped against the bed, my cuffed arm stretched uncomfortably up above my head.

She stood, straightened her jacket, tucked her shirt in, and ran a hand through her hair, smoothing it back down. She cut one more hateful look my way before stomping over to the door and punching some numbers on the keypad. When it didn't open, she banged loudly on its metal surface.

She pushed a button on an intercom and barked, "Open the door!"

She banged again when she got no response. It finally opened, and she stared with disdain at whomever was in the hallway.

"Where were you?" she hissed. "That witch almost killed me!"

"I…" someone said.

"The code doesn't work," she snapped.

"I'm sorry, miss. One of the children needed–" It was Themba.

"I don't care! You're supposed to be here–with me. You do what I say, Themba. You do that and I let you live. That's the deal."

"Yes, miss."

"Now, get in there and get her cleaned up. She smells like death." She glanced over her shoulder and made a disgusted face as she looked at my bloody shirt, then turned and tossed a small set of keys towards him.

"Yes, miss."

"Take the girl to her own room, now."

"Yes, miss."

"Ugh!" Elena rolled her eyes and stormed past Themba. I heard her yell from the hallway, "And fix that code."

He shut the door after she'd gone, testing the code once and shaking his head as the door opened with no problem. He gently lifted me up off the floor and laid me on the cot, being careful of my arm that was cuffed to the rail. His eyes traveled over me, compassion etched on every line. My side was on fire, and I knew that more than one rib was broken. I struggled to take in enough air to fill my lungs. My lip was beginning to swell, and a single hot tear slid down my cheek.

"Oh, Omncane." He hurried over to the sink, running water over a paper towel. He returned to gently wipe the blood from the corner of my mouth. "I'm so sorry."

He'd apologized before, and meant it. It was killing him to obey her; I could feel it. He was torn in half. Something was keeping him here, keeping him bound to her, and I wondered what it was. Could there be salvation for us?

"Will," I said through short shallow breaths. "Is he...is he..."

"I'm sorry, I don't know," he said sadly.

He placed a large, warm hand on my shoulder and whispered gently. "Shhh...sleep now."

I would have slept anyway from the effects of the drug she injected. Through dropping lids, I watched Themba walk over to Amy. He bent over and rubbed her back gently.

"Amy, time to wake."

"Themba?" She yawned and rubbed her eyes.

"Yes, it's Themba. Come, we must go back to your room now." He smiled and took her hand, pulling her up from the cot.

"But...I'm so tired." She sighed and slumped back down.

"Come, hold to me. I will carry you."

She wrapped her arms around his neck, and he lifted her from the cot, holding her securely in his arms. Her head rested on his shoulder. Through drowsy, half-closed eyes she saw me.

"Andy's hurt," she said. "Help her, Themba."

"I'll take care of her, Omncane." He carried her from the room, pushing the door closed behind him.

I was alone, my body broken and muscles weak. I wanted to give in to my emotions and weep, but sobbing would hurt too much. So I simply tried to live through that second, and then the next…and the next. The verses Jacob had asked me to read aloud echoed in my mind. *My soul is downcast within me. Yet this I call to mind, and therefore I have hope; because of the Lord's great love we are not consumed.* As I slipped off into a dreamless and unwanted sleep, I prayed for help.

Help me find a way, Lord; do not let us be consumed. Please let me hold on until You send a way.

CHAPTER 31

"Andromeda."

She'd kept me sedated so I couldn't dream, and I slept for what felt like years. I had no idea how long I'd actually been there, except Themba had brought meals nine times, so I figured three days had passed.

"Shall we give you a new name?" Her red lips twitched, the beginnings of a smile played at the edges. "Who is this Andromeda, anyway? Where is her family? Moved off, left her again. Where are her parents? Dead. Where is her lover? Dead...nothing but ghosts."

The mention of my family sent fire through my veins, and if I could have reached her, I would have ripped her apart with my bare hands. Because of Nadine she knew my history, the nomadic ways of my parents; but she didn't know them now, and she knew nothing of my true identity. Was Will dead? Did she know for sure? She had sent Marco back to–I couldn't even think about it, but was there still hope? There had to be.

My wrist screamed back at me from the bite of the metal handcuff. Elena didn't flinch, confident I was securely restrained. I'd woken chained but dressed in a clean grey t-shirt and grey sweatpants. A tight bandage was wrapped around my ribs, which hurt so badly I could hardly breathe.

My feet were bare, but I wasn't cold. I was furious.

"Everything that made Andromeda is gone. But there is plenty left for you to do. Maybe you don't need a name–how about a number?"

I opened my mouth to scream every vile word I knew at her, but Esther's voice echoed in my head, pleading, commanding. *Remember. Remember what is true.*

Elena was right; they were gone. I felt that familiar comfortable rage begin to settle over my heart, vine-like tentacles reaching, curling, entangling. I wanted to allow it to stay, to root down deep; but that would be the most treacherous of betrayals. If I gave into this emotion, they would truly be lost to me forever, their sacrifice made in vain. I closed my eyes and took a deep, painful breath. My true strength would never come from anger.

Help me control it, Lord. Give me the strength to show her mercy if I can. Please, help me not to hate her–if not for her sake, then for my family. Oh God, I can't be the one to end our legacy–I can't.

If I had to hate something, it would be the evil she'd allowed to take up residence in her heart and poison her mind. I knew it was there; I'd heard its terrible voice with my own ears. Emily's words wafted through my mind with the savory fragrance of wisdom.

The word of God is a double-edged sword. Fight, take captive every thought. I squared my shoulders. Time to tell the truth.

"Andromeda Stone is dead," I said through gritted teeth. "I am a new creation."

Elena turned around sharply. "What did you say?"

"I said, Andromeda Stone doesn't exist. She died to this world; there is nothing you can offer me–nothing you can threaten me with. Nothing. I will not give in to you."

It was risky, but if she attacked me again, I'd eventually pass out, and she couldn't make me do anything for her. Her jaw tensed and her lips became a tight, thin line. She moved and I braced for her attack. She was furious, but something flicked briefly behind the ice in her green eyes and she relaxed, folding her arms across her chest.

"Well, we will just see about that." Her signature smugness returned. She pushed the button on the intercom. "Themba, bring Amy."

Amy? Ice shot up my spine. *Oh no, what have I done?*

Seconds later, the door opened and Themba entered with Amy, who was smiling. When she saw Elena, she instantly cowered behind him.

Themba looked from Elena to me and back again with uncertainty.

"Go and prepare the lab," Elena said.

He didn't move. Amy clung to the fabric of his shirt.

"That will be all, Themba," Elena said, emphasizing each word. She cocked her head to the side as if to send a message only he could understand. "Unless you'd like to bring Thadie instead."

Thadie? Ben's wife? Was she here? I locked eyes with Themba, his wide and pleading. What was happening?

"You promised to leave my daughter alone."

His daughter? Themba wasn't old enough to be Thadie's father. Maybe her brother, but definitely not her father. Marco was too young too. Was I in some kind of time warp—was that a real thing? My heart began to race, and my skin prickled with the adrenaline that was rising to the top, threatening to spill over. But there was something else, too: a whisper, still and small and very familiar.

Get ready, it said.

"Then do as I say," Elena warned.

I could see him struggle with the decision, but finally he turned to leave, placing a soft hand on the top of Amy's head. He stopped and spoke over his shoulder. "What will you do with her?"

"That's up to Andromeda," she said. "As long as she cooperates, everyone will be just fine."

Themba cast one short glance my way, an unspoken request in his eyes. He looked back at Amy and she at him.

"It will be alright, Omncane," he whispered, his long finger gently lifting her chin.

As he walked out, Amy's hand lingered in the air, reaching for him. Something about that scene looked familiar. The stretch of her hand reminded me of the twins in my dream. Siphiwe had held out his hand. He'd called a name.

Themba! That was it! Themba was the chink in her armor. He was the help I had been praying for.

I tried not to let my expression reveal the sudden burst of renewed hope, and sent up a silent request that God would provide the opportunity to speak to Themba alone. For the first time since I'd been pulled away from Will in Elena's office, there was something worth holding onto. Hope.

Elena walked over and took Amy by the arm. The little girl shrunk away from her in fear.

"What do you want from me?" I asked.

"I have a client who needs a little persuasion." She tossed a large envelope towards me, its contents spilled out into my lap.

"What am I, some kind of glorified heavy? You want me to break legs for cash?"

"For now."

"I won't hurt anyone," I said defiantly.

"Ow!" Amy cried when Elena squeezed her arm. Amy jerked and tried to pull away, but Elena just squeezed even harder.

"Oh, look." Elena sneered. "You already are."

"Stop!" I lunged at them, papers scattering across the floor. The chain shook under the strain as I stretched it as far as it would allow. I doubled over, gasping through waves of pain. "Okay! I'll do it–just stop."

"I thought you might."

She headed towards the door Themba had left open, dragging a crying Amy behind her.

"Let her go," I called. "I said I would do what you wanted."

"I'm sure you will, but she stays with me, just in case you need reminding."

"It'll be okay, Amy." I met her frightened eyes.

"Read the file. You have half an hour," she said.

"Half an hour? That's not enough time–"

"I don't think you will have a problem." Amy cried out again as Elena wrenched her arm before disappearing down the hall.

"Amy!" I yelled, but the door slammed shut and I was alone, my body attempting to expel the pain through dry heaves.

I yanked on the handcuff in frustration. The chain clicked and scraped along the metal rail of the cot. My mind raced with so many thoughts, none coming together to make sense. I needed help. Slowly lowering myself down to sit straight on the thin mattress of my cot with my hands resting gingerly on my wrapped ribs, I began to pray, but felt compelled to kneel before God.

So, even though it hurt, I slipped off the mattress and onto the cold tile floor.

Keeping one arm at my injured side, I bowed in reverence.

Lord, I know you are with me. Whatever You will, I accept. But I need help. Please help me save these kids.

I prayed for Themba's favor, somehow knowing he was our best hope. The only other person I had seen besides Amy was Marco, and as far as I could tell, he was as cold and hard as the floor on which I knelt. Like Elena, I doubted there was any humanity left in him at all, but I asked for his favor too. After a final plea for the miracle of seeing Will alive again and a whispered amen, I sat back on my heels.

Something under the bed caught my eye. I reached and felt around. Hanging from one of the springs was a thin piece of metal about the size of a paperclip. I jerked it loose and held it in my palm. I turned my arm, examining the keyhole of the handcuff. I started to unlock it but stopped. *Not yet.* Even if I got the cuffs off, I was still trapped in the room and in the building. There was no way I could run, or climb, or fight. If Elena came back and found me gone, there was no telling what she would do. I didn't know what other good it could do me, but for some reason it seemed like a precious thing, so I slipped the bit of metal into the waistband of my sweatpants, bending the end around the little drawstring opening in hopes that it wouldn't fall out when I moved.

I crawled back onto the cot and studied the intel Elena had given me. Her client was a man named Gregory Farmer. The photo stapled to the document depicted a tall Caucasian man with dark hair and equally dark eyes. He was dressed in a business suit, and had a boring smile on his face.

There was little information provided, but I tried to commit it to memory. Farmer had recently disappeared, hiding somewhere to avoid Elena's retaliation for an offense not mentioned. She hadn't even attempted to locate him yet. He seemed like a small fish; he didn't know anything about Elena or her dealings, really. He posed no threat to her; he simply owed her money. This must be a test. She wanted to know what I could do...what I was willing to do.

The final notes on the last page revealed exactly what Elena Cordova wanted, which was for Farmer to fully understand the extent of her power. She wanted him living in fear, knowing she could reach him anywhere. I was her ethereal muscle, an embarrassing and humiliating use of my gift, as I was sure she intended.

I looked up from the file when the door opened again. Themba stood with his head bowed low.

"Err...Ms. Cordova is ready for you."

I didn't answer or resist as he approached and hesitantly unlocked the restraint. Our eyes met briefly before he stepped aside, and I pulled myself up with a groan. He waited for me at the door. As I passed, I made sure to stop long enough for him to feel uncomfortable and look up at me. I needed him on my side. I touched his arm softly and felt his heartbreak. He was sad, trapped, and afraid.

"This way, Miss." He stepped away and pointed towards the hallway.

I stayed close to his side as we walked. Once again, I was at the top of that peak, just waiting for the cart to roll over and plummet down, sending my racing heart straight up through my throat.

If Themba was the key, maybe we could roll backwards down the incline and back into the gate. Maybe we could finally get off this ride.

I didn't know how long I would have before we reached the "lab" Elena had mentioned. It was time to take a risk. He had taken care of me so far; maybe I could tug at his sympathy.

"Thank you for helping me." My hand rested on my side and the thick bandage under my shirt.

"That wasn't me," he said. "It was Marco."

Marco? Why would Marco have helped? Elena must have told him to. I tried to think of a new plan.

"Your daughter's name is Thadie?"

He glanced at me but didn't speak.

"It means 'loved one,' doesn't it?"

He couldn't hide his surprise.

"I have a friend named Thadie. She has two little twin boys, Sipho and…"

"Siphiwe," he interrupted.

I stopped, but he took my arm, urging us on.

"Keep walking. There are cameras, but she cannot hear."

Small black orbs were sporadically placed near the ceiling on the left side of the hallway. I let him lead me, but noticed his breathing changed as if he were upset. He was debating whether or not to trust me. I was doing the same.

"How do you know them?" I asked, making sure to keep looking ahead.

"My daughter, Thadie, is named after my sister," he whispered.

His sister! Thadie Calloway was Themba's sister. This brought a small bit of clarity, but couldn't possibly be a coincidence.

"I prayed to God for help." Themba's confession snapped me back to the urgency of my mission. *Thank you, Jesus.*

"So did I. You are the help, Themba. You have to help me, please," I said earnestly. We engaged in a fake struggle, an unspoken understanding to buy time. "You're the only chance; we have to get these kids out of here and stop what she's doing to the people in her hospital–she's killing them."

"I know, but I cannot–she has my daughter." There was agony in his voice.

"What does she want with them, with you?"

"She could not find my sister, so she took my daughter and me instead. As for the others, she thinks they will do things."

"What kind of things?"

"She thinks they have…influence…now, or they will in the future." He shook his head, as if trying to make sense of his own words.

"How does she know that?"

"She searches; she has people everywhere looking. She also gets phone calls. They give her names, and she brings them here."

"Calls from who? Who does she work for?"

"I don't know." We kept walking, continuing our charade. I had to get him to tell me where we were. There had to be a way. My tiny sliver of opportunity was slipping away, and a wave of nausea passed over me. That gave me an idea. I wrapped my arms around my stomach and bent over.

"What is wrong?" His voice was laced with panic.

I stopped and turned towards the wall, placing my hand on the cold brick to both support myself and block the camera. Themba stood at my side, a soft hand on my back.

"Miss…are you okay?"

"Themba, please, I need you," I whispered when he was close.

"I can't…my daughter…"

"I promise, I will get her out. Please."

"But how?"

"Just tell me where we are."

He hesitated.

"Themba, please! It's not just your daughter. Sipho and Siphiwe… they're in danger. They're special. She will find them eventually. You know this. She will do whatever it takes to get them and then what will happen to your daughter?"

He sucked in a deep breath.

"It's an underground bunker…abandoned…old."

"In New Orleans? Do you know an address or landmark that it's close to? How would someone recognize it from the outside?"

"Yes, in the city, but…I…I don't know. She doesn't let me leave." His expression was pained, apologetic.

"Is there anything at all you can think of? Please, anything?"

I knew we were running out of time. My fake stomachache was only going to buy us a few more seconds, if that long. Themba squeezed his eyes shut. I turned my head and looked up at him desperately. *Please, God, help him to think of something.* I grabbed his arm, willing him to remember. My fingers felt hot on his skin. His eyes flew open, falling on mine in amazement.

Elena's voice echoed off the stone walls, making both of us jump.

"Themba!" she shouted. "What is the problem?"

"She is sick," he called back.

"Get her in here, now."

He put his arm around my waist, pretending to help me walk.

"The water," he whispered into my ear. "I have seen the water, and boats with sails, and cars on the bridge."

"Thank you."

We stumbled the remaining steps to the door where Elena waited, her arms folded and foot tapping impatiently. She didn't question Themba further. She must have been confident he would never betray her. Themba helped me onto the table to which Elena had pointed, expressing her annoyance with a dramatic eye roll. She huffed and walked over to a counter that was covered with different sizes and shapes of glass vials.

Themba and I watched with anxious curiosity. I nodded at him reassuringly. Elena held a small syringe. When she tapped the end, clear droplets of liquid dripped down a tiny needle.

"I don't need that," I said. "I can fall asleep on my own."

"I'd rather not waste any time." She shoved the needle into my arm, causing me to suck in air sharply.

"Where is Amy?" I rubbed the place where she'd stuck me.

She jerked her head towards a large window high on the opposite wall. Amy's face appeared on the other side, her little hands placed flat on the glass.

"It's okay," I mouthed. She nodded but still looked scared.

I looked back at Elena, who had returned to the counter. "I mean it...I won't hurt anyone."

"You read the file; you know what I want. Just scare him–for now."

"You can't make me keep doing this."

"You'll do whatever I ask, Andromeda," she said, rolling her head towards Amy.

Lord, forgive me. I don't want to do this, but she's leaving me no choice; please let this work.

"Whoa," I said as my head started to swim. "If this is what you gave me before, it's too strong. I won't be able to reach him."

"It's hardly anything. You'll be fine. You have fifteen minutes. Try anything, and whatever happens to Amy will be on you." She cut her eyes to Themba. "Make sure she doesn't move."

Themba stayed by my side, watching and worried. My lids grew heavy and I stretched out a weak hand. Themba took it between his.

"Good luck, Omncane," he said softly.

"What does that mean?" My words slurred together.

"Omncane means 'little one.'"

"What about your name?" I could barely form my words now; my lips and tongue felt like lead.

Themba smiled and leaned over me. "Themba means hope."

I breathed a deep sigh of relief and fell into the darkness of a dream, his last words a melody forming a beautiful song that carried me between worlds.

Chapter 32

Gregory Farmer was surprisingly easy to find. He looked just like his picture: dark suit, bland face.

"Who are you?" he said, clearly spooked. His eyes darted around, and flashes of faces appeared behind him. Among them, I recognized Elena's smug, irksome image.

God, please forgive me.

"Ms. Cordova sends a message," I said, sickened by the words that came out of my mouth.

He backed away a few steps and then turned to run, but he just reappeared again, running towards me. His face was contorted with confusion and fear. Even though I knew he was a criminal, I still wanted no part of this.

I bent on one knee and put my hands to the ground, my fingers splayed wide. I wasn't afraid, but he was. I would have to use his terror to do what I needed to do. I closed my eyes, took a deep breath, and gritted my teeth. Cool water rose, soon covering my hands and approaching my elbows.

"What is that?" I could hear him splashing as he tried to escape. "What are you doing?"

I stood slowly, my eyes remained closed as I drew the water higher. The more fear he felt, the more power I had over the dream.

"She will find you. There is nowhere to hide." My words tasted like poison in my mouth. "She wants the money, all of it. You have three days."

"I...I...I don't..." he stuttered, turning in circles, looking for a way out. The water lapped at our waists. He was trying to lie, but it was impossible. He finally said something true, or as close to the truth as he could get. "Please, give me more time."

"You have three days." I swallowed hard and shook my head. I didn't want to do this, but she would know.

I raised my arms and the water, like a marionette, followed their movement. I waved them back and forth, pushing and pulling the surges, making them rush towards him and away from me. Great waves splashed over him, pushing him down, pulling him up, tossing him like a ragdoll. His screams were silenced as he was hit with a face full of liquid. Delicious heat shot up through my veins as his terror grew. It was almost too easy, and I swirled my hand around as if stirring a spoon in a pot. A pillar of water rose around him, trapping him inside.

I opened my eyes and saw him floating, his face twisted with panic and arms flailing, frantically trying to escape his watery prison. I held him there for thirty seconds...forty-five seconds...sixty seconds. His eyes grew desperately wide. *Stop.*

I dropped my hands and the water fell away, disappearing as fast as it had appeared. He collapsed in a heap on the floor, choking and gasping for air. We were both soaked. I was breathing as heavily as he. When he cowered, I felt a smile curl on my lips. It was such a rush, like a high from a drug. Every part of me was warm and light. *I have to get out of here.*

"You have one hour to contact Ms. Cordova and confirm you have received her message, or I'll be back, and I won't be so patient," I said, following Elena's instructions. She was smart. She made sure there would be proof of delivery.

"One hour!" I said again.

He held up a weak hand in defense, "Okay, okay...I will do it."

I debated staying longer to make sure he was completely clear on the repercussions, but there were only a few minutes left before she would wake me, and only one chance to do what I really came to do.

I turned and ran as fast as I could from the broken Mr. Farmer and the disturbing satisfaction that experience brought. When I was alone in the dark, I steadied myself, concentrating as hard as I could on my next target.

Where are you? Please...please be there.

"Andy?"

Thank you!

I opened my eyes and ran to him. My Uncle Jacob gasped as I hit him with my full weight. I clung to him with every ounce of my strength.

"Jacob–I don't have long. The real patients are in the basement of the hospital. There's a window...uh...right outside the emergency exit. Get there quick. She told Marco to get rid of them."

"Where are you?"

"New Orleans, somewhere. Underground–in an old bunker," I spoke as fast as I could, knowing any second, he would be gone. "You can see the water and sailboats from here...and um, cars, too, on the bridge. You have to hurry; she's got kids here. Themba is helping me, but...we need help, please!"

"I'll do it. We will find you." His image rippled, slipping through my fingers like sand.

"Please hurry...she's making me do things, Jacob, and I don't know how long I can resist. It's...I can't hold out much longer."

I tried to hold onto him, but my hands found nothing solid. *No, no, no!* Elena was waking me up.

"Jacob!" I screamed. "Find us!"

"Andy, Will is..."

He was gone. My eyes flew open and I gasped, my heart racing as I sat up quickly, regretting it immediately and groaning against the pain shooting from my middle. Themba's warm hands were on my shoulders, steadying me.

"It's done," I gasped. "It's done."

Elena was leaning against the wall with her arms crossed, disgustingly satisfied. She looked down at the screen of her phone, and before putting it to her ear, smiled and held it up like she was offering cheers with a champagne glass.

"Yes?" she said into the mouthpiece.

I was still out of breath, both from the dream experience and whatever drug she had administered to bring me out. My eyes met Themba's, and the tiniest of smiles fell across my lips.

We exchanged an unspoken communication, and his eyes lit up with hope. What had Jacob said–something about Will? Was he alive?

Please let that be true!

"Thank you, Mr. Farmer. I look forward to seeing you soon." Elena lowered her phone and pushed herself away from the wall.

"Nicely done, Andromeda. Themba, get a towel and dry that up; she's dripping all over the floor. We have a few more stops to make tonight." She walked to the counter, drawing out five more syringes.

"I can't–" I started to say.

"You can, and you will." She slammed the vial she was holding on the counter and turned sharply. "You think Amy is the only one I can hurt? How many children must suffer for your defiance, Andromeda?"

She was blaming me? That must be what Ben meant when he said "gaslighting." I wasn't falling for it. I might not be able to prevent the destruction, but it wasn't my fault. This was all on her. She stormed over to a small table near the door and grabbed a stack of folders, shoving them forcefully into my hands.

"Your homework."

I shook away angry tears and accepted the towel that Themba was wrapping around my shoulders.

"Miss, please…" Themba begged. "It's too much. Let her rest."

"I'll be back in an hour. Be ready." She cut her eyes sharply to Themba and cocked her head to the side. "Thadie will be joining Amy and I in the observation room."

"No!" I cried.

Elena snapped her fingers, cutting off my plea of resistance. "I can call Marco to handle them instead."

I stiffened and grabbed onto Themba's arm. Elena stood tall, full of pride and self-importance, her chin, as always, tilted slightly upwards as she looked down on everyone around her. Themba's hands felt heavy on my shoulders. He kept his head down and cut his dark eyes sharply up at her.

"I will bring her," he consented, but there was a tone of defiance just beneath the surface and a growing strength in the set of his jaw where before there had been only defeat.

"There is a way that appears to be right, but in the end–it leads to death."

His deep, quiet voice floated quick and smooth across the room, his words almost visible as they reached Elena and wrapped around her like a foggy vine. She fired back a vicious, narrow-eyed glare.

"Is that supposed to be some kind of threat, Themba?" Her voice was ice; it cut and sliced when she spoke.

"Only for some."

Elena may not have recognized the scripture Themba had quoted, but behind her eyes something shifted, and I knew that whatever evil had taken root in her heart certainly did. Themba's words were weapons, ammunition of truth he'd fired against the enemy. I was not fighting alone. There were two of us now. There was hope.

Elena took one last long, cold look at us and walked out of the room. Themba's shoulders sagged. He turned, wiping the back of his hand across his forehead.

"It's okay, Themba." I watched him move towards a small cooler in the corner.

He returned with a bottle of water, which I gratefully accepted. He melted into a chair next to the table, his head falling forward onto his arms.

"I tried to save her." His voice broke. "I have tried so many times."

"Themba."

He lifted his eyes, which were red and shiny with tears that threatened to spill out. My words were a reminder to both of us. "God is good. He is. He will not abandon us. Please, be strong. Help is coming. Have hope."

"Yes, Omncane." He lowered his head again. "God found me once when I was lost. I know He can again."

"Will you tell me?"

"When I was a boy, there was much trouble. My brothers had all gone away to fight. I was to follow them, but God sent a man to my village. The man brought us medicine, food, and books. He also brought to us the word of God. My father was a hard man; his heart…full of pride and fear. He would listen to no one, but God softened his heart, and he listened to the man. Hope had come to our people."

"Hope," I repeated, finding Themba's hand and holding tight.

"Hope." He nodded. "He had a daughter who looked like you. Her name was Emily."

I smiled softly. Of course he would know Emily. Because God was still in control, not Elena Cordova–no matter how much she wished it true.

"I know her." I sighed, laying back and looking up at the bright white ceiling. "She's my friend."

Would I ever get to see Emily again? Would I get to hold her baby in my arms? What else would I have to do for Elena? What was her ultimate plan for me? Question upon question filled my mind, threatening to pull me away from the hope and into a dark pit of nothingness.

Stand firm, Andy. There is yet hope. Do not be consumed.

Themba helped me to sit up. I sucked down the rest of the cool water and opened the first file, praying I would make it through this night without killing anyone, and that tomorrow would bring salvation.

CHAPTER 33

By the time I woke from the fourth dream, my body was shaking beyond control, and I was on the verge of convulsions. Between the sedative used to send me into dreams and the adrenaline to wake me, I was waiting for my heart to burst. Sweat dripped from my forehead and water puddled on the floor. Themba sopped it up with towels and begged Elena to stop, to start again tomorrow night. She had refused, high on the power and basking in the evil satisfaction that each confirming phone call brought.

She eventually had Marco drag Themba away, forcing him to watch helplessly from behind the glass of the observation room. Marco had returned to check my pulse and listen to my heart. He worked silently. I had trouble focusing, but I thought I saw him make eye contact with me once, just for a second. He finished his short exam and walked over to Elena, whispering something in her ear. Her lips formed a tight thin line, and she nodded reluctantly.

She allowed him to draw a syringe full of some other drug and inject it into my arm. When I realized it was a painkiller, I wanted to hug him. It didn't completely erase the pain, but eased it enough so I could breathe.

Hot tears flowed unhindered from my red, raw eyes as they focused on Themba through the glass, Amy and Thadie in his arms. Their faces were hidden against his shoulders, shielded from the horror unfolding before them. If this was how it would end, I thanked God that Themba would still be there to protect them. At least they didn't have to watch as I succumbed more and more to the ecstasy of control. I, too, was drunk on its power, fighting–and losing–to keep it from seeping into every secret part of myself. This was exactly what Taklos had wanted, what he would have done to me. He was rushed and he failed, but Elena had spent the last twenty-two years wondering about the baby that disappeared, preparing, planning. Once she found out the truth about me, she'd engineered the perfect scenario in which I would have no way to escape or resist. I still prayed, though. I was not completely gone; there was still hope. As long as there was life–there was hope. Night was almost over, and dawn was approaching. I just had to wait for the sun.

Elena's phone chimed and a smile spread across her lips.

"Mr. Yokutaki didn't need three days after all," she said. "Well, Andromeda, you must be very persuasive."

She took the last of the syringes and shot a provoking glance at Marco. "You might have some competition, Marco. Shall we find out?"

He grunted but remained seated on a chair in the corner. He was rubbing his hands together, which were bruised and scratched across the knuckles as if he had been in a fight recently.

"You won't…" I whispered.

"What?" she leaned closer.

"You won't win."

Her brows shot together. A hideous scowl formed across her lips as she shoved the picture of the last target in my face. I had read the file, but she reminded me anyway.

"Naveed Hashrami," she spat. "He is hiding something valuable from me. If he refuses to reveal the location, kill him."

"No," I cried, my resistance dwindled to almost nothing. "I won't…I won't."

She jerked me up by my wet shirt, her sharp fingernails scratching deep into my skin. My ribs, though subdued from Marco's merciful pain killer, ached under the strain.

"You will," she hissed through her teeth just inches from my face.

Will…where is Will? Would he have been disappointed in me? I'd give anything to hear his voice, even if it was for him to say that he was.

"What does he have?" I closed my eyes in defeat.

"He knows. You just make sure I get a location."

I was ready to beg, to plead, to promise anything not to have to do this, but what I saw in her eyes told me it would be no use. Her once bright irises had turned a shade of green that was almost black. They were glazed over, and her pupils dilated, having given in to the lust for power–she was gone. I wondered if that was what Jesus saw when he looked into the eyes of Judas Iscariot before that treacherous kiss. Was it what I would see when I looked at my own reflection? Could there yet be redemption for me? What was it Esther had said once–?

Nothing can pluck you from His hand, Joanna.

I prayed that it was true. God holding onto me was my only hope now; my grip was weak and about to slip. Elena walked over and shoved a needle into my arm. I was too exhausted to even cry out. Seconds later, I was in the dark again. At least in my dreamscape, my clothes were dry and clean. I was strong here. After a deep breath, I focused on Naveed Hashrami. Elena knew exactly where he was, physically close by in New Orleans, but I had been too overwhelmed to question. I heard a soft groan and turned around, taken back by what I saw.

A brown-skinned man was seated in a chair, his hands behind him, restrained with thin links of a pad-locked chain. Rope secured his ankles to the legs of the chair.

His head hung forward, shaggy black hair dripping with sweat, and his chin rested on his chest. His clothes were dirty, bloodied, and torn.

What is this?

I stepped forward slowly. "Naveed Hashrami?"

He strained to lift his head, and I gasped. Both eyes were nearly swollen shut; deep cuts, still fresh, split his lips and reddened his cheeks.

"Who are you?" he croaked, his words carrying a thick Middle Eastern accent.

"Ms. Cordova sends a message." My threat was more uncertain than intimidating.

His expression immediately darkened. Though his body was weak, the strength of resolve in his eyes sent me stumbling backwards. I felt villainous under his glare, and he spat in an unspoken and defiant response. I looked down at the splatter of saliva and blood at my feet.

"You can tell her to go to–"

"She wants to know where it is," I interrupted forcefully, then added softer, "Please, just tell me, and I'll go."

He just shook his head, letting it fall back to his chest. "Stop playing nice. I'd rather the other one. Just finish it."

I remembered Marco's bruised and bloody hand. No wonder he was so close; Marco had failed to get the information she wanted, and now Elena was sending me to finish the job. From the intel in Elena's folder, this guy might have deserved that beating.

I knelt and splayed my fingers on the floor, the new ritual I'd established tonight, but the waters wouldn't come. I looked at my hand, put it back down and tried again. Still nothing.

My eyes drifted to Naveed. His head still hung to his chest. He wasn't afraid. Now what?

"Why are you holding out?" I asked. "What is so important about this thing she wants?"

Above his head images flashed. A family. A beautiful mother laughing with her raven-haired daughters, happy and safe.

"Your wife?" I asked.

That caught his attention, and I heard splashes in the distant darkness.

"You want to protect your family?" Cool water lapped at my ankles.

"Who are you?" He jerked against his restraints, consumed with the same desire to tear apart a threat to his family as I'd felt against Elena.

"No one," I answered, surprised by my quick response. How was I able to lie? Unless it wasn't a lie. "Tell me what I want to know, and I won't hurt you. I don't–"

I tried to say 'I don't want to,' but the words were trapped in my mouth.

"I won't tell her where your family is. Trust me. I can just ask you one question, and you'll tell me whether you want to or not."

As the water rose, so did that warm intoxicating feeling I'd been overdosing on for the last several hours. I drank it in. It chased away all my reservations, any guilt or hesitation dissolving like sugar with each rising inch. Nothing remained but a wonderful, easy, nothingness.

The more he resisted, the more his thoughts turned to his family. Soon he was seeing the images too, flashing all around us. Their home, the sign outside of their town, their gray SUV driving up the driveway next to a well-manicured lawn, and his beautiful dark-haired wife climbing out of the driver's side door.

"Stop!" The chains that bound him were strong, despite the delicate melody of their clinking as he struggled.

"Where is it?" I demanded, my hands flat on the water that I'd capped at waist level.

He squeezed his eyes shut, trying to resist, but his mind betrayed him and a single image flashed. It was gone as soon as it appeared, but I had seen enough. Suddenly the water was rising on its own, reaching his chest in seconds.

The image was too familiar. Two little faces. Identical. Dark hair, innocent dark eyes.

"Siphiwe and Sipho," I breathed, staring at the blank space where their faces had been.

My narrowed eyes slid down to Naveed, fire instead of ice blazing through my veins. An ignition of fury built under my skin; I prepared to unleash it and reduce him to ash.

"What have you done with them?" I seethed.

Another image flashed. He was holding their hands, and they smiled up at him, innocent and trusting.

"Stop," he pleaded. Another picture, the boys wrapped in his arms, giggling as he tickled them.

What was this? Trickery? No...it wasn't possible. I felt like I was intruding in a place where I had no right to be. Elena's file was nothing but lies. He wasn't a thief or a murderer. He was a friend–he loved them.

"What is it they can do?" I stilled the tumultuous waters.

He shook his head, setting his jaw tight. A flash of impatience shot through me; I didn't have much time before Elena would jerk me away again.

"Tell me!"

"It's not what they can do, it's what they will become." He grimaced under my compulsion, unable to resist.

"What do you mean?" I forced the water to close in around him, squeezing him tightly. "Tell me everything."

He stiffened under the pressure and spoke through short, pained breaths.

"Their grandfather is the descendant of the last great king, the last of his line...except for the boys. Their father was killed protecting a group of missionaries."

"Their father is Ben Calloway."

"He married their mother, a widow."

"But why does she want them?"

"You work for her–don't you already know?" He fired the accusation through his teeth. His aim was true, and the arrow of his words sliced deep as it pierced its intended target.

"I don't work for– Just tell me!" I shook off his implication.

He resisted, but answering my question wasn't optional.

"Natimala is a Christian nation; one of the few remaining. They influence the entire continent, but many groups are working to destroy the nation and with it, their religion. According to tradition, as twins, the boys will rule together when their grandfather is gone. They can bring peace to the people, strengthen the faith. If the line ends–Natimala falls, and the whole country will be changed. But if the boys are successful, they can restore their nation and end the slavery and persecution. They must be protected."

"How are you involved?"

He shook his head again, but an image of Naveed and Ben, smiling together over a stack of blueprints, flashed over his head. Then another of the two of them ushering a group of blanket-covered women out of a tunnel in the dark.

"What does she want with them?"

"Money, power...and for the Natimala people to end. With them will go the Christian faith in the country. Asia is already in crisis. If Africa falls, Europe will not be far behind."

"And you're telling me Elena Cordova is behind all of this?"

I didn't believe that for a second.

"She's nothing–a minion. It's so much bigger than anyone knows. She's one small part, but whoever she works for...he is a major player."

Now that, I believed. I stared at him. He was telling the truth; he had to be. My mind worked to put it all together. The answer was right there in front of me, but something was holding me back from reaching out and taking hold of it. I felt a sharp pinch, and a tiny red mark appeared just below my elbow. I only had a few minutes. I wanted to ask him about Themba and his daughter, but Elena was already trying to wake me.

"I won't," he said through gritted teeth. "I won't tell her where they are."

"You don't have to." My voice sounded strange, dark and emotionless, as if it belonged to someone else. "I already know where they are."

His eyes were desperate, silently pleading. There was no escape from this, and little time left to decide. If I returned with no answer and left him alive, Marco would only torture him until he was dead or he talked. Elena would hunt down Naveed's family, and they would die too. If she got what she wanted, he would still die, but at least I would have bought a little more time to save the boys.

I moved my hands back and forth, debating, the water swirling with my movement. With each twitch of my fingers, the currents obeyed, releasing hit after hit of powerful endorphins.

"Yesssssss," a soft whispering voice tickled my ear.

"Sssssuch power…" Another voice caressed my mind.

"Ours…be ourssss."

They were wanton and lustful, tempting me with unspeakable desires of control and power. I knew them well; we'd met before in another dark place. And I'd heard them calling my name in the woods near the Prescott cabin. They pursued as I ran, and I'd seen them watching me from behind the cover of trees. Their form was a reflection of what they desired most: me, under their complete control, irrevocably given over.

A great darkness is ahead. You must remember what you know to be true.

I raised and lowered my hands, creating large rolling waves. Naveed had to lift his chin as high as he could to keep the water from covering his face. He stared at me, defiance and conviction his defense. My mind swam with the voices, the water, the power. I had but to raise my hands a few inches higher.

Remember. Remember the power that is in His name.

"Jesus," I whispered then repeated the name louder, calling out for him. "Jesus."

The voices hissed and retreated. Something inside of me snapped like a rubber band that had been stretched too far. It hurt and felt so freeing at the same time. I remembered. God promised to be with me; He would never abandon His beloved. He would always provide a way out, even if that way meant the end of my earthly life. An eternity with my Father would be far better than living with the guilt of what Elena wanted me to do. He wanted my obedience over my sacrifice. I would obey, and rescue as I was called to do.

I clenched my fists and dropped my hands; the waves followed. A sharp pain invaded my side as the rush faded.

Naveed gasped and shook the water off his face. I hurried over to him and squatted down behind his chair, examining the tangle of chains, only a small padlock holding the links together. It didn't budge when I attempted to jerk it loose.

"If I can get you free, can you get out of…wherever you are?"

"I…but how?"

"Can you?" I didn't have time to explain.

"Yes…I think so."

I felt the waistband of my sweatpants and pulled out the little metal piece. I smiled to myself, humored by the way I was so quick to doubt when God had proven Himself to me over and over again.

With trembling fingers, I wiggled the metal pin around and sent up a quick prayer, begging God's forgiveness for my faithless doubting and weakness in letting the high of this power take over. The lock popped open and I helped Naveed untie his legs.

"Will I really be free?" He stood, rubbing the red rings on his wrists.

"I believe so," I said. "I'm…I'm so sorry, Naveed."

"What will you do?" His eyes searched min for assurance. "Will you tell her?"

"No." My head fell forward, accepting the decision I'd already made. "I won't, but she will send Marco back, so you have to get out before he comes. I won't kill you, but he will."

"What about you?"

"I'll be okay. Just go. You have to warn Ben Calloway that his sons are in danger," I said. "And tell Thadie her brother Themba is here, and he needs help."

He nodded and his image wavered.

"Get out," I instructed. "Find my uncle, Jacob Abrams. He will help you."

I told him the phone number, making him repeat it several times. It was a risk, sending him to Jacob, but his damaged face and sincere eyes told me all I needed to know about his true motivations.

He nodded again and reached out, but vanished before our hands touched, the vapor of his gratitude lingering as a wisp of smoke.

CHAPTER 34

The room where Elena had Marco drag me was like all the others–no windows, no way to gauge the passage of time–but it felt like I'd always been there. Memories of a life other than this were only fiction, a fairy tale world where a sun lit the sky and the air didn't reek of despair. My eyes burned from exhaustion, but my heart hadn't stopped racing. She had ordered Marco to hold me down while she shoved bitter white pills in my mouth and poured water down my throat until I swallowed them all.

"She won't be sleeping any time soon," she said with satisfaction as she pushed me off the table into Marco's arms. "Take her below."

"You'll regret this, Andromeda." She grabbed my chin, jerking my face toward hers. I winced as her sharp nails dug into my skin.

I would certainly suffer for my decision, but I would never regret it.

I tried to shake off the trembling in my hands and paced back and forth across the brightly lit room. The clean white light was deceitful as the room was anything but. Evidence of multiple floods littered the entire building. Some rooms had been completely remodeled, but in this room, only the lights had been replaced.

There was nowhere to sit or rest, no comfort to be found.

The floor was covered in a thick layer of grime and debris, and the once-tiled walls were crumbling, revealing ages of neglected earth. I had already searched through the wreckage for anything that might help me escape, finding nothing but broken bricks and disintegrating paper.

I prayed Naveed had better luck. It had taken Marco at least twenty minutes to get me secured in my cell. He'd originally been somewhat gentle, but I'd fought him every step of the way. Any kindness he'd been willing to show quickly disappeared. While I hoped my struggling had bought Naveed a little more time, it had cost me a backhand across the jaw and a very badly sprained wrist. Marco was still an enigma to me. He was hard as stone. He'd shot Will, but didn't finish the job when given the chance–at least, I hoped he hadn't. He'd beaten Naveed, but bandaged my broken ribs and convinced Elena to let him administer a pain killer. I was also quite sure that he'd been the one to transfer at least some of the patients from the hospital before it burned.

He had shoved me into the dirty room but hesitated in the doorway when I was unable to catch my breath from the intense pain in my side, as if unable to ignore my suffering.

"Who are you, really?" I asked him through gritted teeth as I struggled to get up from my knees. He grunted and pushed against the rusted metal door.

"I know you aren't Marco," I said quickly.

He stopped, looking over his shoulder. I continued. As long as he was here, he wasn't hunting down Naveed.

"You can't be. Marco was there with Elena the night she killed my parents. That was over twenty years ago. You can't be more than thirty."

He started to close the door again.

"Do you even know who you are?" I was desperate.

He turned sharply. "I know exactly who I am–and I am Marco. Marco Moreno Dominquez…Junior."

"Junior?" I gasped. "He's your father?"

He didn't answer. I remembered something Elena had said to him on the phone. *There was nothing you could have done.*

"Did he teach you medicine?"

"Yes," he said softly.

"I know you don't want to do this. I know you saved people from the hospital before the explosion."

He didn't answer, only the slightest shake of his head acknowledging that he'd heard me.

"It was you in the alley too, wasn't it?"

His hand turned white from the tightness of his grip on the door.

"What happened to your father; where is he?" I needed to keep him here longer–Naveed needed time.

"He was betrayed." His shoulders stiffened, and he slammed the door shut, leaving me alone.

I'd forced myself to throw up as soon as Marco was gone, but due to my efforts to delay his reunion with Naveed, the pills had already taken effect. Whatever she gave me was meant to keep me awake, and it was working.

Nervous energy kept my mind alert as I picked through everything I'd learned. Elena was working for someone immensely powerful. From what I knew about Amy's father and the twins, a disturbing picture was forming. Someone was systematically trying to end the spread and ultimately the existence of Christianity in the eastern continents. Was it a single person or an entire group? Whoever it was, they must have an extensive network in order to gather all that information and put together such a targeted list. Siphiwe and Sipho were no threat now, but somehow they foresaw their future influence. How many more children had Elena taken over the years–what had become of them?

I had assumed they all had some special gift or ability like me, but now I wondered if they were simply a predicted threat. Clearly, there were two operations occurring simultaneously. Something Elena had said about Nadine finally made sense. *I couldn't have helped her.* Nadine came looking for a trade, even though she didn't get the chance to go through with it. But Elena wasn't ever going to give Nadine anything; she only wanted what Nadine had. What did she say about her collection? All she'd found was useless until me? All these years searching, kidnapping the mentally ill–and not a single thing to show for it. What had she done to deserve such a low position?

The accident–she screwed up. They weren't supposed to die. With Maggie as a prize, there could always be more. An endless supply of gifted offspring–at least that's how it would appear to an unbeliever. Someone who foolishly assumed it was genetic rather than divine. My stomach cramped and I retched again.

Elena had spent the last twenty years paying for her mistake. It was just dumb luck that Nadine stumbled upon her–certainly bad luck for Nadine. Or perhaps it was by design after all. I followed the tumbling dominos in reverse.

If Nadine hadn't plotted to get rid of me, Elena would never have known of her and I would have never met Will. And without Will, I would have never met Esther, never known my lineage or purpose. There was no way to know if my confrontation with Taklos would have had the same outcome, but regardless, I would have never ended up in Elena's bunker. Even though its very walls dripped with despair, somewhere amidst the darkness was the tiniest glimmer of light. The slight chance that God–in His goodness–allowed the awful choices of Nadine, Taklos, and Elena to still work for good to accomplish His plan was enough. It was the reminder that He would always be victorious. It didn't mean that I would come out unscathed, or even survive, but it meant that Amy's pinky promise was true. We would win.

Amy. As grateful as I was that she was unharmed, what possible purpose could there be for keeping her–or the boy? Why keep them alive…unless…they didn't want to simply end their influence, but turn it and use them to fight for the enemy. Amy would be an excellent and effective pawn to make sure John Robins never spoke at the summit.

Naveed said Elena was a nobody, but someone was pulling her strings. Who could it be? Who could be the father of this twisted family? Elena, Marco, Nadine, Taklos…

Father. That word struck something in my mind. I repeated it over and over, in all the languages I knew. *Padre, Pere, Otets…*

"Otets!" I said out loud. Otis. Otis Vranye Goncharov. I slapped my forehead. How could I have missed that? Even his middle name, Vranye, sounded like the Russian word for 'lies.' The truth had been hidden in plain sight the whole time.

Of course, Otis Goncharov was the one behind all of this. I had suspected it all along, but never thought him such a considerable force. The father of lies. Maybe instead of just participating in the experiment that had created Taklos, he was the mastermind. Instead of managing Elena, he recruited her. They wouldn't have known each other, because only the head would know what each of the arms were doing to keep anyone from knowing too much. Too many connections would lead right back to him–that explained all the aliases.

But despite his efforts, they had crossed paths. Nadine's jealousy and hatred of me had connected them, and eventually led me here.

When Elena tracked her down and found out about me, her hope of escaping her lowly position was renewed. I would have been the perfect addition to her collection, and she would have something valuable to raise her status within Goncharov's organization.

I followed the clues to piece together the rest. Elena wouldn't have known of his association with Taklos. If she'd let Nadine live, he might have never known about hers, either. Elena betrayed herself with her lust for blood. All Goncharov had to do was let it play out. If Taklos was successful in procuring my services, his plans would still go forward; if Taklos failed, he could simply let him take the fall. No one had ever suspected Taklos was working for anyone but himself.

My hand fluttered to my lips. Nadine Greyson was dead, and Dovanny Taklos was so deep in a non-existent prison; he would never be heard from again. Otis Goncharov had removed any chance of either of them revealing his involvement. There were too many connections now, though. It wouldn't be long until Elena became too great of a risk and he took care of her and anyone associated with her. That would mean Themba, little Thadie, Amy, and all the others.

Please, let Jacob find them in time.

"I hope it was worth it." Elena's voice at the door startled me. "This will be your life now. I will keep you awake until I decide you can sleep; and believe me, I will make sure you never dream on your own again."

"It doesn't matter what you do to me, you won't win."

"I keep telling you–you're not the only one with something to lose. Why are you so selfish, Andromeda?"

I needed more time. I had to keep her from hurting the others until help arrived. I knew Jacob wouldn't give up until he found us, and if Naveed was successful in reaching him, we stood a chance.

"Let the others go–all of them–and I will do whatever you want." That bargain might require more than I was willing to give, but I offered it anyway.

If I accessed that power too many more times, the darkness would take me. The painful cramps of withdrawal had already begun, even in just the last few hours. My heart belonged to the Lord, but my body would eventually fail. I prayed He would forgive me for whatever I had to do to save the others.

I knew He would be with me until the end, and I would fight until I had nothing left. Whatever purpose He had for giving me this gift, I prayed that I could remain faithful.

"Elena, please. I promise I will do what you want; just let them go." I placed my hands flat on the dirty metal door that separated us and let my forehead fall against it. My wrist ached, and I curled it up against my chest.

She didn't answer right away. I hoped that my promise would be too enticing for her to pass up. With my cooperation, there was no one she couldn't get to, no one she couldn't persuade.

I stepped back at the piercing sound of a harsh metallic scrape. She stood cross-armed in the hallway as Marco pushed the door, her eyes teaming with disgust.

Naveed must have escaped, or Marco wouldn't be back so soon, and she wouldn't be so furious with me. Hope swelled in my heart.

"I accept," she said. As her emerald eyes slid greedily over my broken body, a sinister grin broke the hard line of her lips. "You know, I've been thinking, we could make this a family business."

She stepped back, folding her arms across her chest and ogling me like I was a prize steer.

"What do you think, Marco? I bet you and Andromeda would make beautiful babies." The shock and horror on Marco's face mirrored my own, and she burst into a deafening fit of laughter.

"Oh, come on. Once you clean her up a bit, she's not that bad."

I had to give her credit. She was proficient at finding grains of hope and smashing them to bits under the hard heels of her boots.

"You wouldn't."

Arms still crossed, she leaned close, her nose almost touching mine.

"Try me."

Without taking her eyes off mine, she waved her hand and Marco forcefully jerked me into the hallway. He pulled me along as I stumbled behind the two of them. She never slowed her pace and was soon several yards ahead, Marco and I lagging behind.

"You let him go."

Marco's whispered observation surprised me and I tripped, sliding to my knees on the slimy, wet floor. He dropped to a squat in front of me, his hands on my arms, holding me up, and piercing brown eyes boring into mine.

"Why?" That single word held countless other questions.

My eyes flicked back and forth between his, seeing more than he intended to reveal. Marco was questioning his loyalties, and as far as I could tell hadn't killed anyone…yet.

He walked a dangerous and very fine line between ally and enemy. I crafted a careful answer.

"Because I'm not a killer–and neither are you."

His eyes widened for a beat and then he turned his face, hiding his pained expression. I tried to feel his emotions, to determine his intent, but everything inside of him was so jumbled, I felt nothing but chaos. I suspected Marco felt much like I had once: lost, invisible, and used only for his talents.

"Marco!" Elena's voice reached us from somewhere ahead.

Any possibility of further conversation dissolved as Marco yanked me to my feet. We made our way through the dark, ruined tunnels of the bunker and up rickety metal stairs to the upper level.

I was disappointed when she led us right back to the lab. She meant for me to prove myself right away. Marco threw me up onto the table and marched out of the room.

I rolled onto my side, holding my throbbing wrist close and fighting the urge to throw up again from the pain of my broken ribs. Marco's merciful shot had all but worn off now. Elena snatched a clear vial from her stash and prepared the syringe, my stomach cramping at the sight. How much more of this could my body take before my heart gave out?

Lord, give me strength. Just enough to get them out.

Marco returned minutes later, dragging Themba at gunpoint. Marco's expression remained stoic and hard, but Themba's eyes were wide, matching mine.

"What are you doing?" I turned to Elena, panicked and shaking.

"Simply giving you the proper motivation." She leaned over me with an eerily sweet smile stretching across her lips. "You succeed? Themba and his sweet little daughter go free."

"And if I don't?"

"One or the other, Andromeda." She shrugged, glancing up at Marco, who nodded.

I looked desperately towards Themba. Elena shoved a photograph in my face, breaking our connection. A freezing shock of recognition shot up my spine at the dark eyes that stared back from the paper.

"Dovanny Taklos?"

"This shouldn't be too hard for you," she said. "Consider it a gift. You get to rid the world of one more villain."

"But...he's harmless now."

"Not necessarily." I knew what she meant. It wasn't what he could do anymore, it was what he knew. Apparently even Goncharov couldn't reach him where he was. Even though I was quite certain he was in complete solitary confinement, all he had to do was indicate he had information, and someone would eventually listen. Did she know he was working for the same man? Did she consider that she would eventually be a target as well?

"Eliminate him." She took pleasure in the order.

"There won't be any way to confirm that I did it. You'll never know for sure."

"I guess I'll just have to trust you," she said sarcastically.

I looked at Themba again. His breathing was quick, but his eyes were steady, telling me not to agree.

"Please don't make me do this," I begged.

"One or the other–make your choice." She held up the syringe and Marco jerked Themba closer, pushing the weapon into his side.

Burning salt water escaped my eyes. I was out of time, out of options. If I did this, there was no coming back. Even if I survived everything, even though God would forgive me, I could never forgive myself. I would never be the same.

"Themba," I said. "Be safe."

"No, Andy." His expression was broken, filled with sorrow and regret for things he had power to control.

Elena had already stepped forward, and I winced at the pinch of the needle. The effects were almost immediate.

"Don't...please, Miss...don't make her," Themba pleaded.

"Get him out of here," Elena snapped.

Marco began to drag Themba from the lab as sleep took over.

"Andy!" Themba called as I slipped away. "I know my Lord! I am not afraid–don't give in!"

"Proof that it's done, or he dies in half an hour." Elena's snake-like voice was the last thing I heard before my world went dark.

CHAPTER 35

I didn't even have to kneel. I landed in the water, droplets splashing on my face as if I'd been dropped from a great height. Maybe if I just let the waters rise, they would carry me away. If I never returned, would she still let Themba go? Who was I kidding? Even if I brought back the proof she wanted, she would never release them. I sank to my knees in the rising current. There was no hope–half an hour. What miracle could I expect in just half an hour? Then again, God spoke mankind into being with a single breath. Half an hour for Him might as well have been an eternity. Not all was lost yet.

I let the tears flow, for Themba and the girls, for everyone else that would be swept up in the wake of this destruction. I wanted to save them. I would have given my life, but she wasn't asking for my life, she was asking me to take someone else's. An ugly guttural wail escaped my lips, and I slammed my fists down on the surface of the water, soaking my hair and face as it splashed.

Please, Lord, let there be a way. Please don't let me do this. Please let there be hope. I trust You. I cried and begged, running through every possibility.

"I knew you would come." I recognized his voice immediately.

I stood slowly, wiped my sleeve across my face, and turned to meet the surprisingly sad eyes of Dovanny Taklos.

If he was there, then somewhere inside, I had already decided what I was going to do. I'd found him without even looking.

"Hello Joanna," he said flatly.

"How do you know my name?"

"You told me, don't you remember?"

He looked more like the Dovanny I had seen on the bridge than the skeletal creature I'd met in our dreams. He was utterly human–just a man. We stared at each other.

"How's young William?" he finally said, not that he was much older than Will.

"He's–" I tried to say 'dead,' but the word wouldn't come. Was it because it wasn't true, or because I didn't want to believe it? "Why aren't you surprised to see me?"

"Oh, you mean because you 'died.'" With long, thin fingers he made imaginary quotes in the air. "I knew you were alive."

"How?"

"Because your boyfriend let me live." He shrugged.

"Husband," I corrected.

"Oh…in that case." He spread his arms out and bowed dramatically. "Congratulations then, Mrs. Carter."

"Who have you told?" I asked. "About me–about who I really am?"

"Why? Someone looking for you?" he said with a smirk.

"Did you send someone to look for me?"

"How long are we going to play this little game? Just do what you came to do, and let's be done with it." He stuffed his hands in his pockets and let his shoulders drop.

"I need to know who you told." I needed to know if Jacob was still safe, and Jubal.

"What does it matter? There's no future for people like us. We will all be found, or turned, or killed eventually." A heavy sigh blew through his lips, defeat written across his tipped brows.

"Like Nadine? She's dead, you know." I was harsh; I wanted the news to sting. His expression told me he didn't know. "Do you even care?"

He didn't answer, but something flashed just behind his eyes. Was it… remorse? No. He shouldn't get to feel remorse. If he hadn't made her do all those things, she wouldn't have…

"I never compelled Nadine." He interrupted my tirade.

"How did you–"

He interrupted again by pointing above my head, where an image of Nadine's face hovered, distorted and twisted with disgust.

"I never compelled her to do any of it. She wanted to. I took advantage of her feelings for me, and I used her, but I never forced anything on her."

"Does that really make it better?"

"No." He turned away.

This wasn't the same Dovanny Taklos; this man was broken. I recognized it, because I was broken myself. Even here, in the dream world, where I was strongest, my fingers twitched, longing for the next rush of endorphins from the power I yielded.

"I still need to know who you told about me," I said, twisting my fingers together, trying to quiet their trembling. "I could make you tell me."

"No one, Joanna. I didn't tell anyone you were alive," he said over his shoulder. "Or your true name."

"Why?"

He turned to face me, fists shoved deep in the pockets of his baggy white prison pants. His eyes fell to my hands, and I folded them behind my back.

"I don't know." He shrugged. "A life for a life, I guess."

This was not at all what I expected.

"You could have killed me–should have killed me," he said.

"I wanted to." That was the truth. I had struggled not to kill him, and at one point, I thought I had. That's what sparked my urgent departure from The Agency. I knew when they discovered what I could do, they would use me just like Elena was doing. Was it all for nothing? Should I have just stayed?

"You could have killed me too," I said.

"I know." He looked sad. "I didn't want to. I hoped you would…you were different."

He shuffled his feet and started to say something else, but stopped, shook his head and laughed softly. "Why are you here?"

"Someone sent me." My throat was tight.

"My father." He nodded.

"He's your father?"

Elena actually gave the order, but I suspected it had come down from someone higher.

"He made me, so, for all intents and purposes, yes." I felt his sadness reflected in my own heart. "So, it was Otis?"

"I think so." Just as Elena was using me, I was certain Goncharov was using her to tie up loose ends. He would eventually come for her, too. And then when I was used up–emptied of every good thing–someone would receive an order with my name.

He took in a deep breath, squared his shoulders, and lifted his chin. "Alright, then. Let's get on with it."

"I can't," I said softly.

He considered my response and stepped closer. "If you are here, and not of your own accord, I can assume you're being threatened...or blackmailed?"

I shrugged.

"What are the stakes?"

"What do you care?" My words were sharp. This was all backwards. I hated it. I couldn't believe I was standing here in front of Dovanny Taklos–liar, deceiver, murderer, and of all the people in the world, the one who could understand me the best–and he felt sorry for me.

"Joanna." He looked down and shook his head. My name sounded strange on his lips, natural and too familiar. "I spent most, if not all, of my life in pain, living out the feelings of everyone around me. I did awful, horrible things–unspeakable things. You were supposed to be my greatest conquest, but you...you freed me from that. It almost cost you your life–should have cost me mine. I have spent every moment of the last year just trying to figure out...why."

I turned away from him, hiding. "It wasn't me."

I can't do this. Please don't make me do this. He needed to stop talking; when he was the evil villain trying to take over the world, it was easier.

I flinched when his hand touched my shoulder, and he quickly pulled it away. The last time he'd touched me, his fingers had pressed deep, dark bruises into my skin. I stepped back and spun to face him again. His eyes darted above me, where the flashes of my memories created a playback, reminding him of what he'd done. He was close, his eyes soft and apologetic. I couldn't bear it.

"Who are you trying to save?" he asked.

"My friend, Themba, and his daughter, among others. But there's no use. She's going to kill them anyway. If not her, then Otis, unless…"

"Unless what?"

"Unless help comes soon." My eyes drifted to his curious expression.

"Is that a possibility?"

"I don't know. I hope so," I said, wishing and praying it was possible.

"You need to buy time." He nodded as if accepting a hard truth.

I shrugged again; it didn't matter. Nothing mattered, not even that I was inches away from a man who just over a year ago threatened to kill all my friends and turn me into his personal death dealing monster. I wasn't afraid of him, not even a little. He walked away a few steps. She would be waking me soon, and I would have to face the reality of the inevitable. I wanted to believe God still had a plan; I wanted to know that it was true. *Your ways are not my ways, Your thoughts not my thoughts. Please, help me believe, to have hope.*

"Joanna." His voice was soft; he reached and took my hand. I didn't pull away this time.

"Let me do this, let me give you time," he pleaded.

"What?" His words were foreign, my mind unable to translate and give them meaning.

"Do what you've been sent to do. Maybe…maybe help will come."

"Why would you do that?" I jerked my hand away, eyes narrowed with suspicion.

"I…maybe…to make up for…" His hands found their way to his head, rubbing across his forehead as if smoothing out a sentence.

"I can't." *This can't be the hope I asked for–it can't.*

"You can. I know you can, I've seen it."

"Don't you understand? I can't!" I cried, showing my open, empty hands. "I'll be lost to it; there's no coming back from this! Not for me."

I would sacrifice myself for my friends, there was never any doubt; but this was more than that. This was sacrificing him, and he was lost. Will and Esther's words slipped across my thoughts like a silky ribbon floating through the air. *More than our sacrifice, God wants our obedience.*

What was the command I was supposed to obey? Save my friends, Amy…Themba? Was it to save Dovanny, save Elena? I put my hands over my ears, trying to block out my own questions. I truly didn't know what to do.

"This is no life! I will never see the light of day again, don't you see?

I'm already dead!" He threw his hands up. "It's what I deserve, isn't it?"

His eyes dropped to the floor, where the water had all but receded. There was no point. I heard him walk away. Good. He should walk right out of this nightmare.

"Maybe so." I dropped to my knees. I would just wait now; it wouldn't be long. "Maybe we all deserve it."

Quick footsteps demanded my attention and I looked up the second before he lunged. I yelped; we both fell and he rolled on top of me, straddling my legs, his hands firm on my shoulders.

"What are you doing?" I struggled against him, bucking my hips, trying to throw him off.

He didn't answer. His face was hard and his eyes cold, nothing but a momentary waver in his resolve reminding me that he wasn't the supernatural opponent he once was. I wiggled and thrashed, trying to get out from under him, but he was too strong, too determined. His hands grabbed and twisted and squeezed, blocking all my attempts to push them away.

"Stop!" I screamed.

"Do it!" he screamed back.

He was provoking me, trying to get me to fight back. He had done this before, and it had worked.

"NO!" I put my arms up to block the onslaught of his fists. "I won't!"

He was hitting me, and it hurt, but he wasn't putting his full strength behind it. I brought my knee up hard, drawing a pained groan from his mouth. His grip faltered just enough so I could wriggle out and crawl backwards.

"I know what you're doing," I said through heavy, wheezing breaths.

"Just…do…it! What are you waiting for? I'm trying to help you," he said, still reeling from the blow I'd just delivered.

"No." I tried to catch my breath through sobs and exhaustion. I didn't have much strength left. If he attacked again, I wouldn't be able to fight him off–not without help.

He launched himself at me once again. I threw my arms up and turned my back to shield myself. One of his arms slid under mine and around my neck. With his other hand, he grabbed my wrists and held them down. He squeezed, cutting off my airway. I struggled and pushed back against him with my legs, but he remained solid.

"Stop," I choked. "Please."

His shallow breaths were hot on my neck as he squeezed tighter. Blackness closed in around the edges of my vision and riding on the tail end of a wave of dizziness was a familiar and dangerous emotion: anger.

I rocked back, knocking him enough off balance that he was forced to let go of my hands, but kept a vice across my neck. I grabbed his arms and imagined my hands covered in gloves of blazing fire. A pained howl flew from his mouth but didn't release me. *I can't breathe...I can't...*

I released his arm and stretched out my hands, pulling from the deep. In seconds we were lifted, floating. His suffocating grip remained and my rage swelled. When I threw my hands upward, an instant ocean engulfed us. I kicked against the current, propelling us upward until we were free, gasping as we broke the surface. But he deliberately pulled us both back under, until I thought my lungs would burst and the heat of panic and fury raced up my spine, burning all the way to my ears. I squeezed my fists as hard as I could and then released them, my palms stretched wide. Instantly, the water rushed in all directions, and we crashed to the floor, blue flames flicking the tips of my fingers.

For the second time in my life, I faced off with him, crouched to spring like a lion, our determination and viciousness equally matched. My neck throbbed where his arm had been, and I felt my lip begin to swell from one of his many blows. The coppery taste of blood on my tongue only fueled the rage that grew with each beat of my heart.

I pushed back, digging my heels into an invisible earth–ready–letting him assume our battle would continue. This time, when he sprang forward, I simply put my hand up, and he froze mid-air for a fraction of a second before falling to the ground, groaning from the impact. I was filled with that familiar sweet rush of power, and a sinister smile curled up on my lips. From somewhere far away, a rhythm was trying to reach me, a familiar heartbeat drumming at the edges of my mind. I chose not to hear it.

He didn't stay down long. Pulling himself up, he came for me, and again I stopped him with a subtle wave. I sighed with satisfaction and looked at my hand, eyes wide at its glow and amazed at the power it possessed. That little distraction was just enough for him to try again. He crashed into me, slamming my head back against the ground. A bright light flashed behind my eyes, and pain shot through my skull. His hands were on my throat again in seconds. A visceral growl crept up my throat, and his arms were torn violently away when I moved my hands apart.

With a flick of my wrist, he flew backwards. When he landed, I was there, towering over him, the fury burning hot throughout my body and with it. an unquenchable desire for another hit, and another…and another. The fire raged inside and out, the smell of smoke burning my nose and raising clouds of steam as the remaining moisture evaporated under its heat.

A wall of fire roared up around us, encircling, engulfing. The flames reflected in Dovanny's wide eyes.

"Yesssssssss…" A voice crackled across the flames. It liked my power–so did I.

My hand hovered over him, flat and controlled; his body contorted under the pressure of an invisible force. I pushed from within, and he jerked, an agonized grimace pulling back his lips. One more pulse, and he would be crushed. I took in a long deep breath, preparing for that final and exquisite rush.

"Doooo iiiiit, noooowww…" A whisper caressed my ear, warm and tempting.

Andy… From somewhere far away, someone was shouting my name. *I'm coming! Please let her hear me, Lord. Hold on, Andy!*

I shook my head, but the voice remained. Calling to me, over and over. It was familiar–someone good. Someone who loved me. Someone I once loved, too.

It didn't matter; all that mattered was the sweet, exquisite power coursing through my veins. The fire surged, closing in, air so hot it blurred my view of Dovanny as I smiled victoriously down at his writhing body. I squeezed my eyes shut and when I opened them, they fell on his glassy, terrified eyes.

Joanna, there is hope yet. Do not be overcome with evil, but overcome evil with good. Fiery voices hissed, the flames retreating, flickering low and injured.

What awaited him if I did this? His eternity was dark, hopeless, and lost. I wanted to drop my hand; I wanted to release him, but I felt trapped, held captive by the ecstasy. I needed it as much as I needed air. I searched my heart for something, anything to help me fight. Emily's voice, soft and gentle, from deep in the hidden corners of my heart, echoed in my ears.

For sin shall not have dominion over you, for you are not under law but under grace.

Grace. That word was life. It was light and hope and all things good.

With a painful cry, my hand fell. *He is greater, His grace is greater.*

As air filled his freed lungs, Dovanny gasped and curled his arms up to his chest, rolling over on his side. His image flickered. I dropped to my knees, my labored breaths matching his. The release was painful. It hurt–I crumpled under the agony of loss that reached every nerve. My forehead was pressed to the floor, bones weak from emotion. Ugly cries poured out of my mouth. I felt Dovanny's hands on my shoulders, pushing me up. He faded in and out in front of me. We were destroyed, emptied and broken, both inside and out.

"Why?" His face twisted from pain. "Why?"

"Grace," I gasped between sobs, repeating the words I had said to him the last time we'd met. "Mercy and grace."

He rolled on his side again, groaning, his arms wrapped around himself. His image started to fade, and for once I desperately wished for more time with him. I reached out and touched his flickering figure, making a promise I prayed that I could keep.

"If we live, I will tell you about Him." Just before he disappeared, I whispered, "Don't give up. Where there is life, there is hope."

CHAPTER 36

My chest ached with each heartbeat, and I almost rolled off the table before Marco caught me and pushed me back on. I laid on my side, doubled over as my body twitched and shook. My skin was burning hot and freezing cold at the same time, every nerve ending firing angry, piercing signals to my brain. My head pounded from where Dovanny had slammed me into the ground. It was still hard to swallow, and my wrist was throbbing again. My clothes were soaked, and water dripped into a growing puddle on the floor. There wasn't one good thing left. I'd been here before–on the rocky bank of a river. It had almost ended then, but here I was on the ride again. This time, surely, it had to be coming to an end, even if it meant flying off of the rails and crashing to the ground.

"Well?" Elena said expectantly, her hands on her hips. When I didn't answer, she sent Marco from the room. "Get them."

He disappeared through the lab door and she marched over to where I lay shivering.

"Is it done?" Elena demanded, grabbing a handful of my wet hair and jerking my head back.

"He's gone," I managed through gritted, chattering teeth. "The man you wanted is gone."

Her eyes traveled to my neck, examining the evidence of our struggle. With a disgusted growl, she let go of my hair and pushed a few buttons on her phone.

"We shall see." She was so smug.

I had no idea how she could have found Dovanny; Goncharov's pockets must be very deep. There was definitely a mole in The Agency. Only those who worked at that prison would know its location, and even fewer would know that Dovanny was being held there. I needed to warn her. She was coming up on Goncharov's hit list.

"You'll be next," I croaked.

"You don't scare me." She only rolled her eyes and turned away, unphased. Of course, she thought I was threatening her; her pride wouldn't allow her to recognize it was a warning.

"Yes." A male voice echoed from her speaker.

"What's happening?"

"Medics have been called in. Waiting for a report." His voice was gruff, hushed, and yet...familiar. *Who is it, Andy? Concentrate!*

"Call me back with a confirmation," she said, ending the call.

"I did what you wanted, now let them go," I begged.

"Soon enough," she snapped.

Another sharp pain made my body jerk and I slipped off the table, crashing noisily to the floor. Elena only watched, amused. I was struggling to get up when Marco entered, pulling Themba with little Thadie in his arms. Her face was buried in his shoulder, his hand on the back of her head, pressing her close. Marco urged him forward, and Themba didn't resist. A jerk of Marco's arm revealed the reason for his compliance. Marco held a pistol level at his waist, pressed hard into Themba's side.

"Keep your eyes closed, Omncane, don't look. It will be alright," Themba said softly, the look in his eyes not matching the calm tone of his voice.

"I'm sorry," I mouthed, after glancing at Elena to make sure she wasn't looking. I was so sorry.

Sorry I couldn't kill one person to save another.

Now it was over for all of us; I both dreaded and welcomed the end. I quit trying to get up and slid back down to the floor, covering my mouth with my hand to catch a silent sob.

Did any hope remain? Had I done the right thing by sparing Dovanny? Had I been obedient? Themba closed his eyes and took a deep breath, steadying himself, his lips moving in prayer.

The room was silent. A single shrill ping from Elena's phone echoed off the walls, the ceiling, the floor. Three pairs of eyes followed her movement as she raised the phone to her ear. I knew what answer she would hear, and the narrow-eyed look of pure hatred on her face confirmed it. I didn't want to watch what I knew was coming. I wanted to close my eyes, but they remained open. The next series of events seemed to happen in slow motion, a lapse in time, triggered by the sound of my own breath.

Elena shifted her eyes toward Marco; Marco pushed Themba away and raised his weapon, pointing it at the father and daughter. Themba turned, shielding his little girl's body with his own. Marco flicked his gaze to me for a fraction of a second and in that same instant he turned, pointing the gun at Elena instead. She didn't notice; she wore a sick deadly smile and was focused on Themba.

Confusion flooded my mind when I saw his new target, but an urgent thought rose above the chaos. *If she dies now, she's lost forever.* When a deafening crack split the air and I saw the bright flash of fire from the barrel, I screamed. Without reason, my hands shot out towards both Themba and Elena, wishing, hoping, pleading, praying that somehow God would bend the laws of space and time. Within the boundary of a breath, it was over.

In the next second an army of camouflage burst through the door. Time resumed its normal speed, and instantly, Marco, Elena, and Themba were face down on the floor, their hands being secured with zip ties behind their backs. A wailing Thadie was rushed out of the room, squealing in the arms of one of the soldiers. Elena screamed every foul word imaginable at the soldiers and threatened them with her unnamed employer.

They ignored her. Themba's expression was strange, as though he was going to be sick. Had Marco shot him after all?

"Wait!" I gasped, my words stifled by the tightness in my chest. "He's hurt! Help him!"

Strong hands lifted me. I fought, slipping from their grip and falling on the ground next to Themba. My wrist and ribs screamed as I crawled to him.

"I'm okay…I'm okay, Andy." He grunted under the pressure of a soldier's knee pressing on his back. "I'm not hurt."

From the sound of Elena's voice, she seemed unharmed too. How was this possible? I looked around and saw Marco staring wide-eyed at something on the floor. I followed his gaze and there on the tile was a shiny bullet, still rolling to a stop between him and me. Markings from the barrel were clearly etched on the sides, but it was otherwise unchanged, as if it hadn't struck anything at all. He was less than two yards away from Themba, and even closer to Elena. There was no way he could have missed. I looked up at Marco again, who stared right back at me. Something had changed in his eyes. The storm was still there, but it was breaking. I allowed the mask-covered men to lift me. I didn't know who they were or where'd they'd come from; I was too tired and too broken to care.

"Let Themba go," I pleaded weakly.

They didn't listen. They started to carry me from the room when the crowd of camo-clad bodies parted to let someone through. I stopped squirming, frozen in place.

Brown eyes. Beautiful, deep chocolate brown eyes scanned the room, stopping when they met mine. I greedily took him in, trying to make sense of what I saw. It was him: his dark hair, his strong muscled shoulders, his sweet, crooked smile. It was Will, my Will!

There he was–the good thing that could eclipse all the wrong that existed inside and around me. My knees gave, and I sagged in the arms of the soldiers. He was there in an instant, his arms under mine, holding me up.

"I've got you." His deep soft voice reached through the buzz of surrounding chaos.

"You found me." I stared wide-eyed into his face, unwilling to blink.

He stared back and my eyes drifted down to his mouth, which turned slightly up on one side; his response stole my breath.

"Always."

When my lungs could bear it no more, I sucked in a deep breath and sobbed into his shoulder, pulling him against me, ignoring the sharp stabbing warnings from my side. My hands traveled desperately over him, urgent for proof he was truly corporeal and not some drug-induced hallucination. If he disappeared now, I'd follow right behind.

"You're here." It came out as a squeak. Was all of this still somehow a dream? "Are you really here?"

"I'm here."

He was solid, as always. His hold was secure, but his body tensed as I touched his side and I pushed away, looking him over with concern. His hand moved to his side, tenderly guarding it.

"You were shot!" I grabbed at his shirt, my fingers hovering over the large white bandage covering his side. "How are you here?"

"I'm not sure, honestly." He pulled his shirt down and my hand up to his mouth, brushing his lips across my fingers. "When the team arrived, they found me outside, behind a dumpster. They said it looked like someone had stopped the bleeding already, and if the bullet had been one inch over I wouldn't have even lived that long. The tranquilizer that laced the bullet actually slowed my heart rate and kept me from bleeding out."

"You'll be okay?" I searched his face.

He laughed, brushing my soaked hair back from my face. "I should be asking you that."

His expression changed as he took a good look at me. "Andy, you're shaking...really shaking."

"I'm fi– Whoa." An unexpected wave of dizziness sent my hands flailing; I gripped his arms to keep from falling over. A sudden cramp flamed across my abdomen and searing flashes from my broken ribs caused me to suck in a breath through my teeth.

He helped me back onto the table and barked an order to someone behind him. "Get a medic in here, now!"

"Amy!" I gasped, shaking away the blackness that intruded upon my vision. "There's more kids...more people...I...don't know their names! And the others–the real patients. I...I told Jacob. Did he–"

"Andy–"

"I have to find them!" I tried to push him away, but he didn't budge.

"Baby, we found them. They're safe." He put his hands on the sides of my face, forcing my eyes to meet his.

"Amy?"

"Yes, she's fine. They're all okay. She was the one who led us to you." He spoke softly, his eyes traveling over me, assessing my injuries. "She's amazing, but she's refusing to get into the car."

"Polka-dot peanut butter."

He looked at me the way I'd looked at Amy when she'd said it.

"It's the password. Tell her you know the password, and she will go with you."

Will motioned to one of the men near him and whispered in his ear. Amy was safe; my new friends were safe.

"Themba...he's my friend. He helped me. Tell them to let him go," I pleaded, twisting my hands into the fabric of his shirt. "Please."

Will considered my request and tipped his head towards the soldier who was pulling Themba up.

"Let him go," Will said.

The soldier cut the ties restraining Themba and released him.

Themba reached for me, and Will stepped protectively between us.

"No, it's okay," I said, nodding encouragingly. He stepped aside.

Themba took my hand. "Thank you, Omncane...thank you."

My throat was tight, and my eyes burned with salty tears. I looked to Will. "Please, let him go to his daughter. This is Themba; he's Thadie Calloway's brother."

Will, clearly shocked, nodded again at the soldier, who escorted Themba from the room.

Will faced me as my legs dangled over the edge of the table and I let my head fall against his chest, taking slow, intentional breaths. My hands were still twisted in his shirt, unwilling to let him go. Slowly, he drew lines up and down my back, methodical and calming. *Thank You, Jesus. I don't know how...but thank You.*

I tried to ignore the chaos surrounding us, but a change in its volume forced my attention. I turned to see Elena and Marco being hauled out of the room as a soldier carrying a med kit brushed past them. Elena's glare met mine before she disappeared around the corner; the fiery hate burning behind her intense green eyes sent a shiver up my spine.

My gaze drifted to Marco, whose expression revealed a strange mixture of confusion and disbelief. I started to speak but he shook his head, a movement so subtle, only the two of us noticed, and I closed my mouth as he vanished behind Elena into the hallway.

"Scott," Will called to the young man with the Red Cross patch on his sleeve. "Over here."

Will hovered over the medic as he examined me. The men exchanged a horrified glance when Scott turned my arm over, revealing the numerous red and purple bruises from Elena's rough injections. Will's brown eyes burned, and his jaw clenched as Scott gently lifted my chin to examine even more bruises left by Dovanny's arm. Everything hurt. I needed to focus on something else to endure it.

Scott bore a strange insignia on his jacket and I intentionally investigated every detail. It was a shield bearing the image of two swords crossed behind some kind of animal. I squinted and leaned closer. It was a jackal, maybe–or a fox?

A sharp breath hissed through my teeth when Scott lifted my hand, sending a stinging shock through my injured wrist all the way up to my shoulder.

"Sorry," he said, genuinely apologetic.

After wrapping a bandage around my wrist, he broke a cold pack on the table and placed it gently over the stretchy fabric. He shone a bright penlight in my eyes and took my blood pressure. When he listened to my heart and tried to get me to take deep breaths, I winced, and my hand flew to my side.

"Can you lay back?" he asked.

Will held my shoulders and together, they helped me lay on the table. He pulled up my shirt and tenderly felt around on top of the bandages Marco had wrapped around my ribs and chest. I squeezed Will's arm, both because it hurt and also to keep him from chasing after Elena. His eyes were on fire, and I could tell he was working hard to hold in his fury. As Scott leaned over me, I resumed my distraction efforts and stared at the strange symbol again, tracing the detailed lines with my eyes. When he finished, he motioned for Will to follow him.

Will softly brushed the back of his hand across my cheek. "I'll be right back. Two seconds, okay?"

I nodded, scrutinizing their hushed consultation. The medic leaned in, speaking quietly into Will's ear as he stared at the floor. Scott occasionally flicked his eyes towards me. Whatever news he delivered caused Will to run his hand through his hair and fold his arms tight across his chest. As Scott continued, Will shook his head, as though he were hearing something he didn't agree with. I knew what Scott was saying. He was telling Will that his wife looked like a street fighting drug addict. Will finally nodded, accepting Scott's observations, and placed a hand on the young man's shoulder before dismissing him. With his back to me, Will rested his hands on his hips and stood for a few seconds before returning to the lab. He looked like he had just talked himself into putting on a brave face but kept his distance, hesitant to touch me.

I knew there would be endless questions. I had so many of my own, but in that moment all I wanted to do was hold him, feel the reality of his presence and know for sure he was really there.

Despite his previous assurances, I had to confirm I wasn't still in a dream–that this wasn't a trick. For a few precious seconds, I just wanted everything to be okay, to indulge a sliver of fantasy before I faced the reality that it was definitely not.

"Are you really here? I'm not…I'm not still in a dream?"

He cocked his head, his expression a mix of emotions I couldn't decipher. When he stepped close, leaned over, and put one hand on the table to support himself, an anticipatory breath caught in my throat. A familiar tingle spread out under his touch as he slid his other hand gently along the side of my face, his thumb resting on my cheek.

"Yes, I'm really here."

I pressed my hands to his chest as he hovered, a strong heartbeat thumping against my palm. He was so close. Did he still see me the same– as his wife, a woman he desired, or did he only see a sad, broken thing?

"I want to kiss you and never stop," he breathed. How did he do that? Always answering questions I didn't ask.

In a move that shocked both of us, I seized his shirt and drew him to me, crushing his lips to mine. My ribs hurt, my lips hurt, my wrist hurt…everything hurt, but none of it mattered. To feel his touch, to know he was there, alive and in front of me, was all that mattered. So much passed between us in those long moments as everything else fell away. The soldiers moving about the room, taking pictures, collecting papers and glass vials, the constant coming and going, shouting of orders from the hallway–all of it dissolved into nothing. It was only us, only his lips, warm and tender, on mine. Only his hand twisting up into my hair, pulling me even closer. Only our hearts beating in unison. I was afraid to let go. He finally broke the trance. He smiled, but he didn't pull away.

"I think we're making a scene," he said, his mouth still on mine.

"I don't care," I whispered, pulling him close again.

He sighed and pushed himself back as I groaned in disappointment. His smile was soft, but his eyes were locked intensely on mine.

I knew he was searching to see if I was really there or if I was lost to whatever drugs Elena had been relentlessly injecting over the last several days–or was it weeks? Honestly, I didn't know. I searched his face as well. When he found out all that I'd done–about Dovanny–would he be disappointed? Would he be angry and disgusted or worse, afraid of me?

"Will," I said, my eyes stinging from the tears that were welling up. "I…there are things–"

"No. You did good, Andy," he interrupted. "I'm so proud of you."

I turned away. "You don't know what I've done." A single tear escaped and slid down my cheek.

He took my chin gently and pulled my face back towards his, then wiped another rebellious tear with the back of his hand. "You did what was necessary to save those kids…and you saved me. That's what you've done."

He lowered his forehead until it touched mine and I heard him suck in a deep breath as my uninjured hand slid up and rested on his neck. He placed one finger on my chin, tipped my head up, and softly pressed his lips to mine, taking everything that was wrong and making it right.

Soldiers waited; there were questions to be answered, statements to give, evidence to collect. It all could wait. The growing unease in my stomach told me that my battle was far from over. But right now, nothing was more important than Will's arms which circled around me protectively, healing and mending my brokenness. God had answered my prayers yet again. He made a way when there was none. He pulled me out of the darkness and into the light one more time. From the very deepest part of my heart, I poured out praise to my Father in heaven for His mercy. I heard my praises echoed back in my ears as Will whispered his own words of thankfulness.

CHAPTER 37

I knew this place well. I didn't even have to open my eyes. A clean antiseptic smell, low hum of hushed voices, occasional click of a closing door, rhythmic roll of wheels on a tiled floor: I was back inside The Agency. At least, I was dreaming that I was. The last time I had been in the medical wing, I was recovering from being left to die in the woods by Nadine Greyson. This was where I'd met Will, really met him. He'd never left my side. I'd kept my eyes closed then too, just to enjoy the simple ecstasy of being alive and warm. If I opened them, I would see Will in a day-old blue suit sitting on the couch, his arm stretched over the back, tie loosened, head turned to gaze out of the window.

Sure enough, when my lids finally fluttered open, he was there. I smiled; this was one of my best memories. I'd welcome this dream any day. He was so kind, so safe. I knew even then that I could trust him, though I fought it for a long time afterwards.

But he wasn't wearing his blue suit. He was dressed in jeans and a dark grey t-shirt. His dark hair was freshly washed and still wet, longer on the sides and top than before. I looked down.

My arms rested on top of a white blanket that was tucked up around me and my wristband said Stone, A., but there was a set of rings on my left hand. Wedding rings. This was not the same memory; it was different–and different was almost always bad.

I shifted, my body tensing immediately. I hurt all over, every muscle sore, every nerve tender and screaming. My wrist was wrapped, but in a different bandage than medic Scott had used. That wasn't right.

This wasn't a dream. This was real. Despite the pain, I sat up quickly, tugging at the clear plastic lines pumping fluids into my body. Will's hands were on mine in an instant, just like before.

"We have to go," I said frantically, my voice hushed. "I can't be here."

"Andy, it's okay," Will said calmly.

"No…no…I have to go; we have to go." I fought, but I was down one hand, my ribs were still broken, and he was much stronger. He held my good wrist and sat on the bed next to me.

"Stop fighting me, baby, you're going to hurt yourself," he said. His voice was steady. How could he be so calm?

"Will," I pleaded. "I can't be here."

"Andy, you're safe. Just let me explain," he said, still holding onto me.

I felt a familiar sting in my eyes as the tears threatened. They'd done something to him. He would never take me back here, never! *Lord, when will this end?* I had to get out, and then I would somehow figure out how to get him back. I needed a distraction. I scanned the room. It was a typical hospital room. I didn't see anything that could help; only my clothes, washed and folded neatly on a chair in the corner. I needed a plan. He was still holding my good hand, so I reached up with my injured one to touch my necklace, a habit I'd developed since my grandmother gave it to me. It wasn't there.

Will's free hand was on mine, pulling it gently away from where I was frantically feeling around for the comfort of my little silver lion.

"I found your rings, but your necklace wasn't there. I'm sorry," he said softly.

"Where's Jacob?" Surely, he would help me. He knew what they wanted to do–what they would make me do.

"He's just down the hall. Do you want me to get him?"

I nodded. Plan formed.

"You promise not to try and pull these out again?"

I nodded again, sitting back. He looked skeptical, but slowly released my hand, leaned over, and kissed my forehead. Plan executed.

"I'll be right back." He stepped through the door, looking back before disappearing down the hall.

I waited a few seconds, painfully ripped the IV out of my arm, and dove for my clothes, fighting off a wave of nausea and lightheadedness. Everything was there but my shoes. I'd just have to go without them. Unsure of how quickly he would return, I didn't take the time to change, planning to slip into an empty room as soon as I could. Clothes tucked under my good arm, I peeked and found the hallway clear. I slipped out and sprinted towards the double doors at the end of the hall. From what I remembered, they would open to a staircase, where I could head up to the main floor or down towards the research sector. Medical was just above Research, where I had worked, and two floors below the lobby. There was an emergency room entrance at the rear, but I'd have to go past the nurse's station and the conference room to get there. I'd escaped from this place once. I could do it again…if I could stay conscious. My head was swimming, blackness edging my vision.

I took the stairs two at a time and turned off onto the administrative floor one level above medical, but had to grab the rail at the top of the flight to keep from passing out. The first room to the left was empty; I slipped inside and closed the door softly.

It took me less than two minutes to change and hide my hospital gown under some papers in the trash can. From there, I didn't have a good plan, and simply pressed my body against the cool wood of the door.

A beaten-up barefoot girl in jeans and a t-shirt was sure to be noticed if I simply walked down the hallway. If Will had already returned with Jacob and found me gone, he would have called the lobby and had them watch the doors. There was one option, but it was risky–as were most of my decisions.

I opened the door just enough to scope out my exit. One agent approached, but he was busy examining a document. Once he turned into an office, the way was clear. I squeezed out of the room and tiptoed down the carpeted hallway, headed for my target. I ducked under office windows as I sprinted to the end of the hall, jerked down the fire alarm, and tucked myself under an empty desk as people poured out of their offices. Being curled up so tightly sent sharp pains up and down my sides. I couldn't take in a full breath, but I only needed to wait a few more seconds.

When the last of the agents filed out, I crawled out and looked around, grabbing at the desk as yet another wave of blackness passed over me. Once again, I fought to stay standing. I shook my head, finding enough clarity to keep going. Someone had left a blazer hanging on the back of her chair. I slipped it on, stumbling towards the door through which the agents had just exited.

There was a crowd still gathered, slowly making their way down the stairs to the medical emergency exit. I folded myself in, hoping no one would notice my lack of footwear.

As we walked, I twisted the long strands of my hair up into a floppy bun and secured it with a pencil from the jacket's pocket.

I hid my bandaged arm inside the stolen blazer, keeping close to the others in the herd. We quickly shuffled through double doors at the bottom of the stairs. Just ahead I could see the exit. Once I got out, I could head for the woods. When I'd worked for The Agency before, I'd spent many hours exploring the grounds, and because of a vague warning from a trusted professor, I'd developed a variety of escape routes. Last time, I headed for the highway; this time I'd head Northeast–towards the suburbs.

Hopefully, Will would go back to my original path, and I could use the confusion of the fire alarm to my advantage.

My group merged seamlessly with medical staff and I worked my way to the far-left edge of the mob. When they all turned right out of the door to file into the open parking lot, I turned sharply left into the covered garage and disappeared into the shadows.

I planned to sprint across the garage, ducking behind cars, but a cold sweat broke out across my forehead and my stomach began to cramp. I was barely able to walk, much less run. I finally made it to the end and climbed on the hood of a car to hoist myself up and over the concrete wall. There was a small opening between the wall and the roof of the garage just big enough for me to shimmy through on my stomach.

Andy, what are you doing? Between episodes of dizziness and doubling over from pain, I wasn't moving very fast. Somewhere in my mind a voice of reason told me to go back, that there was something really wrong, but I ignored it. The stronger voice of panic gave me a different command. *Run, keep running.*

There was a thick patch of trees just ahead, which was where I needed to be, and quickly. They would have started searching the building now and would soon discover that someone pulled the alarm.

I hoped all the attention was still focused on the interior and if Will was outside, he would be searching the crowd.

I took a deep breath and with my good hand cradling my bandaged arm against my stomach, I hobbled towards the trees. My heart was pounding, sending strong, silent pulses of pressure to my ears. Just inside the cover of woods, I collapsed and crawled on my elbows, hiding behind one of the larger trees.

Beads of sweat ran down my face, stinging my eyes. My hands were shaking, my throat so dry I couldn't swallow. It was hard to think; my mind was racing, and I felt like my heart was about to explode. *What is wrong with me?*

A seizing cramp sent me reeling against the rough bark of the tree, dry heaving. I would never make it to the next group of trees, much less out of the woods and to the maze of endless identical subdivision streets, but I couldn't stay there. The Agency was no better than Elena. How could this be happening? Did I go through all of this only to end back up where I started? How could this be God's plan? I was on the verge of panic–my clammy palms burned, and thin, wispy tendrils of smoke rose up from my fingertips, a convincing hallucination. I knew if I gave into this hysteria, I'd collapse there on the ground, never able to get up.

Keep going, Andy…just keep moving forward.

I took a deep breath and glanced around the tree back towards the building. It was clear.

"I'm always finding you in the woods."

I jumped, coming face to face with a smirking Will Carter. His smile vanished when he registered the paralyzing turmoil on my face and the truly awful state of my condition. I shook my head, backing up into the rough, unmoving bark of a tree. He was going to haul me back. *No…no, no, no.*

His hands flew up disarmingly, brows knit together with extreme concern. Awareness of my fear and determination not to be caught spread across his face. I would do anything–risk anything–not to be turned into a monster by that institution behind me.

"Andy, why do you always run? I promise you're safe. Just let me explain." His voice was low and pleading. He stepped forward, hesitating when I flinched, but gently wrapped his hands around my trembling arms. I had nowhere to run.

He could easily overpower me; I could never outrun him, even at full strength. But he wasn't trying to force anything on me. He was asking, giving me the choice–just like he'd always done. Could I really leave him there alone to deal with whatever they'd done to him? Didn't we promise to stick together, no matter what?

"Baby, please," he begged, melting what was left of my resolve.

I sagged against his chest with a sob and he folded me into his arms. He was safe, the solid thing I'd clung to during every impossible minute for the past year. This was the same Will, the same heartbeat drumming in his chest. Surely, he was not deceiving me.

He drew back, sliding his hand along my jaw just under my ear. At the warmth of his hand, I felt instant peace. My heart raced as I searched his eyes. He looked like my Will; his eyes that same warm chocolate brown I'd always known. There was nothing but honesty behind his gaze. He was telling the truth. He lowered his head until our foreheads met and took a deep breath.

"Please trust me," he whispered. "I know why you want to run; I do. But I would never do anything to hurt you. Never."

I wanted to believe that, so badly.

"I trust you," I breathed. I had to. He'd given me a choice, but even though I'd resisted, there was never really another option. "I go where you go."

He sighed, relief flooding out from his spirit, but he didn't lift his head.

"I assume you pulled the fire alarm, or do we need to evacuate?" he asked, amusement playing at the edge of his words.

"No, I pulled it." My last words came out as a groan and I squeezed my eyes shut when another sharp pain sliced across my abdomen.

He stood up straight, shifting his jaw as I breathed through the cramp. His curious eyes drifted up, taking in the makeshift bun secured by a yellow number two pencil. He pulled it out, sending my long red locks cascading around my shoulders. He smiled as he tucked a strand behind my ear.

"So brave," he said, holding the pencil up like he'd found a hidden prize. "I almost didn't find you."

"That's not true." I snatched it from his hand, blushing from humiliation.

"Okay, you're right, but it was a good effort."

What was to become of us? Our eyes searched each other as the question hung there between us, heavy and foreboding. His smile faded, replaced by something much more serious and intense.

He lowered his head, his lips hovering just above mine, waiting…asking permission. I lifted my chin, my kiss describing every intense emotion I couldn't explain with words. The agony of seeing him dying on the office floor, the sinking feeling of his blood on my hands, the desperation at the sound of his shallow breaths and the unending, unbearable, excruciating heartbreak at the idea that he was gone. All of these memories burned through my heart and poured out of my eyes, painful and consuming, but extinguished in an instant by the vision of his brown eyes appearing in a sea of camouflage.

The grief and loss, the searching and praying, and then the incredible relief–it all crashed over us in waves as we clung to each other, and I could tell that he felt all of it every bit as intensely as I. He finally broke away, breathless and softly smiling, his eyes still closed. He shook his head as if chasing away a thought and then opened his beautiful eyes, bathing my face in warmth.

"Come on." He slid his arm around my shoulders, leading us back to the building. When we were about halfway there, his arm dropped to my waist to better support me, careful and cautious of my tender ribs. When I tripped and my knees gave out, he simply scooped me up without comment and carried me back to the building, only putting me down when we neared the entrance so I could walk in on my own. He didn't need to mention it–it was clear. I was in bad shape. Something was definitely wrong; this was far more serious than simple exhaustion and a couple of broken ribs.

We remained quiet as we walked the short distance to my room where Jacob was waiting outside, leaning against the wall, arms folded. I rushed to him and he opened his arms, gratefully receiving my embrace.

"Is this really okay?" I asked quietly, my mouth close to his ear.

"I hope so," he said, then as if to answer my unspoken question, he added, "I trust Will."

After I was sufficiently hooked back up to my IVs, vitals checked, and received permission to remain dressed in my street clothes after a heated discussion with the nurse, I turned to Will expectantly.

"Explain." I sat up on the bed, my legs crisscrossed as I nervously crunched a spoonful of ice chips. "Did you find the rest of the patients? How did I get here? Am I an agent again?"

He grinned and lowered himself onto the bed, reaching out for my hand.

"No." He played with my fingers as he talked. "I mean yes, we found all the patients."

"Were they alright? Did she give them that–whatever that drug was called?"

"No. It was actually really strange. There was a supply of what was labeled Clozophinol. It was marked on their charts as having been administered, but none of them had it in their system, and when we tested the actual pills, it was only a placebo."

Marco. It had to be. I almost said his name, but something told me to keep it myself for now.

"Why does my wrist band say Stone?"

Will glanced at Jacob.

"We thought it was best if you were exactly who they always thought you were. Andromeda Stone."

"Back from the dead? How'd you pull that off?"

Will's throat moved as he swallowed hard and bobbed his head in a slight nod. "I followed your example and just told the truth. We faked your death, changed your name, and moved away."

"Who do they think you are?" I looked at Jacob.

"Kindly church groundskeeper turned father figure." Jacob's brow lifted, humored at his own cleverness.

"Sneaky," I muttered. "So…am I an agent?"

"Only if you want to be."

I shifted uncomfortably. He raised my hand to his lips, softly kissing the back of it, flashing that same reassuring smile he had the first time we sat in this room together.

"How are we here, though?"

"After she took off with you, the New Orleans Agency team found me within a few minutes. If you hadn't left that card, I wouldn't have made it, even though–" He shook his head, as if trying to remember something. "The damage wasn't that bad, but I would have bled out soon."

The sound of his words in my ears made me sick, the memory of him lying there bleeding to death was too overwhelming, and my throat grew tight with emotion. When he noticed my reaction, he slid close, letting me wrap my arm around him.

"Hey," he said. "I'm okay, really."

I sat back and shifted my eyes to Jacob, who seemed relaxed where he sat on the couch. He nodded as if to confirm Will's statement.

"I called Jacob. He met me at the hospital."

"Yeah, he almost had to come bail me out of jail first, though." Jacob's smile told me he found his brush with the law more humorous than serious.

"Sorry." Will chuckled. "While he was talking his way out of an arrest, they patched me up, and we started searching for you right away. I finally convinced Jacob to get some sleep. We were hoping you'd find one of us, and you did. From what you told him, we were able to narrow down your location to a few places. Then Jacob got a phone call from a man named...Naveed?"

"Did you find him?" My eyes widened. "Is he safe?"

"Yes, we sent a team to pick him up, and he's being taken care of. He told us more about Elena and Marco, and we headed towards the canal."

"I don't know how, but Will just knew where to go. He led them right to the bunker." Jacob leaned forward, resting his elbows on his knees.

"That's what he does." I smiled, looking up at Will through my lashes.

Seeing my smile brought one to Will's face, and he seemed to relax a little.

"We found little Amy first and she led us to the others, then told us about the lab where you were. I was just so worried we wouldn't make it in time," he said, his smile fading. "I was praying you would hold on, that somehow you would know I was coming."

"I think...I think that I heard you...it was close," I said softly. "But that doesn't explain why we are back here."

"I agreed to let them bring you here. You were in bad shape, Andy. There would be too many questions I couldn't answer at a civilian hospital, so this seemed like the best place for you to get the help you needed. I had to make a choice." His eyes shifted to Jacob, who looked down at the ground.

"What?" I said, looking between the two of them. "What are you not telling me?"

"Andy, what Elena did..." His head dropped and when he looked back up, a familiar fire burned in his eyes. "Whatever she gave you, it's highly addictive."

I looked from Will to Jacob and back. They both looked defeated.

"I feel fine. Well, aside from every muscle in my body being sore."

That wasn't exactly true, but I didn't want to accept what he was implying. Will looked at me, his head cocked to the side; he didn't believe me, either.

"They're trying to help flush your system by giving you little doses at a time. That's why you've been asleep so long," Will said, his eyes searching mine for understanding.

"How long have I been asleep?"

"Four days."

Four days?

Four.

Days.

That couldn't be right. I looked to Jacob, and he nodded, confirming what Will had said.

"Honestly, I'm amazed you could stand, much less have the strength to get all the way out of the building," Will said, not trying to hide his admiration.

I couldn't really believe it either, but shrugged in response. "So, what's going to happen?"

"They'll slowly decrease the amount and interval of the dose, and then you'll have to withdraw on your own." Will wouldn't look at me; it hurt him to tell me this.

"How long will it take?"

"There's no way to know. That'll really be up to you, I guess."

I considered his words. My throat was dry, and my stomach was already beginning to cramp again. I felt a cold chill creep up my spine and spread across my skin, followed by that familiar dull ache at the base of my skull, signaling the impending arrival of a terrific headache. On the wall, just over my shoulder, a little pump whirred, pushing clear liquid through a tube into my arm. The cramp slowly faded.

I wondered how bad it would be when that merciful pump no longer whirred, when there was no reprieve from the pain. Would it be worse than what I felt in the woods? Would I need a straitjacket and a padded room?

"Will you stay with me?" I asked Will.

His eyes shot up, glistening slightly.

"Of course." He scooted forward, drawing me tight into his arms. "Of course, I will. Every second. I promise."

"What did you mean earlier? When you said I could be an agent if I wanted."

He sat back and glanced over at Jacob. They were going to have to stop doing that.

"Naveed confirmed our suspicion that there's more to Elena's employer, much more. The Agency wants to get involved in tracking down the rest of the organization. They've asked us to help."

I wondered if they'd come to all the same conclusions as I had. I'd have to tell Will everything I'd learned when I wasn't so concerned with his immediate employment.

"Did you say yes?"

"I didn't say anything. I was waiting for you."

"You know I can't work for them again. They know what I can do." I shook my head. "They'll make me…"

"They've agreed not to force you, not to even ask you," he interrupted. He looked sincere.

"Why would they do that?"

"Because you are valuable, even without…the things you can do."

I cocked my head at him suspiciously. "More like *you* are valuable. You made a deal, didn't you?"

"Not yet." His lips twitched, a smile threatening to break through his business-like expression.

"How do you know they'll keep their word?"

"I've got it in writing."

I had so many questions, but even that magical clear juice dripping through the IV hadn't managed to get rid of my growing migraine. I put my thumb and finger on my good hand up to my forehead, squeezing them hard into my temples.

I was about to ask how long I had to decide when the nurse came in. She insisted it was time to rest; Will and Jacob were ordered to either leave or be quiet. Will said leaving wasn't an option, so he retreated to the couch next to Jacob as the nurse injected something else into my IV. I felt relaxed and warm after just a few minutes, and slumped back against the pillows. My eyes grew heavy; I let them close without resistance.

"Jacob?" I asked, my eyes remaining closed.

"Mmm," he answered.

"What was in the basement?"

"Elena's basement?"

"No…Marco's basement."

"Oh," he said, and I heard him chuckle softly. "Nothing really, just boxes. The missing box of Clozophinol, oddly enough. I actually–"

I heard him get up and opened my eyes. He looked around as if to see if anyone else was watching. "I took something."

He walked over to the corner of the room, opened a duffle bag, and fished around inside. When he found what he was looking for, he stood but didn't turn around. I glanced over at Will, who shrugged. Finally, Jacob turned and walked to the side of the bed. He hesitated for a second more before handing me a little plush lion.

I watched my hands reach out and take the toy. I felt a strange familiarity when my fingers slid through the soft synthetic fur. Its faded brown plastic eyes stared wide and friendly back at me.

"I don't know why I took it," Jacob said. "It was in a baby's diaper bag in some random box of what looked like garage sale items."

I stroked the fur around its ears. It was old but well cared for, waiting many long years to find its way back home.

I couldn't stop staring at its smiling yellow face. I knew Jacob and Will were in the room, but they felt a million miles away.

"I do," I said finally.

"What do you mean, Andy?" Will asked.

"This was mine," I whispered.

"What did she say?" Will asked Jacob.

I slowly looked back and forth between them.

"This was mine." I was getting sleepy and spoke frankly, as if we were talking about something as meaningless as the weather. "I saw it in our dream; it was in my diaper bag. I saw it on the floor of the car."

Jacob stepped back suddenly. Will reached out to catch him before he tripped. He sank down onto the couch. I watched, but my brain didn't fully register what was happening. Jacob's hand was covering his mouth. He took a long, deep breath.

"I bought that for you…before you were even born."

None of us spoke. There was nothing to say. It was completely unbelievable and so obviously simple at the same time. Elena took the bag from the car that night, and for some reason, she kept the one thing that would mean so much to us. Maybe somewhere deep down she thought it was bait, maybe it was a reminder of this terrible thing she had done, maybe a souvenir of her atrocious act, maybe I would never know. Or maybe she hadn't kept it at all; it had been in Marco's basement. Maybe his father had been an unwilling participant, too.

"Thank you, Jacob," I said.

He nodded, his expression still reading disbelief.

I tucked the soft body of the toy under my chin and reached for Will. He moved a chair close to the bed and took my outstretched hand.

"We've been here before," I said, really starting to feel groggy.

"I remember." Will smiled, sympathy thick in his tone. "Sleep, Andy. I won't let anything happen to you."

"You said that before, too." My eyes wouldn't stay open, and my brain felt loopy.

"I know." His thumb was making little circles on my palm. "I'm doing my best to keep that promise. You certainly don't make it easy."

"I'll do it," I said, although I didn't know if he could understand me at that point.

"Do what?"

"I'll be a super-secret agent spy person..." I mumbled.

"You don't have to decide right now." He laughed, but it sounded like he was in another room–a tunnel room.

"I have a condition, though."

"What's your condition?" Someone's hand was on my head, brushing my hair back away from my face and tucking strands behind my ear.

"I need to see Dovanny." I was falling away from the world, floating slowly down in a gentle, feathery swing. "He needs to know..."

"What did she say?" A deep voice spoke, his words drawn and slow. It sounded a little like my Uncle Jacob.

"Dovanny? She wants to see Dovanny Taklos," another slow deep voice replied.

"What in the world could she possibly want to see him for?"

I didn't hear the reply, because I was comfortably wrapped in a warm blanket of deep, dreamless sleep.

EPILOGUE

"She was so proud of you, Andy." Jacob's voice sounded far away. "Her last words were a prayer of thanks to God for letting her know you."

We gathered in the innermost part of the garden on the grounds of Christ Chapel. I had sprinkled half of the ashes from the urn over a patch of lilies, and Jacob scattered the rest under Esther's favorite oak.

Will stood quietly beside me, protective and solid as always. It was warm; the sun was shining, and the sweet smell of spring filled the air, but I felt disconnected–out of place, as if I weren't really there. I could feel the pressure of my feet on the ground, the smooth cool surface of the ceramic urn in my hands, the heat of the sun on my skin, but none of it reached below the surface. I knew there was more, much more to be done, to endure, before I could finally return and be fully present here.

"Thank you both," I said finally, the words feeling foreign in my mouth. "You saved my life…in so many ways."

Vivid flashbacks from that emotional day in the hotel room blinked across my mind. I'd been so angry. Memories of the poisonous plant I'd allowed to take root made me squirm. I'd have surely succumbed to its toxin if Jacob hadn't explained that emotions were just emotions, feelings that would come and go–but our response, our reactions, were ours to control, ours to submit to God. He'd set me free with truth, even though it hurt to hear. If he hadn't, our story would have had a much different outcome. Would Esther be so proud if she'd known that?

Will's hand brushed my elbow, bringing me from past to present.

"I think you should write her story." He held the brown leather journal in which Esther had recorded our history. My hands wouldn't move to accept, and he added, "When you're ready."

The book waited, balanced on his palms–desiring to return home, to be taken into the arms of one of its own. It called to me, a soft whisper in the wind, a single word that spoke volumes.

Remember.

My trembling fingers touched the soft edges of its binding, curling around the spine before drawing it in close to my chest.

A sudden figure appeared on the path ahead. It was a young Esther, wearing a smile so brilliant her entire face glowed. Silken gowns of white hung perfectly formed to her shape, the fabric floating around her like wings. Her strawberry blond hair fell in thick waves over her shoulders. Delicately placed atop her head was the most beautiful crystal crown adorned with jewels of all colors. One sparkled as she turned, a deep green emerald, cut to perfection by expert hands. I knew that if I looked closely, my name would be etched lovingly across its surface. She had shared her faith so passionately, so honestly. They were her prayers that had covered me all my life, even across two decades of unknowns. Her faith had become my faith, a legacy I intended to continue. My name was recorded in my Father's book because of His grace and her willingness.

"Thank you, Esther," I whispered.

Her delicate hand lifted, a gesture abundant with grace, and with an expectant twinkle in her crystal blue eyes, she vanished. Esther was gone. I knew she had been since her beautiful eyes closed for the last time, whisked away to spend a blissful eternity with her Savior. Still I hoped somehow she could feel the depth of my gratitude, and sent a silent prayer of thanks to God for giving me that beautiful mirage to settle my worried mind.

From the open door of the sanctuary, organ music floated across the grounds into our ears. As Jacob began to softly sing the words to Esther's favorite hymn, I let my tears flow freely.

I'd stay in the garden with Him,
Though the night around me be falling.
But He bids me go; through the voice of woe
His voice to me is calling.

And He walks with me and He talks with me,
And He tells me I am His own;
And the joy we share as we tarry there;
None other has ever known.

My dreams were blissful: full of smiling faces, warm happy feelings, and pleasant memories. We had both fallen asleep easily after a long but wonderful day, but a sudden cold, dark curtain fell over my sleeping mind, jerking me awake.

I sat up and swung my legs over the side of the bed, rubbing my eyes, not yet fully awake. Hoping I'd been quiet enough not to wake my sleeping spouse, I glanced over my shoulder, surprised to find the other side empty.

I was instantly alert, and the icy chill from my dreams spread across my skin. The room was quiet, which calmed me a little, but my eyes searched the dark, stopping on the closed bathroom door. It was edged with light, and I sighed in relief. I flopped back onto my pillow and folded my arms behind my head, waiting. Several minutes passed. What was taking so long?

A soft rhythmic thumping drew my attention towards the bathroom. I walked slowly to the door and knocked softly. No answer; just that same continual thump, thump, thump. I turned the knob, which wasn't locked, and opened the door a crack. Any calmness that I'd felt before was gone in an instant.

"Andy!" I dove to her side.

Her small body was twitching, convulsing horribly, one clenched fist hitting the side of the bathtub, creating that sickening repetitive thump. My hands hovered over her, unsure of what to do. *Oh God...what do I do? Lord, please help me.*

I jumped up and ran to my bedside table, grabbing my cell phone. I tried to keep my shaking fingers under control long enough to dial three numbers. As the phone rang, I threw open my bedroom door and yelled down the hall.

"Jacob!" *Ring, ring.* "Jacob! We need you!"

"9-1-1, what is your emergency?" A calm female voice spoke.

Jacob appeared in the doorway, disheveled and half asleep. I pointed towards the bathroom as I rambled to the operator. He scooped Andy into his lap and held her head still as she shook, tenderly wiping her sweat-soaked hair away from her face.

"Stay on the line, sir; a team is en route right now. Is your wife breathing?"

"Yes," I answered without thinking.

"Is someone with you, sir?"

"Yes."

"They are one minute away; can you make sure the door is open for them?"

"Yes." I couldn't take my eyes off of her. Her pale skin, her eyes rolled back, her small delicate hands clenched so tightly I could see red marks on her palms from her nails. This wasn't happening, this couldn't be happening; she was fine all day. They said she would be fine. I could find her when she was lost, overpower anyone who wanted to hurt her, outsmart a villain, or even throw myself in front of a bullet. But this...I had no control. I couldn't save her from this. For the first time in my life, I froze.

"Sir, they are at the door," the operator said. "Sir!"

"Yes."

I could hear pounding, but nothing reached my brain to send it into action. Jacob was yelling my name; I could only see her. She continued shaking as he laid her gently on the floor. Someone was shaking me and cut off my view of Andy.

"Will! Snap out of it! She needs you!" Jacob yelled in my face before running out the door and down the hall.

His words had an immediate effect and I jumped into action, rushing to her again. I scooped her up in my arms and brought her to the bed. When I pried her fingers open, the deep and fiery red grooves her nails had cut in her skin made me wince, and I let her hands clamp around my own. Her grip was so strong, she crushed my bones together, but I didn't care; she could break every bone in my body if it would stop this.

I wanted to take all of it, to bear every bit of whatever was torturing her so she would be free.

"Come on, baby," I said through panicked breaths. "Andy... Oh, God, please save her from this, Jesus...please."

Two paramedics ran through our door and started working on her while asking question after question about what she had eaten, her medical history, and if she had taken any drugs.

"Uh...pasta...no allergies, I don't..."

I looked up at Jacob.

"Go," he said, taking my place by her side and fielding the questions as best he could.

I grabbed my cell phone from the floor where I'd dropped it and stumbled into the hallway, running my hands through my hair in desperate frustration.

"Will?" A sleepy voice answered after the third ring. "What's wrong?"

"Matt...I need you...Andy needs you." I repeated the words I'd said to him over a year before from the payphone at a small service station miles outside of the village where Andy had been bitten by a poisonous snake. When would it end?

"I'm coming," he said, fully alert. "Have them take her to St. Mark's. It's closest; I'll call in the protocol."

"Matt?"

"I know, Will...I know."

The water was warm, perfectly clear, with the most beautiful green-blue tint. I floated effortlessly on the surface, gently rocked by the slightest of waves. Though the sun was bright, it was not uncomfortable. I'd been floating there forever, but I wasn't tired of the water–my fingers weren't even wrinkled.

The perfectly content sigh that had been growing in my chest escaped, peeling back my lips to expose a toothy grin. Delicious healing rays of sun bathed my skin, soaking deep into the bones beneath. I took a breath and dove under, gliding through the cooler temperatures below the surface. My kicking feet forced my descent, continuing downward until my hands sank into wet powdery-soft sand. I crawled along the bottom, watching a naturally choreographed dance performed by creatures that lived there. Colorful schools of fish darted back and forth, flicking quickly out my reach and kicking up little clouds from the sandy floor. I stayed as long as my lungs would allow before pushing off against the sand with my feet, shooting upwards.

As my head broke the surface, a long refreshing breath filled my needy lungs. A sound, whispered but clear, caused me to turn quickly, seeking its source.

"Andy..."

There it was again. What was that? Someone calling from far away? The quiet of my solitude was pleasant; preferring its companionship, I took another breath, preparing to dive back under.

"Joanna!"

The authority of this voice halted my escape. It fell on my ears as if the speaker was within inches, but I remained alone. The water grew cold and a dark cloud appeared, covering the sun. I looked up to the bluff that surrounded my perfect beach.

Atop the high cliffs, where dark, sharp edges cut harshly against the blue sky, stood a man. Though details were concealed by shadow, there was such familiarity, an unexplainable knowledge that I'd known him my whole life. That somehow, I belonged to him. He was safe and good–the One from whom all good things came. Yet, I feared his power, in the way one would tremble in the center of a cyclone. Completely safe within, yet unquestionably aware of the force surrounding, with walls of wrath that were awesome and terrible. A wrath composed neither of anger nor vengeance, but of righteousness.

The ocean chilled further, raising goosebumps on my skin. But where he walked, there was warmth. I should go to him. I longed to be with him, so much that it ached, yet...I resisted.

The climb up to the edge where he stood looked arduous and dangerous; the journey would take a lifetime to complete. Between the beach and cliffs stretched a labyrinth of cedar forest, the path through dark and unknown. My beach and the ocean where I swam, though cold, was familiar. It was comfortable. Even as a sudden wind began to stir up the sand into a swirling, tornadic whirlwind that most certainly would consume me if I wandered near...I still resisted leaving it behind.

The figure stretched out his gentle hand, pointing to where the forest met the sand, beckoning me onward.

And something stirred among the trees. There was danger where he called. I couldn't see what waited beyond the open shore.

A momentary break in the clouds let the sun through, and a sparkle reflected its light. I lifted my hand up out of the water. A tiny heart shaped diamond on a white gold band was perfectly wrapped around my finger, the symbol of a covenant made before God and man. A promise that led to more promises. Promises that must be kept. A sharp jolt of recognition shot up through my body, reviving a force that had long been slumbering. Just before I dove under the water in a direct course for the shore, a low growl, wild and strong, rumbled across the sky. It carried a command I could not resist.

"Awake, oh sleeper."

FROM THE AUTHOR

W hat Andy failed to realize for almost this entire book was that although she had become a believer and had chosen to follow Christ–she would still fail. The same is true for all believers. We will still fall short, all.the.time.

Christ's capacity and authority to forgive, renew, and transform will never run out. This does not give us free reign to sin, but instead, gives us freedom from sin. We are no longer slaves to ourselves if we choose to enslave ourselves instead to the One who loves us more than anything!

That means we are free to forgive, because we don't own the vengeance nor the offense; we never have. All sin is against the one who made the law: that is God. It is not against us, therefore–we can be free from anger, from bitterness and resentment–free to live in peace.

It is always my first and foremost goal to share the Good News of Jesus with my readers. If this story has resonated with you on any level, please reach out and let me know!

You can send me an email at authorcarriecotten@gmail.com or find me on one of the many social media platforms.

If you want to know the kind of assurance that I have, the kind that allows me to boldly walk into battle without fear because I know that I fight for the One who has overcome the world, don't stop asking until you find out.

It's the most important question you'll ever ask.

Find out more at www.carriecotten.com/gospel

AWAKEN

A Dreamwalker Novel: Book 3

PROLOGUE

O tis stared at the printed photograph. The bright auburn hair and crystal blue eyes gazing back at him struck a chord deep within, a string that he'd long since severed, suddenly reconnected. It made him uncomfortable, a feeling he was not accustomed to.

"How could I have not known about this?" Still gripping the picture, he slammed his fist on the hard, slick surface of his desk.

"I'm sorry, sir. Cordova kept her activity concealed."

"This is…unacceptable." Otis smoothed the wrinkles on the page his outburst had caused and let his eyes trace the lines of the young woman's face as he decided on the best course of action.

He chastised himself for not eliminating the incompetent Cordova years ago. He'd been too merciful–banishing her had only caused him trouble. Now she'd been captured, and would possibly bring his whole organization down with her. All that he'd worked for, all the sacrifices…

Otis slammed his fist again, making the already hesitant man opposite him jump.

"I thought you'd be pleased; we'd been told she was dead."

Otis glared at the thin-framed man, his trim black suit masking the trembling coward underneath.

"Pleased, Eagle?" Otis scoffed, disgusted by the regal code name this imbecile had managed to ascertain. Buzzard would have been better. "Am I pleased she's alive–yes. Am I pleased that a highly trained operative failed to bring in a single target and the other held her in secret, damaging her nearly beyond repair? I'm beyond outraged."

"I won't fail you, sir." Eagle straightened his posture, putting forth a false confidence that only made Otis cringe.

"No. You won't. Because I'm going to tell you exactly what to do. Sit."

Otis reached behind and pulled his own chair towards the desk, then searched through the remaining stack of surveillance photos.

His employee hesitantly scooted forward in the sleek metal and leather chair that perfectly coordinated with the rest of Otis' office, silently asking permission before resting his elbow on the desk.

"Where was this image taken?" Otis flashed another photograph from the pile.

"Outside of The Agency medical entrance."

"Who is the other man? The older one with the beard?" His finger tapped the face of the man in question. In the image, the woman was being wheeled on a gurney into the facility. On one side of her, a man Otis recognized as her husband, and on the other, the man he'd asked about. The way his hand rested on hers…it was intimate, caring. This was someone who knew her well.

"The caretaker of the church where the Carters currently reside," Eagle replied. "No one of consequence, as far as I know."

"What is his name?" Otis picked up the photo, holding it at an angle so the last remaining rays of setting sun illuminated the paper.

"Er…" Eagle leaned back, fumbling with the papers in a folder that rested on his lap. "That information is not in the file."

"Of course," Otis mused to himself, not at all surprised at the complete ineptness of the entire situation.

"Do you want me to find out more about him? Is he important?"

"Possibly." Otis dropped the photo onto the desk, pushing a thin finger on the likeness of his real interest.

Eagle bent his head and shot Otis a questioning glance. Otis was pointing to the dark-haired agent, Will Carter. "The boy scout?"

"This." He looked up, making sure Eagle was paying attention. "This is your in. Do exactly what I tell you, and we will have both of them on our side."

A flash of greedy excitement passed across Eagle's smirking face, and he leaned even closer to the man he both feared and admired.

"Now this, I have to see."

Made in the USA
Middletown, DE
22 July 2022

69892278R00201